The Night Operator

Frank L. Packard

The Night Operator

Copyright © 2020 Bibliotech Press
All rights reserved

ISBN: 978-1-64799-795-3

TO
CHARLES AGNEW MACLEAN

iii

FOREWORD

Summed up short, the Hill Division is a vicious piece of track; also, it is a classic in its profound contempt for the stereotyped equations and formulæ of engineering. And it is that way for the very simple reason that it could not be any other way. The mountains objected, and objected strenuously, to the process of manhandling. They were there first, the mountains, that was all, and their surrender was a bitter matter.

So, from Big Cloud, the divisional point, at the eastern fringe of the Rockies, to where the foothills of the Sierras on the western side merge with the more open, rolling country, the right of way performs gyrations that would not shame an acrobatic star. It sweeps through the rifts in the range like a freed bird from the open door of its cage; clings to cañon edges where a hissing stream bubbles and boils eighteen hundred feet below; burrows its way into the heart of things in long tunnels and short ones; circles a projecting spur in a dizzy whirl, and swoops from the higher to the lower levels in grades whose percentages the passenger department does not deem it policy to specify in its advertising literature, but before which the men in the cabs and the cabooses shut their teeth and try hard to remember the prayers they learned at their mothers' knees. Some parts of it are worse than others, naturally; but no part of it, to the last inch of its single-tracked mileage, is pretty—leaving out the scenery, which is grand. That is the Hill Division.

And the men who man the shops, who pull the throttles on the big, ten-wheel mountain racers, who swing the pick and shovels in the lurching cabs, who do the work about the yards, or from the cupola of a caboose stare out on a string of wriggling flats, boxes and gondolas, and, at night-time, watch the high-flung sparks sail heavenward, as the full, deep-chested notes of the exhaust roar an accompaniment in their ears, are men with calloused, horny hands, toilers, grimy of face and dress, rough if you like, not gentle of word, nor, sometimes, of action—but men whose hearts are big and right, who look you in the face, and the grip of whose paws, as they are extended after a hasty cleansing on a hunk of more or less greasy waste, is the grip of men.

Many of these have lived their lives, done their work, passed on, and left no record, barely a memory, behind them, as other men in other places and in other spheres of work have done and always will do; but others, for this or that, by circumstance, or personality, or opportunity, have woven around themselves the very legends and traditions of their environment.

And so these are the stories of the Hill Division and of the men who wrought upon it; the stories of those days when it was young and in the making; the stories of the days when Carleton, "Royal" Carleton, was superintendent, when gruff, big-hearted, big-paunched Tommy Regan was master mechanic, when the grizzled, gray-streaked Harvey was division

iv

engineer, and little Doctor McTurk was the Company surgeon, and Riley was the trainmaster, and Spence was the chief despatcher; the stories of men who have done brave duty and come to honor and glory and their reward—and the stories of some who have gone into Division for the last time on orders from the Great Trainmaster, and who will never railroad any more. F. L. P.

CONTENTS

Chapter I

THE NIGHT OPERATOR

Toddles, in the beginning, wasn't exactly a railroad man—for several reasons. First, he wasn't a man at all; second, he wasn't, strictly speaking, on the company's pay roll; third, which is apparently irrelevant, everybody said he was a bad one; and fourth—because Hawkeye nicknamed him Toddles.

Toddles had another name—Christopher Hyslop Hoogan—but Big Cloud never lay awake at nights losing any sleep over that. On the first run that Christopher Hyslop Hoogan ever made, Hawkeye looked him over for a minute, said, "Toddles," short-like—and, short-like, that settled the matter so far as the Hill Division was concerned. His name was Toddles.

Piecemeal, Toddles wouldn't convey anything to you to speak of. You'd have to see Toddles coming down the aisle of a car to get him at all—and then the chances are you'd turn around after he'd gone by and stare at him, and it would be even money that you'd call him back and fish for a dime to buy something by way of excuse. Toddles got a good deal of business that way. Toddles had a uniform and a regular run all right, but he wasn't what he passionately longed to be—a legitimate, dyed-in-the-wool railroader. His paycheck, plus commissions, came from the News Company down East that had the railroad concession. Toddles was a newsboy. In his blue uniform and silver buttons, Toddles used to stack up about the height of the back of the car seats as he hawked his wares along the aisles; and the only thing that was big about him was his head, which looked as though it had got a whopping big lead on his body—and didn't intend to let the body cut the lead down any. This meant a big cap, and, as Toddles used to tilt the vizor forward, the tip of his nose, bar his mouth which was generous, was about all one got of his face. Cap, buttons, magazines and peanuts, that was Toddles—all except his voice. Toddles had a voice that would make you jump if you were nervous the minute he opened the car door, and if you weren't nervous you would be before he had reached the other end of the aisle—it began low down somewhere on high G and went through you shrill as an east wind, and ended like the shriek of a brake-shoe with everything the Westinghouse equipment had to offer cutting loose on a quick stop.

Hawkeye? That was what Toddles called his beady-eyed conductor in retaliation. Hawkeye used to nag Toddles every chance he got, and, being Toddles' conductor, Hawkeye got a good many chances. In a word, Hawkeye, carrying the punch on the local passenger, that happened to be the run Toddles was given when the News Company sent him out from the East, used to think he got a good deal of fun out of Toddles—only his idea of fun and Toddles' idea of fun were as divergent as the poles, that was all.

Toddles, however, wasn't anybody's fool, not by several degrees—not

1

even Hawkeye's. Toddles hated Hawkeye like poison; and his hate, apart from daily annoyances, was deep-seated. It was Hawkeye who had dubbed him "Toddles." And Toddles repudiated the name with his heart, his soul—and his fists.

Toddles wasn't anybody's fool, whatever the division thought, and he was right down to the basic root of things from the start. Coupled with the stunted growth that nature in a miserly mood had doled out to him, none knew better than himself that the name of "Toddles," keeping that nature stuff patently before everybody's eyes, damned him in his aspirations for a bona fide railroad career. Other boys got a job and got their feet on the ladder as call-boys, or in the roundhouse; Toddles got—a grin. Toddles pestered everybody for a job. He pestered Carleton, the super. He pestered Tommy Regan, the master mechanic. Every time that he saw anybody in authority Toddles spoke up for a job, he was in deadly earnest—and got a grin. Toddles with a basket of unripe fruit and stale chocolates and his "best-seller" voice was one thing; but Toddles as anything else was just—Toddles.

Toddles repudiated the name, and did it forcefully. Not that he couldn't take his share of a bit of guying, but because he felt that he was face to face with a vital factor in the career he longed for—so he fought. And if nature had been niggardly in one respect, she had been generous in others; Toddles, for all his size, possessed the heart of a lion and the strength of a young ox, and he used both, with black and bloody effect, on the eyes and noses of the call-boys and younger element who called him Toddles. He fought it all along the line— at the drop of the hat—at a whisper of "Toddles." There wasn't a day went by that Toddles wasn't in a row; and the women, the mothers of the defeated warriors whose eyes were puffed and whose noses trickled crimson, denounced him in virulent language over their washtubs and the back fences of Big Cloud. You see, they didn't understand him, so they called him a "bad one," and, being from the East and not one of themselves, "a New York gutter snipe."

But, for all that, the name stuck. Up and down through the Rockies it was—Toddles. Toddles, with the idea of getting a lay-over on a siding, even went to the extent of signing himself in full—Christopher Hyslop Hoogan— every time his signature was in order; but the official documents in which he was concerned, being of a private nature between himself and the News Company, did not, in the very nature of things, have much effect on the Hill Division. Certainly the big fellows never knew he had any name but Toddles— and cared less. But they knew him as Toddles, all right! All of them did, every last one of them! Toddles was everlastingly and eternally bothering them for a job. Any kind of a job, no matter what, just so it was real railroading, and so a fellow could line up with everybody else when the paycar came along, and look forward to being something some day.

Toddles, with time, of course, grew older, up to about seventeen or so, but he didn't grow any bigger—not enough to make it noticeable! Even Toddles' voice wouldn't break—it was his young heart that did all the breaking there was done. Not that he ever showed it. No one ever saw a tear in the boy's eyes. It was clenched fists for Toddles, clenched fists and passionate attack.

2

And therein, while Toddles had grasped the basic truth that his nickname militated against his ambitions, he erred in another direction that was equally fundamental, if not more so.

And here, it was Bob Donkin, the night despatcher, as white a man as his record after years of train-handling was white, a railroad man from the ground up if there ever was one, and one of the best, who set Toddles— But we'll come to that presently. We've got our "clearance" now, and we're off with "rights" through.

No. 83, Hawkeye's train—and Toddles'—scheduled Big Cloud on the eastbound run at 9.05; and, on the night the story opens, they were about an hour away from the little mountain town that was the divisional point, as Toddles, his basket of edibles in the crook of his arm, halted in the forward end of the second-class smoker to examine again the fistful of change that he dug out of his pants pocket with his free hand.

Toddles was in an unusually bad humor, and he scowled. With exceeding deftness he separated one of the coins from the others, using his fingers like the teeth of a rake, and dropped the rest back jingling into his pocket. The coin that remained he put into his mouth, and bit on it—hard. His scowl deepened. Somebody had presented Toddles with a lead quarter.

It wasn't so much the quarter, though Toddles' salary wasn't so big as some people's who would have felt worse over it, it was his amour propre that was touched—deeply. It wasn't often that any one could put so bald a thing as lead money across on Toddles. Toddles' mind harked back along the aisles of the cars behind him. He had only made two sales that round, and he had changed a quarter each time—for the pretty girl with the big picture hat, who had giggled at him when she bought a package of chewing gum; and the man with the three-carat diamond tie-pin in the parlor car, a little more than on the edge of inebriety, who had got on at the last stop, and who had bought a cigar from him.

Toddles thought it over for a bit; decided he wouldn't have a fuss with a girl anyway, balked at a parlor car fracas with a drunk, dropped the coin back into his pocket, and went on into the combination baggage and express car. Here, just inside the door, was Toddles', or, rather, the News Company's chest. Toddles lifted the lid; and then his eyes shifted slowly and travelled up the car. Things were certainly going badly with Toddles that night.

There were four men in the car: Bob Donkin, coming back from a holiday trip somewhere up the line; MacNicoll, the baggage-master; Nulty, the express messenger—and Hawkeye. Toddles' inventory of the contents of the chest had been hurried—but intimate. A small bunch of six bananas was gone, and Hawkeye was munching them unconcernedly. It wasn't the first time the big, hulking, six-foot conductor had pilfered the boy's chest, not by many— and never paid for the pilfering. That was Hawkeye's idea of a joke.

Hawkeye was talking to Nulty, elaborately simulating ignorance of Toddles' presence—and he was talking about Toddles.

"Sure," said Hawkeye, his mouth full of banana, "he'll be a great railroad man some day! He's the stuff they're made of! You can see it sticking out all over him! He's only selling peanuts now till he grows up and—"

3

Toddles put down his basket and planted himself before the conductor.

"You pay for those bananas," said Toddles in a low voice—which was high.

"When'll he grow up?" continued Hawkeye, peeling more fruit. "I don't know—you've got me. The first time I saw him two years ago, I'm hanged if he wasn't bigger than he is now—guess he grows backwards. Have a banana?" He offered one to Nulty, who refused it.

"You pay for those bananas, you big stiff!" squealed Toddles belligerently.

Hawkeye turned his head slowly and turned his little beady, black eyes on Toddles, then he turned with a wink to the others, and for the first time in two years offered payment. He fished into his pocket and handed Toddles a twenty-dollar bill—there always was a mean streak in Hawkeye, more or less of a bully, none too well liked, and whose name on the payroll, by the way, was Reynolds.

"Take fifteen cents out of that," he said, with no idea that the boy could change the bill.

For a moment Toddles glared at the yellow-back, then a thrill of unholy glee came to Toddles. He could just about make it, business all around had been pretty good that day, particularly on the run west in the morning.

Hawkeye went on with the exposition of his idea of humor at Toddles' expense; and Toddles went back to his chest and his reserve funds. Toddles counted out eighteen dollars in bills, made a neat pile of four quarters—the lead one on the bottom—another neat pile of the odd change, and returned to Hawkeye. The lead quarter wouldn't go very far toward liquidating Hawkeye's long-standing indebtedness—but it would help some.

Hawkeye counted the bills carefully, and crammed them into his pocket. Toddles dropped the neat little pile of quarters into Hawkeye's hand—they counted themselves—and Hawkeye put those in his pocket. Toddles counted out the odd change piece by piece, and as Hawkeye put that in his pocket—Toddles put his fingers to his nose.

Queer, isn't it—the way things happen? Think of a man's whole life, aspirations, hopes, ambitions, everything, pivoting on—a lead quarter! But then they say that opportunity knocks once at the door of every man; and, if that be true, let it be remarked in passing that Toddles wasn't deaf!

Hawkeye, making Toddles a target for a parting gibe, took up his lantern and started through the train to pick up the fares from the last stop. In due course he halted before the inebriated one with the glittering tie-pin in the smoking compartment of the parlor car.

"Ticket, please," said Hawkeye.

"Too busy to buysh ticket," the man informed him, with heavy confidence. "Whash fare Loon Dam to Big Cloud?"

"One-fifty," said Hawkeye curtly. The man produced a roll of bills, and from the roll extracted a two-dollar note.

Hawkeye handed him back two quarters, and started to punch a cash-fare slip. He looked up to find the man holding out one of the quarters insistently, if somewhat unsteadily.

4

"What's the matter?" demanded Hawkeye brusquely.

"Bad," said the man.

A drummer grinned; and an elderly gentleman, from his magazine, looked up inquiringly over his spectacles.

"Bad!" Hawkeye brought his elbow sharply around to focus his lamp on the coin; then he leaned over and rang it on the window sill—only it wouldn't ring. It was indubitably bad. Hawkeye, however, was dealing with a drunk—and Hawkeye always did have a mean streak in him.

"It's perfectly good," he asserted gruffly. The man rolled an eye at the conductor that mingled a sudden shrewdness and anger, and appealed to his fellow travellers. The verdict was against Hawkeye, andHawkeye ungraciously pocketed the lead piece and handed over another quarter.

"Shay," observed the inebriated one insolently, "shay, conductor, I don't like you. You thought I was—hic!—s'drunk I wouldn't know—eh? Thash where you fooled yerself!"

"What do you mean?" Hawkeye bridled virtuously for the benefit of the drummer and the old gentleman with the spectacles.

And then the other began to laugh immoderately.

"Same ol' quarter," said he. "Same—hic!—ol' quarter back again. Great system—peanut boy—conductor—hic! Pass it off on one—other passes it off on some one else. Just passed it off on—hic!—peanut boy for a joke. Goin' to give him a dollar when he comes back."

"Oh, you did, did you!" snapped Hawkeye ominously. "And you mean to insinuate that I deliberately tried to—"

"Sure!" declared the man heartily.

"You're a liar!" announced Hawkeye, spluttering mad. "And what's more, since it came from you, you'll take it back!" He dug into his pocket for the ubiquitous lead piece.

"Not—hic!—on your life!" said the man earnestly. "You hang onto it, old top. I didn't pass it off on you."

"Haw!" exploded the drummer suddenly. "Haw—haw, haw!"

And the elderly gentleman smiled.

Hawkeye's face went red, and then purple.

"Go 'way!" said the man petulantly. "I don't like you. Go 'way! Go an' tell peanuts I—hic!—got a dollar for him."

And Hawkeye went—but Toddles never got the dollar. Hawkeye went out of the smoking compartment of the parlor car with the lead quarter in his pocket—because he couldn't do anything else—which didn't soothe his feelings any—and he went out mad enough to bite himself. The drummer's guffaw followed him, and he thought he even caught a chuckle from the elderly party with the magazine and spectacles.

Hawkeye was mad; and he was quite well aware, painfully well aware that he had looked like a fool, which is about one of the meanest feelings there is to feel; and, as he made his way forward through the train, he grew madder still. That change was the change from his twenty-dollar bill. He had not needed to be told that the lead quarter had come from Toddles. The only question at all in doubt was whether or not Toddles had put the counterfeit

5

coin over on him knowingly and with malice aforethought. Hawkeye, however, had an intuition deep down inside of him that there wasn't any doubt even about that, and as he opened the door of the baggage car his intuition was vindicated. There was a grin on the faces of Nulty, MacNicoll and Bob Donkin that disappeared with suspicious celerity at sight of him as he came through the door.

There was no hesitation then on Hawkeye's part. Toddles, equipped for another excursion through the train with a stack of magazines and books that almost hid him, received a sudden and vicious clout on the side of the ear.

"You'd try your tricks on me, would you?" Hawkeye snarled. "Lead quarters—eh?" Another clout. "I'll teach you, you blasted little runt!"

And with the clouts, the stack of carefully balanced periodicals went flying over the floor; and with the clouts, the nagging, and the hectoring, and the bullying, that had rankled for close on two years in Toddles' turbulent soul, rose in a sudden all-possessing sweep of fury. Toddles was a fighter—with the heart of a fighter. And Toddles' cause was just. He couldn't reach the conductor's face—so he went for Hawkeye's legs. And the screams of rage from his high-pitched voice, as he shot himself forward, sounded like a cageful of Australian cockatoos on the rampage.

Toddles was small, pitifully small for his age; but he wasn't an infant in arms—not for a minute. And in action Toddles was as near to a wild cat as anything else that comes handy by way of illustration. Two legs and one arm he twined and twisted around Hawkeye's legs; and the other arm, with a hard and knotty fist on the end of it, caught the conductor a wicked jab in the region of the bottom button of the vest. The brass button peeled the skin off Toddles' knuckles, but the jab doubled the conductor forward, and coincident with Hawkeye's winded grunt, the lantern in his hand sailed ceiling-wards, crashed into the center lamps in the roof of the car, and down in a shower of tinkling glass, dripping oil and burning wicks, came the wreckage to the floor.

There was a yell from Nulty; but Toddles hung on like grim death. Hawkeye was bawling fluent profanity and seeing red. Toddles heard one and sensed the other—and he clung grimly on. He was all doubled up around Hawkeye's knees, and in that position Hawkeye couldn't get at him very well; and, besides, Toddles had his own plan of battle. He was waiting for an extra heavy lurch of the car.

It came. Toddles' muscles strained legs and arms and back in concert, and for an instant across the car they tottered, Hawkeye staggering in a desperate attempt to maintain his equilibrium—and then down—speaking generally, on a heterogeneous pile of express parcels; concretely, with an eloquent squnch, on a crate of eggs, thirty dozen of them, at forty cents a dozen.

Toddles, over his rage, experienced a sickening sense of disaster, but still he clung; he didn't dare let go. Hawkeye's fists, both in an effort to recover himself and in an endeavor to reach Toddles, were going like a windmill; and Hawkeye's threats were something terrifying to listen to. And now they rolled over, and Toddles was underneath; and then they rolled over again; and then a hand locked on Toddles' collar, and he was yanked, terrier-fashion, to his feet.

His face white and determined, his fists doubled, Toddles waited for Hawkeye to get up—the word "run" wasn't in Toddles' vocabulary. He hadn't long to wait.

Hawkeye lunged up, draped in the broken crate—a sight. The road always prided itself on the natty uniforms of its train crews, but Hawkeye wasn't dressed in uniform then—mostly egg yolks. He made a dash for Toddles, but he never reached the boy. Bob Donkin was between them.

"Cut it out!" said Donkin coldly, as he pushed Toddles behind him. "You asked for it, Reynolds, and you got it. Now cut it out!"

And Hawkeye "cut it out." It was pretty generally understood that Bob Donkin never talked much for show, and Bob Donkin was bigger than Toddles, a whole lot bigger, as big as Hawkeye himself. Hawkeye "cut it out."

Funny, the egg part of it? Well, perhaps. But the fire wasn't. True, they got it out with the help of the hand extinguishers before it did any serious damage, for Nulty had gone at it on the jump; but while it lasted the burning oil on the car floor looked dangerous. Anyway, it was bad enough so that they couldn't hide it when they got into Big Cloud—and Hawkeye and Toddles went on the carpet for it the next morning in the super's office.

Carleton, "Royal" Carleton, reached for a match, and, to keep his lips straight, clamped them firmly on the amber mouthpiece of his brier, and stumpy, big-paunched Tommy Regan, the master mechanic, who was sitting in a chair by the window, reached hurriedly into his back pocket for his chewing and looked out of the window to hide a grin, as the two came in and ranged themselves in front of the super's desk—Hawkeye, six feet and a hundred and ninety pounds, with Toddles trailing him, mostly cap and buttons and no weight at all.

Carleton didn't ask many questions—he'd asked them before—of Bob Donkin—and the despatcher hadn't gone out of his way to invest the conductor with any glorified halo. Carleton, always a strict disciplinarian, said what he had to say and said it quietly; but he meant to let the conductor have the worst of it, and he did—in a way that was all Carleton's own. Two years' picking on a youngster didn't appeal to Carleton, no matter who the youngster was. Before he was half through he had the big conductor squirming. Hawkeye was looking for something else—besides a galling and matter-of-fact impartiality that accepted himself and Toddles as being on exactly the same plane and level.

"There's a case of eggs," said Carleton at the end. "You can divide up the damage between you. And I'm going to change your runs, unless you've got some good reason to give me why I shouldn't?"

He waited for an answer.

Hawkeye, towering, sullen, his eyes resting bitterly on Regan, having caught the master mechanic's grin, said nothing; Toddles, whose head barely showed over the top of Carleton's desk, and the whole of him sizing up about big enough to go into the conductor's pocket, was equally silent—Toddles was thinking of something else.

"Very good," said Carleton suavely, as he surveyed the ridiculous incongruity before him. "I'll change your runs, then. I can't have you two men brawling and prize-fighting every trip."

There was a sudden sound from the window, as though Regan had got some of his blackstrap juice down the wrong way.

Hawkeye's face went black as thunder.

Carleton's face was like a sphinx.

"That'll do, then," he said. "You can go, both of you."

Hawkeye stamped out of the room and down the stairs. But Toddles stayed.

"Please, Mr. Carleton, won't you give me a job on—" Toddles stopped.

So had Regan's chuckle. Toddles, the irrepressible, was at it again—and Toddles after a job, any kind of a job, was something that Regan's experience had taught him to fly from without standing on the order of his flight. Regan hurried from the room.

Toddles watched him go—kind of speculatively, kind of reproachfully. Then he turned to Carleton.

"Please give me a job, Mr. Carleton," he pleaded. "Give me a job, won't you?"

It was only yesterday on the platform that Toddles had waylaid the super with the same demand—and about every day before that as far back as Carleton could remember. It was hopelessly chronic. Anything convincing or appealing about it had gone long ago—Toddles said it parrot-fashion now. Carleton took refuge in severity.

"See here, young man," he said grimly, "you were brought into this office for a reprimand and not to apply for a job! You can thank your stars and Bob Donkin you haven't lost the one you've got. Now, get out!"

"I'd make good if you gave me one," said Toddles earnestly. "Honest, I would, Mr. Carleton."

"Get out!" said the super, not altogether unkindly. "I'm busy."

Toddles swallowed a lump in his throat—but not until after his head was turned and he'd started for the door so the super couldn't see it. Toddles swallowed the lump—and got out. He hadn't expected anything else, of course. The refusals were just as chronic as the demands. But that didn't make each new one any easier for Toddles. It made it worse.

Toddles' heart was heavy as he stepped out into the hall, and the iron was in his soul. He was seventeen now, and it looked as though he never would get a chance—except to be a newsboy all his life. Toddles swallowed another lump. He loved railroading; it was his one ambition, his one desire. If he could ever get a chance, he'd show them! He'd show them that he wasn't a joke, just because he was small!

Toddles turned at the head of the stairs to go down, when somebody called his name.

"Here—Toddles! Come here!"

Toddles looked over his shoulder, hesitated, then marched in through the open door of the despatchers' room. Bob Donkin was alone there.

8

"What's your name—Toddles?" inquired Donkin, as Toddles halted before the despatcher's table.

Toddles froze instantly—hard. His fists doubled; there was a smile on Donkin's face. Then his fists slowly uncurled; the smile on Donkin's face had broadened, but there wasn't any malice in the smile.

"Christopher Hyslop Hoogan," said Toddles, unbending.

Donkin put his hand quickly to his mouth—and coughed.

"Um-m!" said he pleasantly. "Super hard on you this morning—Hoogan?"

And with the words Toddles' heart went out to the big despatcher: "Hoogan"—and a man-to-man tone.

"No," said Toddles cordially. "Say, I thought you were on the night trick."

"Double-shift—short-handed," replied Donkin. "Come from New York, don't you?"

"Yes," said Toddles.

"Mother and father down there still?"

It came quick and unexpected, and Toddles stared for a moment. Then he walked over to the window.

"I haven't got any," he said.

There wasn't any sound for an instant, save the clicking of the instruments; then Donkin spoke again—a little gruffly:

"When are you going to quit making an ass of yourself?"

Toddles swung from the window, hurt. Donkin, after all, was like all the rest of them.

"Well?" prompted the despatcher.

"You go to blazes!" said Toddles bitterly, and started for the door. Donkin halted him.

"You're only fooling yourself, Hoogan," he said coolly. "If you wanted what you call a real railroad job as much as you pretend you do, you'd get one."

"Eh?" demanded Toddles defiantly; and went back to the table.

"A fellow," said Donkin, putting a little sting into his words, "never got anywhere by going around with a chip on his shoulder fighting everybody because they called him Toddles, and making a nuisance of himself with the Big Fellows until they got sick of the sight of him."

It was a pretty stiff arraignment. Toddles choked over it, and the angry blood flushed to his cheeks.

"That's all right for you!" he spluttered out hotly. "You don't look too small for the train crews or the roundhouse, and they don't call you Toddles so's nobody 'll forget it. What'd you do?"

"I'll tell you what I'd do," said Donkin quietly. "I'd make everybody on the division wish their own name was Toddles before I was through with them, and I'd make a job for myself."

Toddles blinked helplessly.

"Getting right down to a cash fare," continued Donkin, after a moment,

9

as Toddles did not speak, "they're not so far wrong, either, about you sizing up pretty small for the train crews or the roundhouse, are they?"

"No-o," admitted Toddles reluctantly; "but—"

"Then why not something where there's no handicap hanging over you?" suggested the despatcher—and his hand reached out and touched the sender. "The key, for instance?"

"But I don't know anything about it," said Toddles, still helplessly.

"That's just it," returned Donkin smoothly. "You never tried to learn."

Toddles' eyes widened, and into Toddles' heart leaped a sudden joy. A new world seemed to open out before him in which aspirations, ambitions, longings all were a reality. A key! That was real railroading, the top-notch of railroading, too. First an operator, and then a despatcher, and—and—and then his face fell, and the vision faded.

"How'd I get a chance to learn?" he said miserably. "Who'd teach me?"

The smile was back on Donkin's face as he pushed his chair from the table, stood up, and held out his hand—man-to-man fashion.

"I will," he said. "I liked your grit last night, Hoogan. And if you want to be a railroad man, I'll make you one—before I'm through. I've some old instruments you can have to practise with, and I've nothing to do in my spare time. What do you say?"

Toddles didn't say anything. For the first time since Toddles' advent to the Hill Division, there were tears in Toddles' eyes for some one else to see. Donkin laughed.

"All right, old man, you're on. See that you don't throw me down. And keep your mouth shut; you'll need all your wind. It's work that counts, and nothing else. Now chase yourself! I'll dig up the things you'll need, and you can drop in here and get them when you come off your run to-night."

Spare time! Bob Donkin didn't have any spare time those days! But that was Donkin's way. Spence sick, and two men handling the despatching where three had handled it before, didn't leave Bob Donkin much spare time—not much. But a boost for the kid was worth a sacrifice. Donkin went at it as earnestly as Toddles did—and Toddles was in deadly earnest.

When Toddles left the despatcher's office that morning with Donkin's promise to teach him the key, Toddles had a hazy idea that Donkin had wings concealed somewhere under his coat and was an angel in disguise; and at the end of two weeks he was sure of it. But at the end of a month Bob Donkin was a god! Throw Bob Donkin down! Toddles would have sold his soul for the despatcher.

It wasn't easy, though; and Bob Donkin wasn't an easy-going taskmaster, not by long odds. Donkin had a tongue, and on occasions could use it. Short and quick in his explanations, he expected his pupil to get it short and quick; either that, or Donkin's opinion of him. But Toddles stuck. He'd have crawled on his knees for Donkin anywhere, and he worked like a major—not only for his own advancement, but for what he came to prize quite as much, if not more, Donkin's approval.

Toddles, mindful of Donkin's words, didn't fight so much as the days went by, though he found it difficult to swear off all at once; and on his runs

10

he studied his Morse code, and he had the "calls" of every station on the division off by heart right from the start. Toddles mastered the "sending" by leaps and bounds; but the "taking" came slower, as it does for everybody—but even at that, at the end of six weeks, if it wasn't thrown at him too fast and hard, Toddles could get it after a fashion.

Take it all around, Toddles felt like whistling most of the time; and, pleased with his own progress, looked forward to starting in presently as a full-fledged operator. He mentioned the matter to Bob Donkin—once. Donkin picked his words and spoke fervently. Toddles never brought the subject up again.

And so things went on. Late summer turned to early fall, and early fall to still sharper weather, until there came the night that the operator at Blind River muddled his orders and gave No. 73, the westbound fast freight, her clearance against the second section of the eastbound Limited that doomed them to meet somewhere head-on in the Glacier Cañon; the night that Toddles—but there's just a word or two that comes before.

When it was all over, it was up to Sam Beale, the Blind River operator, straight enough. Beale blundered. That's all there was to it; that covers it all— he blundered. It would have finished Beale's railroad career forever and a day—only Beale played the man, and the instant he realized what he had done, even while the tail lights of the freight were disappearing down the track and he couldn't stop her, he was stammering the tale of his mistake over the wire, the sweat beads dripping from his wrist, his face gray with horror, to Bob Donkin under the green-shaded lamp in the despatchers' room at Big Cloud, miles away.

Donkin got the miserable story over the chattering wire—got it before it was half told—cut Beale out and began to pound the Gap call. And as though it were before him in reality, that stretch of track, fifteen miles of it, from Blind River to the Gap, unfolded itself like a grisly panorama before his mind. There wasn't a half mile of tangent at a single stretch in the whole of it. It swung like the writhings of a snake, through cuts and tunnels, hugging the cañon walls, twisting this way and that. Anywhere else there might be a chance, one in a thousand even, that they would see each other's headlights in time—here it was disaster quick and absolute.

Donkin's lips were set in a thin, straight line. The Gap answered him; and the answer was like the knell of doom. He had not expected anything else; he had only hoped against hope. The second section of the Limited had pulled out of the Gap, eastbound, two minutes before. The two trains were in the open against each other's orders.

In the next room, Carleton and Regan, over their pipes, were at their nightly game of pedro. Donkin called them—and his voice sounded strange to himself. Chairs scraped and crashed to the floor, and an instant later the super and the master mechanic were in the room.

"What's wrong, Bob?" Carleton flung the words from him in a single breath.

Donkin told them. But his fingers were on the key again as he talked. There was still one chance, worse than the thousand-to-one shot; but it was

11

the only one. Between the Gap and Blind River, eight miles from the Gap, seven miles from Blind River, was Cassil's Siding. But there was no night man at Cassil's, and the little town lay a mile from the station. It was ten o'clock—Donkin's watch lay face up on the table before him—the day man at Cassil's went off at seven—the chance was that the day man might have come back to the station for something or other!

Not much of a chance? No—not much! It was a possibility, that was all; and Donkin's fingers worked—the seventeen, the life and death—calling, calling on the night trick to the day man at Cassil's Siding.

Carleton came and stood at Donkin's elbow, and Regan stood at the other; and there was silence now, save only for the key that, under Donkin's fingers, seemed to echo its stammering appeal about the room like the sobbing of a human soul.

"CS—CS—CS," Donkin called; and then, "the seventeen," and then, "hold second Number Two." And then the same thing over and over again.

And there was no answer.

It had turned cold that night and there was a fire in the little heater. Donkin had opened the draft a little while before, and the sheet-iron sides now began to pur red-hot. Nobody noticed it. Regan's kindly, good-humored face had the stamp of horror in it, and he pulled at his scraggly brown mustache, his eyes seemingly fascinated by Donkin's fingers. Everybody's eyes, the three of them, were on Donkin's fingers and the key. Carleton was like a man of stone, motionless, his face set harder than face was ever carved in marble.

It grew hot in the room; but Donkin's fingers were like ice on the key, and, strong man though he was, he faltered.

"Oh, my God!" he whispered—and never a prayer rose more fervently from lips than those three broken words.

Again he called, and again, and again. The minutes slipped away. Still he called—with the life and death—the "seventeen"—called and called. And there was no answer save that echo in the room that brought the perspiration streaming now from Regan's face, a harder light into Carleton's eyes, and a chill like death into Donkin's heart.

Suddenly Donkin pushed back his chair; and his fingers, from the key, touched the crystal of his watch.

"The second section will have passed Cassil's now," he said in a curious, unnatural, matter-of-fact tone. "It'll bring them together about a mile east of there—in another minute."

And then Carleton spoke—master railroader, "Royal" Carleton, it was up to him then, all the pity of it, the ruin, the disaster, the lives out, all the bitterness to cope with as he could. And it was in his eyes, all of it. But his voice was quiet. It rang quick, peremptory, his voice—but quiet.

"Clear the line, Bob," he said. "Plug in the roundhouse for the wrecker—and tell them to send uptown for the crew."

Toddles? What did Toddles have to do with this? Well, a good deal, in one way and another. We're coming to Toddles now. You see, Toddles, since his fracas with Hawkeye, had been put on the Elk River local run that left Big

12

Cloud at 9.45 in the morning for the run west, and scheduled Big Cloud again on the return trip at 10.10 in the evening.

It had turned cold that night, after a day of rain. Pretty cold—the thermometer can drop on occasions in the late fall in the mountains—and by eight o'clock, where there had been rain before, there was now a thin sheeting of ice over everything—very thin—you know the kind—rails and telegraph wires glistening like the decorations on a Christmas tree—very pretty—and also very nasty running on a mountain grade. Likewise, the rain, in a way rain has, had dripped from the car roofs to the platforms—the local did not boast any closed vestibules—and had also been blown upon the car steps with the sweep of the wind, and, having frozen, it stayed there. Not a very serious matter; annoying, perhaps, but not serious, demanding a little extra caution, that was all.

Toddles was in high fettle that night. He had been getting on famously of late; even Bob Donkin had admitted it. Toddles, with his stack of books and magazines, an unusually big one, for a number of the new periodicals were out that day, was dreaming rosy dreams to himself as he started from the door of the first-class smoker to the door of the first-class coach. In another hour now he'd be up in the despatcher's room at Big Cloud for his nightly sitting with Bob Donkin. He could see Bob Donkin there now; and he could hear the big despatcher growl at him in his bluff way: "Use your head—use your head—Hoogan!" It was always "Hoogan," never "Toddles." "Use your head"—Donkin was everlastingly drumming that into him; for the despatcher used to confront him suddenly with imaginary and hair-raising emergencies, and demand Toddles' instant solution. Toddles realized that Donkin was getting to the heart of things, and that some day he, Toddles, would be a great despatcher—like Donkin. "Use your head, Hoogan"—that's the way Donkin talked—"anybody can learn a key, but that doesn't make a railroad man out of him. It's the man when trouble comes who can think quick and think right. Use your—"

Toddles stepped out on the platform—and walked on ice. But that wasn't Toddles' undoing. The trouble with Toddles was that he was walking on air at the same time. It was treacherous running, they were nosing a curve, and in the cab, Kinneard, at the throttle, checked with a little jerk at the "air." And with the jerk, Toddles slipped; and with the slip, the center of gravity of the stack of periodicals shifted, and they bulged ominously from the middle. Toddles grabbed at them—and his heels went out from under him. He ricochetted down the steps, snatched desperately at the handrail, missed it, shot out from the train, and, head, heels, arms and body going every which way at once, rolled over and over down the embankment. And, starting from the point of Toddles' departure from the train, the right of way for a hundred yards was strewn with "the latest magazines" and "new books just out to-day."

Toddles lay there, a little, curled, huddled heap, motionless in the darkness. The tail lights of the local disappeared. No one aboard would miss Toddles until they got into Big Cloud—and found him gone. Which is Irish for saying that no one would attempt to keep track of a newsboy's idiosyncrasies on a train; it would be asking too much of any train crew; and, besides, there was no mention of it in the rules.

13

It was a long while before Toddles stirred; a very long while before consciousness crept slowly back to him. Then he moved, tried to get up—and fell back with a quick, sharp cry of pain. He lay still, then, for a moment. His ankle hurt him frightfully, and his back, and his shoulder, too. He put his hand to his face where something seemed to be trickling warm—and brought it away wet. Toddles, grim little warrior, tried to think. They hadn't been going very fast when he fell off. If they had, he would have been killed. As it was, he was hurt, badly hurt, and his head swam, nauseating him.

Where was he? Was he near any help? He'd have to get help somewhere, or—or with the cold and—and everything he'd probably die out here before morning. Toddles shouted out—again and again. Perhaps his voice was too weak to carry very far; anyway, there was no reply.

He looked up at the top of the embankment, clamped his teeth, and started to crawl. If he got up there, perhaps he could tell where he was. It had taken Toddles a matter of seconds to roll down; it took him ten minutes of untold agony to get up. Then he dashed his hand across his eyes where the blood was, and cried a little with the surge of relief. East, down the track, only a few yards away, the green eye of a switch lamp winked at him.

Where there was a switch lamp there was a siding, and where there was a siding there was promise of a station. Toddles, with the sudden uplift upon him, got to his feet and started along the track—two steps—and went down again. He couldn't walk, the pain was more than he could bear—his right ankle, his left shoulder, and his back—hopping only made it worse—it was easier to crawl.

And so Toddles crawled.

It took him a long time even to pass the switch light. The pain made him weak, his senses seemed to trail off giddily every now and then, and he'd find himself lying flat and still beside the track. It was a white, drawn face that Toddles lifted up each time he started on again—miserably white, except where the blood kept trickling from his forehead.

And then Toddles' heart, stout as it was, seemed to snap. He had reached the station platform, wondering vaguely why the little building that loomed ahead was dark—and now it came to him in a flash, as he recognized the station. It was Cassil's Siding—and there was no night man at Cassil's Siding! The switch lights were lit before the day man left, of course. Everything swam before Toddles' eyes. There—there was no help here. And yet—yet perhaps—desperate hope came again—perhaps there might be. The pain was terrible—all over him. And—and he'd got so weak now—but it wasn't far to the door.

Toddles squirmed along the platform, and reached the door finally—only to find it shut and fastened. And then Toddles fainted on the threshold.

When Toddles came to himself again, he thought at first that he was up in the despatcher's room at Big Cloud with Bob Donkin pounding away on the battered old key they used to practise with—only there seemed to be something the matter with the key, and it didn't sound as loud as it usually did—it seemed to come from a long way off somehow. And then, besides, Bob was working it faster than he had ever done before when they were practising.

14

"Hold second"—second something—Toddles couldn't make it out. Then the "seventeen"—yes, he knew that—that was the life and death. Bob was going pretty quick, though. Then "CS—CS—CS"—Toddles' brain fumbled a bit over that—then it came to him. CS was the call for Cassil's Siding. Cassil's Siding! Toddles' head came up with a jerk.

A little cry burst from Toddles' lips—and his brain cleared. He wasn't at Big Cloud at all—he was at Cassil's Siding—and he was hurt—and that was the sounder inside calling, calling frantically for Cassil's Siding—where he was.

The life and death—the seventeen—it sent a thrill through Toddles' pain-twisted spine. He wriggled to the window. It, too, was closed, of course, but he could hear better there. The sounder was babbling madly.

"Hold second—"

He missed it again—and as, on top of it, the "seventeen" came pleading, frantic, urgent, he wrung his hands.

"Hold second"—he got it this time—"Number Two."

Toddles' first impulse was to smash in the window and reach the key. And then, like a dash of cold water over him, Donkin's words seemed to ring in his ears: "Use your head."

With the "seventeen" it meant a matter of minutes, perhaps even seconds. Why smash the window? Why waste the moment required to do it simply to answer the call? The order stood for itself—"Hold second Number Two." That was the second section of the Limited, east-bound. Hold her! How? There was nothing—not a thing to stop her with. "Use your head," said Donkin in a far-away voice to Toddles' wobbling brain.

Toddles looked up the track—west—where he had come from—to where the switch light twinkled green at him—and, with a little sob, he started to drag himself back along the platform. If he could throw the switch, it would throw the light from green to red, and—and the Limited would take the siding. But the switch was a long way off.

Toddles half fell, half bumped from the end of the platform to the right of way. He cried to himself with low moans as he went along. He had the heart of a fighter, and grit to the last tissue; but he needed it all now—needed it all to stand the pain and fight the weakness that kept swirling over him in flashes.

On he went, on his hands and knees, slithering from tie to tie—and from one tie to the next was a great distance. The life and death, the despatcher's call—he seemed to hear it yet—throbbing, throbbing on the wire.

On he went, up the track; and the green eye of the lamp, winking at him, drew nearer. And then suddenly, clear and mellow through the mountains, caught up and echoed far and near, came the notes of a chime whistle ringing down the gorge.

Fear came upon Toddles then, and a great sob shook him. That was the Limited coming now! Toddles' fingers dug into the ballast, and he hurried—that is, in bitter pain, he tried to crawl a little faster. And as he crawled, he kept his eyes strained up the track—she wasn't in sight yet around the curve—not yet, anyway.

Another foot, only another foot, and he would reach the siding switch—

15

in time—in plenty of time. Again the sob—but now in a burst of relief that, for the moment, made him forget his hurts. He was in time!

He flung himself at the switch lever, tugged upon it—and then, trembling, every ounce of remaining strength seeming to ooze from him, he covered his face with his hands. It was locked—padlocked.

Came a rumble now—a distant roar, growing louder and louder, reverberating down the cañon walls—louder and louder—nearer and nearer. "Hold second Number Two. Hold second Number Two"—the "seventeen," the life and death, pleading with him to hold Number Two. And she was coming now, coming—and—and—the switch was locked. The deadly nausea racked Toddles again; there was nothing to do now—nothing. He couldn't stop her—couldn't stop her. He'd—he'd tried—very hard—and—and he couldn't stop her now. He took his hands from his face, and stole a glance up the track, afraid almost, with the horror that was upon him, to look. She hadn't swung the curve yet, but she would in a minute—and come pounding down the stretch at fifty miles an hour, shoot by him like a rocket to where, somewhere ahead, in some form, he did not know what, only knew that it was there, death and ruin and—

"Use your head!" snapped Donkin's voice to his consciousness.

Toddles' eyes were on the light above his head. It blinked red at him as he stood on the track facing it; the green rays were shooting up and down the line. He couldn't swing the switch—but the lamp was there—and there was the red side to show just by turning it. He remembered then that the lamp fitted into a socket at the top of the switch stand, and could be lifted off—if he could reach it!

It wasn't very high—for an ordinary-sized man—for an ordinary-sized man had to get at it to trim and fill it daily—only Toddles wasn't an ordinary-sized man. It was just nine or ten feet above the rails—just a standard siding switch.

Toddles gritted his teeth, and climbed upon the base of the switch—and nearly fainted as his ankle swung against the rod. A foot above the base was a footrest for a man to stand on and reach up for the lamp, and Toddles drew himself up and got his foot on it—and then at his full height the tips of his fingers only just touched the bottom of the lamp. Toddles cried aloud, and the tears streamed down his face now. Oh, if he weren't hurt—if he could only shin up another foot—but—but it was all he could do to hang there where he was.

What was that! He turned his head. Up the track, sweeping in a great circle as it swung the curve, a headlight's glare cut through the night—and Toddles "shinned" the foot. He tugged and tore at the lamp, tugged and tore at it, loosened it, lifted it from its socket, sprawled and wriggled with it to the ground—and turned the red side of the lamp against second Number Two.

The quick, short blasts of a whistle answered, then the crunch and grind and scream of biting brake-shoes—and the big mountain racer, the 1012, pulling the second section of the Limited that night, stopped with its pilot nosing a diminutive figure in a torn and silver-buttoned uniform, whose hair was clotted red, and whose face was covered with blood and dirt.

16

Masters, the engineer, and Pete Leroy, his fireman, swung from the gangways; Kelly, the conductor, came running up from the forward coach.

Kelly shoved his lamp into Toddles' face—and whistled low under his breath.

"Toddles!" he gasped; and then, quick as a steel trap: "What's wrong?"

"I don't know," said Toddles weakly. "There's—there's something wrong. Get into the clear—on the siding."

"Something wrong," repeated Kelly, "and you don't—"

But Masters cut the conductor short with a grab at the other's arm that was like the shutting of a vise—and then bolted for his engine like a gopher for its hole. From down the track came the heavy, grumbling roar of a freight. Everybody flew then, and there was quick work done in the next half minute— and none too quickly done—the Limited was no more than on the siding when the fast freight rolled her long string of flats, boxes and gondolas thundering by.

And while she passed, Toddles, on the platform, stammered out his story to Kelly.

Kelly didn't say anything—then. With the express messenger and a brakeman carrying Toddles, Kelly kicked in the station door, and set his lamp down on the operator's table.

"Hold me up," whispered Toddles—and, while they held him, he made the despatcher's call.

Big Cloud answered him on the instant. Haltingly, Toddles reported the second section "in" and the freight "out"—only he did it very slowly, and he couldn't think very much more, for things were going black. He got an order for the Limited to run to Blind River and told Kelly, and got the "complete"— and then Big Cloud asked who was on the wire, and Toddles answered that in a mechanical sort of a way without quite knowing what he was doing—and went limp in Kelly's arms.

And as Toddles answered, back in Big Cloud, Regan, the sweat still standing out in great beads on his forehead, fierce now in the revulsion of relief, glared over Donkin's left shoulder, as Donkin's left hand scribbled on a pad what was coming over the wire.

Regan glared fiercely—then he spluttered:

"Who in hell's Christopher Hyslop Hoogan—h'm?"

Donkin's lips had a queer smile on them.

"Toddles," he said.

Regan sat down heavily in his chair.

"What?" demanded the super.

"Toddles," said Donkin. "I've been trying to drum a little railroading into him—on the key."

Regan wiped his face. He looked helplessly from Donkin to the super, and then back again at Donkin.

"But—but what's he doing at Cassil's Siding? How'd he get there—h'm? H'm? How'd he get there?"

"I don't know," said Donkin, his fingers rattling the Cassil's Siding call again. "He doesn't answer any more. We'll have to wait for the story till they make Blind River, I guess."

And so they waited. And presently at Blind River, Kelly, dictating to the operator—not Beale, Beale's day man—told the story. It lost nothing in the telling—Kelly wasn't that kind of a man—he told them what Toddles had done, and he left nothing out; and he added that they had Toddles on a mattress in the baggage car, with a doctor they had discovered amongst the passengers looking after him.

At the end, Carleton tamped down the dottle in the bowl of his pipe thoughtfully with his forefinger—and glanced at Donkin.

"Got along far enough to take a station key somewhere?" he inquired casually. "He's made a pretty good job of it as the night operator at Cassil's."

Donkin was smiling.

"Not yet," he said.

"No?" Carleton's eyebrows went up. "Well, let him come in here with you, then, till he has; and when you say he's ready, we'll see what we can do. I guess it's coming to him; and I guess"—he shifted his glance to the master mechanic—"I guess we'll go down and meet Number Two when she comes in, Tommy."

Regan grinned.

"With our hats in our hands," said the big-hearted master mechanic.

Donkin shook his head.

"Don't you do it," he said. "I don't want him to get a swelled head."

Carleton stared; and Regan's hand, reaching into his back pocket for his chewing, stopped midway.

Donkin was still smiling.

"I'm going to make a railroad man out of Toddles," he said.

18

Chapter II

OWSLEY AND THE 1601

His name was Owsley—Jake Owsley—and he was a railroad man before ever he came to Big Cloud and the Hill Division—before ever the Hill Division was even advanced to the blue-print stage, before steel had ever spider-webbed the stubborn Rockies, before the Herculean task of bridging a continent was more than a thought in even the most ambitious minds.

Owsley was an engineer, and he came from the East, when they broke ground at Big Cloud for a start toward the western goal through the mighty range, a comparatively young man—thirty, or thereabouts. Then, inch by inch and foot by foot, Owsley, with his ballast cars and his boxes and his flats bumping material behind him, followed the construction gangs as they burrowed and blasted and trestled their way along—day in, day out, month in, month out, until the years went by, and they were through the Rockies, with the Coast and the blue of the Pacific in sight.

First over every bridge and culvert, first through every cut, first through every tunnel shorn in the bitter gray rock of the mountain sides, the pilot of Owsley's engine nosed its way; and, when the rough of the work was over, and in the hysteria of celebration, the toll of lives, the hardships and the cost were forgotten for the moment, and the directors and their guests crowded the cab and perched on running boards and footplates till you couldn't see the bunting they'd draped the engine with, and the mahogany coaches behind looked like the striped sticks of candy the kids buy on account of more bunting, and then some, and the local band they'd brought along from Big Cloud got the mouthpieces of their trombones and cornets mixed up with the necks of champagne bottles, and the Indian braves squatted gravely at different points along the trackside and thought their white brothers had gone mad, Owsley was at the throttle for the first through run over the division—it was Owsley's due.

Then other years went by, and the steel was shaken down into the permanent right of way that is an engineering marvel to-day, and Owsley still held a throttle on a through run—just kept growing a little older, that was all—but one of the best of them, for all that—steadier than the younger men, wise in experience, and with a love for his engine that was like the love of a man for a woman.

It's a strange thing, perhaps, a love like that; but, strange or not, there was never an engineer worth his salt who hasn't had it—some more than others, of course—as some men's love for a woman is deeper than others. With Owsley it came pretty near being the whole thing, and it was queer enough to see him when they'd change his engine to give him a newer and more improved type for a running mate. He'd refuse point-blank at first to be

19

separated from the obsolete engine, that was either carded for some local jerk-water, mixed-freight run, or for a construction job somewhere.

"Leave her with me," he'd say to Regan, the master mechanic. "Leave me with her. You can give my run to some one else, Regan, d'ye mind? It's little I care for the swell run; me and the old girl sticks. I'll have nothing else."

But the bluff, fat, big-hearted, good-natured, little master mechanic, knew his man—and he knew an engineer when he saw one. Regan would no more have thought of letting Owsley get away from the Imperial's throttle than he would have thought of putting call boys in the cabs to run his engines.

"H'm!" he would say, blinking fast at Owsley. "Feel that way, do you? Well, then, mabbe it's about time you quit altogether. I didn't offer you your choice, did I? You take the Imperial with what I give you to take her with—or take nothing. Think it over!"

And Owsley, perforce, had to "think it over"—and, perforce, he stayed on the limited run.

Came then the day when changes in engine types were not so frequent, and a fair maximum in machine-design efficiency had been obtained—and Owsley came to love, more than he had ever loved any engine before, his big, powerful, 1600-class racer, with its four pairs of massive drivers, that took the curves with the grace of a circling bird, that laughed in glee at anything lower than a three per cent grade, and tackled the "fives" with no more than a grunt of disdain—Owsley and the 1601, right from the start, clipped fifty-five minutes off the running time of the Imperial Limited through the Rockies, where before it had been nip and tuck to make the old schedule anywhere near the dot.

For three years it was Owsley and the 1601; for three years east and west through the mountains—and a smile in the roundhouse at him as he nursed and cuddled and groomed his big flyer, in from a run. Not now—they don't smile now about it. It was Owsley and the 1601 for three years—and at the end it was still Owsley and the 1601. The two are coupled together—they never speak of one on the Hill Division without the other—Owsley and the 1601.

Owsley! One of the old guard who answered the roll call at the birth of the Hill Division! Forty years a railroader—call boy at ten—twenty years of service, counting the construction period, on the Hill Division! Straight and upright as a young sapling at fifty-odd, with a swing through the gangway that the younger men tried to imitate; hair short-cropped, a little grizzled; gray, steady eyes; a beard whose color, once brown, was nondescript, kind of shading tawny and gray in streaks; a slim, little man, overalled and jumpered, with greasy, peaked cap—and, wifeless, without kith or kin save his engine, the star boarder at Mrs. McCann's short-order house. Liked by everybody, known by everybody on the division down to the last Polack construction hand, quiet, no bluster about him, fall of good-humored fun, ready to take his part or do his share in anything going, from a lodge minstrel show to sitting up all night and playing trained nurse to anybody that needed one—that was Owsley.

Oh, you, in your millions, who ride in trains by day and night, do you ever give a thought to the men into whose keeping you hand your lives? Does it ever occur to you that they are not just part of the equipment of iron and wood and steel and rolling things to be accepted callously, as bought and paid for with the strip of ticket that you hold, animate only that you may voice your grumblings and your discontent at some delay that saves you probably from being hurled into eternity while you chafe impatiently and childishly at something you know nothing about—that they, like you, are human too, with hopes achieved and aspirations shattered, and plans and interests in life? Have you ever thought that there was a human side to railroading, and that—but we were speaking of Owsley, Jake Owsley, perhaps you'll understand a little better farther on along the right of way.

Elbow Bend, were it not for the insurmountable obstacles that Dame Nature had seen fit to place there—the bed of the Glacier River on one side and a sheer rock base of mountain on the other—would have been a black mark against the record of the engineering corps who built the station. Speaking generally, it's not good railroad practice to put a station on a curve—when it can be helped. Elbow Bend, the whole of it, main line and siding, made a curve—that's how it got its name. And yet, in a way, it wasn't the curve that was to blame; though, too, in a way, it was—Owsley had a patched eye that night from a bit of steel that had got into it in the afternoon, nothing much, but a patch on it to keep the cold and the sweep of the wind out.

It was the eastbound run, and, to make up for the loss of time a slow order over new construction work back a dozen miles or so had cost him, the 1601 was hitting a pretty fast clip as he whistled for Elbow Bend. Owsley checked just a little as he nosed the curve—the Imperial Limited made no stop at Elbow Bend—and then, as the 1601 sort of got her footing, so to speak, on the long bend, he opened her out again, and the storm of exhausts from her short, stubby stack went echoing through the mountains like the play of artillery.

The light of the west-end siding switch flashed by like a scintillating gem in the darkness. Brannigan, Owsley's fireman, pulled his door, shooting the cab and the heavens full of leaping, fiery red, and swung to the tender for a shovelful of coal. Owsley, crouched a little forward in his seat, his body braced against the cant of the mogul on the curve, was "feeling" the throttle with careful hand, as he peered ahead through the cab glass. Came the station lights; the black bulk of a locomotive, cascading steam from her safety, on the siding; and then the thundering reverberation as the 1601 began to sweep past a long, curving line of boxes, flats and gondolas, the end of which Owsley could not see—for the curve.

Owsley relaxed a little. That was right—Extra No. 49, west, was to cross him at Elbow Bend—and she was on the siding as she should be. His headlight, streaming out at a tangent to the curve, played its ray kaleidoscopically along the sides of the string of freights, now edging the roof of a box car, now opening a hole to the gray rock of the cut when a flat or two intervened—and then, sudden, quick as doom, with a yell from his fireman ringing in his ears, Owsley, his jaws clamping like a steel trap, flung his arm

21

forward, jamming the throttle shut, while with the other hand he grabbed at the "air."

Owsley had seen it, too—as quick as Brannigan—a figure, arms waving frantically, for a fleeting second strangely silhouetted in the dancing headlight's glare on the roof of one of the box cars. A wild shout from the man, fluttering, indistinguishable, reached them as they roared by—then the grind and scream of brake-shoes as the "air" went on—the answering shudder vibrating through the cab of the big racer—the meeting clash of buffer plates echoing down the length of the train behind—and a queer obstructing blackness dead ahead ere the headlight, tardy in its sweep, could point the way—but Owsley knew now—too late.

Brannigan screamed in his ear.

"She ain't in the clear!" he screamed. "It's a swipe! She ain't in the clear!" he screamed again—and took a flying leap through the off-side gangway.

Owsley never turned his head—only held there, grim-faced, tight-lipped, facing what was to come—facing it with clear head, quick brain, doing what he could to lessen the disaster, as forty years had schooled him to face emergency. Owsley—for forty years with his record, until that moment, as clean and unsmirched as the day he started as a kid calling train crews back in the little division town on the Penn in the far East! Strange it should come to Owsley, the one man of all you'd never think it would! It's hard to understand the running orders of the Great Trainmaster sometimes—isn't it? And sometimes it doesn't help much to realize that we never will understand this side of the Great Divide—does it?

The headlight caught it now—seemed to gloat upon it in a flood of blazing, insolent light—the rear cars of the freight crawling frantically from the main line to the siding—then the pitiful yellow from the cupola of the caboose, the light from below filtering up through the windows. It seared into Owsley's brain lightning quick, but vivid in every detail in a horrible, fascinating way. It was a second, the fraction of a second since Brannigan had jumped—it might have been an hour.

The front of the caboose seemed to leap suddenly at the 1601, seemed to rise up in the air and hurl itself at the straining engine as though in impotent fury at unwarranted attack. There was a terrific crash, the groan and rend of timber, the sickening grind and crunch as the van went to matchwood—the débris hurtling along the running boards, shattering the cab glass in flying splinters—and Owsley dropped where he stood—like a log. And the pony truck caught the tongue of the open switch, and, with a vicious, nasty lurch, the 1601 wrenched herself loose from her string of coaches, staggered like a lost and drunken soul a few yards along the ties—and turned turtle in the ditch.

It was a bad spill, but it might have been worse, a great deal worse—a box car and the van for the junk heap, and the 1601 for the shops to repair fractures—and nobody hurt except Owsley.

But they couldn't make head or tail of the cause of it. Everybody went on the carpet for it—and still it was a mystery. The main line was clear at the west end of the siding, and the switch was right; everybody was agreed on

22

that, and it showed that way on the face of it—and that was as it should have been. The operator at Elbow Bend swore that he had shown his red, and that it was showing when the Limited swept by. He said he knew it was going to be a close shave whether the freight, a little late and crowding the Limited's running time, would be clear of the main line without delaying the express, and he had shown his red before ever he had heard her whistle—his red was showing. The engine crew and the train crew of Extra No. 49, west, backed the operator up—the red was showing.

Brannigan, the fireman, didn't count as a witness. The only light he'd seen at all was the west-end switch light, the curve had hidden anything ahead until after he'd pulled his door and turned to the tender for coal, and by then they were past the station. And Owsley, pretty badly smashed up, and in bed down in Mrs. McCann's short-order house, talked kind of queer when he got around to where he could talk at all. They asked him what color light the station semaphore was showing, and Owsley said white—white as the moon. That's what he said—white as the moon. And they weren't quite sure he understood what they were driving at.

For a week that's all they could make out of it, and then, with Regan scratching his head over it one day in confab with Carleton, the superintendent, it came more by chance than anything else.

"Blamed if I know what to make of it!" he growled. "Ordinary, six men's words would be the end of it, but Owsley's the best man that ever latched a throttle in our cabs, and for twenty years his record's cleaner than a baby's. What he says now don't count, because he ain't right again yet; but what you can't get away from is the fact that Owsley's not the man to have slipped a signal. Either the six of them are doing him cold to save their own skins, or there's something queer about it."

Carleton, "Royal" Carleton, in his grave, quiet way, shook his head.

"We've been trying hard enough to get to the bottom of it, Tommy," he said. "I wish to the Lord we could. I don't think the men are lying—they tell a pretty straight story. I've been wondering about that patch Owsley had on his eye, and—"

"What's that got to do with it?" cut in the blunt little master mechanic, who made no bones about his fondness for the engineer. "He isn't blind in the other, is he?"

Carleton stared at the master mechanic for a moment, pulling ruminatively at his brier; then—they were in the super's office at the time—his fist came down with a sudden bang upon the desk.

"I believe you've got it, Tommy!" he exclaimed.

"Believe I've got it!" echoed Regan, and his hand halfway to his mouth with his plug of chewing stopped in mid-air. "Got what? I said he wasn't blind in the other, and neither he is—you know that as well as I do."

"Wait!" said Carleton. "It's very rare, I know, but it seems to me I've heard of it. Wait a minute, Tommy." He was leaning over from his chair and twirling the little revolving bookcase beside the desk, as he spoke—not a large library was Carleton's, just a few technical books, and his cherished Britannica. He pulled out a volume of the encyclopedia, laid it upon his desk, and began to turn the leaves. "Yes, here it is," he said, after a moment. "Listen"—and he commenced to read rapidly:

"'The most common form of Daltonism'—that's colorblindness you know, Tommy—'depends on the absence of the red sense. Great additions to our knowledge of this subject, if only in confirmation of results already deduced from theory, have been obtained in the last few years by Holmgren, who has experimented on two persons, each of whom was found to have one color-blind eye, the other being nearly normal.'"

"Color-blind!" spluttered the master mechanic.

"In one eye," said Carleton, sort of as though he were turning a problem over in his mind. "That would account for it all, Tommy. As far as I know, one doesn't go color-blind—one is born that way—and if this is what's at the bottom of it, Owsley's been color-blind all his life in one eye, and probably didn't know what was the matter. That would account for his passing the tests, and would account for what happened at Elbow Bend. It was the patch that did it—you remember what he said—the light was white as the moon."

"And he's out!" stormed Regan. "Out for keeps—after forty years. Say, d'ye know what this'll mean to Owsley—do you, eh, do you? It'll be hell for him, Carleton—he thinks more of his engine than a woman does of her child."

Carleton closed the volume and replaced it mechanically in the bookcase.

Regan's teeth met in his plug and jerked savagely at the tobacco.

"I wish to blazes you hadn't read that!" he muttered fiercely. "What's to be done now?"

"I'm afraid there's only one thing to be done," Carleton answered gravely. "Sentiment doesn't let us out—there's too many lives at stake every time he takes out an engine. He'll have to try the color test with a patch over the same eye he had it on that night. Perhaps, after all, I'm wrong, and—"

"He's out!" said the master mechanic gruffly. "He's out—I don't need any test to know that now. That's what's the matter, and no other thing on earth. It's rough, damn rough, ain't it—after forty years?"—and Regan, with a short laugh, strode to the window and stood staring out at the choked railroad yards below him.

And Regan was right. Three weeks later, when he got out of bed, Owsley took the color test under the queerest conditions that ever a railroad man took it—with his right eye bandaged—and failed utterly.

But Owsley didn't quite seem to understand—and little Doctor McTurk, the company surgeon, was badly worried, and had been all along. Owsley was a long way from being the same Owsley he was before the accident. Not physically—that way he was shaping up pretty well, but his head seemed to bother him—he seemed to have lost his grip on a whole lot of things. They gave him the test more to settle the point in their own minds, but they knew before they gave it to him that it wasn't much use as far as he was concerned one way or the other. There was more than a mere matter of color wrong with Owsley now. And maybe that was the kindest thing that could have happened to him, maybe it made it easier for him since the colors barred him anyway from ever pulling a throttle again—not to understand!

24

They tried to tell him he hadn't passed the color test—Regan tried to tell him in a clumsy, big-hearted way, breaking it as easy as he could—and Owsley laughed as though he were pleased—just laughed, and with a glance at the clock and a jerky pull at his watch for comparison, a way he had of doing, walked out of Riley's, the trainmaster's office, and started across the tracks for the roundhouse. Owsley's head wasn't working right—it was as though the mechanism was running down—the memory kind of tapering off. But the 1601, his engine—stuck. And it was train time when he walked out of Riley's office that afternoon—the first afternoon he'd been out of bed and Mrs. McCann's motherly hands since the night at Elbow Bend.

Perhaps you'll smile a little tolerantly at this, and perhaps you'll say the story's "cooked." Well, perhaps! If you think that way about it, you'll probably smile more broadly still, and with the same grounds for a smile, before we make division and sign the train register at the end of the run. Anyway, that afternoon, as Owsley, out for the first time, walked a little shakily across the turntable and through the big engine doors into the roundhouse, the 1601 was out for the first time herself from the repair shops, and for the first time since the accident was standing on the pit, blowing from a full head of steam, and ready to move out and couple on for the mountain run west, as soon as the Imperial Limited came in off the Prairie Division from the East. Is it a coincidence to smile at? Yes? Well, then, there is more of the same humor to come. They tell the story on the Hill Division this way, those hard, grimy-handed men of the Rockies, in the cab, in the caboose, in the smoker, if you get intimate enough with the conductor or brakeman, in the roundhouse and in the section shanty—but they never smile themselves when they tell it.

Paxley, big as two of Owsley, promoted from a local passenger run, had been given the Imperial—and the 1601. He was standing by the front-end, chatting with Clarihue, the turner, as Owsley came in.

Owsley didn't appear to notice either of the men—didn't answer either of them as they greeted him cheerily. His face, that had grown white from his illness, was tinged a little red with excitement, and his eyes seemed trying to take in every single detail of the big mountain racer all at once. He walked along to the gangway, his shoulders sort of bracing further back all the time, and then with the old-time swing he disappeared into the cab. He was out again in a minute with a long-spouted oil can, and, just as he always did, started in for an oil around.

Paxley and Clarihue looked at each other. And Paxley sort of fumbled aimlessly with the peak of his cap, while Clarihue couldn't seem to get the straps of his overalls adjusted comfortably. Brannigan, Owsley's old fireman, joined them from the other side of the engine. None of them spoke. Owsley went on oiling—making the round slowly, carefully, head and shoulders hidden completely at times as he leaned in over the rod, poking at the motion-gear. And Regan, who had followed Owsley, coming in, got the thing in a glance—and swore fiercely deep down in his throat.

Not much to choke strong men up and throw them into the "dead-center"? Well, perhaps not. Just a railroad man for forty years, just an engineer, and the best of them all—out!

25

Owsley finished his round, and, instead of climbing into the cab through the opposite gangway, came back to the front-end and halted before Jim Clarihue.

"I see you got that injector valve packed at last," said he approvingly. "She looks cleaner under the guard-plates than I've seen her for a long time, too. Give me the 'table, Jim."

Not one of them answered. Regan said afterward that he felt as though there'd been a head-on smash somewhere inside of him. But Owsley didn't seem to expect any answer. He went on down the side of the locomotive, went in through the gangway, and the next instant the steam came purring into the cylinders, just warming her up for a moment, as Owsley always did before he moved out of the roundhouse.

It was Clarihue then who spoke—with a kind of catchy jerk:

"She's stiff from the shops. He ain't strong enough to hold her on the 'table."

Regan looked at Paxley—and tugged at his scraggly little brown mustache.

"You'll have to get him out of there, Bob," he said gruffly, to hide his emotion. "Get him out—gently."

The steam was coming now into the cylinders with a more businesslike rush—and Paxley jumped for the cab. As he climbed in, Brannigan followed, and in a sort of helpless way hung in the gangway behind him. Owsley was standing up, his hand on the throttle, and evidently puzzled a little at the stiffness of the reversing lever, that refused to budge on the segment with what strength he had in one hand to give to it.

Paxley reached over and tried to loosen Owsley's hand on the throttle.

"Let me take her, Jake," he said.

Owsley stared at him for a moment in mingled perplexity and irritation.

"What in blazes would I let you take her for?" he snapped suddenly, and attempted to shoulder Paxley aside. "Get out of here, and mind your own business! Get out!" He snatched his wrist away from Paxley's fingers and gave a jerk at the throttle—and the 1601 began to move.

The 'table wasn't set, and Paxley had no time for hesitation. More roughly than he had any wish to do it, he brushed Owsley's hand from the throttle and latched the throttle shut.

And then, quick as a cat, Owsley was on him.

It wasn't much of a fight—hardly a fight at all—Owsley, from three weeks on his back, was dropping weak. But Owsley snatched up a spanner that was lying on the seat, and smashed Paxley with it between the eyes. Paxley was a big man physically—and a bigger man still where it counts most and doesn't show—with the blood streaming down his face, and half blinded, regardless of the blows that Owsley still tried to rain upon him, he picked the engineer up in his arms like a baby, and with Brannigan, dropping off the gangway and helping, got Owsley to the ground.

Owsley hadn't been fit for excitement or exertion of that kind—for any kind of excitement or exertion. They took him back to his boarding house, and Doctor McTurk screwed his eyes up over him in the funny way he had when things looked critical, and Mrs. McCann nursed him daytimes, and Carleton and Regan and two or three others took turns sitting up with him nights—for a month. Then Owsley began to mend again, and began to talk of getting back on the Limited run with the 1601—always the 1601. And most times he talked pretty straight, too—as straight as any of the rest of them—only his memory seemed to keep that queer sort of haze over it—up to the time of the accident it seemed all right, but after that things blurred woefully.

Regan, Carleton and Doctor McTurk went into committee over it in the super's office one afternoon just before Owsley was out of bed again.

"What d'ye say—h'm? What d'ye say, doc?" demanded Regan.

Doctor McTurk, scientific and professional in every inch of his little body, lined his eyebrows up into a ferocious black streak across his forehead, and talked medicine in medical terms into the superintendent and the master mechanic for a good five minutes.

When he had finished, Carleton's brows were puckered, too, his face was a little blank, and he tapped the edge of his desk with the end of his pencil somewhat helplessly.

Regan tugged at both ends of his mustache and sputtered.

"What the blazes!" he growled. "Give it to us in plain railroading! Has he got rights through—or hasn't he? Does he get better—or does he not? H'm?"

"I don't know, I tell you!" retorted Doctor McTurk. "I don't know—and that's flat. I've told you why a minute ago. I don't know whether he'll ever be better in his head than he is now—otherwise he'll come around all right."

"Well, what's to be done?" inquired Carleton.

"He's got to work for a living, I suppose—eh?" Doctor McTurk answered. "And he can't run an engine any more on account of the colors, no matter what happens. That's the state of affairs, isn't it?"

Carleton didn't answer; Regan only mumbled under his breath.

"Well then," submitted Doctor McTurk, "the best thing for him, temporarily at least, to build him up, is fresh air and plenty of it. Give him a job somewhere out in the open."

Carleton's eyebrows went up. He looked across at Regan questioningly.

"He wouldn't take it," said Regan slowly. "There's nothing to anything for Owsley but the 1601."

"Wouldn't take it!" snapped the little doctor. "He's got to take it. And if you care half what you pretend you do for him, you've got to see that he does."

"How about construction work with McCann?" suggested Carleton. "He likes McCann, and he's lived at their place for years now."

"Just the thing!" declared Doctor McTurk heartily. "Couldn't be better."

Carleton looked at Regan again.

"You can handle him better than any one else, Tommy. Suppose you see what you can do? And speaking of the 1601, how would it do to tell him what's happened in the last month. Maybe he wouldn't think so much of her as he does now."

"No!" exclaimed Doctor McTurk quickly. "Don't you do it!"

"No," said Regan, shaking his head. "It would make him worse. He'd

27

blame it on Paxley, and we'd have trouble on our hands before you could bat an eyelash."

"Yes; perhaps you're right," agreed Carleton. "Well, then, try him on the construction tack, Tommy."

And so Regan went that afternoon from the super's office over to Mrs. McCann's short-order house, and up to Owsley's room.

"Well, how's Jake to-day?" he inquired, in his bluff, cheery way, drawing a chair up beside the bed.

"I'm fine, Regan," said Owsley earnestly. "Fine! What day is this?"

"Thursday," Regan told him.

"Yes," said Owsley, "that's right—Thursday. Well, you can put me down to take the old 1601 out Monday night. I'm figuring to get back on the run Monday night, Regan."

Regan ran his hand through his short-cropped hair, twisted a little uneasily in his chair—and coughed to fill in the gap.

"I wouldn't be in a hurry about it, if I were you, Jake," he said. "In fact, that's what I came over to have a little talk with you about. We don't think you're strong enough yet for the cab."

"Who don't?" demanded Owsley antagonistically.

"The doctor and Carleton and myself—we were just speaking about it."

"Why ain't I?" demanded Owsley again.

"Why, good Lord, Jake," said Regan patiently, "you've been sick—dashed near two months. A man can't expect to get out of bed after a lay-off like that and start right in again before he gets his strength back. You know that as well as I do."

"Mabbe I do, and mabbe I don't," said Owsley, a little uncertainly. "How'm I going to get strong?"

"Well," replied Regan, "the doc says open-air work to build you up, and we were thinking you might like to put in a month, say, with Bill McCann up on the Elk River work—helping him boss Polacks, for instance."

Owsley didn't speak for a moment, he seemed to be puzzling something out; then, still in a puzzled way:

"And then what about after the month?"

"Why then," said Regan, "then"—he reached for his hip pocket and his plug, pulled out the plug, picked the heart-shaped tin tag off with his thumb nail, decided not to take a bite, and put the blackstrap back in his pocket again. "Why then," said he, "you'll—you ought to be all right again."

Owsley sat up in bed.

"You playing straight with me, Regan?" he asked slowly.

"Sure," said Regan gruffly. "Sure, I am."

Owsley passed his hand two or three times across his eyes.

"I don't quite seem to get the signals right on what's happened," he said. "I guess I've been pretty sick. I kind of had a feeling a minute ago that you were trying to side-track me, but if you say you ain't, I believe you. I ain't going to be side-tracked. When I quit for keeps, I quit in the cab with my boots on—no way else. I'll tell you something, Regan. When I go out, I'm going out with my hand on the throttle, same as it's been for more'n twenty years. And

28

me and the old 1601, we're going out together—that's the way I want to go when the time comes—and that's the way I'm going. I've known it for a long time."

"How do you mean you've known it for a long time?" Regan swallowed a lump in his throat, as he asked the question—Owsley's mind seemed to be wandering a little.

"I dunno," said Owsley, and his hand crept to his head again. "I dunno—I just know." Then abruptly: "I got to get strong for the old 1601, ain't I? That's right. I'll go up there—only you give me your word I get the 1601 back after the month."

Regan's eyes, from the floor, lifted and met Owsley's steadily.

"You bet, Jake!" he said.

"Give me your hand on it," said Owsley happily.

And Regan gripped the engineer's hand.

Regan left the room a moment or two after that, and on his way downstairs he brushed the back of his hand across his eyes.

"What the hell!" he growled to himself. "I had to lie to him, didn't I?"

And so, on the Monday following, Owsley went up to the new Elk River road work, and— But just a moment, we've over-run our holding orders a bit, and we've got to back for the siding. The 1601 crosses us here.

Superstition is a queer thing, isn't it? Speaking generally, we look on it somewhat from the viewpoint of the old adage that all men are mortal save ourselves; that is, we can accept, with more or less tolerant condescension, the existence of superstition in others, and, with more or less tolerant condescension, put it down to ignorance—in others. But we're not superstitious ourselves, so we've got to have something better to go on than that, as far as the 1601 is concerned. Well, the 1601 was pretty badly shaken up that night in the spill at Elbow Bend, and when they overhauled her in the shops, while they made her look like new, perhaps they missed something down deep in her vitals in the doing of it; perhaps she was weakened and strained where they didn't know she was; perhaps they didn't get clean to the bottom of all her troubles; perhaps they made a bad job of a job that looked all right under the fresh paint and the gold leaf. There's nothing superstitious about that, is there? It's logical and reasonable enough to satisfy even the most hypercritical crank amongst us anti-superstitionists—isn't it?

But that doesn't go in the cabs, and the roundhouses, and the section shanties on the Hill Division. You could talk and reason out there along that line until you were blue in the face from shortness of breath, and they'd listen to you while they wiped their hands on a hunk of waste—they'd listen, but they've got their own notions.

It was the night at Elbow Bend that Owsley and the 1601 together first went wrong; and both went into hospital together and came out together to the day—the 1601 for her old run through the mountains, and Owsley with no other idea in life possessing his sick brain than to make the run with her. Owsley had a relapse that day—and that day, twenty miles west of Big Cloud, the 1601 blew her cylinder head off. And from then on, while Owsley lay in bed again at Mrs. McCann's, the 1601, when she wasn't in the shops from an endless series of mishaps, was turning the hair gray on a despatcher or two, and had got most of Paxley's nerve.

But what's the use of going into all the details—there was enough paper used up in the specification repair-sheets! Going slow up a grade and around a curve that was protected with ninety-pound guard-rails, her pony truck jumped the steel where a baby carriage would have held the right of way; she broke this, she broke that, she was always breaking something; and rare was the night that she didn't limp into division dragging the grumbling occupants of the mahogany sleepers after her with her schedule gone to smash. And then, finally, putting a clincher on it all, she ended up, when she was running fifty miles an hour, by shedding a driving wheel, and nearly killing Paxley as the rod ripped through and through, tearing the right-hand side of the cab into mangled wreckage—and that finished her for the Limited run. Do you recall that Owsley, too, was finished for the Limited run?

Superstition? You can figure it any way you like—they've got their own notions on the Hill Division.

When the 1601 came out of the shops again after that, the marks of authority's disapprobation were heavy upon her—the gold leaf of the passenger flyer was gone; the big figures on the tender were only yellow paint.

Regan scowled at her as they ran her into the yards.

"Damn her!" said Regan fervently; and then, as he thought of Owsley, he scowled deeper, and yanked at his mustache. "Say," said Regan heavily, "it's queer, ain't it? Blamed queer—h'm—when you come to think of it?"

And so, while the 1601, disfranchised, went to hauling extra freights, kind of a misfit doing spare jobs, anything that turned up, no regular run any more, Owsley, kind of a misfit, too, without any very definite duties, because there wasn't anything very definite they dared trust him with, went up on the Elk River work with Bill McCann, the husband of Mrs. McCann, who kept the short-order house.

Owsley told McCann, as he had told Regan, that he was only up there getting strong again for the 1601—and he went around on the construction work whistling and laughing like a schoolboy, and happy as a child—getting strong again for the 1601!

McCann couldn't see anything very much the matter with Owsley—except that Owsley was happy. He studied the letter Regan had sent him, and watched the engineer, and scratched at his bullet head, and blinked fast with his gray Irish eyes.

"Faith," said McCann, "it's them that's off their chumps—not Owsley. Hark to him singin' out there like a lark! An', bedad, ut's mesilf'll tell 'em so!"

And he did. He wrote his opinion in concise, forceful, misspelled English on the back of a requisition slip, and sent it to Regan. Regan didn't say much—just choked up a little when he read it. McCann wasn't strong on diagnosis.

It was still early spring when Owsley went to the new loop they were building around the main line to tap a bit of the country south, and the chinook, blowing warm, had melted most of the snow, and the creeks, rivers and sluices were running full—the busiest time in all the year for the trackmen and section hands. It was a summer's job, the loop—if luck was with them—and the orders were to push the work, the steel was to be down before the snow flew again. That was the way it was put up to McCann when he first moved into construction camp, a short while before Owsley joined him.

"Then give me the stuff," said McCann. "Shoot the material along, an' don't lave me bitin' me finger nails for the want av ut—d'ye moind?"

So the Big Cloud yards, too, had orders—standing orders to rush out all material for the Elk River loop as fast as it came in from the East.

In a way, of course, that was how it happened—from the standing orders. It was just the kind of work the 1601 was hanging around waiting to do—the odd jobs—pulling the extras. Ordinarily, perhaps, somebody would have thought of it, and maybe they wouldn't have sent her out—maybe they would. You can't operate a railroad wholly on sentiment—and there were ten cars of steel and as many more of ties and conglomerate supplies helping to choke up the Big Cloud yards when they should have been where they were needed a whole lot more—in McCann's construction camp.

But there had been two days of bad weather in the mountains, two days of solid rain, track troubles, and troubles generally, and what with one thing and another, the motive-power department had been taxed to its limit. The first chance they got in a lull of pressure, not the storm, they sent the material west with the only spare engine that happened to be in the roundhouse at the time—the 1601—and never thought of Owsley. Regan might have, would have, if he had known it; but Regan didn't know it—then. Regan wasn't handling the operating.

Perhaps, after all, they needn't have been in a belated hurry that day—McCann and his foreigners had done nothing but hug their shanties and listen to the rain washing the ballast away for two days and a half, until, as it got dark on that particular day, barely a week after Owsley had come to the work, they listened, by way of variation, to the chime whistle of an engine that came ringing down with the wind.

McCann and Owsley shared a little shanty by themselves, and McCann was trying to initiate Owsley into the mysteries of that grand old game so dear to the hearts of Irishmen—the game of forty-five. But at the first sound of the whistle, the cards dropped from Owsley's hands, and he jumped to his feet.

"D'ye hear that! D'ye hear that!" he cried.

"An' fwhat av ut?" inquired McCann. "Ut'll be the material we'd be hung up for, if 'twere not for the storm."

Owsley leaned across the table, his head turned a little sideways in a curious listening attitude—leaned across the table and gripped McCann's shoulders.

"It's the 1601!" he whispered. He put his finger to his lips to caution silence, and with the other hand patted McCann's shoulder confidentially. "It's the 1601!" he whispered—and jumped for the door—out into the storm.

"For the love av Mike!" gasped McCann, staggering to his feet as the lamp flared up and out with the draft. "Now, fwhat the divil—from this, an' the misfortunate way he picks up forty-foive, mabbe, mabbe I was wrong, an'

31

mabbe ut's queer after all, he is, an'—" McCann was still muttering to himself as he stumbled to the door.

There was no sign of Owsley—only a string of boxes and flats, backed down, and rattling and bumping to a halt on the temporary track a hundred yards away—then the joggling light of a trainman running through the murk and, evidently, hopping the engine pilot, for the light disappeared suddenly and McCann heard the locomotive moving off again.

McCann couldn't see the main line, or the little station they had erected there since the work began for the purpose of operating the construction trains, but he knew well enough what was going on. Off the main line, in lieu of a turntable and to facilitate matters generally, they had built a Y into the construction camp; and the work train, in from the East, had dropped its caboose on the main line between the arms of the Y, gone ahead, backed the flats and boxes down the west-end arm of the Y into the camp, left them there in front of him, and the engine, shooting off on the main line again, via the east-end arm of the Y, would be heading east, and had only to back up the main line and couple on the caboose for the return trip to Big Cloud—there were no empties to go back, he knew.

It was raining in torrents, pitilessly, and, over the gusts of wind, the thunder went racketing through the mountains like the discharge of heavy guns. McCann swore with sincerity as he gazed from the doorway, didn't like the look of it, and was minded to let Owsley go to the devil; but, instead, after getting into rubber boots, a rubber coat, and lighting a lantern, he put his head down to butt the storm, goat fashion, and started out.

"Me conscience 'ud not be clear av anything happened the man," communed McCann, as he battered and sloshed his way along. "'Tis wan hell av a night!"

McCann lost some time. He could have made a shortcut over to the main line and the station; but, instead, thinking Owsley might have run up the track beside the camp toward the front-end of the construction train and the engine, he kept along past the string of cars. There was no Owsley; and the only result he obtained from shouting at the top of his lungs was to have the wind slap his voice back in his teeth. McCann headed then for the station. He took the west-end arm of the Y, that being the nearer to his destination. Halfway across, he heard the engine backing up on the main line, and, a moment later, saw her headlight and the red tail lights of the caboose as she coupled on.

Of course, it was against the rules—but rules are broken sometimes, aren't they? It was a wicked night, and the station, diminutive and makeshift as it was, looked mighty hospitable and inviting by comparison. The engine crew, Matt Duggan and Greene, his fireman, thought it sized up better while they were waiting for orders than the cab of the 1601 did, and they didn't see why the train crew, MacGonigle, the conductor, and his two brakemen, should have any the better of it—so they left their engine and crowded into the station, too.

There wasn't much room left for McCann when he came in like an animated shower bath. He heard Merle, the young operator—they'd probably been guying him—snap at MacGonigle:

"I ain't got any orders for you yet, but you'd better get into the clear on the Y—the Limited, east, is due in four minutes."

"Say!" panted McCann. "Say—" and that was as far as he got. Matt Duggan, making a wild dash for the door, knocked the rest of his breath out of him.

And after Duggan, in a mad and concerted rush, sweeping McCann along with it, the others burst through the door and out on the platform, as, volleying through the storm, came suddenly the quick, staccato bark of engine exhaust.

For a moment, huddled there, trying to get the rights of it, no one spoke—then it came in a yell from Matt Duggan.

"She's gone!" he screamed—and gulped for his breath. "She's gone!"

McCann looked, and blinked, and shook the rain out of his face. Two hundred yards east down the track, and disappearing fast, were the twinkling red tail lights of the caboose.

"By the tokens av all the saints," stammered McCann. "Ut's—ut's—" He grabbed at Matt Duggan. "Fwhat engine is ut?"

It was MacGonigle who answered, as they crowded back inside again for shelter—and answered quick, getting McCann's dropped jaw.

"The 1601. What's wrong with you, McCann?"

"Holy Mither!" stuttered McCann miserably. "That settles ut! Ut's Owsley! 'Twas the whistle, d'ye moind—the whistle!"

Merle, young and hysterical, was up in the air.

"The Limited! The Limited!" he burst out, white-faced. "There ain't three minutes between them! She's coming now!"

MacGonigle, grizzled old veteran, cool in any emergency, whirled on the younger man.

"Then stop her!" he drawled. "Don't make a fool of yourself! Show your red and hold her here until you get Big Cloud on the wire—they're both running the same way, aren't they, you blamed idiot! Everything's out of the road far enough east of here on account of the Limited to give 'em time at headquarters to take care of things. Let 'em have it at Big Cloud."

And Big Cloud got it. Spence, the despatcher, on the early night trick, got it—and Carleton and Regan, at their homes, got it in a hurried call from Spence over their private keys, that brought them running to headquarters.

"I've cleared the line," said Spence. "The Limited is holding at Elk River till Brook's Cut reports Owsley through—then she's to trail along."

Carleton nodded, and took a chair beside the despatcher's table. Regan, as ever with him in times of stress, tugged at his mustache, and paced up and down the room.

He stepped once in front of Carleton and laughed shortly—and there was more in his words, a whole lot more, than he realized then.

"The Lord knows where he'll stop now with the bit in his teeth, but suppose he'd been heading the other way into the Limited—h'm!" Head-on—

33

instead of just tying up all the blamed traffic between here and the Elk—what? We can thank God for that!"

Carleton didn't answer, except by another nod. He was listening to Spence at the key, asking Brook's Cut why they didn't report Owsley through.

The rain rattled at the window panes, and the sashes shook under the gusts of wind; out in the yards below the switch lights showed blurred and indistinct. Regan paced the room more and more impatiently. Carleton's face began to go hard. Spence hung tensely over the table, his fingers on the key, waiting for the sounder to break, waiting for the Brook's Cut call.

It was only seven miles from Elk River, where the stalled passengers of the Limited—will you remember this?—grumbled and complained, pettish in their discontent at the delay, only seven miles from there to Brook's Cut, the first station east—only seven miles, but the minutes passed, and still Brook's Cut answered: "No." And Carleton's face grew harder still, and Regan swore deep down under his breath from a full heart, and Spence grew white and rigid in his chair. And so they waited there, waited with the sense of disaster growing cold upon them—waited—but Brook's Cut never reported Owsley "in" or "out" that night.

Owsley? Who knows what was in the poor, warped brain that night? He had heard her call to him, and they had brought him back the 1601, and she was standing there, alone, deserted—and she had called to him. Who knows what was in his mind, as, together, he and the 1601 went tearing through that black, storm-rent night, when the rivers, and the creeks, and the sluices were running full, and the Elk River, that paralleled the right of way for a mile or two to the crossing, was a raging torrent? Who knows if he ever heard the thundering crash with which the Elk River bridge went out? Who knows, as he swung the curve that opened the bridge approach, without time for any man, Owsley or another, to have stopped, if the headlight playing on the surge of maddened waters meant anything to him? Who knows? That was where they found them, beneath the waters, Owsley and the 1601—and Owsley was smiling, his hand tight-gripped upon the throttle that he loved.

"I dunno," says Regan, when he speaks of Owsley, "if the mountains out here have anything to do with making a man think harder. I dunno— sometimes I think they do. You get to figuring that the Grand Master mabbe goes a long way back, years and years, to work things out—if it hadn't been for Owsley the Limited would have gone into the Elk that night with every soul on board. Owsley? That's the way he wanted to go out, wasn't it?—with the 1601. Mabbe the Grand Master thought of him, too."

Chapter III

THE APOTHEOSIS OF SAMMY DURGAN

The only point the Hill Division, from Carleton, the super, to the last car tink, would admit it was at all hazy on as far as Sammy Durgan was concerned, was why in the everlasting name of everything the man stuck to railroading. When the Hill Division got up against that point it was floored and took the count.

Sammy Durgan wore the belt. He held a record never equalled before or since. Tommy Regan, the master mechanic, who had a warped gift for metaphor, said the man was as migratory on jobs as a flock of crows in a poor year for corn, only a blamed sight harder to get rid of.

As far back as anybody could remember they remembered Sammy Durgan. Somewhere on the division you were bound to bump up against him—but rarely twice in the same place. There wasn't any one in authority, even so mild an authority as a section boss, who hadn't fired Sammy Durgan so often that it had grown on them like a habit. Not that it made much difference, however; for, ejected from the roundhouse, Sammy Durgan's name would be found decorating the pay roll next month in the capacity of baggage master, possibly, at some obscure spot up the line; and here, for example, a slight mix-up of checks in the baggage of a tourist family, that divided the family against itself and its baggage as far as the East is from the West—and Sammy Durgan moved on again. What the Hill Division said about him would have been complimentary if it hadn't been for the grin; they said he was an all-round railroad man. Shops, roundhouse, train crews, station work and construction gangs, Sammy Durgan knew them all; and they knew Sammy Durgan. Eternally and everlastingly in trouble—that was Sammy Durgan.

Nothing much else the matter with him—just trouble. Brains all right; only, as far as the Hill Division could make out, the last thing Sammy Durgan ever thought of doing was to give his brains a little exercise to keep them in condition. But, if appalling in his irresponsibility, Sammy Durgan nevertheless had a saving grace—no cork ever bobbed more buoyantly on troubled waters than Sammy Durgan did on his sea of adversity. Sammy Durgan always came up smiling. He had a perennial sort of cheerfulness on his leathery face that infected his guileless blue eyes, while a mop of fiery red hair like a flaming halo kind of guaranteed the effect to be genuine. One half of you felt like kicking the man violently, and the other half was obsessed with an insane desire to hobnob with him just as violently. Sammy Durgan, to say the least of it, was a contradictory proposition. He had an ambition—he wanted a steady job.

He mentioned the matter to Regan one day immediately following that period in his career when, doing odd jobs over at the station, he had, in filling up the fire buckets upstairs, inadvertently left the tap running. The sink being small and the flooring none too good, a cherished collection of Regan's blue-prints in the room below were reduced to a woebegone mass of sticky pulp. Sammy Durgan mentioned his ambition as a sort of corollary, as it were, to the bitter and concise remarks in which the fat little master mechanic had just couched Sammy Durgan's ubiquitous discharge.

Regan didn't stop breathing—he had dealt with Sammy Durgan before. Regan smiled as though it hurt him.

"A steady job, is it?" said Regan softly. "I've been thinking so hard daytimes trying to place you in a railroad job and still keep railroading safe out in this part of the world that I've got to dreaming about it at nights. Last night I dreamt I was in a foundry and there was an enormous vat of red, bubbling, liquid iron they'd just drawn off the furnace, and you came down from the ceiling on a spider web and hung over it. And then I woke up, and I was covered with cold sweat—for fear the web wouldn't break."

"Regan," said Sammy Durgan, blinking fast, "you don't know a man when you see one. You're where you are because you've had the chance to get there. Mind that! I've never had a chance. But it'll come, Regan. And the day'll come, Regan, when you'll be down on your knees begging me to take what I'm asking for now, a steady job on your blessed railroad."

"Mabbe," said Regan, chewing absently on his blackstrap; and then, as a sort of afterthought: "What kind of a job?"

"A steady one," said Sammy Durgan doggedly. "I dunno just what, but—"

"H'm!" said Regan solicitously. "Well, don't make up your mind in a hurry, Durgan—I don't want to press you. When you've had a chance to look around a little more, mabbe you'll be able to decide better—what? Get out!"

Sammy Durgan backed to the door. There he paused, blinking fast again:

"Some day I'll show you, Regan, you and all the rest of 'em, and—"

"Get out!" said the little master mechanic peremptorily.

And Sammy Durgan got out. He was always getting out. That was his forte. When he got in, it was only to get out.

"Some day," said Sammy Durgan—and the Hill Division stuck its tongue in its cheek. But Sammy Durgan had his answer to the blunt refusal that invariably greeted his modest request for a fresh job.

"Listen here," said Sammy Durgan, with a firm hold on the overalls' strap of, it might be, the bridge foreman he was trying to wheedle a time check out of. "'Twas Regan fired me first, but he was in a bad humor at the time; 'twas the steam hose I was washing out boiler tubes with in the roundhouse got away from me, and it was accidental, though mabbe for the moment it was painful for him. It just shows that if you get fired once it sticks to you. And as for them baggage checks out to Moose Peak, they weren't no family, they was a tribe, about eighteen kids besides the pa and ma, and fourteen baggage cars full of trunks. He was a little bow-legged fellow with a scared look, and he whispers where he wants the checks for about three minutes before train time, then she comes in, bigger'n two elephants, scorches him through a pair of glasses she carries on a handle, and orders 'em checked somewhere else. Say, was I to blame if some of them checks in the hurry didn't get the first name I'd written on 'em scratched out? And over there to the station the time Regan's office got flooded 'twasn't my fault. If you get fired once, you keep on getting fired no matter what you do. I turned the tap off. It was one of them little devils of call boys turned it on again. But do you think any one would believe that? They would not—or I'd have mentioned it at the time. If there's any trouble anywhere and I'm around it's put onto me. And there's Mrs. Durgan back there to Big Cloud. She ain't very well. Cough's troubling her more'n usual lately, and worrying about the rent not being paid ain't helping her any. Say, you'll give me a job, won't you?"

Sammy Durgan got the job.

Now, as may be inferred, Sammy Durgan did not always adhere strictly to the truth—not that he swerved from it with vicious intent, but that, like some other things, trouble for instance, the swerving had grown, as it were, to be a habit. Mrs. Durgan did not have a cough, neither was she worrying about the unpaid rent. Mrs. Durgan, speaking strictly in a physical sense, was mightiest among women in Big Cloud, and on the night the story proper opens—a very black night for Sammy Durgan—Sammy Durgan was sitting on Mrs. Durgan's front door step, and the door was locked upon him. Sammy Durgan, paradoxical as it may sound, though temporarily out of a job again and with no job to be fired from, was being fired at that moment harder than he had ever been fired before in his life—and the firing was being done by Mrs. Durgan. It had been threatening for quite a while, quite a long while, two or three years, but it none the less came to Sammy Durgan with something of a shock, and he gasped.

Mrs. Durgan was intensely Irish, from purer stock than Sammy Durgan, and through the window Mrs. Durgan spoke barbed words:

"'Tis shame yez should take to yersilf, Sammy Durgan, if yez had the sinse to take annything—the loikes av yez, a big strong man! 'Tis years I've put up wid yez, whin another woman would not, but I'll put up wid yez no more! 'Tis the ind this night, Sammy Durgan, an' the Holy Mither be praised there's no children to blush fer the disgrace yez are!"

"Maria," said Sammy Durgan craftily, for this had worked before, "do I drink?"

Mrs. Durgan choked in her rage.

"I do not," said Sammy Durgan soothingly. "And who but me lays the pay envelopes on your lap without so much as tearing 'em to count the insides of 'em? Listen here, Maria, listen—"

"Is ut mocking me, yez are!" shrieked Mrs. Durgan. "'Tis little good the opening av 'em would do! Listen, is ut, to the smooth tongue av yez! I've listened till me fingers are bare to the bone wid the washtubs to kape a roof over me head. I'll listen no more, Sammy Durgan, moind thot!"

"Maria," said Sammy Durgan, with a softness that was meant to turn away wrath, "Maria, open the door."

"I will not," said Mrs. Durgan, with a truculent gasp. "Niver! Not while yez live, Sammy Durgan—fer yez funeral mabbe, but fer no less than thot, an' thin only fer the joy av bein' a widdy!"

It sounded inevitable. There was a sort of cold uncompromise even in the fire of Mrs. Durgan's voice. Sammy Durgan rose heavily from the doorstep.

"Some day," said Sammy Durgan sadly, "some day, Maria, you'll be sorry for this. You'll break your heart for it, Maria! You wait! 'Tis no fault of mine, the trouble. Everybody's against me—and now my wife. But you wait. Once in the life of every man he gets his chance. Mine ain't come yet. But you wait! It's the man who rises to an emergency that counts, and—"

There was a gurgling sound from Mrs. Durgan's throat. Then the window slammed down—hard.

Sammy Durgan stared, stared a little blankly as the lamp retreated from the window and the front of the house grew black.

"I guess," said Sammy Durgan a little wistfully to himself, "I guess I'm fired all around for fair." He turned and walked slowly out to the street and headed downtown toward the railroad yards. And as he walked he communed with himself somewhat bitterly: "Any blamed little thing that comes up, that, if 'twere anybody else, nobody'd pay any attention to it, and everybody yells 'fire Sammy Durgan.' That's me—'fire Sammy Durgan.' And why? Because I never get a chance—that's why!" Sammy Durgan grew earnest in his soliloquy. "Some day," said he, as he reached the station platform, "I'll show 'em—I'll show Maria! It'll come, every man gets his chance. Give me the chance to rise to an emergency, that's all I ask—just give me that and I'll show 'em!"

Sammy Durgan walked up the deserted platform with no very definite destination in view, and stopped abruptly in front of the freight shed as he suddenly remembered that it was very late. He sat down on the edge of the platform, and kicked at the main-line rail with the toe of his boot. Sammy Durgan was bedless, penniless, wifeless and jobless. It was a very black night indeed for Sammy Durgan.

Sammy Durgan's mind catalogued those in authority in Big Cloud in whose gift a job was, and he went over the list—but it did not take him long, as he had need to hesitate over no single name. Big Cloud and a job for Sammy Durgan were separated by a great gulf. Sammy Durgan, however, his perennial optimism gaining the ascendancy again, found solace even in that fact. In view of his present marital difficulties a job in Big Cloud would be an awkward thing anyhow. In fact, for the first time in his life, he would have refused a job in Big Cloud. Sammy Durgan had a certain pride about him. Given the opportunity, the roundhouse, the shops, the yards, and the train crews, once they discovered the little impasse that had arisen in the Durgan family, might be safely trusted to make capital out of it—at his expense.

Sammy Durgan's mind in search of a job went further afield. This was quite a different proposition, for the mileage of the Hill Division was big. For an hour Sammy Durgan sat there, scratching at his red hair, puckering his leathery face, and kicking at the rail to the detriment of the toe-cap of his boot. He knew the division well, very well—too well. At the moment, he could not place any spot upon it that he did not know, or, perhaps what was more to the point, that was not intimately acquainted with him. Road work, bridge work, yard work, station work passed in review before him, but always and with each one arose a certain well-remembered face whose expression, Biblically speaking, was not like unto a father's on the prodigal's return.

And then at last Sammy Durgan sighed in relief. There was Pat Donovan! True, he and Pat Donovan had had a little misunderstanding incident to the premature explosion of a keg of blasting powder that had wrecked the construction shanty, but that was two years ago and under quite different conditions. Pat Donovan now was a section boss on a desolate stretch of track about five stations up the line, and his only companions were a few Polacks who spoke English like parrots—voluble enough as far as it went, but not entirely soul-filling to an Irishman of the sociable tendencies of Pat Donovan. He could certainly get a job out of Pat Donovan.

The matter ultimately settled, Sammy Durgan stood up. Across the yards they were making up the early morning freight. That solved the transportation question. A railroad man, whether he was out of a job or not, could always get a lift in any caboose that carried the markers or the tail lights of old Bill Wallis' train. Sammy Durgan got a lift that morning up to Dam River; and there, a little further along the line, he ran Pat Donovan and his Polacks to earth where they were putting in some new ties.

Donovan, a squat, wizened, red eye-lidded little man, with a short, bristling crop of sandy whiskers circling his jaws like an ill-trimmed hedge, hurriedly drew back the hand he had extended as he caught the tail end of Sammy Durgan's greeting.

"Oh, a job is ut?" he inquired without enthusiasm, from his seat on a pile of ties beside the track.

"Listen, here, Pat," said Sammy Durgan brightly. "Listen to—"

"Yez have yer nerve wid yez!" observed the section boss caustically. "Yez put me in moind av a felley I had workin' fer me wance, for yez are the dead spit av him, Sammy Durgan, that blew the roof off av the construction shanty, an'—"

"That was two years ago, Donovan," interposed Sammy Durgan hurriedly, "and you've no blasting powder on this job, and it was no fault of mine. I would have explained it at the time, but you were a bit hot under the collar, Pat, and you would not listen. I was but testing the detonator box, and 'twas yourself told me the connections were not made."

"Did I?"—the section boss was watching his chattering gang of foreigners with gradually narrowing eyes.

"You did," asserted Sammy Durgan earnestly, "and—"

Sammy Durgan stopped. Donovan had leaped from his seat, and was gesticulating fiercely at his gold-earringed, greasy-haired laboring crew.

"Yez are apes!" he yelled, dancing frantically up and down. "Yez are oorang-ootangs! An' yez talk like a cageful av monkeys! Yez look loike men, but yez are not! Yez are annything that has no brains! Have I not told yez till me throat's cracked doin' ut thot yez are not rayquired to lift the whole dombed right av way to put in a single measly tie? Is ut a hump loike a camel's back yez are tryin' to make in the rail? Here! Dig—here!"—the little section boss, with wrathful precision, indicated the exact spot with the toe of his boot.

He returned to his seat, and regarded Sammy Durgan helplessly.

"'Tis a new lot," said he sadly, "an' the worst, bar none, that iver I had."

"But an Irishman, and one that can talk your own tongue, you won't hire when he's out of a job," insinuated Sammy Durgan reproachfully.

The section boss scrubbed reflectively at his chin whiskers.

"An' how's Mrs. Durgan?" he asked, with some cordiality.

"She's bad," said Sammy Durgan, suddenly mournful and shaking his head. "She's worse than ever she's been, Donovan. I felt bad at leaving her last night, Donovan—I did that. But what could I do? 'Twas a job I had to get, Donovan, bad as I felt at leaving her, Donovan."

"Sure now, is thot so?" said the little section boss sympathetically. "'Tis cruel harrd luck yez have, Durgan. But yez'll moind I've not much in the way av jobs—'tis a desolate bit av country, an' mostly track-walkin' at a dollar-tin a day."

"Donovan," said Sammy Durgan from a full heart, "the day'll come, Donovan, when I'll keep the grass green on your grave for this. I knew you'd not throw an old friend down."

"'Tis glad I am to do ut," said Donovan, waving his hand royally. "An' yez can start in at wance."

And Sammy Durgan started. And for a week Sammy Durgan assiduously tramped his allotted mileage out and back to the section shanty each day—and for a week Sammy Durgan and trouble were asunder.

Trouble? Where, from what possible source, could there be any trouble? Not a soul for miles around the section shanty, just mountains and track and cuts and fills, and nothing on earth for Sammy Durgan to do but keep a paternal eye generally on the roadbed. Trouble? It even got monotonous for Sammy Durgan himself.

"'Tis not," confided Sammy Durgan to himself one morning, after a week of this, that found him plodding along the track some two miles east of the section shanty, "'tis not precisely the job I'd like, for it's a chance I'm looking for to show 'em, Maria, and Regan, and the rest of 'em, and there'll be no chance here—but temporarily it'll do. 'Tis not much of a job, and beneath me at that, but have I not heard that them as are faithful in little will some day be handed much? There'll be no one to say"—he glanced carefully around him in all directions—"that Sammy Durgan was not a good track-walker."

Sammy Durgan sat down on the edge of the embankment, extracted a black cutty from his pocket, charged it with very black tobacco, lit it, tamped the top of the bowl with a calloused forefinger, and from another pocket extracted a newspaper—one of a bundle that the train crew of No. 7 thoughtfully heaved at the section shanty door each morning on their way up the line.

It was a warm, bright morning; one of those comfortable summer mornings with just enough heat to lift a little simmering haze from the rails, and just enough sun to make a man feel leisurely, so to speak. Sammy Durgan, the cutty drawing well, wormed a comfortable and inviting hollow in the gravel of the embankment, propped his back against an obliging tie, and opened his paper.

"Track-walking," said Sammy Durgan, "is not much of a job, and 'tis not what I'm looking for, but there are worse jobs."

Somebody had read the paper before Sammy Durgan, hence the sheet that first presented itself to his view was a page of classified advertisements. His eye roved down the column of "Situations Vacant"—and held on one of them.

MEN WANTED for grading work at The Gap. Apply at Engineers' Office, Big Cloud, or to T. H. MacMurtrey, foreman, at The Gap.

Sammy Durgan pursed his lips.

"There's no telling," said Sammy Durgan thoughtfully, "when I'll be looking for a new job, so I'll bear it in mind. Not that they'd give me a job at the office, for they would not; but by the name of him this T. H. MacMurtrey 'll be a new man and unknown to me, which is quite another matter—and I'll keep it in mind."

Sammy Durgan turned the sheet absently—and then, forgetful of the obliging tie that propped his back, he sat bolt upright with a jerk.

"For the love of Mike!" observed Sammy Durgan breathlessly, with his eyes glued to the paper.

It leaped right out at him in the biggest type the Big Cloud Daily Sentinel had to offer, which, if it had its limitations, was not to be despised, since it had acquired a second-hand font or two from a metropolitan daily east that made no pretense at being modest in such matters.

Sammy Durgan's eyes began to pop, and his leathery face to screw up.

GHASTLY RAILROAD TRAGEDY

UNKNOWN MAN MURDERED IN STATEROOM
OF EASTBOUND FLYER

No Clue to Assassin

Sammy Durgan's eyes bored into the fine print of the "story." If the style was a trifle provincial and harrowing, Sammy Durgan was not fastidious enough to be disturbed thereby—it was intensely vivid. Sammy Durgan's mouth was half open, as he read.

One of the most atrocious, daring and bloody murders in the annals of the country's crime was perpetrated last night in a compartment of the sleeping car on No. 12, the eastbound through express. It is a baffling mystery, though suspicion is directed against a passenger who gave his name as Samuel Starke of New York. The details, gathered by the Sentinel staff from Conductor Hurley, and Clements, the porter, on the arrival of the train at Big Cloud, are as follows:

41

The car was a new-type compartment car, with the compartment doors opening off the corridor that runs along one side of the length of the car. As the train was passing Dam River, Clements, the porter, at the forward end of the car, thought he heard two revolver shots from somewhere in the rear. Clements says he thought at first he had been mistaken, for the train was travelling fast and making a great uproar, and he did not at once make any effort to investigate. Then he heard a compartment door open, and he started down the corridor. Starke was standing in the doorway of B compartment where the murdered man was, and Starke yelled at Clements. "Here, porter, quick!" is what Clements says Starke said to him: "There's a man been shot in here! My compartment's next to this, you know, and I heard two shots and rushed in."

It was a horrible and unnerving sight that greeted the porter's eyes. Mr. Clements was still visibly affected by it as he talked to the Sentinel reporter in Big Cloud. The unknown murdered man lay pitifully huddled on the floor, lifeless and dead, a great bullet wound in one temple and another along the side of his neck that must have severed the jugular vein. It was as though blood had rained upon the victim. He was literally covered with it. He was already past aid, being quite dead. Conductor Hurley was quickly summoned. But investigation only deepened the mystery. Suicide was out of the question because there was no weapon to be found. Mr. Starke, at his own request, was searched, but had no revolver. Mr. Starke, however, has been held by the police.

The Sentinel, without wishing to infringe upon the sphere of the authorities or cast aspersions upon their acumen, but in the simple furtherance of justice, offers the suggestion that, as the compartment window was open, the assassin, whoever he was, hurled the revolver out of the window after committing his dastardly and unspeakable crime; and the Sentinel hereby offers Twenty-five Dollars Reward for the recovery of the revolver. Lawlessness and crime, we had fondly believed, was stamped out of the West, and we raise our voice in protest against the return of desperadoes, bandits, and train robbers, and we solemnly warn all those of that caliber that they will not be tolerated in the new West, and we call upon all public-spirited citizens in whose veins red blood flows to rise up and put them down with an iron and merciless—

There were still three columns. Sammy Durgan read them voraciously. At the end, he sucked hard on the black cutty. The black cutty was out.

"To think of the likes of that!" muttered Sammy Durgan heavily, as he dug for a match. "The fellow that wrote the piece—'twill be that little squint-eyed runt Labatt—is not the fool I thought him. It's right, he is; what with murders and desperadoes no man's life's safe—it is not! And to think of it right on this same railroad! And who knows"—Sammy Durgan rose with sudden haste—"but 'twas right on this same spot where I am this blessed minute, for the paper says it was close to Dam River, that the poor devil was shot dead and foully killed! And— The match flamed over the bowl of the cutty, but Sammy Durgan's attention was not on it.

42

Sammy Durgan, in a sort of strained way, descended the embankment. The match burned his fingers, and Sammy Durgan dropped it. Sammy Durgan rubbed his eyes—yes, it was still glistening away there in the sunlight. He stooped, and from the grass, trembling a little with excitement, picked up a heavy-calibered, nickel-trimmed revolver.

"Holy Christmas!" whispered Sammy Durgan, blinking fast. "'Tis the same! There's no doubt of it—'tis the same that done the bloody deed! And 'tis the first bit of luck I've had since I was born! Twenty-five dollars reward!" He said it over very softly again: "Twenty-five dollars reward!"

Sammy Durgan returned to the track, and resumed his way along it; though, as far as his services to the road were concerned, he might just as well have remained where he was. Sammy Durgan's thoughts were not of loosened spikes and erring fishplates, and neither were his eyes intent on their discovery—his mind, thanks to Labatt, of the Big Cloud Daily Sentinel, teemed with scenes of violence vividly portrayed, midnight murders, corpses in grotesque attitudes on gore-bespattered compartment floors, desperadoes of all descriptions, train bandits and train robbers in masks holding up trains.

"'Tis true," said Sammy Durgan to himself. "'Tis a lawless country, these same Rockies. I mind 'twas only a year ago that Black Dempsey and his gang tried to wreck Number Two in the Cut near Coyote Bend—I mind it well."

Sammy Durgan walked on down the track. At intervals he took the revolver from his pocket and put it back again, as though to assure himself beyond peradventure of doubt that it was in his possession.

"Twenty-five dollars reward!" communed Sammy Durgan, grown arrogant with wealth. "'Tis near a month's pay at a dollar-ten—and all for the picking of it up. I called it luck—but it is not luck. An ordinary trackwalker would have walked it by and not seen it. 'Tis what you get for keeping your eyes about you, and besides the twenty-five 'tis promotion, too, mabbe I'll get. 'Twill show 'em that there's track-walkers and track walkers. I'll say to Regan: 'Regan,' I'll say, 'you've said hard words to me, Regan, but I ask you, Regan, how many track-walkers would have brought a bloody murderer to justice by keeping their eyes about them in the faithful performance of their duty, Regan? 'Tis but the chance I ask. 'Tis the man in an emergency that counts, and if ever I get a chance at an emergency I'll show you.' And Regan'll say: 'Sammy,' he'll say, 'you—'"

Sammy Durgan paused in his engrossing soliloquy as the roar of an approaching train fell on his ears, and he scrambled quickly down from the right of way to the bottom of the embankment. Just ahead of him was a short, narrow, high-walled rock cut, and at the farther end the track swerved sharply to the right, side-stepping, as it were, the twist of the Dam River that swung in, steep-banked, to the right of way.

"I'll wait here," said Sammy Durgan, "'till she's through the cut."

Sammy Durgan waited. The train came nearer and nearer—and then Sammy Durgan cocked his head in a puzzled way and stared through the cut. He couldn't see anything, of course, for the curve, but from the sound she had stopped just beyond the cut.

"Now, what the devil is she stopping there for?" inquired Sammy Durgan of the universe in an injured tone.

He started along through the cut. And then Sammy Durgan stopped himself—as though he were rooted to the earth—and a sort of grayish white began to creep over his face. Came echoing through the cut a shout, a yell, another, a chorus of them—then a shot, another shot, a fusilade of them—and then a din mingling the oaths, the yells, and the shots into a hideous babel that rang terror in Sammy Durgan's ears.

Sammy Durgan promptly sidled in and hugged up against the rock wall that towered above him. Here he hesitated an instant, then he crept cautiously forward. Where he could not see, it was axiomatic that he could not be seen; and where he could not be seen, it was equally logical that he would be safe.

Sammy Durgan's face, quite white now, was puckered as it had never been puckered before, and his lips moved in a kind of twitching, jerky way as he crept along. Then suddenly, a voice, that seemed nearer than the others, but which from the acoustic properties of the cut he could not quite locate, bawled out fiercely over the confusion, prefaced with an oath:

"Get that express car door open, and be damned quick about it! Go on, shoot along the side of the train every time you see a head in a window!"

Sammy Durgan's mouth went dry, and his heart lost a beat, then went to pounding like a trip-hammer. Labatt and the Big Cloud Daily Sentinel hadn't drawn any exaggerated picture. A hold-up—in broad daylight!

"Holy Mither!" whispered Sammy Durgan.

He crept farther forward, very cautiously—still farther—and then he lay full length, crouched against the rock wall at the end of the cut. He could see now, and the red hair of Sammy Durgan kind of straggled down damp over his forehead, and his little black eyes lost their pupils.

It was a passenger train; one side of it quite hidden by the sharp curve of the track, the other side presented almost full on to Sammy Durgan's view—the whole length of it. And Sammy Durgan, gasping, stared. Not ten yards away from the mouth of the cut a huge pile of ties were laid across the rails, with the pilot of the stalled engine almost nosing them. Down the embankment, a very steep embankment where the Dam River swirled along, marched there evidently at the revolver's point, the engine crew stood with their hands up in the air—at the revolver's point with a masked man behind it. Along the length of the train, two or three more masked men were shooting past the windows in curt intimation to the passengers that the safest thing they could do was to stay where they were; and farther down, by the rear coach, the conductor and two brakemen, like their mates of the engine crew, held their hands steadfastly above their heads as another bandit covered them with his weapon. And through the open door of the express car Sammy Durgan could see bobbing heads and straining backs, and the express company's safe being worked across the floor preparatory to heaving it out on the ground.

It takes long to tell it—Sammy Durgan got it all as a second flies. And something, a bitter something, seemed to be gnawing at Sammy Durgan's vitals.

"Holy Mither!" he mumbled miserably. "'Tis an emergency, all right—but 'tis not the right kind of an emergency. What could any one man do against a lot of bloodthirsty, desperate devils like that, that'd sooner cut your throat than look at you!"

Sammy Durgan's hand inadvertently rubbed against his right-hand coat pocket—and his revolver. He drew it out mechanically, and it seemed to put new life into Sammy Durgan, for, as he stared again at the scene before him, Sammy Durgan quivered with a sudden, fierce elation.

"I was wrong," said Sammy Durgan grimly. "'Tis the right kind of an emergency, after all—and 'tis the man that uses his head and rises to one that counts. I'll show 'em, Maria, and Regan, and the rest of 'em! Begorra, it can be done! 'Tis no one 'll notice me while I'm getting to the engine and climbing in on the other side, and, by glory, if I back her out quick enough them thieving hellions in the express car can either jump for it or ride back to the arms of authority at the next station—but the safe 'll be there, and 'twill be Sammy Durgan that kept it there!"

But Sammy Durgan still lay on the ground and stared—while the safe was being pushed to the express car door, and one edge of it already protruded out from the car.

"Go on, Sammy Durgan!" urged Sammy Durgan anxiously to himself. "Don't you be skeered, Sammy, you got a revolver. 'Tis yourself, and not Maria, that'll do the locking of the doors hereafter, and 'tis Regan you can pass with fine contempt. Think of that, Sammy Durgan! And all for a bit of a run that'll not take the time of a batting of an eyelash, and with no one to notice you doing it. 'Tis a clever plan you've devised, Sammy Durgan—it is that. Go on, Sammy; go on!"

Sammy Durgan wriggled a little on the ground, cocked his revolver—and wriggled a little more.

"I will!" said Sammy Durgan with a sudden pinnacling of determination—and he sprang to his feet.

Some loosened shale rattled down behind him. Sammy Durgan dashed through the mouth of the cut—and then for a moment all was a sort of chaos to Sammy Durgan. From the narrow edge of the embankment, just clear of the cut, a man stepped suddenly out. Sammy Durgan collided with him, his cocked revolver went off, and, jerked from his grasp by the shock, sailed riverwards through the air, while, echoing its report from the express car door, a man screamed wildly and grabbed at a bullet-shattered wrist; and the man with whom Sammy Durgan had collided, having but precarious footing at best, reeled back from the impact, smashed into another man behind him, and with a crash both rolled down the almost perpendicular embankment. Followed a splash and a spout of water as they struck the river—and from every side a tornado of yells and curses.

"'Tis my finish!" moaned Sammy Durgan—but his feet were flying. "I—I've done it now! If I ran back up the cut they'd chase me and finish me—'tis my finish, anyway, but the engine 'll be the only chance I got."

Sammy Durgan streaked across the track, hurdled, tumbled, fell, and

45

sprawled over the pile of ties, recovered himself, regained his feet, and made a frantic spring through the gangway and into the cab.

With a sweep Sammy Durgan shot the reversing lever over into the back notch, and with a single yank he wrenched the throttle wide. There was nothing of the craftsman in engine-handling about Sammy Durgan at that instant—only hurry. The engine, from a passive, indolent and inanimate thing, seemed to rise straight up in the air like an aroused and infuriated beast that had been stung. With one mad plunge it backed crashing into the buffer plates of the express car behind it, backed again, and once again, and the tinkle of breaking glass sort of ricochetted along the train as one car after another added its quota of shattered window panes, while the drivers, slipping on the rails, roared around like gigantic and insensate pinwheels.

Sammy Durgan snatched at the cab frame for support—and then with a yell he snatched at a shovel. A masked face showed in the gangway. Sammy Durgan brought the flat of the shovel down on the top of the man's head.

The gangway was clear again. There was life for it yet! The train was backing quickly now under the urgent, prodding bucks of the engine. Sammy Durgan mopped at his face, his eyes warily on the gangways. Another man made a running jump for it—again Sammy Durgan's shovel swung—and again the gangway was clear.

Shovel poised, lurching with the lurch of the cab, red hair flaming, half terrified and half defiant, eyes shooting first to one gangway and then the other, Sammy Durgan held the cab. A minute passed with no renewal of attack. Sammy Durgan stole a quick glance over his shoulder through the cab glass up the track—and, with a triumphant shout, he flung the shovel clanging to the iron floor-plates, and, leaning far out of the gangway, shook his fist. Strewn out along the right of way masked men yelled and shouted and cursed, but Sammy Durgan was beyond their reach—and so was the express company's safe.

"Yah!" screamed Sammy Durgan, wildly derisive and also belligerent in the knowledge of his own safety. "Yah! Yah! Yah! 'Twas me, ye bloody hellions, that turned the trick on ye! 'Twas me, Sammy Durgan, and I'll have you know it! 'Twas—"

Sammy Durgan turned, as the express car opened, and Macy, the conductor, hatless and wild-eyed, appeared on the platform.

"'S'all right, Macy!" Sammy Durgan screeched reassuringly. "'S'all right—it's me, Sammy Durgan."

Macy jumped from the platform to the tender, jumped over the water tank, and came down into the cab with an avalanche of coal. His mouth was twitching and jerking, but for a moment he could not speak—and then the words came like an explosion, and he shook his fist under Sammy Durgan's nose.

"You—you damned fathead!" he roared. "What in the double-blanked, blankety-blanked son of blazes are you doing!"

"Fathead, yourself!" retorted Sammy Durgan promptly—and there was spice in the way Sammy Durgan said it. "I'm doing what you hadn't the nerve or the head to do, Macy—unless mabbe you're in the gang yourself! I'm saving that safe back there in the express car, that's what I'm doing."

"Saving nothing!" bellowed Macy crazily, as he slammed the throttle shut. "There! Look there!" He reached for Sammy Durgan's head, and with both hands twisted it around, and fairly flattened Sammy Durgan's nose against the cab glass.

"What—what is it?" faltered Sammy Durgan, a little less assertively.

Macy was excitable. He danced upon the cab floor as though it were a hornets' nest.

"What is it!" he echoed in a scream. "What is it! It's moving pictures, you tangle-brained, rusty-headed idiot! That's what it is!"

A sort of dull gray film seemed to spread itself over Sammy Durgan's face. Sammy Durgan stared through the cab glass. The track ahead was just disappearing from view as the engine backed around a curve, but what Sammy Durgan saw was enough—two dripping figures were salvaging a wrecked and bedraggled photographic outfit on the river bank, close to the entrance of the cut where he had been in collision with them; an excited group of train bandits, without any masks now, were gesticulating around the marooned engineer and fireman; and in the middle distance, squatting on a rail, a man, coatless, his shirt sleeve rolled up, was making horrible grimaces as a companion bandaged his wrist.

Macy's laugh rang hollow—it wasn't exactly a laugh.

"I don't know how much it costs," stuttered the conductor demoniacally, "but there's about four million dollars' worth of film they're fishing out of the river there, and they paid a thousand dollars for the train and thirty-five minutes between stations to clear Number Forty, and there's about eight thousand car windows gone, and one vestibule and two platforms in splinters, and a man shot through the wrist, and if that crowd up there ever get their hands on you they'll—"

"I think," said Sammy Durgan hurriedly, "that I'll get off."

He edged back to the gangway and peered out. The friendly bend of the road hid the "outlaws." The train was almost at a standstill—and Sammy Durgan jumped. Not on the river side—on the other side. Sammy Durgan's destination was somewhere deep in the wooded growth that clothed the towering mountain before him.

There is an official record for cross-country mileage registered in the name of some one whose name is not Sammy Durgan—but it is not accurate. Sammy Durgan holds it. And it was far up on the mountain side that he finally crossed the tape and collapsed, breathless and gasping, on a tree stump. He sat there for quite a while, jabbing at his streaming face with the sleeve of his jumper; and there was trouble in Sammy Durgan's eyes, and plaint in his voice when at last he spoke.

"Twenty-five dollars reward," said Sammy Durgan wistfully. "And 'twas as good as in my pocket, and now 'tis gone. 'Tis hard luck, cruel hard luck. It is that!"

Sammy Durgan's eyes roved around the woods about him and grew thoughtful.

"I was minded at the time," said Sammy Durgan, "that 'twas not the right kind of an emergency, and when he hears of it Regan will be displeased. And now what'll I do? 'Twill do no good to return to the section shanty, for they'll be telegraphing Donovan to fire Sammy Durgan. That's me—fire Sammy Durgan. 'Tis trouble dogs me and cruel hard luck—and all I'm asking for is a steady job and a chance."

Sammy Durgan relapsed into mournful silence and contemplation for a spell—and then his face began to clear. Sammy Durgan's optimism was like the bobbing cork.

"'Tis another streak of cruel hard luck, of bitter, cruel hard luck I've had this day, but am I down and out for the likes of that?" inquired Sammy Durgan defiantly of himself.

"I am not!" replied Sammy Durgan buoyantly to Sammy Durgan. "'Tis not the first time I've been fired, and did I not read that there's MacMurtrey begging for men up at The Gap? And him being a new man and unknown to me, 'tis a job sure. 'Tis only my name might stand in the way, for 'tis likely 'twill be mentioned in his hearing on account of the bit of trouble down yonder. But 'tis the job I care for and not the name. I'll be working for MacMurtrey to-morrow morning—I will that! And what's more," added Sammy Durgan, beginning to blink fast, "I'll show 'em yet, Maria, and Regan, and the rest of 'em. Once in every man's life he gets his chance. Mine ain't come yet. I thought it had to-day, but I was wrong. But it'll come. You wait! I'll show 'em some day!"

Sammy Durgan lost himself in meditation. After a little, he spoke again.

"I'm not sure about the law," said Sammy Durgan, "but on account of the fellow that the bullet hit, apart from MacMurtrey taking note of it, 'twould be as well, anyway, if I changed my name temporarily till the temper of all concerned is cooled down a bit." Sammy Durgan rose from the stump. "I'll start West," said Sammy Durgan, "and get a lift on the first way-freight before the word is out. I'm thinking they'll be asking for Sammy Durgan down at Big Cloud."

And they were. It was quite true. Down at headquarters they were earnestly concerned about Sammy Durgan. Sammy Durgan had made no mistake in that respect.

"Fire Sammy Durgan," wired the roadmaster to the nearest station for transmission by first train to Pat Donovan, the section boss—and he got this answer back the next morning:

I. P. Spears, Roadmaster, Big Cloud:
Sammy Durgan missing.
P. DONOVAN."

Missing—that was it. Just that, nothing more—as though the earth had opened and swallowed him up, Sammy Durgan had disappeared. And while Carleton grew red and apoplectic over the claim sheet for damages presented by the moving-picture company, and Regan fumed and tugged at his scraggly

48

brown mustache at thought of the damage to his rolling stock—Sammy Durgan was just missing, that was all—just missing.

Nobody knew where Sammy Durgan had gone. Nobody had seen him. Station agents, operators, road bosses, section bosses, construction bosses and everybody else were instructed to report—and they did. They reported—nothing. Regan even went so far as to ask Mrs. Durgan.

"Is ut here to taunt me, yez are!" screamed Mrs. Durgan bitterly—and slammed the door in the little master mechanic's face.

"I guess," observed Regan to himself, as he gazed at the uncommunicative door panels, "I guess mabbe the neighbors have been neighborly—h'm? But I guess, too, we're rid of Sammy Durgan at last; and I dunno but what that comes pretty near squaring accounts for window glass and about a million other incidentals. Only," added the little master mechanic, screwing up his eyes, as he walked back to the station, "only it would have been more to my liking to have got my hands on him first—and got rid of him after!"

But Regan, and Carleton, and Mrs. Durgan, and the Hill Division generally were not rid of Sammy Durgan—far from it. For a week he was missing, and then one afternoon young Hinton, of the division engineer's staff, strolled into the office, nodded at Carleton, and grinned at the master mechanic, who was tilted back in a chair with his feet on the window sill.

"I dropped off this morning to look over the new grading work at The Gap," said Hinton casually. "And I thought you might be interested to know that MacMurtrey's got a man working for him up there by the name of Timmy O'Toole."

"Doesn't interest me," said Regan blandly, chewing steadily on his blackstrap. "Try and spring it on the super, Hinton. He always bites."

"Who's Timmy O'Toole?" smiled Carleton.

Hinton squinted at the ceiling.

"Sammy Durgan," said Hinton—casually.

There wasn't a word spoken for a minute. Regan lifted his feet from the window sill and lowered his chair legs softly down to the floor as though he were afraid of making a noise, and the smile on Carleton's face sort of faded away as though a blight had withered it.

"What was the name?" said Carleton presently, in a velvet voice.

"Timmy O'Toole," said Hinton.

Carleton's hand reached out, kind of as though of its own initiative, kind of as though it were just habit, for a telegraph blank—but Regan stopped him. It wasn't often that the fat, good-natured little master mechanic was vindictive, but there were times when even Regan's soul was overburdened.

"Wait!" said Regan, with ferocious grimness. "Wait! I'll make a better job of it than that, Carleton. I'm going up the line myself to-morrow morning on Number Three—and I'll drop off at The Gap. Timmy O'Toole now, is it? I'll make him sick!" Regan clenched his pudgy fist. "When I'm through with him he'll never have to be fired again—not on this division. Still looking for an emergency to rise to, eh? Well, I'll accommodate him! He'll run up against the hottest emergency to-morrow morning he ever heard of!"

And Regan was right—that was exactly what Sammy Durgan did. Only it wasn't quite the sort of emergency that Regan— But just a moment till the line's clear, there go the cautionaries against us.

If it had been any other kind of a switch it would never have happened—let that be understood from the start. And how it ever came to be left on the main line when modern equipment was installed is a mystery, except perhaps that as it was never used it was therefore never remembered by anybody. Nevertheless, there it stood, an old weather-beaten, two-throw, stub switch of the vintage of the ark. Two-throw, mind you, when a one-throw switch, even in the days of its usefulness, would have answered the purpose just as well, better for that matter. No modern drop-handle, interlocking safety device about it. Not at all! A handle sticking straight out like a sore thumb that could creak around on a semicircular guide, with a rusty pin dangling from a rusty chain to lock it—if some itinerant section hand didn't forget to jab the pin back into the hole it had the habit of worming its way out of! It stood about a quarter of the way down the grade of The Gap, which is to say about half a mile from the summit, a deserted sentinel on guard over a deserted spur that, in the old construction days, had been built in a few hundred yards through a soft spot in the mountain side for camp and material stores.

As for The Gap itself, it was not exactly what might be called a nice piece of track. Officially, the grade is an average of 4.2; practically, it is likened to a balloon descension by means of a parachute. It begins at the east end and climbs up in a wriggling, twisting way, hugging gray rock walls on one side, and opening a cañon on the other that, as you near the summit, would make you catch your breath even to look at over the edge—it is a sheer drop. And also the right of way is narrow, very narrow; just clearance on one side against the rock walls, and a whole cañon full of nothingness at the edge of the other rail, and— But there's our "clearance" now.

MacMurtrey's camp was at the summit; and MacMurtrey's work, once the camp was fairly established and stores in, was to shave the pate of the summit, looking to an amelioration in The Gap's grade average—that is, its official grade average. But on the morning that Regan left Big Cloud on No. 3, the work was not very far along—only the preliminaries accomplished, so to speak, which were a siding at the top of the grade, with storehouse and camp shanties flanking it.

And on the siding, that morning, just opposite the storehouse which, it might be remarked in passing, had already received its first requisition of blasting materials for the barbering of the grade that was to come, a hybrid collection of Polacks, Swedes, and Hungarians were emptying an oil-tank car and discharging supplies from some flats and box cars; while on the main line track a red-haired man, with leathery face, was loading some grade stakes on a handcar.

MacMurtrey, tall, lanky and irascible, shouted at the red-haired man from a little distance up the line.

"Hey, O'Toole!"

The red-haired man paid no attention.

50

"O'Toole!" It came in a bellow from the road boss. "You, there, O'Toole, you wooden-headed mud-picker, are you deaf!"

Sammy Durgan looked up to get a line on the disturbance—and caught his breath.

"By glory!" whispered Sammy Durgan to himself. "I was near forgetting—'tis me he's yelling at."

"O'Too—"

"Yes, sir!" shouted Sammy Durgan hurriedly.

"Oh, you woke up, have you?" shrilled MacMurtrey. "Well, when you've got those stakes loaded, take 'em down the grade and leave 'em by the old spur. And take it easy on the grade, and mind your brakes going down—understand?"

"Yes, sir," said Sammy Durgan.

Sammy Durgan finished loading his handcar, and, hopping aboard, started to pump it along. At the brow of the grade he passed the oil-tank car, and nodded sympathetically at a round-faced, tow-headed Swede who was snatching a surreptitious drag at his pipe in the lee of the car.

Like one other memorable morning in Sammy Durgan's career, it was sultry and warm with that same leisurely feeling in the air. Sammy Durgan and his handcar slid down the grade—for about an eighth of a mile—rounded a curve that hid Sammy Durgan and the construction camp one from the other, continued on for another hundred yards—and came to a stop.

Sammy Durgan got off. On the cañon side there was perhaps room for an agile mountain goat to stretch its legs without falling off; but on the other side, if a man squeezed in tight enough and curled his legs Turk fashion, the rock wall made a fairly comfortable backrest.

"'Twas easy, he said, to take it on the grade," said Sammy Durgan reminiscently. "And why not?"

Sammy Durgan composed himself against the rock wall, and produced his black cutty.

"'Tis a better job than track-walking," said Sammy Durgan judicially, "though more arduous."

Sammy Durgan smoked on.

"But some day," said Sammy Durgan momentously, "I'll have a better one. I will that! It's a long time in coming mabbe, but it'll come. Once in every man's life a chance comes to him. 'Tis patience that counts, that and rising to the emergency that proves the kind of a man you are, as some day I'll prove to Maria, and Regan, and the rest of 'em."

Sammy Durgan smoked on. It was a warm summer morning, sultry even, as has been said, but it was cool and shady against the rock ledge. Peace fell upon Sammy Durgan—drowsily. Also, presently, the black cutty fell, or, rather, slipped down into Sammy Durgan's lap—without disturbing Sammy Durgan.

A half hour, three-quarters of an hour passed—and MacMurtrey, far up at the extreme end of the construction camp, let a sudden yell out of him and started on a mad run toward the tank-car and the summit of the grade, as a series of screeches in seven different varieties of language smote his ears, and a great burst of black smoke rolling skyward met his startled gaze. But fast as he ran, the Polacks, Swedes and Hungarians were faster—pipe smoking under discharging oil-tank cars and in the shadow of a dynamite storage shed they were accustomed to, but to the result, a blazing oil-tank car shooting a flame against the walls of the dynamite shed, they were not—they were only aroused to action with their lives in peril, and they acted promptly and earnestly—too earnestly. Some one threw the main line open, and the others crowbarred the blazing car like mad along the few feet of siding to get it away from the storage shed, bumped it on the main line, and then their bars began to lose their purchase under the wheels—the grade accommodatingly took a hand.

MacMurtrey, tearing along toward the scene, yelled like a crazy man:

"Block her! Block the wheels! You—you—" His voice died in a gasp. "D'ye hear!" he screamed, as he got his breath again. "Block the wheels!"

And the Polacks, the Swedes, the Hungarians and the What-Nots, scared stiff, screeched and jabbered, as they watched the tank-car, gaining speed with every foot it travelled, sail down the grade. And MacMurtrey, too late to do anything, stopped dead in his tracks—his face ashen. He pulled his watch, licked dry lips, and kind of whispered to himself.

"Number Three 'll be on the foot of the grade now," whispered MacMurtrey, and licked his lips again. "Oh, my God!"

Meanwhile, down the grade around the bend, Sammy Durgan yawned, sat up, and cocked his ear summit-wards.

"Now what the devil are them crazy foreigners yelling about!" complained Sammy Durgan unhappily. "'Tis always the way with them, like a cageful of screeching cockatoos, they are—but being foreigners mabbe they can't help it, 'tis their nature to yell without provocation and—"

Sammy Durgan's ear caught a very strange sound, that mingled the clack of fast-revolving wheels as they pounded the fish-plates with a roar that hissed most curiously—and then Sammy Durgan's knees went loose at the joints and wobbled under him.

Trailing a dense black canopy of smoke, wrapped in a sheet of flame that spurted even from the trucks, the oil-tank car lurched around the bend and plunged for him—and for once, Sammy Durgan thought very fast. There was no room to let it pass—on one side was just nothing, barring a precipice; and on the rock side, no matter how hard he squeezed back from the right of way, there wasn't any room to escape that spurting flame that even in its passing would burn him to a crisp. And with one wild squeak of terror Sammy Durgan flung himself at his handcar, and, pushing first like a maniac to start it, sprang aboard. Then he began to pump.

There were a hundred yards between the bend and the scene of Sammy Durgan's siesta—only the tank-car had momentum, a whole lot of it, and Sammy Durgan had not. By the time Sammy Durgan had the handcar started the hundred yards was twenty-five, and the monster of flame and smoke behind him was travelling two feet to his one.

Sammy Durgan pumped—for his life. He got up a little better speed— but the tank-car still gained on him. Down the grade he went, the handcar rocking, swaying, lurching, and up and down on the handle, madly, frantically, desperately, wildly went Sammy Durgan's arms, shoulders and head—his hat blew off, and his red hair sort of stood straight up in the wind, and his face was like chalk.

Down he went, faster and faster, and the handcar, reeling like a drunken thing, took a curve with a vicious slew, and the off wheels hung in air for an instant while Sammy Durgan bellowed in panic, then found their base again and shot along the straight. And faster and faster behind him, on wings of fire it seemed, spitting flame tongues, vomiting its black clouds of smoke like an inferno, roaring like a mighty furnace in blast, came the tank-car. It was initial momentum and mass against Sammy Durgan's muscles on a handcar pump handle—and the race was not to Sammy Durgan.

He cast a wild glance behind, and squeaked again, and his teeth began to go like castanets, as the hot breath of the thing fanned his back.

"'Tis my finish," wheezed and stuttered Sammy Durgan through bursting lungs and chattering teeth. "'Tis a dead man, I am—oh, Holy Mither—'tis a dead man I am!"

Ahead and to either side swept Sammy Durgan's eyes like a hunted rat's—and they held, fascinated, on where the old spur track led off from the main line. But it was not the spur track that interested Sammy Durgan—it was that the rock wall, diverging away from his elbow, as it were, presented a wide and open space.

"It's killed I am, anyway," moaned Sammy Durgan. "But 'tis a chance. If—if mabbe I could jump far enough there where there's room to let it pass, I dunno—but 'tis killed, I'll be, anyway—oh, Holy Mither—but 'tis a chance—oh, Holy Mither!"

Hissing in its wind-swept flames, belching its cataract of smoke that lay behind it up the grade like a pall of death, roaring like some insensate demon, the tank-car leaped at him five yards away. And, screaming now in a paroxysm of terror that had his soul in clutch, crazed with it, blind with it, Sammy Durgan jumped—blindly—just before he reached the spur.

Like a stone from a catapult, Sammy Durgan went through the air, and with a sickening thud his body crashed full into the old stub switch-stand and into the switch handle, whirled around, and he ricochetted, a senseless, bleeding, shattered Sammy Durgan, three yards away.

It threw the switch. The handcar, already over it, sailed on down the main line and around the next bend, climbed up the front end of the 508 that was hauling No. 3 up the grade, smashed the headlight into battered ruin, unshipped the stack, and took final lodgment on the running board, its wheels clinging like tentacles to the 508's bell and sand-box; but the tank-car, with a screech of wrenching axles, a frightened, quivering stagger, took the spur, rushed like a Berserker amuck along its length, plowed up sand and gravel and dirt and rock where there were no longer any rails, and toppled over, a spent and buckled thing, on its side.

It was a flying switch that they talk of yet on the Hill Division. No. 3, suspicious of the handcar, sniffed her way cautiously around the curve, and there, passengers, train crew, engine crew and Tommy Regan, made an excited exodus from the train—just as MacMurtrey, near mad with fear,

53

Swedes, Hungarians and Polacks stringing out along the right of way behind him, also arrived on the scene.

Who disclaims circumstantial evidence! Regan stared at the burning oil-tank up the spur, stared at the bleeding, senseless form of Sammy Durgan—and then he yelled for a doctor.

But a medical man amongst the passengers was already jumping for Sammy Durgan; and MacMurtrey was clawing at the master mechanic's arm, stuttering out the tale of what had happened.

"And—and if it hadn't been for Timmy O'Toole there," stuttered MacMurtrey, flirting away the sweat that stood out in great nervous beads on his face, "I—it makes me sick to think what would have happened when the tank struck Number Three. Something would have gone into the cañon sure. Timmy O'Toole's a—"

"His name's Sammy Durgan," said Regan, kind of absently.

"I don't give a blamed hoot what his name is!" declared MacMurtrey earnestly. "He's a man with grit from the soles up, and a head on him to use it with. It was three-quarters of an hour ago that I sent him down, so he must have been near the top on his way back when he saw the tank-car coming—and he took the one chance there was—to try and beat it to the spur here to save Number Three; and it was so close on him, for it's a cinch he hadn't time to stop, that he had to jump for the switch with about one chance in ten for his own life—see?"

"A blind man could see it," said Regan heavily, "but—Sammy Durgan!" He reached uncertainly toward his hip pocket for his chewing—and then, with sudden emotion, the big-hearted, fat, little master mechanic bent over Sammy Durgan.

"God bless the man!" blurted out Regan. And then, to the doctor: "Will he live?"

"Oh, yes; I think so," the doctor answered. "He's pretty badly smashed up, though."

Sammy Durgan's lips were moving. Regan leaned close to catch the words.

"A steady job," murmured Sammy Durgan. "Never get a chance. But some day it'll come. I'll show 'em, Maria, and Regan, and the rest of 'em!"

"You have, Sammy," said Regan, in a low, anxious voice. "It's all right, Sammy. It's all right, old boy. Just pull around and you can have any blamed thing you want on the Hill Division."

The doctor smiled sympathetically at Regan.

"He's delirious, you know," he explained kindly. "What he says doesn't mean anything."

Regan looked up with a kind of a grim smile.

"Don't it?" inquired Regan softly. Then he cleared his throat, and tugged at his scraggly brown mustache—both ends of it. "That's what I used to think myself," said the fat little master mechanic, sort of as though he were apostrophizing the distant peaks across the cañon; and not as though he were talking to the doctor at all. "But I guess—I guess I know Sammy Durgan better than I did. H'm?"

Chapter IV

THE WRECKING BOSS

Opinions, right or wrong, on any subject are a matter of individuality—there have been different opinions about Flannagan on the Hill Division. But the story is straight enough—from car-tink to superintendent, there has never been any difference of opinion about that.

Flannagan was the wrecking boss.

Tommy Regan said the job fitted Flannagan, for it took a hard man for the job, and Flannagan, bar none, was the hardest man on the payroll; hardest at crooking elbows in MacGuire's Blazing Star Saloon, hardest with his fists, and hardest of all when it came to getting at the heart of some scalding, mangled horror of death and ruin that a man wouldn't be called a coward to turn from—sick.

Flannagan looked it. He stood six feet one in his stockings, and his chest and shoulders were like the front-end view you'd get looking at a sturdy, well-grown ox. He wasn't pretty. His face was scarred with cuts and burns enough to stall any German duelling student on a siding till the rails rusted, and the beard he grew to hide these multitudinous disfigurements just naturally came out in tussocks; he had black eyes that could go coal black and lose their pupils, and a shock of black hair that fell into them half the time; also, he had a tongue that wasn't elegant. That was Flannagan—Flannagan, the wrecking boss.

There's no accounting for the way some things come about—and it's pretty hard to call the turn of the card when Dame Fortune deals the bank. It's a trite enough saying that it is the unexpected that happens in life, but the reason it's trite is because it's immeasurably true. Flannagan growled and swore and cursed one night, coming back from a bit of a spill up the line, because they stalled him and his wrecking outfit for an hour about half a mile west of Big Cloud—the reason being that, like the straw that broke the camel's back, a circus train in from the East, billed for a three days' lay-off at Big Cloud, had, seeking siding, temporarily choked the yards, already glutted with traffic, until the mix-up Gleeson, the yardmaster, had to wrestle with would have put a problem in differential calculus into the kindergarten class.

Flannagan was very dirty, and withal very tired, and when, finally, they gave him the "clear" and his flat and caboose and his staggering derrick rumbled sullenly down toward the roundhouse and shops, the sight of gilded cages, gaudily decorated cars, and converted Pullmans that were second-class-tourist equipment painted white, did not assuage his feelings; neither was there enchantment for him in the roars of multifarious beasts, nor in the hybrid smells that assailed his nostrils from the general direction of the menagerie. Flannagan, for an hour's loss of sleep, with heartiness and

55

abandon, consigned that particular circus, also all others and everything thereunto pertaining, from fangless serpents to steam calliopes, to regions that are popularly credited with being somewhat warmer than the torrid zone on the hottest day in midsummer. But then—Flannagan did not know.

Opinions differ. Flannagan was about the last man on earth that any one on the Hill Division would have picked out for a marrying man; and, equally true the other way round, about the last man they would have picked out as one a pretty girl would want to marry. With her, maybe, it was the strength of the man, since they say that comes first with women; with him, maybe, it was just the trim little brown-eyed, brown-haired figure that could ride with the grace of a fairy. Anyway, the only thing about it that didn't surprise any one was the fact that, when it came, it came as sudden and quick as a head-on smash around a ninety-degree curve. That was Flannagan's way, for Flannagan, if he was nothing else, was impulsive.

That night Flannagan cursed the circus; the next day he saw Daisy MacQueen riding in the street parade and—but this isn't the story of Flannagan's courtship, not but that the courtship of any man like Flannagan would be worth the telling—only there are other things.

At first, Big Cloud winked and chuckled slyly to itself; and then, when the circus left and Flannagan got a week off and left with it, it guffawed outright—but when, at the end of that week, Flannagan brought back Mrs. Flannagan, née Daisy MacQueen, Big Cloud stuck its tongue in its cheek, wagged its head and waited developments.

This is the story of the developments.

Maybe that same impulsiveness of Flannagan's, that could be blind and bullheaded, coupled with a passion that was like a devil's when aroused, was to blame; maybe the women of Big Cloud, following the lead of Mrs. MacAloon, the engineer's wife and the leader of society circles, who shook her fiery red head and turned up her Celtic nose disdainfully at Daisy MacQueen, had something to do with it; maybe Daisy herself had a little pride—but what's the use of speculating? It all goes back to the same beginning—opinions differ.

Tongues wagged; Flannagan listened—that's the gist of it. But, once for all, let it be said and understood that Daisy MacQueen was as straight as they make them. She hadn't been brought up the way Mrs. MacAloon and her coterie had, and she liked to laugh, liked to play, liked to live, and not exist in a humdrum way ever over washtubs and a cook stove—though, all credit to her who hadn't been used to them, she never shirked one nor the other. The women's ideas about circuses and circus performers were, putting it mildly, puritanical; but the men liked Daisy MacQueen—and took no pains to hide it. They clustered around her, and, before long, she ruled them all imperially with a nod of her pretty head; and, as a result, the women's ideas from puritanical became more so—which is human nature, Big Cloud or anywhere else.

At first, Flannagan was proud of the little wife he had brought to Big Cloud—proud of her for the very attitude adopted toward her by his mates; but, as the months went by, gradually the wagging tongues got in their work, gradually Flannagan began to listen, and the jealousy that was his by nature above the jealousy of most men commenced to smolder into flame. Just a rankling jealousy, directed against no one in particular—just jealousy. Things up at the little house off Main Street where the Flannagans lived weren't as harmonious as they had been.

In the beginning, Daisy, not treating the matter seriously, answered Flannagan with a laugh; finally, she answered him not at all. And that stage, unfortunately far from unique in other homes than Flannagan's the world over, was reached where only some one act, word or deed was needed to bring matters to a head.

Perhaps, after all, there was poetic justice in Flannagan's cursing of the circus, for it was the circus that supplied that one thing needed. Not that the circus came back to town—it didn't—but a certain round, little, ferret-eyed, short, pompadour-haired, waxed-mustached, perfumed Signor Ferraringi, the ringmaster, did.

Ferraringi was a scoundrel—what he got he deserved, there was never any doubt about that; but that night Flannagan, when he walked into the house, saw only Ferraringi on his knees before Daisy, heard only impassioned, flowery words, and, in the blind fury that transformed him from man to beast, the scorn, contempt and horror in Daisy's eyes, the significance of the rigid little figure with tight-clenched hands, was lost. Ferraringi had been in love with Daisy. Flannagan knew that, and his seething brain remembered that. The circus people had told him so; Daisy had told him so; Ferraringi had told him so with a snarl and a threat—and he had laughed—then.

One instant Flannagan hung upon the threshold. He was not a pretty sight. Back from a wreck, he was still in his overalls, and these were smeared with blood—four carloads of steers had gone into premature shambles in the ditch. One instant Flannagan hung there, his face working convulsively—and then he jumped. His left hand locked into the collar of the ringmaster's coat, his arm straightened like the tautening chains of his own derrick crane, and, as the other came off his knees and upright from the yank, Flannagan's right swung a terrific full-arm smash that, landing a little above the jaw, plastered one side of that tonsorial work of art, the waxed and curled mustache, flat into Ferraringi's cheek.

Ferraringi's answer, as he wriggled free, was a torrent of malediction— and a blinding flash. Daisy screamed. The shot missed, but the powder singed Flannagan's face.

It was the only shot that Ferraringi fired! With a roar, high-pitched like the maddened trumpeting of an elephant amuck, Flannagan with a single blow sent the revolver sailing ceiling high—then his arms, like steel piston rods, worked in and out, and his fists drummed an awful, merciless tattoo upon the ringmaster.

The smoke from the shot filled the room with pungent odor. Chairs and furniture, overturned, broken, crashed to the floor. Daisy, wild-eyed, with parted lips, dumb with terror, crouched against the wall, her hands clasped to her breast—but before Flannagan's eyes all was red—red.

A battered, bruised, reeling, staggering form before him curled up suddenly and slid in a heap at his feet. Flannagan, with groping hands and twitching fingers, reached for it—and then, with a rush, other forms, many of them, came between him and what was on the floor.

It was very good for Ferraringi, very good, for that was all that saved him—Flannagan was seeing only red.

The neighbors lifted the stunned ringmaster, limp as rags, to his feet. Flannagan brushed his great fist once across his eyes in a half-dazed way, and glared at the roomful of people. Suddenly, he heaved forward, pushing those nearest him violently toward the door.

"Get out of here!" he bellowed hoarsely. "Get out, curse you, d'ye hear! Get out!"

There were men in that little crowd, men besides the three or four women, Mrs. MacAloon amongst them; men not reckoned overfaint of spirit in Big Cloud by those who knew, but they knew Flannagan, and they went— went, half carrying, half dragging the ringmaster, oiled and perfumed now in a fashion grimly different than before.

"Get out!" roared Flannagan again to hurry them, and, as the last one disappeared, he whirled on Daisy. "And you, too!" he snarled. "Get out!"

Terrified, shaken by the scene as she was, his words, their implication, their injustice, whipped her into scorn and anger. White-lipped, she stared at him for an instant.

"You dare," she burst out, "you dare to—"

"Get out!" Flannagan's voice in his passion was a thick, stumbling, guttural whisper. "Get out! Go back! to your circus—go where you like! Get out!" His hand dove into his pocket, and its contents, bills and coins, what there was of them, he flung upon the table. "Get out—as far as all I've got will take you!"

Daisy MacQueen was proud—perhaps, though, not above the pride of other women. The blood was hot in her cheeks; her big, brown eyes had a light in them near to that light with which she had faced Ferraringi but a short time before; her breath came in short, hard, little gasps. For a full minute she did not speak—and then the words came cold as death.

"Some day—some day, Michael Flannagan, you'll get what you deserve."

"That's what I'm gettin' now—what I deserve," he flung back; then, halting in the doorway: "You understand, eh? Get out! I'm lettin' you down easy. Get out of Big Cloud! Get out before I'm back. Number Fifteen 'll be in in an hour—you'd better take her."

Flannagan stepped out on the street. A curious little group had collected two houses down in front of Mrs. MacAloon's. Flannagan glanced at them, muttered a curse; and then, head down between his shoulders, clenched fists rammed in his pockets, he headed in the other direction toward Main Street. Five minutes later, he pushed the swinging doors of the Blazing Star open, and walked down the length of the room to where Pete MacGuire, the proprietor, lounged across the bar.

"Pete"—he jerked out his words hoarsely—"next Tuesday's pay day—is my face good till then?"

MacGuire looked at him curiously. The news of the fracas had not yet reached the Blazing Star.

"Why, sure," said he. "Sure it is, Flannagan, if you want it. What's—"

"Then let 'em come my way," Flannagan rapped out, with a savage laugh; "an' let 'em come—fast."

Flannagan was the wrecking boss. A hard man, Regan had called him, and he was—a product of the wild, rough, pioneering life, one of those men who had followed the grim-faced, bearded corps of engineers as they pitted their strength against the sullen gray of the mighty Rockies from the eastern foothills to the plains of the Sierras, fighting every inch of their way with indomitable perseverance and daring over chasms and gorges, through tunnels and cuts, in curves and levels and grades, against obstacles that tried their souls, against death itself, taping the thin steel lines they left behind them with their own blood. Hard? Yes, Flannagan was hard. Uncultured, rough, primal, he undoubtedly was. A brute man, perhaps, full of the elemental—fiery, hot-headed, his passions alone swayed him. That side of Flannagan, the years, in the very environment in which he had lived them, had developed to the full—the other side had been untouched. What Flannagan did that night another might not have done—or he might. The judging of men is a grave business best let alone.

Flannagan let go his hold then; not at once, but gradually. That night spent in the Blazing Star was the first of others, others that followed insidiously, each closer upon the former's heels. Daisy had gone—had gone that night—where, he did not know, and told himself he did not care. He grew moody, sullen, uncompanionable. Big Cloud took sides—the women for Flannagan; the men for the wife. Flannagan hated the women, avoided the men—and went to the Blazing Star.

There was only one result—the inevitable one. Regan, kindly for all his gruffness, understanding in a way, stood between Flannagan and the super and warned Flannagan oftener than most men were warned on the Hill Division. Nor were his warnings altogether without effect. Flannagan would steady up—temporarily—maybe for a week—then off again. Steady up just long enough to keep putting off and postponing the final reckoning. And then one day, some six months after Daisy Flannagan had gone away, the master mechanic warned him for the last time.

"I'm through with you, Flannagan," he said. "Understand that? I'm out from under, and next time you'll talk to Carleton—and what he'll have to say won't take long—about two seconds. You know Carleton, don't you? Well, then—what?"

It was just a week to a day after that that Flannagan cut loose and wild again. He made a night and a day of it, and then another. After that, though by that time Flannagan was quite unaware of the fact, some of the boys got him home, dumped him on his bed and left him to his reflections—which were a blank.

Flannagan slept it off, and it took about eighteen hours to do it. When he came to himself he was in a humor that, far from being happy, was atrocious; likewise, there were bodily ailments—Flannagan's head was bad, and felt as though a gang of boiler-makers, working against time, were driving rivets in it. He procured himself a bracer and went back to bed. This resulted in a decidedly improved physical condition, but when he arose late in the afternoon any improvement there might have been in his mental state was speedily dissipated—Flannagan found a letter shoved under his door, postmarked the day before, and with it an official manila envelope from the super's office.

He opened the letter and read it—read it again while his jaws worked and the red surged in a passion into his face; then, with an oath, he tore it savagely into shreds, flung the bits on the floor and stamped upon them viciously with his heavy nail-heeled boot.

The official manila he did not open at all. A guess was enough for that— a curt request to present himself in the super's office, probably. Flannagan glared at it, then grabbed his hat, and started down for the station. There was no idea of shirking it; Flannagan wasn't that kind at any time, and just now his mood, if anything, spurred him on rather than held him back. Flannagan welcomed the prospect of a row about anything with anybody at that moment—if only a war of words.

Carleton's office was upstairs over the ticket office and next to the despatchers' room then, for the station did duty for headquarters and everything else—not now, it's changed now, and there's a rather imposing gray-stone structure where the old wooden shack used to be; but, no matter, that's the way it was then, for those were the early days when the road was young and in the making.

Flannagan reached the station, climbed the stairs, and pushed Carleton's door open with little ceremony.

"You want to see me?" he demanded gruffly, as he stepped inside.

Carleton, sitting at his desk, looked up and eyed the wrecking boss coolly for a minute.

"No, Flannagan," he said curtly. "I don't."

"Then what in blazes d'ye send for me for?" Flannagan flung out in a growl.

"See here, Flannagan," snapped Carleton, "I've no time to talk to you. You can read, can't you? You're out!"

Flannagan blinked.

"Was that what was in the letter?"

"It was—just that," said Carleton grimly.

"Hell!" Flannagan's short laugh held a jeering note of contempt. "I didn't open it—or mabbe I'd have known, eh?"

Carleton's eyes narrowed.

"Well, you know now, don't you?"

"Sure!" Flannagan scowled and licked his lips. "I'm out, thrown out, and—"

"Then, get out!" Carleton cut in sharply. "You've had more chances than any man ever got before from me, thanks to Regan; but you've had your last, and talking won't do you any good now."

Flannagan stepped nearer to the desk.

"Talkin'! Who's talkin'?" he flared in sudden bravado. "Didn't I tell you I didn't read your damned letter? Didn't I, eh, didn't I? D'ye think I'd crawl to you or any man for a job? I'm out, am I? D'ye think I came down to ask you to take me back? I'd see you rot first! T'hell with the job—see!"

Few men on the Hill Division ever saw Carleton lose his temper—it wasn't Carleton's way of doing things. He didn't lose it now, but his words were like trickling drops of ice water.

"Sometimes, Flannagan," he said, "to make a man like you understand one has to use your language. You say you'd see me rot before you asked me for the job back again—very well. I'd rot before I gave it to you after this. Now, will you get out—or be thrown out?"

For a moment it looked as though Flannagan was going to mix it there and then. His eyes went ugly, and his fists, horny and gnarled, doubled into knots, as he glared viciously at the super.

Carleton, who was afraid of no man, or any aggregation of men, his face stern-set and hard, leaned back in his swivel chair and waited.

A tense minute passed. Then Flannagan's better sense weighed down the balance, and, without so much as a word, he turned, went out of the room, and stamped heavily down the stairs.

Goaded into it, or through unbridled, ill-advised impulse, men say rash things sometimes—afterward, both Flannagan and Carleton were to remember their own and the other's words—and the futility of them. Nor was it to be long afterward—without warning, without so much as a premonition, quick and sudden as doom, things happen in railroading.

It was half past five when Flannagan went out of the super's office; it was but ten minutes later when, before he had decanted a drop from the bottle he had just lifted to fill his glass, he slapped the bottle back on the bar of the Blazing Star with a sudden jerk. From down the street in the direction of the yards boomed three long blasts from the shop whistle—the wrecking signal. It came again and again. Men around him began to move. Chairs from the little tables were pushed hurriedly back. The bell in the English chapel took up the alarm. It stirred the blood in Flannagan's veins, and whipped it to his cheeks in fierce excitement—it was the call to arms!

He turned from the bar—and stopped like a man stunned. There had been times in the last six months when he had not responded to that call, because, deaf to everything, he had not heard it. Then, it had been his call—the call for the wrecking crew, and, first of all, for the wrecking boss; now—there was a dazed look on his face, and his lips worked queerly. It was not for him, he was barred—out.

Slowly he turned back to the bar, rested his foot on the rail, and, with a mirthless laugh and a shrug of his shoulders, reached for the bottle again. He poured the whisky glass full to the brim—and laughed once more and shrugged his shoulders as his fingers curled around it. He raised the glass—and held it poised halfway to his lips.

Quick-running steps came up the street, the swinging doors of the Blazing Star burst open and a call boy shoved in his head.

"Wreckers out! Wreckers out!" he bawled. "Number Eighty's gone to glory in Spider Cut. Everybody's killed"—and he was gone, a grimy-faced harbinger of death and disaster; gone, speeding with his summons to wherever men were gathered throughout the little town.

An instant Flannagan stood motionless as one transformed from flesh to sculptured clay—then the glass slid from his fingers and crashed into tinkling splinters on the floor. The liquor splashed his boots. Number Eighty was the eastbound Coast Express! Like one who moves in unknown places through the dark, so, then, Flannagan moved toward the door. Men looked at him in amazement, and stood aside to let him pass. Something was tugging at his heart, beating at his brain, impelling him forward; a force irresistible, that, in its first, sudden, overwhelming surge he could not understand, could not grasp, could not focus into concrete form—could only obey.

He passed out through the doors, and then for the first time a cry rang from his lips. There were no halting, stumbling, uncertain steps now. Men running down the street called to Flannagan as he sped past them. Flannagan made no answer, did not look their way; his face, strained and full of dumb anguish, was set toward the station.

He gained the platform and raced along it. Shouts came from across the yards. Up and down the spurs fluttered the fore-shortened little yard engine, coughing sparks and wheezing from her exhaust as she bustled the wrecking train together; lamps swung and twinkled like fireflies, for it was just opening spring and the dark fell early; and in front of the roundhouse, the 1014, blowing hard from her safety under a full head of steam, like a thoroughbred that scents the race, was already on the table.

With a heave of his great shoulders and a sweep of his arms, Flannagan won through the group of trainmen, shop hands, and loungers clustered around the door, and took the stairs four at a leap.

A light burned in the super's office, but the voices came from the despatchers' room. And there in the doorway Flannagan halted—halted just for a second's pause while his eyes swept the scene before him.

Regan, the master mechanic, by the window, was mouthing curses under his breath as men do in times of stress; Spence, the despatcher, white-faced, the hair straggling into his eyes, was leaning over the key under the green-shaded lamp, over the key clearing the line while the sounder clicked in his ears of ruin and of lives gone out. Harvey, the division engineer, was there, pulling savagely at a brier with empty bowl. And at the despatcher's elbow stood Carleton, a grim commander, facing tidings of disaster, his shoulders braced and bent a little forward as though to take the blow, his jaws clamped tight till the lips, compressed, were bloodless, and the chiselled lines on his face told of the bitterness in his heart.

Then Flannagan stepped forward.

"Carleton," he cried, and his words came like panting sobs, "Carleton, give me back my job."

It was no place for Flannagan.

Carleton's cup was already full to overflowing, and he swung on Flannagan like a flash. His hand lifted and pointed to the door.

"Get out of here!" he said between his teeth.

"Carleton," cried Flannagan again, and his arms went out in

supplication toward the super, "Carleton, give me back my job—give it back to me for to-night—just for tonight."

"No!" the single word came from Carleton's lips like a thunder clap.

Flannagan shivered a little and shrank back.

"Just for to-night," he mumbled hoarsely. "Just for—"

"No!" Carleton's voice rang hard as flint. "I tell you, no! Get out of here!"

Harvey moved suddenly, threateningly, toward Flannagan—and, as suddenly, Flannagan, roused by the act, brushed the division engineer aside like a plaything, sprang forward, and, with a quick, fierce grip, caught Carleton's arms and pinioned them, vise-like, to his sides.

"And I tell you, yes!" his voice rose dominant with the power, the will that shook him now to the depths of his turbulent soul. As a man who knows no law, no obstacle, no restraint, as a man who would batter down the gates of hell itself to gain his end, so then was Flannagan. "I tell you, yes! I tell you, yes! My wife and baby's in that wreck to-night!"

Turmoil, shouts, the short, quick intermittent hiss of steam as the 1014, her cylinder cocks open, backed down to the platform, the clash of coupling cars, a jumbled medley of sounds, floated up from the yard without—but within the little room, the chattering sounder for the moment stilled, there fell a silence as of death, and no man among them moved or spoke.

Flannagan, gray-faced, gasping, his mighty grip still on Carleton, his head thrown forward close to the other's, stared into the super's face—and, for a long minute, in the twitching muscles of the big wrecker's face, in the look that man reads seldom in his fellows' eyes, Carleton drew the fearful picture, lived the awful story that the babbling wire had told. "Royal" Carleton, square man and big of heart, his voice broke.

"God help you, Flannagan—go."

No word came from Flannagan's lips—only a queer choking sound, as his hands dropped to his sides—only a queer choking sound, as he turned suddenly and jumped for the door.

On the stairs, Dorsay, the driver of the 1014, coming up for his orders, passed Flannagan.

"Bad spill, I hear," growled the engineer, as he went by. "The five hundred and five's pony truck jumped the rails on the lower curve and everything's in the ditch. Old Burke's gone out and a heap of the passengers with him. I—"

Flannagan heard no more—he was on the platform now. Coupled behind the derrick crane and the tool car were two coaches, improvised ambulances, and into these latter, instead of the tool car, the men of the wrecking gang were piling—a bad smash brought luxury for them. Shouts, cries, hubbub, a babel of voices were around him, but in his brain, repeated and repeated over and over again, lived only a phrase from the letter he had torn to pieces, stamped under heel that afternoon—the words were swimming before his eyes: "Michael, dear, we've both been wrong; I'm bringing baby back on the Coast Express Friday night."

Men with little black bags brushed by him and tumbled into the rear

63

coach—the doctors of Big Cloud to the last one of them. Dorsay came running from the station, a bit of tissue, his orders, fluttering in his hand, and sprang for the cab. 1014's exhaust burst suddenly into quick, deafening explosions, the sparks shot volleying heavenward from her short stack, the big, whirling drivers were beginning to bite—and then, through the gangway, after the engineer, into the cab swung Flannagan—Flannagan, the wrecking boss.

Spider Cut is the Eastern gateway of the Rockies, and it lies, as the crows fly, sixteen miles west of Big Cloud; but the right of way, as it twists and turns, circling and dodging the buttes that grow from mounds to foothills, makes it on the blue-prints twenty-one decimal seven. The running time of the fast fliers on this stretch is—but what of that? Dorsay that night smashed all records, and the medical men in the rear coach tell to this day how they clung for life and limb to their seats and to each other, and most of them will admit—which is admitting much—that they were frightened, white-lipped men with broken nerves.

As the wreck special, with a clash and clatter, shattered over the switches in the upper yard and nosed the main line, Stan Willard, who had the shovel end of it, with a snatch at the chain swung open the furnace door and a red glow lighted up the heavens. Dorsay turned in his seat and looked at the giant form of the wrecking-boss behind him—they had told him the story in the office.

The eyes of the two men met. Flannagan's lips moved dumbly; and, with a curious, pleading motion, he gestured toward the throttle.

Dorsay opened another notch. He laughed a grim, hard laugh.

"I know," he shouted over the roar. "I know. Leave it to me, Flannagan."

The bark of the exhaust came quicker and quicker, swelled and rose into the full, deep-toned thunder of a single note. Notch by notch, Dorsay opened out the 1014, notch by notch, and the big mountain racer, answering like a mettlesome steed to the touch of the whip, leapt forward, ever faster, into the night.

Now the headlight played on shining steel ahead; now suddenly threw a path of light across the short, yellow stubble of a rising butte, and Dorsay checked grudgingly for an instant as they swung the curve—just for an instant—then into the straight again, with wide-flung throttle.

It was mad work, and in that reeling, dizzy cab no man spoke. The sweep of the singing wind, the wild tattoo of beating trucks, the sullen whir of flying drivers; was in their ears; while behind, the derrick crane, the tool car and the coaches writhed and wriggled, swayed and lurched, tearing at their couplings, bouncing on their trucks, jerking viciously as each slue took up the axle play, rolling, pitching crazily like cockleshells tossed on an angry sea.

Now they tore through a cut, and the walls took up the deafening roar and echoed and reëchoed it back in volume a thousandfold; now into the open, and the sudden contrast was like the gasping breath of an imprisoned thing escaped; now over culverts, trestles, spans, hollow, reverberating—the speed was terrific.

Over his levers, bounding on his seat, Dorsay, tense and strained, leaned far forward following the leaping headlight's glare; while staggering

64

like a drunken man to keep his balance, the sweat standing out in glistening beads upon his grimy face, Stan Willard watched the flickering needle on the gauge, and his shovel clanged and swung; and in the corner, back of Dorsay, bent low to brace himself, thrown backward and forward with every lurch, in the fantastic, dancing light like some tigerish, outraged animal crouched to spring, Flannagan, with head drawn into his shoulders, jaws outthrust, stared over the engineer's back, stared with never a look to right or left, stared through the cab glass to the right of way ahead—stared toward Spider Cut.

Again and again, with sickening, giddy shock, wheel-base lifted from the swing, the 1014 struck the tangents, hung a breathless space, and, with a screech of crunching flanges, found the rails once more.

Again and again—but the story of that ride is the doctors' story—they tell it best. Dorsay made the run that night from Big Cloud to Spider Cut, twenty-one point seven miles, in nineteen minutes.

There have been bad spills on the Hill Division, bad spills—but there have never been worse than on that Friday night when the 505 jumped the rails at the foot of the curve coming down the grade just east of Spider Cut, shot over the embankment and piled the Coast Express, mahogany sleepers and all, into splintered wreckage forty feet below the right of way.

As Dorsay checked and with screaming brake-shoes the 1014 slowed, Flannagan, with a wild cry, leaped from the cab and dashed up the track ahead of the still-moving pilot. It was light enough—the cars of the wreck nearest him, the mail and baggage cars, had caught, and, fanned by the wind into yellow flames, were blazing like a huge bonfire. Shouts arose from below; cries, anguished, piercing, from those imprisoned in the wreck; figures, those of the crew and passengers who had made their escape, were moving hither and thither, working as best they might, pulling others through shattered windows and up-canted doors, laying those who were past all knowing beside the long row of silent forms already tenderly stretched upon the edge of the embankment.

A man, with face cut and bleeding, came running toward Flannagan. It was Kingsley, conductor of Number Eighty. Flannagan jumped for him, grasped him by the shoulders and stared without a word into his face.

But Kingsley shook his head.

"I don't know, Flannagan," he choked. "She was in the first-class just ahead of the Pullmans. There's—there's no one come out of that car yet"—he turned away his head—"we couldn't get to it."

"Couldn't get to it"—Flannagan's lips repeated the phrase mechanically. Then he looked—and understood the grim significance of the words. He laughed suddenly, jarring hoarse, as it is not good to hear men laugh—and with that laugh Flannagan went into the fight.

The details of that night no one man knows. There in the shadow of the gray-walled Rockies, men, flint-hearted, calloused, rough and ready though they were, sobbed as they toiled; and while the derrick tackles creaked and moaned, axe and pick and bar swung and crashed and tore through splintering glass and ripping timber.

What men could do they did—and through the hours Flannagan led

65

them. Tough, grizzled men, more than one dropped from sheer weariness; but ever Flannagan's great arms rose and fell, ever his mighty shoulders heaved, ever he led them on. What men could do they did—but it was graying dawn before they opened a way to the heart of the wreck—the first-class coach that once ahead of the Pullmans was under them now.

Flannagan, gaunt, burned and bleeding, a madman with reeling brain, staggered toward the jagged hole that they had torn in the flooring of the car. They tried to hold him back, the man who had spurred them through the night alternately with lashing curse and piteous prayer, the man who had worked with demon strength as no three men among them had worked, the man who was tottering now at the end in mind and body, they tried to hold him back— for mercy's sake. But Flannagan shook them off and went—went laughing again the same fearful laugh with which he had begun the fight.

He found her there—found her with a little bundle lying in the crook of her outstretched arm. She moaned and held it toward him—but Flannagan had gone his limit, his work was done, the tension broke.

And when they worked their way to the far end of the car after him, those hard, grim-visaged followers of Flannagan, they found a man squatted on an up-ended seat, a woman beside him, death and desolation and huddled shapes around him, dandling a tiny infant in his arms, crooning a lullaby through cracked lips, crooning a lullaby—to a little one long hushed already in its last sleep.

Opinions differ. But Big Cloud to-day sides about solid with Regan.

"Flannagan?" says the master mechanic. "Flannagan's a pretty good wrecking boss, pretty good, I don't know of any better—since the Almighty had him on the carpet. He's got a plot up on the butte behind the town, he and Daisy, with a little mound on it. They go up there together every Sunday— never've known 'em to miss. A man ain't likely to fall off the right of way again as long as he does that, is he? Well, then, forget it, he's been doing that for a year now—what?"

Chapter V

THE MAN WHO SQUEALED

Back in the early days the payroll of the Hill Division was full of J. Smiths, T. Browns and H. Something-or-others—just as it is to-day. But to-day there is a difference. The years have brought a certain amount of inevitable pedigree, as it were—a certain amount of gossip, so to speak, over the back fences of Big Cloud. It's natural enough. There's a possibility, as a precedent, that one or two of the passengers on the Mayflower didn't have as much blue blood when they started on the voyage as their descendants have got now—it's possible. The old hooker, from all accounts, had a pretty full passenger list, and there may have been some who secured accommodations with few questions asked, and a subsequent coat of glorified whitewash that they couldn't have got if they'd stayed at home where they were intimately known—that is, they couldn't have got the coat of glorified whitewash.

It's true that there's a few years between the landing of the Mayflower and the inception of Big Cloud, but the interval doesn't count—the principle is the same. Out in the mountains on the Hill Division, "Who's Who" begins with the founding of Big Cloud—it is verbose, unprofitable and extremely bad taste to go back any farther than that—even if it were possible. There's quite a bit known about the J. Smiths, the T. Browns and the H. Something-or-others now, with the enlightenment of years upon them—but there wasn't then. There were a good many men who immigrated West to help build the road through the Rockies, and run it afterwards—for reasons of their own. There weren't any questions asked. Plain J. Smith, T. Brown or H. Something-or-other went—that was all there was to it.

He said his name was Walton—P. Walton. He was tall, hollow-cheeked, with skin of an unhealthy, colorless white, and black eyes under thin, black brows that were unnaturally bright. He dropped off at Big Cloud one afternoon—in the early days—from No. 1, the Limited from the East, climbed upstairs in the station to the super's room, and coughed out a request to Carleton for a job.

Carleton, "Royal" Carleton, the squarest man that ever held down a divisional swivel chair, looked P. Walton over for a moment before he spoke. P. Walton didn't size up much like a day's work anyway you looked at him.

"What can you do?" inquired Carleton.

"Anything," said P. Walton—and coughed.

Carleton reached for his pipe and struck a match.

"If you could," said he, sucking at the amber mouthpiece between words, "there wouldn't be any trouble about it. For instance, the construction gangs want men to—"

"I'll go—I'll do anything," cut in P. Walton eagerly. "Just give me a chance."

"Nope!" said Carleton with a grin. "I'm not hankering to break the Sixth Commandment—know what that is?"

P. Walton licked dry lips with the tip of his tongue.

"Murder," said he. "But you might as well let it come that way as any other. I'm pretty bad here"—he jerked his thumb toward his lungs—"and I'm broke here"—he turned an empty trouser's pocket inside out.

"H'm!" observed Carleton reflectively. There was something in the other that touched his sympathy, and something apart from that that appealed to him—a sort of grim, philosophical grit in the man with the infected lungs.

"I came out," said P. Walton, looking through the window, and kind of talking to himself, "because I thought it would be healthier for me out here than back East."

"I dare say," said Carleton kindly; "but not if you start in by swinging a pick. Maybe we can find something else for you to do. Ever done any railroading?"

Walton shook his head.

"No," he answered. "I've always worked on books. I'm called pretty good at figures, if you've got anything in that line."

"Clerk, eh? Well, I don't know," said Carleton slowly. "I guess, perhaps, we can give you a chance. My own clerk's doing double shift just at present; you might help him out temporarily. And if you're what you say you are, we'll find something better for you before the summer's over. Thirty dollars a month—it's not much of a stake—what do you say?"

"It's a pretty big stake for me," said P. Walton, and his face lighted up as he turned it upon Carleton.

"All right," said Carleton. "You'd better spend the rest of the afternoon then in hunting up some place to stay. And here"—he dug into his pocket and handed P. Walton two five-dollar gold pieces—"this may come in handy till you're on your feet."

"Say," said P. Walton huskily, "I—" he stopped suddenly, as the door opened and Regan, the master mechanic, came in.

"Never mind," smiled Carleton. "Report to Halstead in the next room to-morrow morning at seven o'clock."

P. Walton hesitated, as though to complete his interrupted sentence, and then, with an uncertain look at Regan, turned and walked quietly from the room.

Regan wheeled around and stared after the retreating figure. When the door had closed he looked inquiringly at Carleton.

"Touched you for a loan, eh?" he volunteered quizzically.

"No," said Carleton, still smiling; "a job. I gave him the money as an advance."

"More fool you!" said the blunt little master mechanic. "Your security's bad—he'll never live long enough to earn it. What sort of a job?"

"Helping Halstead out to begin with," replied Carleton.

"H'm!" remarked Regan. "Poor devil."

"Yes, Tommy," said Carleton. "Quite so—poor devil."

Regan, big-hearted, good-natured for all his bluntness, walked to the front window and watched P. Walton's figure disappear slowly, and a little haltingly, down the platform. The fat little master mechanic's face puckered.

"We get some queer cards out here," he said. "He looks as though he'd had a pretty hard time of it—kind of a discard in the game, I guess. Out here to die—pleasant, what? I wonder where he came from?"

"He didn't say," said Carleton dryly.

"No," said Regan; "I dare say he didn't—none of 'em do. I wonder, though, where he came from?"

And in this the division generally were in accord with Regan. They didn't ask—which was outside the ethics; and P. Walton didn't say—which was quite within his rights. But for all that, the division, with Regan, wondered. Ordinarily, they wouldn't have paid much attention to a new man one way or the other, but P. Walton was a little more than just a new man—he was a man they couldn't size up. That was the trouble. It didn't matter who any one was, or where he came from, if they could form an opinion of him—which wasn't hard to form in most instances—that would at all satisfactorily fill the bill. But P. Walton didn't bear the earmarks of a hard case "wanted" East, or show any tendency toward deep theological thought; therefore opinions were conflicting—which wasn't satisfying.

Not that P. Walton refused to mix, or held himself aloof, or anything of that kind; on the contrary, all hands came to know him pretty well—as P. Walton. As a matter of cold fact, they had more chances of knowing him than they had of knowing most new-comers; and that bothered them a little, because, somehow, they didn't seem to make anything out of their opportunities. As assistant clerk to the super, P. Walton was soon a familiar enough figure in the yards, the roundhouse and the shops, and genial enough, and pleasant enough, too; but they never got past the pure, soft-spoken, perfect English, and the kind of firm, determined swing to the jaw that no amount of emaciation could eliminate. They agreed only on one thing—on the question of therapeutics—they were unanimous on that point with Regan—P. Walton, whatever else he was, or wasn't, was out there to die. And it kind of looked to them as though P. Walton had through rights to the Terminal, and not much of any limit to speak of on his permit.

Regan put the matter up to Carleton one day in the super's office, about a month after P. Walton's advent to Big Cloud.

"I said he was a queer card the first minute I clapped eyes on him," observed the master mechanic. "And I think so now—only more so. What in blazes does a white man want to go and live in a two-room pigsty, with a family of Polacks and about eighteen kids, for?"

Carleton tamped down the dottle in his pipe with his forefinger musingly.

"How much a week, Tommy," he inquired, "is thirty dollars a month, with about a third of the time out for sick spells?"

"I'm not a mathematician," growled the little master mechanic. "About five dollars, I guess."

"It's a good guess," said Carleton quietly. "He bought new clothes you remember with the ten I gave him—and he needed them badly enough." Carleton reached into a drawer of his desk, and handed Regan an envelope that was torn open across the end. "I found this here this afternoon after the paycar left," he said.

Regan peered into the envelope, then extracted two five-dollar gold pieces and a note. He unfolded the note, and read the two lines written in a hand that looked like steel-plate engraving.

> With thanks and grateful appreciation.
> P. WALTON.

Regan blinked, handed the money, note, and envelope back to Carleton, and fumbled a little awkwardly with his watch chain.

"He's the best hand with figures and his pen it's ever been my luck to meet," said Carleton, kind of speculatively. "Better than Halstead; a whole lot better. Halstead's going back East in a couple of weeks into the general office—got the offer, and I couldn't stand in his way. I was thinking of giving P. Walton the job, and breaking some young fellow in to relay him when he's sick. What do you think about it, Tommy?"

"I think," said Regan softly, "he's been getting blamed few eggs and less fresh air than he ought to have had, trying to make good on that loan. And I think he's a better man than I thought he was. A fellow that would do that is white enough not to fall very far off the right of way. I guess you won't make any mistake as far as trusting him goes."

"No," said Carleton, "I don't think I will."

And therein Carleton and Regan were both right and wrong. P. Walton wasn't—but just a minute, we're over-running our holding orders—P. Walton is in the block ahead.

The month hadn't helped P. Walton much physically, even if it had helped him more than he, perhaps, realized in Carleton's estimation. And the afternoon following Regan's and Carleton's conversation, alone in the room, for Halstead was out, he was hanging over his desk a pretty sick man, though his pen moved steadily with the work before him, when the connecting door from the super's office opened, and Bob Donkin, the despatcher, came hurriedly in.

"Where's the super?" he asked quickly.

"I don't know," said P. Walton. "He went out in the yards with Regan half an hour ago. I guess he'll be back shortly."

"Well, you'd better try and find him, and give him this. Forty-two'll be along in twenty minutes." Donkin slapped a tissue on the desk, and hurried back to his key in the despatchers' room.

P. Walton picked up the tissue and read it. It was from the first station west on the line.

Gopher Butte, 3.16 P. M.
J. H. CARLETON, Supt. Hill Division:

70

No. 42 held up by two train robbers three miles west of here. Express messenger Nulty in game fight killed one and captured the other in the express car. Arrange for removal of body, and have sheriff on hand to take prisoner into custody on arrival in Big Cloud. Everything O.K.

McCURDY, Conductor.

P. Walton, with the telegram in his hand, rose from his chair and made for the hall through the super's room, reading it a second time as he went along. There had been some pretty valuable express stuff on the train, as he knew from the correspondence that had passed through his hands—and he smiled a little grimly.

"Well, they certainly missed a good one," he muttered to himself. "I think I'd rather be the dead one than the other. It'll go hard with him. Twenty years, I guess."

He stepped out into the hall to the head of the stairs—and met Carleton coming up.

Carleton, quick as a steel trap, getting the gist of the message in a glance, brushed by P. Walton, hurried along the hall to the despatchers' room—and the next moment a wide-eyed call boy was streaking uptown for the sheriff, and breathlessly imparting the tale of the hold-up, embellished with gory imagination, to every one he met.

By the time Forty-two's whistle sounded down the gorge, there was a crowd on the platform bigger than a political convention, and P. Walton, by virtue of his official position, rather than from physical qualifications, together with his chief, Regan, the ticket agent, the baggage master and Carruthers, the sheriff, were having a hard time of it to keep themselves from being shoved off on the tracks, let alone trying to keep a modest breadth of the platform clear. And when the train came to a stop with screeching brake-shoes, and the side door of the express car was shot back with a dramatic bang by some one inside, the crowd seemed to get altogether beyond P. Walton's control, and surged past him. As they handed out a hard-visaged, bullet-headed customer, whose arms were tightly lashed behind him, P. Walton was pretty well back by the ticket-office window with the crowd between him and the center of attraction—and P. Walton was holding his handkerchief to his lips, flecking the handkerchief with a spot or two of red, and coughing rather badly. Carleton found him there when the crowd, trailing Carruthers and his prisoner uptown, thinned out—and Carleton sent him home.

P. Walton, however, did not go home, though he started in that direction. He followed in the rear of the crowd up to Carruthers' place, saw steel bracelets replace the cords around the captive's wrists, saw the captive's legs securely bound together, and the captive chucked into Carruthers' back shed—this was in the early days, and Big Cloud hadn't yet risen to the dignity of a jail—with about as much formality as would be used in handling a sack of meal. After that, Carruthers barred the door by slamming the long, two-inch-thick piece of timber, that worked on a pivot in the center, home into its iron rests with a flourish of finality, as though to indicate that the show was over—

71

and the crowd dispersed—the men heading for the swinging doors of the Blazing Star; and the women for their own back fences.

P. Walton, with a kind of grim smile on his lips, retraced his steps to the station, climbed the stairs, and started through the super's room to reach his own desk.

Carleton removed his pipe from his mouth, and stared angrily as the other came in.

"You blamed idiot!" he exploded. "I thought I told you to go home!"

"I'm feeling better," said P. Walton. "I haven't got those night orders out yet for the roundhouse. There's three specials from the East to-night."

"Well, Halstead can attend to them," said Carleton, a kindliness creeping into the tones that he tried to make gruff. "What are you trying to do—commit suicide?"

"No," said P. Walton, with a steady smile, "just my work. It was a little too violent exercise trying to hold the crowd, that was all. But I'm all right now."

"You blamed idiot!" grunted Carleton again. "Why didn't you say so? I never thought of it, or I wouldn't have let—"

"It doesn't matter," said P. Walton brightly. "I'm all right now"—and he passed on into his own room.

When he left his desk again it was ten minutes of six, and Carleton had already gone. P. Walton, with his neatly written order sheets, walked across the tracks to the roundhouse, handed them over to Clarihue, the night turner, who had just come in, and then hung around, toying in an apparently aimless fashion with the various tools on the workbenches till the whistle blew, while the fitters, wipers and day gang generally washed up. After that he plodded across the fields to the Polack quarters on the other side of the tracks from the town proper, stumbled into the filthy, garlic smelling interior of one of the shacks, and flung himself down on the bunk that was his bedroom.

"Lord!" he muttered. "I'm pretty bad to-night. Guess I'll have to postpone it. Might be as well, anyway."

He lay there for an hour, his bright eyes fastened now on the dirty, squalling brood of children upon the floor, now on the heavy, slatternly figure of their mother, and now on the tin bowl of boiled sheep's head that awaited the arrival of Ivan Peloff, the master of the house—and then, with abhorrent disgust, he turned his eyes to the wall.

"Thank God, I get into a decent place soon!" he mumbled once. "It's the roughest month I ever spent. I'd rather be back where"—he smiled sort of cryptically to himself—"where I came from." A moment later he spoke again in a queer, kind of argumentative, kind of self-extenuating way—in broken sentences. "Maybe I put it on a little too thick boarding here so's to stand in with Carleton and pay that ten back quick—but, my God, I was scared—I've got to stand in with somebody, or go to the wall."

It was after seven when Ivan Peloff came—smelling strong of drink, and excitement heightening the flush upon his cheek.

"Hello, Meester Walton!" he bubbled out with earnest inebriety. "We rise hell to-night—by an' by. Get him goods by midnight." Ivan Peloff drew his fingers around his throat, and, in lieu of English that came hard to him at any time, jerked his thumb dramatically up and down in the air.

"Who?" inquired P. Walton, without much enthusiasm.

"Dam' robber—him by train come in," explained Ivan Peloff laboriously.

"Oh," said P. Walton, "talking of stringing him up—is that it?"

Ivan Peloff nodded his head delightedly.

P. Walton swung himself lazily from his bunk.

"Eat?" invited Ivan Peloff, moving toward the table.

"No," said P. Walton, moving toward the door. "I'm not hungry; I'm going out for some air."

Ivan Peloff pulled two bottles of a deadly brand from under his coat, and set them on the table.

"Me eat," he grinned. "By an' by have drinks all 'round"—he waved his hands as though to embrace the whole Polack quarter—"den we comes—rise hell—do him goods by midnight."

P. Walton halted in the doorway.

"Who put you up to this, Peloff?" he inquired casually.

"Cowboys," grinned Peloff, lunging at the sheep's head. "Plenty drink. Say have fun."

"The cowboys, eh?" observed P. Walton. "So they're in town, are they—and looking for fun?"

"We fix him goods by midnight," repeated Ivan Peloff, wagging his head; then, with a sudden scowl: "You not tell—eh, Meester Walton?"

P. Walton smiled disinterestedly—but there wasn't any doubt in P. Walton's mind that devilment was in the wind—Big Cloud, in the early days, knew its full share of that.

"I?" said P. Walton quietly, as he went out. "No; I won't tell. It's no business of mine, is it?"

It was fall, and already dark. P. Walton made his way out of the Polack quarters, reached the tracks, crossed them—and then headed out through the fields to circle around the town to the upper end again, where it dwindled away from cross streets to the houses flanking on Main Street alone.

"I guess," he coughed—and smiled, "I won't postpone it till to-morrow night, after all."

It was a long walk for a man in P. Walton's condition, and it was a good half hour before he finally stopped in the rear of Sheriff Carruthers' back shed and listened—there were no fences here, just a procession of buttes and knolls merging the prairie country into the foothills proper of the Rockies—neither was there any sound. P. Walton stifled a cough, and slipped like a shadow through the darkness around to the front of the shed, shifted the wooden bar noiselessly on its pivot, opened the door, and, as he stepped inside, closed it softly behind him.

"Butch!" he whispered.

A startled ejaculation, and a quick movement as of a man suddenly shifting his position on the floor, answered him.

"Keep quiet, Butcher—it's all right," said P. Walton calmly—and, stooping, guiding his knife blade by the sense of touch, cut away the rope from the other's ankles. He caught at the steel-linked wrists and helped the man to his feet. "Come on," he said. "Slip around to the back of the shed—talk later."

P. Walton pushed the door open, and the man he called the Butcher, lurching a little unsteadily from cramped ankles, passed out. P. Walton carefully closed the door, coolly replaced the bar in position, and joined the other.

"Now, run for it!" he said—and led the way straight out from the town.

For two hundred yards, perhaps a little more, they raced—and then P. Walton stumbled and went down.

"I'm—I'm not very well to-night," he gasped. "This will do—it's far enough."

The Butcher, halted, gazed at the prostrate form.

"Say, cull, what's yer name?" he demanded. "I owe you something for this, an' don't you forget it."

P. Walton made no answer. His head was swimming, lights were dancing before his eyes, and there was a premonitory weakness upon him whose issue he knew too well—unless he could fight it off.

The Butcher bent down until his face was within an inch of P. Walton's.

"So help me!" he informed the universe in unbounded amazement. "It's de Dook!"

"Sit down there opposite me, and hold out your hands," directed P. Walton, with an effort. "We haven't got any time to waste."

The Butcher, heavy with wonderment, obeyed mechanically—and P. Walton drew a rat-tail file from his pocket.

"I saw you in the express car this afternoon, and I went to the roundhouse for this when I left the office," P. Walton said, as he set to work on the steel links. "But I was feeling kind of down and out, and was going to leave you till to-morrow night—only I heard they were going to lynch you at midnight."

"Lynch me!" growled the Butcher. "What fer? They don't lynch a fellow 'cause he's nipped in a hold-up—we didn't kill no one."

"Some of the cowboys are looking for amusement," said P. Walton monotonously. "They've distributed redeye among the Polacks, for the purpose, I imagine, of putting the blame—on the Polacks."

"I get you!" snarled the Butcher, with an oath. "It's de Bar K Ranch—we took their payroll away from 'em two weeks ago. Lynchin', eh? Well, some of 'em 'll dance on air fer this themselves, blast 'em! Dook, yer white—an' you always was. I thought me luck was out fer keeps to-day when Spud—you saw Spud, didn't you?"

"Yes," said P. Walton, filing steadily.

"Spud always had a soft spot in his heart," said the Butcher. "Instead of drilling that devil, Nulty, when he had the chance, Nulty filled Spud full of holes, an' we fluked up—yer gettin' a bit of my wrist, Dook, with that damned file. Well, as I said, I thought me luck was out fer keeps—an' you show up. Gee! Who'd have thought of seein' de Angel Dook, de prize penman, de gem of forgers! How'd you make yer getaway—you was in fer twenty spaces, wasn't you?"

"I think they wanted to save the expense of burying me," said P. Walton. "The other wrist, Butch. I got a pardon."

"What's de matter with you, Dook?" inquired the Butcher solicitously.

"Lungs," said P. Walton tersely. "Bad."

"Hell!" said the Butcher earnestly.

There was silence for a moment, save only for the rasping of the file, and then the Butcher spoke again.

"What's yer lay out here, Dook?" he asked.

"Working for the railroad in the super's office—and keeping my mouth shut," said P. Walton.

"There's nothin' in that," said the Butcher profoundly. "Nothin' to it!"

"Not much," agreed P. Walton. "Forty a month, and—oh, well, forty a month."

"I'll fix that fer you, Dook," said the Butcher cheerily. "You join de gang. There's de old crowd from Joliet up here in de mountains. We got a swell layout. There's Larry, an' Big Tom, an' Dago Pete—Spud's cashed in—an' they'll stand on their heads an' yell Salvation Army songs when they hear that de slickest of 'em all—that's you, Dook—is buyin' a stack an' settin' in."

"No," said P. Walton. "No, Butch, I guess not—it's me for the forty per."

"Eh!" ejaculated the Butcher heavily. "You don't mean to say you've turned parson, Dook? You wouldn't be lettin' me loose if you had."

"No; nothing like that," replied P. Walton. "I'm sitting tight because I have to—until some one turns up and gives my record away—if I'm not dead first. I'm too sick, Butch, to be any use to you—I couldn't stand the pace."

"Sure, you could," said the Butcher reassuringly. "Anyway, I'm not fer leavin' a pal out in de cold, an'—" He stopped suddenly, and leaned toward P. Walton. "What was it you said you was doin' in de office?" he demanded excitedly.

"Assistant clerk to the superintendent," said P. Walton—and his file bit through the second link. "You'll have to get the bracelets off your wrists when you get back to the boys—your hands are free."

"Say," said the Butcher breathlessly, "it's a cinch! You see de letters, an' know what's goin' on pretty familiar-like, don't you?"

"Yes," said P. Walton.

"Well, say, can you beat it!" Once more the Butcher invoked the universe. "You're de inside man, see? Gee—it's a cinch! We only knew there was mazuma on de train to-day by a fluke, just Spud an' me heard of it, too late to plant anything fancy an' get de rest of de gang. You see what happened? After this we don't have to take no chances. You passes out de word when there's a good juicy lot of swag comin' along, we does de rest, and you gets your share—equal. An' that ain't all. They'll be sendin' down East fer de Pinkertons, if they ain't done it already, an' we gives 'em de laugh—you tippin' us off on de trains de 'dicks' are ridin' on, an' puttin' us wise to 'em generally. An' say"—the Butcher's voice dropped suddenly to a low, sullen, ugly growl—"you give us de lay de first crack we make when that low-lived, snook-nosed Nulty's aboard. He goes out fer Spud—an' he goes out quick. He's fired a gun de last time he'll ever fire one—see?"

75

P. Walton felt around on the ground, picked up the bit of chain he had filed from the handcuffs, and handed it, with the file, to the Butcher.

"Put these in your pocket, Butch," he said, "and throw them in the river where it's deep when you get a chance—especially the file. I guess from the way you put it I could earn my stake with the gang."

"Didn't I tell you, you could!" The Butcher, with swift change of mood, grinned delightedly. "Sure, you can! Larry's an innocent-lookin' kid, an' he's not known in de town. He'll float around an' get de bulletins from you—you'll know ahead when there's anything good comin' along, won't you?"

"When it leaves the coast," said P. Walton. "Thirty-six hours—sometimes more."

"An' I thought me luck was out fer keeps!" observed the Butcher, in an almost awe-struck voice.

"Well, don't play it too hard by hanging around here until they get you again," cautioned P. Walton dryly. "The further you get away from Big Cloud in the next few hours, the better you'll like it to-morrow."

"I'm off now," announced the Butcher, rising to his feet. "Dook, you're white—all de way through. Don't forget about Nulty, blast him!" He wrung P. Walton's hand with emotion. "So long, Dook!"

"So long, Butch!" said P. Walton.

P. Walton watched the Butcher disappear in the darkness, then he began to retrace his steps toward the Polack quarters. His one thought now was to reach his bunk. He was sick, good and sick, and those premonitory symptoms, if they had been arrested, were still with him. The day had been too much for him—the jostling on the platform, mostly when he had fought his way through the rear of the crowd for fear of an unguarded recognition on the part of the Butcher; then the walking he had done; and, lastly, that run from the sheriff's shed.

P. Walton, with swimming head and choking lungs, reeled a little as he went along. It was farther, quite a lot farther, to go by the fields, and he was far enough down from Carruthers' now so that it would not make any difference anyhow, even if the Butcher's escape had been discovered—which it hadn't, the town was too quiet for that. P. Walton headed into a cross street, staggered along it, reached the corner of Main Street—and, fainting, went suddenly down in a heap, as the hemorrhage caught him, and the bright, crimson "ruby" stained his lips.

Coming up the street from a conference in the super's office, Nulty, the express messenger, big, brawny, hard-faced, thin-lipped, swung along, dragging fiercely at his pipe, scowling grimly as he reviewed the day's happenings. He passed a little knot of Polacks, quite obviously far gone in liquor—and almost fell over P. Walton's body.

"Hullo!" said Nulty. "What the deuce is this!" He bent down for a look into the unconscious man's face. "The super's clerk!" he exclaimed—and stared around for help.

There was no one in sight, save the approaching Polacks—but one of these hurriedly, if unsteadily, lurched forward.

"Meester Walton!" announced Ivan Peloff genially. "Him be sick—yes?"

76

"Where's he live?" demanded Nulty, without waste of words.

"Him by me live," said Ivan Peloff, tapping his chest proudly as he swayed upon his feet. He called to his companions, and reached for P. Walton's legs. "We take him by us home."

"Let him alone!" said Nulty gruffly, as the interior of a Polack shanty pictured itself before his eyes.

"Him by me live," repeated Ivan Peloff, still reaching doggedly, if uncertainly, for P. Walton's legs.

"Let him alone, I tell you, you drunken Guinea!" roared Nulty suddenly, and his arm went out with a sweep that brushed Ivan Peloff back to an ultimate seat in the road three yards away. Without so much as a glance in the direction taken by the other, Nulty stepped up to the rest of the Polacks, stared into their faces, and selecting the one that appeared less drunk than the others, unceremoniously jerked the man by the collar into the foreground. "You know me!" he snapped. "I'm Nulty—Nulty. Say it!"

"Nultee," said the bewildered foreigner.

"Yes," said Nulty. "Now you run for the doctor—and you run like hell. If he ain't at home—find him. Tell him to come to Nulty—quick. Understand?"

The Polack nodded his head excitedly.

"Doctor—Nultee," he ejaculated brightly.

"Yes," said Nulty. "Go on, now—run!" And he gave the Polack an initial start with a vigorous push that nearly toppled the man forward on his nose.

Nulty stooped down, picked up P. Walton in his arms as though the latter were a baby, and started toward his own home a block away.

"My God," he muttered, "a railroad man down there in a state like this—he'd have a long chance, he would! Poor devil, guess he won't last out many more of these. Blast it all, now if the wife was home she'd know what to do—blamed if I know!"

For all that, however, Nulty did pretty well. He put P. Walton to bed, and started feeding him cracked ice even before the doctor came—after that Nulty went on feeding cracked ice.

Along toward midnight, Gleason, the yard-master, burst hurriedly into the house.

"Say, Nulty, you there!" he bawled. "That blasted train robber's got away, and—oh!" He had stepped from the hall over the threshold of the bedroom door, only to halt abruptly as his eyes fell upon the bed. "Anything I can do—Nulty?" he asked in a booming whisper, that he tried to make soft.

Nulty, sitting in a chair by the bed, shook his head—and Gleason tiptoed in squeaky boots out of the house.

P. Walton, who had been lying with closed eyes, opened them, and looked at Nulty.

"What did he say?" he inquired.

"Says the fellow we got to-day has got away," said Nulty shortly. "Shut up—the doctor says you're not to talk."

P. Walton's bright eyes made a circuit of the room, came back, and rested again on Nulty.

"Would you know him again if you saw him?" he demanded.

77

"Would I know him!" exclaimed Nulty. "It's not likely I wouldn't, is it? I was dead-heading him down from Gopher Butte, wasn't I?"

"I think," said P. Walton slowly, "if it were me I'd be scared stiff that he got away—afraid he'd be trying to revenge that other fellow, you know. You want to look out for him."

"I'd ask nothing better than to meet him again," said Nulty grimly. "Now, shut up—you're not to talk."

P. Walton was pretty sick. Nulty sat up all that night with him, laid off from his run the next day, and sat up with P. Walton again the next night. Then, having sent for Mrs. Nulty, who was visiting relatives down the line, Mrs. Nulty took a hand in the nursing. Mrs. Nulty was a little, sweet-faced woman, with gray Irish eyes and no style about her—Nulty's pay-check didn't reach that far—but she knew how to nurse; and if her hands were red and the knuckles a little swollen from the washtub, she could use them with a touch that was full enough of tender sympathy to discount anything a manicure might have reason to find fault with on professional grounds. She didn't rate Nulty for turning her home into a hospital, and crowding her train-sheet of work, already pretty full, past all endurance—Mrs. Nulty, God bless her, wasn't that kind of a woman! She looked at her husband with a sort of happy pride in her eyes; looked at P. Walton, and said, "Poor man," as her eyes filled—and went to work. But for all that, it was touch and go with P. Walton—P. Walton was a pretty sick man.

It's queer the way trouble of that sort acts—down and out one day with every signal in every block set dead against you; and the next day a clear track, with rights through buttoned in your reefer, a wide-flung throttle, and the sweep of the wind through the cab glass whipping your face till you could yell with the mad joy of living. It's queer!

Five days saw P. Walton back at the office, as good, apparently, as ever he was—but Mrs. Nulty didn't stop nursing. Nulty came down sick in place of P. Walton and took to bed—"to give her a chance to keep her hand in," Nulty said. Nulty came down, not from overdoing it on P. Walton's account—a few nights sitting up wasn't enough to lay a man like Nulty low—Nulty came down with a touch of just plain mountain fever.

It wasn't serious, or anything like that; but it put a stop order, temporarily at least, on the arrangements Nulty had cussed P. Walton into agreeing to. P. Walton was to come and board with the Nultys at the same figure he was paying Ivan Peloff until he got a raise and could pay more. And so, while Nulty was running hot and cold with mountain fever, P. Walton, with Mrs. Nulty in mind, kept his reservations on down in the Polack quarters, until such time as Nulty should get better—and went back to work at the office.

On the first night of his convalescence, P. Walton had a visitor—in the person of Larry, the brains and leader of the gang. Larry did not come inside the shack—he waited outside in the dark until P. Walton went out to him.

"Hullo, Dook!" said Larry. "Tough luck, eh? Been sick? Gee, I'm glad to see you! All to the mustard again? Couldn't get into town before, but a fellow uptown said you'd been bad."

"Hello, Larry," returned P. Walton, and he shook the other's hand cordially. "Glad to see you, too. Yes; I guess I'm all right—till next time."

"Sure, you are!" said Larry heartily. "Anything good doing?"

"Well," said P. Walton, "I don't know whether you'd call it good or not, but there was a new order went into effect yesterday to remain in force until further notice—owing to the heavy passenger traffic. They are taking the mail and express cars off the regular afternoon east-bound trains, and running them as a through extra on fast time. They figure to land the mails East quicker, and ease up on the equipment of the regular trains so as to keep them a little nearer schedule. So now the express stuff comes along on Extra No. 34, due Spider Cut at eight-seventeen p. m., which is her last stop before Big Cloud."

"Say," said Larry dubiously, "'taint going to be possible to board a train like that casual-like, is it?" Then, brightening suddenly: "But say, when you get to thinking about it, it don't size up so bad, neither. I got the lay, Dook—I got it for fair—listen! Instead of a train-load of passengers to handle there won't be no one after the ditching but what's left of the train crew and the mail clerks; a couple of us can stand the stamp lickers up easy, while the two others pinches the swag. We'll stop her, all right! We ditch the train—see? There's a peach of a place for it about seven miles up the line from here. We tap the wires, Big Tom's some cheese at that, and then cuts them as soon as we know the train has passed Spider Cut, and is wafting its way toward us. Say, it's good, Dook, it's like a Christmas present—I was near forgetting the registered mail."

P. Walton laughed—and coughed.

"I guess it's all right, Larry," he said. "According to a letter I saw in the office this afternoon, there's a big shipment of banknotes that some bank is remitting, and that will be on board night after next."

"Say that again," said Larry, sucking in his breath quickly. "I ain't deaf, but I'd like to hear it just once more."

"I was thinking," said P. Walton, more to himself than to his companion, "that I'd like to get down to Northern Australia—up Queensland way. They say it's good for what ails me—bakes it out of one."

"Dook," said Larry, shoving out his hand, "you can buy your ticket the day after the night after next—you'll get yours, and don't you forget it, I'll see to that. We'll move camp to-morrow down handy to the place I told you about, and get things ready. And say, Dook, is that cuss Nulty on the new run?"

"I don't know anything about Nulty," said P. Walton.

"Well, I hope he is," said Larry, with a fervent oath. "We're going to cut the heart out of him for what he did to Spud. The Butcher was for coming into town and putting a bullet through him anyway, but I'm not for throwing the game. It won't hurt Spud's memory any to wait a bit, and we won't lose any enthusiasm by the delay, you can bet your life on that! And now I guess I'll mosey along. The less I'm seen around here the better. Well, so long, Dook—I got it straight, eh? Night after to-morrow, train passes Spider Cut eight-seventeen—that right?"

"Eight-seventeen—night after to-morrow—yes," said P. Walton. "Good luck to you, Larry."

"Same to you, Dook," said Larry—and slipped away in the shadows.

P. Walton went uptown to sit for an hour or two with Nulty—turn about being no more than fair play. Also on the following night he did the same—and on this latter occasion he took the opportunity, when Mrs. Nulty wasn't around to hear and worry about it, to turn the conversation on the hold-up, after leading up to it casually.

"When you get out and back on your run again, Nulty, I'd keep a sharp look-out for that fellow whose pal you shot," he said.

"You can trust me for that," said Nulty anxiously. "I'll bet he wouldn't get away a second time!"

"Unless he saw you first," amended P. Walton evenly. "There's probably more where those two came from—a gang of them, I dare say. They'll have it in for you, Nulty."

"Don't you worry none about me," said Nulty, and his jaw shot out. "I'm able to take care of myself."

"Oh, well," said P. Walton, "I'm just warning you, that's all. Anyway, there isn't any immediate need for worry. I guess you're safe enough—so long as you stay in bed."

The next day P. Walton worked assiduously at the office. If excitement or nervousness in regard to the events of the night that was to come was in any wise his portion, he did not show it. There was not a quiver in the steel-plate hand in which he wrote the super's letters, not even an inadvertent blur on the tissue pages of the book in which he copied them. Only, perhaps, he worked a little more slowly—his work wasn't done when the shop whistle blew and he came back to the office after supper. It was close on ten minutes after eight when he finally finished, and went into the despatcher's room with the sheaf of official telegrams to go East during the night at odd moments when the wires were light.

"Here's the super's stuff," he said, laying the papers on the despatcher's desk.

"All right," said Spence, who was sitting in on the early trick. "How's P. Walton to-night?"

"Pretty fair," said P. Walton, with a smile. "How's everything moving?"

"Slick as clockwork," Spence answered. "Everything on the dot. I'll get some of that stuff off for you now."

"Good," said P. Walton, moving toward the door. "Good-night, Spence."

"'Night, old man," rejoined Spence, and picking up the first of the super's telegrams began to rattle a call on his key like the tattoo of a snare drum.

P. Walton, in possession of the information he sought—that Extra No. 34 was on time—descended the stairs to the platform, and started uptown.

"I think," he mused, as he went along, "that about as good a place as any for me when this thing breaks will be sitting with Nulty."

P. Walton noticed the light burning in Nulty's bedroom window as he reached the house; and, it being a warm night, found the front door wide open. He stepped into the hall, and from there into the bedroom, Mrs. Nulty was sitting in a rocking-chair beside the lamp, mending away busily at a pair of Nulty's overalls—but there wasn't anybody else in the room.

"Hello!" said P. Walton cheerily. "Where's the sick man?"

"Why, didn't you know?" said Mrs. Nulty a little anxiously, as she laid aside her work and rose from her chair. "The express company sent word this morning that if he was able they particularly wanted to have him make the run through the mountains to-night on Extra Number Thirty-four—I think there was some special shipment of money. He wasn't at all fit to go, and I tried to keep him home, but he wouldn't listen to me. He went up to Elk River this morning to meet Thirty-four and come back on it. I've been worrying all day about him."

P. Walton's eyes rested on the anxious face of the little woman before him, dropped to the red, hard-working hands that played nervously with the corner of her apron, then travelled to Nulty's alarm clock that ticked raucously upon the table—it was 8.17. P. Walton smiled.

"Now, don't you worry, Mrs. Nulty," he said reassuringly. "A touch of mountain fever isn't anything one way or the other—don't you worry, it'll be all right. I didn't know he was out, and I was going to sit with him for a little while, but what I really came for was to get him to lend me a revolver—there's a coyote haunting my end of the town that's kept me awake for the last two nights, and I'd like to even up the score. If Nulty hasn't taken the whole of his armament with him, perhaps you'll let me have one.

"Why, yes, of course," said Mrs. Nulty readily. "There's two there in the top bureau drawer. Take whichever one you want."

"Thanks," said P. Walton—and stepped to the bureau. He took out a revolver, slipped it into his pocket, and turned toward the door. "Now, don't you worry, Mrs. Nulty," he said encouragingly, "because there's nothing to worry about. Tell him I dropped in, will you?—and thank you again for the revolver. Good-night, Mrs. Nulty."

P. Walton's eyes strayed to the clock as he left the room—it was 8.19. On the sidewalk he broke into a run, dashed around the corner and sped, with instantly protesting lungs, down Main Street, making for the railroad yards. And as he ran P. Walton did a sum in mental arithmetic, while his breath came in gasps.

If you remember Flannagan, you will remember that the distance from Spider Cut to Big Cloud was twenty-one decimal seven miles. P. Walton figured it roughly twenty-two. No. 34, on time, had already left Spider Cut at 8.17—and the wires were cut. Her running time for the twenty-two miles was twenty-nine minutes—she made Big Cloud at 8.46. Counting Larry's estimate of seven miles to be accurate, No. 34 had fifteen miles to go from Spider Cut before they piled her in the ditch, and it would take her a little over nineteen minutes to do it. With two minutes already elapsed—three now—and allowing, by shaving it close, another five before he started, P. Walton found that he was left with eleven minutes in which to cover seven miles.

It took P. Walton four of his five-minute allowance to reach the station platform; and here, for just an instant, he paused while his eyes swept the

81

twinkling switch lights in the yards. Then he raced along the length of the platform, jumped from the upper end to the ground, and ran, lurching a little, up the main line track to where the fore-shortened, unclassed little switching engine—the 229—was grunting heavily, and stealing a momentary rest after having sent a string of flats flying down a spur under the tender guidance of a brakeman or two. And as P. Walton ran, he reached into his pocket and drew out Nulty's revolver.

There wasn't much light inside the cab—there was only the lamp over the gauges—but it was light enough to show P. Walton's glittering eyes, fever bright, the deadly white of his face, the deadly smile on his lips, and the deadly weapon in his hand, as he sprang through the gangway.

"Get out!" panted P. Walton coldly.

Neither Dalheen, the fireman, nor Mulligan, fat as a porpoise, on the right-hand side, stood upon the order of their going. Dalheen ducked, and took a flying leap through the left-hand gangway; and Mulligan, with a sort of anxious gasp that seemed as though he wished to convey to P. Walton the fact that he was hurrying all he could, squeezed himself through the right-hand gangway and sat down on the ground.

P. Walton pulled the throttle open with an unscientific jerk.

With a kind of startled scream from the hissing steam, the sparks flying from madly racing drivers as the wheel tires bit into the rails, the old 229, like a frightened thoroughbred at the vicious lash of a yokel driver, reared and plunged wildly forward. The sudden, violent start from inertia pitched P. Walton off his feet across the driver's seat, and smashed his head against the reversing lever that stood notched forward in the segment. He gained his feet again, and, his head swimming a little from the blow, looked behind him.

Yells were coming from half a dozen different directions; forms, racing along with lanterns bobbing up and down, were tearing madly for the upper end of the yard toward him; there was a blur of switch lights, red, white, purple and green—then with a wicked lurch around a curve darkness hid them, and the sweep of the wind, the roar of the pounding drivers deadened all other sounds.

P. Walton smiled—a strange, curious, wistful smile—and sat down in Mulligan's seat. His qualifications for a Brotherhood card had been exhausted when he had pulled the throttle—engine driving was not in P. Walton's line. P. Walton smiled at the air latch, the water glass, the gauges and injectors, whose inner workings were mysteries to him—and clung to the window sill of the cab to keep his seat. He understood the throttle—in a measure—he had ridden up and down the yards in the switchers once or twice during the month that was past—that was all.

Quicker came the bark of the exhaust; quicker the speed. P. Walton's eyes were fixed through the cab glass ahead, following the headlight's glare, that silvered now the rails, and now flung its beams athwart the stubble of a butte as the 229 swung a curve. Around him, about him, was dizzy, lurching chaos, as, like some mad thing, the little switcher reeled drunkenly through the night—now losing her wheel-base with a sickening slew on the circling

82

track, now finding it again with a staggering quiver as she struck the tangent once more.

It was not scientific running—P. Walton never eased her, never helped her—P. Walton was not an engineer. He only knew that he must go fast to make the seven miles in eleven minutes—and he was going fast. And, mocking every formula of dynamics, the little switcher, with no single trailing coach to steady it, swinging, swaying, rocking, held the rails.

P. Walton's lips were still half parted in their strange, curious smile. A deafening roar was in his ears—the pound of beating trucks on the fish-plates; the creek and groan of axle play; the screech of crunching flanges; the whistling wind; the full-toned thunder now of the exhaust—and reverberating back and forth, flinging it from butte to butte, for miles around in the foothills the still night woke into a thousand answering echoes.

Meanwhile, back in Big Cloud, things were happening in the super's office. Spence, the despatcher, interrupting Carleton and Regan at their nightly pedro, came hastily into the room.

"Something's wrong," he said tersely. "I can't get anything west of here, and—" He stopped suddenly, as Mulligan, flabby white, came tumbling into the room.

"He's gone off his chump!" screamed Mulligan. "Gone delirious, or mad, or—"

"What's the matter?" Carleton was on his feet, his words cold as ice.

"Here!" gasped the engineer. "Look!" He dragged Carleton to the side window, and pointed up the track—the 229, sparks volleying skyward from her stack, was just disappearing around the first bend. "That's—that's the two-twenty-nine!" he panted. "P. Walton's in her—drove me and Dalheen out of the cab with a revolver."

For an instant, no more than a breathing space, no one spoke; then Spence's voice, with a queer sag in it, broke the silence:

"Extra Thirty-four left Spider Cut eight minutes ago."

Carleton, master always of himself, and master always of the situation, spoke before the words were hardly out of the despatcher's mouth:

"Order the wrecker out, Spence—jump! Mulligan, go down and help get the crew together." And then, as Spence and Mulligan hurried from the room, Carleton looked at the master mechanic. "Well, Tommy, what do you make of this?" he demanded grimly.

Regan, with thinned lips, was pulling viciously at his mustache.

"What do I make of it!" he growled. "A mail train in the ditch, and nothing worth speaking of left of the two-twenty-nine—that's what I make of it!"

Carleton shook his head.

"Doesn't it strike you as a rather remarkable coincidence that our wires should go out, and P. Walton should go off his head with delirium at the same moment?"

"Eh!" snapped Regan sharply. "Eh!—what do you mean?"

"I don't mean anything," Carleton answered, clipping off his words. "It's strange, that's all—I think we'll go up with the wrecker, Tommy."

"Yes," said Regan slowly, puzzled; then, with a scowl and a tug at his mustache: "It does look queer, queerer every minute—blamed queer! I wonder who P. Walton is, and where he came from anyhow?"

"You asked me that once before," Carleton threw back over his shoulder, moving toward the door. "P. Walton never said."

And while Regan, still tugging at his mustache, followed Carleton down the stairs to the platform, and ill-omened call boys flew about the town for the wrecking crew, and the 1018, big and capable, snorting from a full head of steam, backed the tool car, a flat, and the rumbling derrick from a spur to the main line, P. Walton still sat, smiling strangely, clinging to the window sill of the laboring 229, staring out into the night through the cab glass ahead.

"You see," said P. Walton to himself, as though summing up an argument dispassionately, "ditching a train travelling pretty near a mile a minute is apt to result in a few casualties, and Nulty might get hurt, and if he didn't, the first thing they'd do would be to pass him out for keeps, anyway, on Spud's account. They're not a very gentle lot—I remember the night back at Joliet that Larry and the Butcher walked out with the guards' clothes on, after cracking the guards' skulls. They're not a very gentle lot, and I guess they've been to some little trouble fixing up for to-night—enough so's they won't feel pleasant at having it spoiled. I guess"—P. Walton coughed—"I won't need that ticket for the heat of Northern Queensland. I guess"—he ended gravely—"I guess I'm going to hell."

P. Walton put his head out through the window and listened—and nodded his head.

"Sound carries a long way out here in the foothills," he observed. "They ought to hear it on the mail train as soon as we get close—and I guess we're close enough now to start it."

P. Walton got down, and, clutching at the cab-frame for support, lifted up the cover of the engineer's seat—there was sure to be something there among the tools that would do. P. Walton's hand came out with a heavy piece of cord. He turned then, pulled the whistle lever down, tied it down—and, screaming now like a lost soul, the 229 reeled on through the night.

The minutes passed—and then the pace began to slacken. Dalheen was always rated a good fireman, and a wizard with the shovel, but even Dalheen had his limitations—and P. Walton hadn't helped him out any. The steam was dropping pretty fast as the 229 started to climb a grade.

P. Walton stared anxiously about him. It must be eleven minutes now since he had started from the Big Cloud yards, but how far had he come? Was he going to stop too soon after all? What was the matter? P. Walton's eyes on the track ahead dilated suddenly, and, as suddenly, he reached for the throttle and slammed it shut—he was not going to stop too soon—perhaps not soon enough.

Larry, the Butcher, Big Tom, and Dago Pete had chosen their position well. A hundred yards ahead, the headlight played on a dismantled roadbed and torn-up rails, then shot off into nothingness over the embankment as the right of way swerved sharply to the right—they had left no single loophole for

Extra No. 34, not even a fighting chance—the mail train would swing the curve and be into the muck before the men in her cab would be able to touch a lever.

Screaming hoarsely, the 229 slowed, bumped her pony truck on the ties where there were no longer any rails, jarred, bounced, and thumped along another half dozen yards—and brought up with a shock that sent P. Walton reeling back on the coal in the tender.

A dark form, springing forward, bulked in the left-hand gangway—and P. Walton recognized the Butcher.

"Keep out, Butch!" he coughed over the scream of the whistle—and the Butcher in his surprise sort of sagged mechanically back to the ground.

"It's de Dook!" he yelled, with a gasp; and then, as other forms joined him, he burst into a torrent of oaths. "What de blazes are you doin'!" he bawled. "De train 'll be along in a minute, if you ain't queered it already—cut out that cursed whistle! Cut it out, d'ye hear, or we'll come in there an' do it for you in a way you won't like—have you gone nutty?"

"Try it," invited P. Walton—and coughed again. "You won't have far to come, but I'll drop you if you do. I've changed my mind—there isn't going to be any wreck to-night. You'd better use what time is left in making your getaway."

"So that's it, is it!" roared another voice. "You dirty pup, you'd squeal on your pals, would you, you white-livered snitch, you! Well, take that!"

There was a flash, a lane of light cut streaming through the darkness, and a bullet lodged with an angry spat on the coal behind P. Walton's head. Another and another followed. P. Walton smiled, and flattened himself down on the coal. A form leaped for the gangway—and P. Walton fired. There was a yell of pain and the man dropped back. Then P. Walton heard some of them running around behind the tender, and they came at him from both sides, firing at an angle through both gangways. Yells, oaths, revolver shots and the screech of the whistle filled the air—and again P. Walton smiled—he was hit now, quite badly, somewhere in his side.

His brain grew sick and giddy. He fired once, twice more unsteadily—then the revolver slipped from his fingers. From somewhere came another whistle—they weren't firing at him any more, they were running away, and—P. Walton tried to rise—and pitched back unconscious.

Nulty, the first man out from the mail train, found him there, and, wondering, his face set and grim, carried P. Walton to the express car. They made a mattress for him out of chair cushions, and laid him on the floor—and there, a few minutes later, Regan and Carleton, from the wrecker, after a look at the 229 and the wrecked track that spoke eloquently for itself, joined the group.

Carleton knelt and looked at P. Walton—then looked into Nulty's face.

Nulty, bending over P. Walton on the other side, shook his head.

"He's past all hope," he said gruffly.

P. Walton stirred, and his lips moved—he was talking to himself.

"If I were you, Nulty," he murmured, and they stooped to catch the words, "I'd look out for—for—that—"

The words trailed off into incoherency.

Regan, tugging at his mustache, swallowed a lump in his throat, and turned away his head.

"It's queer!" he muttered. "How'd he know—what? I wonder where he came from, and who he was?"

But P. Walton never said. P. Walton was dead.

Chapter VI

THE AGE LIMIT

As its scarred and battle-torn colors are the glory of a regiment, brave testimony of hard-fought fields where men were men, so to the Hill Division is its tradition. And there are names there, too, on the honor roll—not famous, not world-wide, not on every tongue, but names that in railroading will never die. The years have gone since men fought and conquered the sullen gray-walled Rockies and shackled them with steel and iron, and laid their lives on the altar of one of the mightiest engineering triumphs the world has ever known; but the years have dimmed no memory, have only brought achievement into clearer focus, and honor to its fullness where honor is due. They tell the stories of those days yet, as they always will tell them—at night in the roundhouse over the soft pur of steam, with the yellow flicker of the oil lamps on the group clustered around the pilot of a 1600-class mountain greyhound—and the telling is as though men stood erect, bareheaded, at "salute" to the passing of the Old Guard.

Heroes? They never called themselves that—never thought of themselves in that way, those old fellows who have left their stories. Their uniform was a suit of overalls, their "decorations" the grime that came with the day's work—just railroad men, hard-tongued, hard-fisted, hard-faced, rough, without much polish, perhaps, as some rank polish, with hearts that were right and big as a woman's—that was all.

MacCaffery, Dan MacCaffery, was one of these. This is old Dan MacCaffery's story.

MacCaffery? Dan was an engineer, one of the old-timers, blue-eyed, thin—but you'd never get old Dan that way, he wouldn't look natural! You've got to put him in the cab of the 304, leaning out of the window, way out, thin as a bent toothpick, and pounding down the gorge and around into the straight making for the Big Cloud yards, with a string of buff-colored coaches jouncing after him, and himself bouncing up and down in his seat like an animated piece of rubber. Nobody ever saw old Dan inside the cab, that is, all in—he always had his head out of the window—said he could see better, though the wind used to send the water trickling down from the old blue eyes, and generally there were two little white streaks on his cheeks where no grime or coal dust ever got a chance at a strangle hold on the skin crevices. For the rest, what you could see sticking out of the cab over the whirling rod as he came down the straight, was just a black, greasy peaked cap surmounting a scanty fringe of gray hair, and a wizened face, with a round little knob in the center of it for a nose.

But that isn't altogether old Dan MacCaffery, either—there was Mrs. MacCaffery. Everybody liked Dan, with his smile, and the cheery way he had of puckering up his lips sympathetically and pushing back his cap and scratching near his ear where the hair was, as he listened maybe to a hard-luck story; everybody liked Dan—but they swore by Mrs. MacCaffery. Leaving out the railroaders who worshipped her anyway, even the worst characters in Big Cloud, and there were some pretty bad ones in those early days, hangers-on and touts for the gambling hells and dives, used to speak of the little old lady in the lace cap with a sort of veneration.

Lace cap? Yes. Sounds queer, doesn't it? An engineer's wife, keeping his shanty in a rough and ready, half baked bit of an uncivilized town in the shadow of the Rockies, and a lace cap don't go together very often, that's a fact. But it is equally a fact that Mrs. MacCaffery wore a lace cap—and somehow none of the other women ever had a word to say about her being "stuck up" either. There was something patrician about Mrs. MacCaffery—not the cold, stand-offish effect that's only make-believe, but the real thing. The Lord knows, she had to work hard enough, but you never saw her rinsing the washtub suds from her hands and coming to the door with her sleeves rolled up—not at all. The last thing you'd ever think there was in the house was a washtub. Little lace cap over smoothly-parted gray hair, little black dress with a little white frill around the throat, and just a glad look on her face whether she'd ever seen you before or not—that was Mrs. MacCaffery.

As far back as any one could remember she had always looked like that, always a little old lady—never a young woman, although she and Dan had come there years before, even before the operating department had got the steel shaken down into anything that might with justice be called a permanent right of way. Perhaps it was the gray hair—Mrs. MacCaffery's hair had been gray then, when it ought to have been the glossy, luxuriant brown that the old-fashioned daguerreotype, hanging in the shanty's combination dining and sitting room, proclaimed that it once was.

Big Cloud, of course, didn't call her patrician—because they didn't talk that way out there. They said there was "some class" to Mrs. MacCaffery—and if their expression was inelegant, what they meant by it wasn't. Not that they ranked her any finer than Dan, for the last one of them ranked Dan as one of God's own noblemen, and there's nothing finer than that, only they figured, at least the women did, that back in the Old Country she'd been brought up to things that Dan MacCaffery hadn't.

Maybe that accounted for their sending young Dan East, and pinching themselves pretty near down to bed rock to give the boy an education and a start. Not that Mrs. MacCaffery had any notions that railroading and overalls and dirt was plebeian and beneath her—far from it! She was proud of old Dan, proud of his work, proud of his record; she'd talk about Dan's engine to you by the hour just as though it were alive, just as Dan would, and she would have hung chintz curtains on the cab windows and put flower pots on the running boards if they had let her. It wasn't that—Mrs. MacCaffery wasn't that kind. Only there were limitations to a cab, and she didn't want the boy, he was the only one they had, to start out with limitations of any kind that would put a slow order on his reaching the goal her mother's heart dreamed of. What goal? Who knows? Mothers always dream of their boy's future in that gentle, loving,

88

all-conquering, up-in-the-clouds kind of a way, don't they? She wanted young Dan to do something, make a name for himself some day.

And young Dan did. He handed a jolt to the theory of heredity that should, if it didn't, have sent the disciples of that creed to the mat for the full count. When he got through his education, he got into a bank and backed the brain development, the old couple had scrimped to the bone to give him, against the market—with five thousand dollars of the bank's money. Old Dan and Mrs. MacCaffery got him off—Mrs. MacCaffery with her sweet old face, and Dan with his grim old honesty. The bank didn't prosecute. The boy was drowned in a ferryboat accident the year after. And old Dan had been paying up ever since.

He was always paying up. Five thousand dollars, even in instalments for a whole lot of years, didn't leave much to come and go on from his monthly pay check. He talked some of dropping the benefit orders he belonged to, and he belonged to most of them, but Mrs. MacCaffery talked him out of that on account of the insurance, she said, but really because she knew that Dan and his lodge rooms and his regalias and his worshipful titles were just part and parcel of each other, and that he either was, or was just going to be, Supreme High Chief Illustrious Something-or-other of every Order in town. Besides, after all, it didn't cost much compared with the other, just meant pinching a tiny bit harder—and so they pinched.

Old Dan and Mrs. MacCaffery didn't talk about their troubles. You'd never get the blues on their account, no matter how intimate you got with them. But everybody knew the story, of course, for everybody knows a thing like that; and everybody knew that dollars were scarce up at the MacCafferys' shanty for, though they didn't know how much old Dan sent East each year, they knew it had to be a pretty big slice of what was coming to him to make much impression on that five thousand dollars at the other end—and they wondered, naturally enough, how the MacCafferys got along at all. But the MacCafferys got along somehow, outwardly without a sign of the hurt that was deeper than a mere matter of dollars and cents, got along through the years— and Mrs. MacCaffery got a little grayer, a little more gentle and patient and sweet-faced, and old Dan's hair narrowed to a fringe like a broken tonsure above his ears, and—but there's our "clearance" now, and we're off with a clean-swept track and "rights through" into division.

Dan was handling the cab end of one of the local passenger runs when things broke loose in the East—a flurry in Wall Street. But Wall Street was a long, long way from the Rockies, and, though the papers were full of it, there didn't seem to be anything intimate enough in a battle of brokers and magnates, bitter, prolonged, and to the death though it might be, to stir up any excitement or enthusiasm on the Hill Division. The Hill Division, generally speaking, had about all it could do to mind its own affairs without bothering about those of others', for the Rockies, if conquered, took their subjection with bad grace and were always in an incipient state of insurrection that kept the operating, the motive power and the maintenance-of-way departments close to the verge of nervous prostration without much let-up to speak of. But when the smoke cleared away down East, the Hill Division and

Big Cloud forgot their bridge troubles and their washouts and their slides long enough to stick their tongues in their cheeks and look askance at each other; and Carleton, in his swivel chair, pulled on the amber mouthpiece of his brier and looked at Regan, who, in turn, pulled on his scraggly brown mustache and reached for his hip pocket and his plug. The system was under new control.

"Who's H. Herrington Campbell when he's at home?" spluttered Regan.

"Our new general manager, Tommy," Carleton told him for the second time.

Regan grunted.

"I ain't blind! I've read that much. Who is he—h'm? Know him?"

Carleton took the pipe from his mouth—a little seriously.

"It's the P. M. & K. crowd, Tommy. Makes quite an amalgamation, doesn't it—direct eastern tidewater connection—what? They're a younger lot, pretty progressive, too, and sharp as they make them."

"I don't care a hoot who owns the stock," observed Regan, biting deeply at his blackstrap. "It's the bucko with the overgrown name in the center that interests me—who's he? Do you know him?"

"Yes," said Carleton slowly. "I know him." He got up suddenly and walked over to the window, looked out into the yards for a moment, then turned to face the master mechanic. "I know him, and I know most of the others; and I'll say, between you and me, Tommy, that I'm blamed sorry they've got their fingers on the old road. They're a cold, money-grabbing crew, and Campbell's about as human as a snow man, only not so warm-blooded. I fancy you'll see some changes out here."

"I turned down an offer from the Penn last week," said the fat little master mechanic reminiscently, "mabbe I—"

Carleton laughed—he could afford to. There was hardly a road in the country but had made covetous offers for the services of the cool-eyed master of the Hill Division, who was the idol of his men down to the last car tink.

"No; I guess not, Tommy. Our heads are safe enough, I think. When I go, you go—and as the P. M. & K. have been after me before, I guess they'll let me alone now I'm on their pay roll."

"What kind of changes, then?" inquired Regan gruffly.

"I don't know," said Carleton. "I don't know, Tommy—new crowd, new ways. We'll see."

And, in time, Regan saw. Perhaps Regan himself, together with Riley, the trainmaster, were unwittingly the means of bringing it about a little sooner than it might otherwise have come—perhaps not. Ultimately it would have been all the same. Sentiment and H. Herrington Campbell were not on speaking terms. However, one way or the other, in results, it makes little difference.

It was natural enough that about the first official act of the new directors should be a trip to look over the new property they had acquired; and if there was any resentment on the Hill Division at the change in ownership, there was no sign of it in Big Cloud when the word went out of what was coming. On the contrary, everybody sort of figured to make a kind of holiday affair of it, for the special was to lay off there until afternoon to give

90

the Big Fellows a chance to see the shops. Anyway, it was more or less mutually understood that they were to be given the best the Hill Division had to offer.

Regan kept his pet flyer, the 1608, in the roundhouse, and tinkered over her for two days, and sent for Dan MacCaffery—there'd been a good deal of speculation amongst the engine crews as to who would get the run, and the men were hot for the honor.

Regan squinted at old Dan—and squinted at the 1608 on the pit beside him.

"How'd you think she looks, Dan?" he inquired casually.

The old engineer ran his eyes wistfully over the big racer, groomed to the minute, like the thoroughbred it was.

"She'll do you proud, Regan," he said simply.

And then Regan's fat little hand came down with a bang on the other's overalled shoulder—that was Regan's way.

"And you, too, Dan," he grinned. "I got you slated for the run."

"Me!" said MacCaffery, his wizened face lighting up.

"You—sure!" Regan's grin expanded. "It's coming to you, ain't it? You're the senior engineer on the division, ain't you? Well, then, what's the matter with you? Riley's doing the same for Pete Chartrand—he's putting Pete in the aisles. What?"

Old Dan looked at Regan, then at the 1608, and back at Regan again.

"Say," he said a little huskily, "the missus 'll be pleased when I tell her. We was talking it over last night, and hoping—just hoping, mind you, that mabbe—"

"Go tell her, then," said the little master mechanic, who didn't need any word picture to make him see Mrs. MacCaffery's face when she heard the news—and he gave the engineer a friendly push doorwards.

Not a very big thing—to pull the latch of the Directors' Special? Nothing to make a fuss over? Well no, perhaps not—not unless you were a railroad man. It meant quite a bit to Dan MacCaffery, though, and quite a bit to Mrs. MacCaffery because it was an honor coming to Dan; and it meant something to Regan, too. Call it a little thing—but little things count a whole lot, too, sometimes in this old world of ours, don't they?

There had been a sort of little programme mapped out. Regan, as naturally fell to his lot, being master mechanic, was to do the honors of the shops, and Carleton was to make the run up through the Rockies and over the division with the new directors; but at the last moment a telegram sent the superintendent flying East to a brother's sick bed, and the whole kit and caboodle of the honors, to his inward consternation and dismay, fell to Regan.

Regan, however, did the best he could. He fished out the black Sunday suit he wore on the rare occasions when he had time to know one day of the week from the other, wriggled into a boiled shirt and a stiff collar that was yellow for want of daylight, and, nervous as a galvanic battery, was down on the platform an hour before the train was due. Also, by the time the train rolled in, Regan's handkerchief was wringing wet from the sweat he mopped off his forehead—but five minutes after that the earnest little master mechanic, as he afterwards confided to Carleton, "wouldn't have given a whoop for two trainloads of 'em, let alone the measly lot you could crowd into one private car." Somehow, Regan had got it into his head that he was going on his mettle before a crowd of up-to-the-minute, way-up railroaders; but when he found there wasn't a practical railroad man amongst them, bar H. Herrington Campbell, to whom he promptly and whole-heartedly took a dislike, Regan experienced a sort of pitying contempt, which, if it passed over the nabobs' heads without doing them any harm, had at least the effect of putting the fat little master mechanic almost superciliously at his ease.

Inspect the shops? Not at all. They were out for a joy ride across the continent and the fun there was in it.

"How long we got here? Three hours? Wow!" boomed a big fellow, stretching his arms lazily as he gazed about him.

"Let's paint the town, boys," wheezed an asthmatic, bowlegged little man of fifty, who sported an enormous gold watch chain. "Come on and look the natives over!"

Regan, who had been a little hazy on the etiquette of chewing in select company, reached openly for his plug—and kind of squinted over it non-committingly, as he bit in, at H. Herrington Campbell, who stood beside him. Carleton had sized the new general manager up pretty well—cold as a snow man—and he looked it. H. Herrington Campbell was a spare-built man, with sharp, quick, black eyes, a face like a hawk, and lips so thin you wouldn't know he had any if one corner of his mouth hadn't been pried kind of open, so to speak, with the stub of a cigar.

"Go ahead and amuse yourselves, boys." H. Herrington Campbell talked out of the corner of his mouth where the cigar was. "We pull out at twelve-thirty sharp." Then to Regan, curtly: "We'll look the equipment and shops over, Mr. Regan."

"Yes—sure," agreed Regan, without much enthusiasm, and led the way across the tracks toward the roundhouse as a starting point for the inspection tour.

The whole blamed thing was different from the way Regan had figured it out in his mind beforehand; but Regan set out to make himself agreeable—and H. Herrington Campbell listened. H. Herrington Campbell was the greatest listener Regan had ever met, and Regan froze—and then Regan thawed out again, but not on account of H. Herrington Campbell. Regan might have an unresponsive audience, but then Regan didn't require an audience at all to warm him up when it came to his roundhouse, and his big mountain racers, and the shops he lay awake at night planning and thinking about. Here and there, H. Herrington Campbell shot out a question, crisp, incisive, unexpected, and lapsed into silence again—that was all.

They inspected everything, everything there was to inspect; but when they got through Regan had about as good an idea of what impression it had made on H. Herrington Campbell as he had when he started out, which is to say none at all. The new general manager just listened. Regan had done all the talking.

Not that H. Herrington Campbell sized up as a misfit, not by any means, far from it! Regan didn't make that mistake for a minute. He didn't need to be told that the other knew railroading from the ground up, he could feel it; but he didn't need to be told, either, that the other was more a high-geared efficiency machine than he was a man, he could feel that, too.

One word of praise Regan wanted, not for himself, but for the things he loved and worked over and into which he put his soul. And the one word, where a thousand were due, Regan did not get. The new general manager had the emotional instincts of a wooden Indian. Regan, toward the end of the morning, got to talking a little less himself, that is, aloud—inwardly he grew more eloquent than ever, cholerically so.

It was train time when they had finished, and the 1608, with old Dan MacCaffery, half out of the cab window as usual, had just backed down and coupled on the special, as Regan and the new general manager came along the platform from the upper freight sheds. And Regan, for all his inward spleen, couldn't help it, as they reached the big, powerful racer, spick and span from the guard-plates up.

"I dunno where you'll beat that, East or West," said Regan proudly, with a wave of his hand at the 1608. "Wish we had more of that type out here—we could use 'em. What do you think of her, Mr. Campbell—h'm?"

H. Herrington Campbell didn't appear to take any notice of the masterpiece of machine design to speak of. His eyes travelled over the engine, and fixed on Dan MacCaffery in the cab window. Dan had an old, but spotless, suit of overalls on, spotless because Mrs. MacCaffery, who was even then modestly sharing her husband's honors from the back of the crowd by the ticket-office window, had made them spotless with a good many hours' work the day before, for grease sticks hard even in a washtub; and on old Dan's wizened face was a genial smile that would have got an instant response from anybody—except H. Herrington Campbell. H. Herrington Campbell didn't smile, neither did he answer Regan's question.

"How old are you?" said he bluntly to Dan MacCaffery.

"Me?" said old Dan, taken aback for a moment. Then he laughed: "Blest if I know, sir, it's so long since I've kept track of birthdays. Sixty-one, I guess—no, sixty-two."

H. Herrington Campbell didn't appear to hear the old engineer's answer, any more than he had appeared to take any notice of the 1608. He had barely paused in his walk, and he was pulling out his watch now and looking at it as he continued along the platform—only to glance up again as Pete Chartrand, the senior conductor, gray-haired, gray-bearded, but dapper as you please in his blue uniform and brass buttons, hurried by toward the cab with the green tissue copy of the engineer's orders in his hand.

Regan opened his mouth to say something—and, instead, snapped his jaws shut like a steel trap. The last little bit of enthusiasm had oozed out of the usually good-natured little master mechanic. Two days' tinkering with the 1608, the division all keyed up to a smile, everybody trying to do his best to please, a dozen little intimate plans and arrangements talked over and worked out, were all now a matter of earnest and savage regret to Regan.

"By Christmas," growled Regan to himself, as he elbowed his way through the crowd on the platform—for the town, to the last squaw with a papoose strapped on her back, had turned out to see the Directors' Special off—"by Christmas, if 'twere not for Carleton's sake, I'd tell him, the little tin god that he thinks he is, what I think of him! And mabbe," added Regan viciously, as he swung aboard the observation car behind H. Herrington Campbell, "and mabbe I will yet!"

But Regan's cup, brimming as he held it to be, was not yet full. It was a pretty swell train, the Directors' Special, that the crowd sent off with a burst of cheering that lasted until the markers were lost to view around a butte; a pretty swell train, about the swellest that had ever decorated the train sheet of the Hill Division—two sleepers, a diner and observation, mostly mahogany, and the baggage car a good enough imitation to fit into the color scheme without outraging even the most esthetic taste, and the 1608 on the front end, gold-leafed, and shining like a mirror from polished steel and brass. As far as looks went there wasn't a thing the matter with it, not a thing; it would have pulled a grin of pride out of a Polack section hand—which is pulling some. And there wasn't anything the matter with the send-off, either, that was propitious enough to satisfy anybody; but, for all that, barring the first hour or so out of Big Cloud, trouble and the Directors' Special that afternoon were as near akin as twin brothers. Nothing went right; everything went wrong— except the 1608, that ran as smooth as a full-jewelled watch, when old Dan, for the mix-up behind him, could run her at all. The coupling on the diner broke—that started it. When they got that fixed, something else happened; and then the forward truck of the baggage car developed a virulent attack of hot box.

The special had the track swept for her clean to the Western foothills, and rights through. But she didn't need them. Her progress was a crawl. The directors, in spite of their dollar-ante and the roof of the observation car for the limit, began to lose interest in their game.

"What is this new toy we've bought?" inquired one of them plaintively. "A funeral procession?"

Even H. Herrington Campbell began to show emotion—he shifted his cigar stub at intervals from one corner of his mouth to the other. Regan was hot—both ways—inside and out; hotter a whole lot than the hot box he took his coat off to, and helped old Pete Chartrand and the train crew slosh buckets of water over every time the Directors' Special stopped, which was frequently.

It wasn't old Pete's fault. It wasn't anybody's fault. It was just blamed hard luck, and it lasted through the whole blamed afternoon. And by the time they pulled into Elk River, where Regan had wired for another car, and had transferred the baggage, the Directors' Special, as far as temper went, was as touchy as a man with a bad case of gout. As they coupled on the new car, Regan spoke to old Dan in the cab—spoke from his heart.

"We're two hours late, Dan—h'm? For the love of Mike, let her out and do something. That bunch back there's getting so damned polite to me you'd think the words would melt in their mouths—what?"

Old Dan puckered his face into a reassuring smile under the peak of his greasy cap.

"I guess we're all right now we've got rid of that car," he said. "You leave it to me. You leave it to me, Regan."

Pete Chartrand, savage as though the whole matter were a personal and direct affront, reached up with a new tissue to the cab window.

"Two hours and ten minutes late!" he snapped out. "Nice, ain't it! Directors' Special, all the swells, we're doing ourselves proud! Oh, hell!"

"Keep your shirt on, Pete," said Regan, somewhat inconsistently. "Losing your hair over it won't do any good. You're not to blame, are you? Well then, forget it!"

Two hours and ten minutes late! Bad enough; but, in itself, nothing disastrous. It wasn't the first time in railroading that schedules had gone aglimmering. Only there was more to it than that. There were not a few other trains, fast freights, passengers, locals and work trains, whose movements and the movements of the Directors' Special were intimately connected one with the other. Two hours and ten minutes was sufficient, a whole lot more than sufficient, to play havoc with a despatcher's carefully planned meeting points over a hundred miles of right of way, and all afternoon Donkin had been chewing his lips over his train sheet back in the despatcher's office at Big Cloud, until the Directors' Special, officially Special 117, had become a nightmare to him. Orders, counter orders, cancellations, new orders had followed each other all afternoon—and now a new batch went out, as the rehabilitated Special went out of Elk River, and Bob Donkin, with a sigh of relief at the prospect of clear sailing ahead, pushed the hair out of his eyes and relaxed a little as he began to give back the "completes."

It wasn't Donkin's fault; there was never so much as a hint that it was. The day man at Mitre Peak—forgot. That's all—but it's a hard word, the hardest there is in railroading. There was a lot of traffic moving that afternoon, and with sections, regulars, and extras all trying to dodge Special 117, they were crowding each other pretty hard—and the day man at Mitre Peak forgot.

It was edging dusk as old Pete Chartrand, from the Elk River platform, lifted a finger to old Dan MacCaffery in the cab, and old Dan, with a sort of grim smile at the knowledge that the honor of the Hill Division, what there was left of it as far as Special 117 was concerned, was up to him, opened out the 1608 to take the "rights" they'd given him afresh for all there was in it.

From Elk River to Mitre Peak, where the right of way crosses the Divide, it is a fairly stiff climb—from Mitre Peak to Eagle Pass, at the cañon bed, it is an equally emphatic drop; and the track in its gyrations around the base of the towering, jutting peaks, where it clings as a fly clings to a wall, is an endless succession of short tangents and shorter curves. The Rockies, as has been said, had been harnessed, but they had never been tamed—nor never will be. Silent, brooding always, there seems a sullen patience about them, as though they were waiting warily—to strike. There are stretches, many of them, where no more than a hundred yards will blot utterly one train from the sight of another; where the thundering reverberations of the one, flung echoing back and forth from peak to peak, drown utterly the sounds of the other. And west of Mitre Peak it is like this—and the operator at Mitre Peak forgot the holding order for Extra Freight No. 69.

It came quick, quick as the winking of an eye, sudden as the crack of doom. Extra Freight No. 69 was running west, too, in the same direction as the Directors' Special; only Extra No. 69 was a heavy train and she was feeling her way down the grade like a snail, while the Directors' Special, with the spur and prod of her own delinquency and misbehavior, was hitting up the fastest clip that old Dan, who knew every inch of the road with his eyes shut, dared to give within the limits of safety on that particular piece of track.

It came quick. Ten yards clear on the right of way, then a gray wall of rock, a short, right-angled dive of the track around it—and, as the pilot of the 1608 swung the curve, old Dan's heart for an instant stopped its beat—three red lights focussed themselves before his eyes, the tail lights on the caboose of Extra No. 69. There was a yell from little Billy Dawes, his fireman.

"My God, Dan, we're into her!" Dawes yelled. "We're into her!"

Cool old veteran, one of the best that ever pulled a throttle in any cab, there was a queer smile on old Dan MacCaffery's lips. He needed no telling that disaster he could not avert, could only in a measure mitigate, perhaps, was upon them; but even as he checked, checked hard, and checked again, the thought of others was uppermost in his mind—the train crew of the freight, some of them, anyway, in the caboose. Dawes was beside him now, almost at his elbow, as nervy and as full of grit as the engineer he'd shovelled for for five years and thought more of than he did of any other man on earth—and for the fraction of a second old Dan MacCaffery looked into the other's eyes.

"Give the boys in the caboose a chance for their lives, Billy, in case they ain't seen or heard us," he shouted in his fireman's ear. "Hold that whistle lever down."

Twenty yards, fifteen between them—the 1608 in the reverse bucking like a maddened bronco, old Dan working with all the craft he knew at his levers—ten yards—and two men, scurrying like rats from a sinking ship, leaped from the tail of the caboose to the right of way.

"Jump!" The word came like a half sob from old Dan. There was nothing more that any man could do. And he followed his fireman through the gangway.

It made a mess—a nasty mess. From the standpoint of traffic, as nasty a mess as the Hill Division had ever faced. The rear of the freight went to matchwood, the 1608, the baggage and two Pullmans turned turtle, derailing the remaining cars behind; but, by a miracle, it seemed, there wasn't any one seriously hurt.

Scared? Yes—pretty badly. The directors, a shaken, white-lipped crowd, poured out of the observation car to the track side. There was no cigar in H. Herrington Campbell's mouth.

It was dark by then, but the wreckage caught fire and flung a yellow glow far across the cañon, and in a shadowy way lighted up the immediate surroundings. Train crews and engine crews of both trains hurried here and there, torches and lanterns began to splutter and wink, hoarse shouts began to echo back and forth, adding their quota to a weird medley of escaping steam and crackling flame.

Regan, from a hasty consultation with old Dan MacCaffery and old Pete Chartrand, that sent the two men on the jump to carry out his orders, turned—to face H. Herrington Campbell.

"Nobody hurt, sir—thank God!" puffed the fat little master mechanic, in honest relief.

H. Herrington Campbell's eyes were on the retreating forms of the engineer and conductor.

"Oh, indeed!" he said coldly. "And the whole affair is hardly worth mentioning, I take it—quite a common occurrence. You've got some pretty old men handling your trains out here, haven't you?"

Regan's face went hard.

"They're pretty good men," he said shortly. "And there's no blame coming to them for this, Mr. Campbell, if that's what you mean."

H. Herrington Campbell's fingers went tentatively to his vest pocket for a cigar, extracted the broken remains of one—the relic of his own collision with the back of a car seat where the smash had hurled him—and threw it away with an icy smile.

"Blame?" expostulated H. Herrington Campbell ironically. "I don't want to blame any one; I'm looking for some one to congratulate—on the worst run division and the most pitiful exemplification of near-railroading I've had any experience with in twenty years—Mr. Regan."

For a full minute Regan did not speak. He couldn't. And then the words came away with a roar from the bluff little master mechanic.

"By glory!" he exploded. "We don't take that kind of talk out here even from general managers—we don't have to! That's straight enough, ain't it? Well, I'll give you some more of it, now I've started. I don't like you. I don't like that pained look on your face. I've been filling up on you all morning, and you don't digest well. We don't stand for anything as raw as that from any man on earth. And you needn't hunt around for any greased words, as far as I'm concerned, to do your firing with—you can have my resignation as master mechanic of the worst run division you've seen in twenty years right now, if you want it—h'm?"

H. Herrington Campbell was gallingly preoccupied.

"How long are we stalled here for—the rest of the night?" he inquired irrelevantly.

Regan stared at him a moment—still apoplectic.

"I've ordered them to run the forward end of the freight to Eagle Pass, and take you down," he said, choking a little. "There's a couple of flats left whole that you can pile yourselves and your baggage on, and down there they'll make up a new train for you."

"Oh, very good," said H. Herrington Campbell curtly.

And ten minutes later, the Directors' Special, metamorphosed into a string of box cars with two flats trailing on the rear, on which the newly elected board of the Transcontinental sat, some on their baggage, and some with their legs hanging over the sides, pulled away from the wreck and headed down the grade for Eagle Pass. Funny, the transition from the luxurious leather upholstery of the observation to an angry, chattering mob of magnates, clinging to each others' necks as they jounced on the flooring of an old flat? Well perhaps—it depends on how you look at it. Regan looked at it—and Regan grinned for the pure savagery that was in him.

"But I guess," said Regan to himself, as he watched them go, "I guess mabbe I'll be looking for that job on the Penn after all—h'm?"

Everybody talked about the Directors' Special run—naturally. And, naturally, everybody wondered what was going to come from it. It was an open secret that Regan had handed one to the general manager without any candy coating on the pill, and the Hill Division sort of looked to see the master mechanic's head fall and Regan go. But Regan did not go; and, for that matter, nothing else happened—for a while.

Carleton came back and got the rights of it from Regan—and said nothing to Regan about his reply to H. Herrington Campbell's letter, in which he had stated that if they were looking for a new master mechanic there would be a division superintendency vacant at the same time. The day man at Mitre Peak quit railroading—without waiting for an investigation. Old Dan MacCaffery and Billy Dawes went back to their regular run with the 304. And the division generally settled down again to its daily routine—and from the perspective of distance, if the truth be told, got to grinning reminiscently at the run the Big Bugs had had for their money.

Only the grin came too soon.

A week or so passed, pay day came and went—and the day after that a general order from the East hit the Hill Division like a landslide.

Carleton slit the innocent-looking official manila open with his paper knife, chucked the envelope in the waste-basket, read the communication, read it again with gathering brows—and sent for Regan. He handed the form to the master mechanic without a word, as the latter entered the office.

Regan read it—read it again, as his chief had—and two hectic spots grew bright on his cheeks. It was brief, curt, cold—for the good of the service, safety, and operating efficiency, it stated. In a word, on and after the first of the month the services of employees over the age of sixty years would no longer be required. Those were early days in railroading; not a word about pensions, not a word about half-pay; just sixty years and—out!

The paper crackled in Regan's clenched fists; Carleton was beating a tattoo on his teeth with the mouthpiece of his pipe—there wasn't another sound in the office for a moment. Then Regan spoke—and his voice broke a little.

"It's a damned shame!" he said, through his teeth. "It's that skunk Campbell."

"How many men does it affect?" asked Carleton, looking through the window.

"I don't know," said the little master mechanic bitterly; "but I know one that it'll hit harder than all the rest put together—and that's old Dan MacCaffery."

There was hurt in the super's gray eyes, as he looked at the big-hearted little master mechanic's working face.

"I was thinking of old Dan myself," he said, in his low, quiet way.

"He hasn't a cent!" stormed Regan. "Not a cent—not a thing on earth to fall back on. Think of it! Him and that little old missus of his, God bless her sweet old face, that have been scrimping all these years to pay back what that blasted kid robbed out of the bank. It ain't right, Carleton—it ain't right—it's hell, that's what it is! Sixty years! There ain't a better man ever pulled a latch in a cab, there ain't a better one pulling one anywhere to-day than old Dan MacCaffery. And—and I kind of feel as though I were to blame for this, in a way."

"To blame?" repeated Carleton.

"I put him on that run, and Riley put old Pete Chartrand on. It kind of stuck them under Campbell's nose. The two of them together, the two oldest men—and the blamedest luck that ever happened on a run! H'm?"

Carleton shook his head.

"I don't think it would have made any difference in the long run, Tommy. I told you there'd be changes as soon as the new board got settled in the saddle."

Regan tugged viciously at his scraggly brown mustache.

"Mabbe," he growled fiercely; "but Campbell's seen old Dan now, or I'd put one over on the pup—I would that! There ain't any birth register that I ever heard of out here in the mountains, and if Dan said he was fifty I'd take his word for it."

"Dan wouldn't say that," said Carleton quietly, "not even to hold his job."

"No, of course he wouldn't!" spluttered the fat little master mechanic, belligerently inconsistent. "Who said he would? And, anyway, it wouldn't do any good. Campbell asked him his age, and Dan told him. And—and—oh, what's the use! I know it, I know I'm only talking, Carleton."

Neither of them said anything for a minute; then Regan, pacing up and down the room, spoke again:

"It's a clean sweep, eh? Train crews, engine crews, everything—there ain't any other job for him. Over sixty is out everywhere. A white man—one of the whitest"—Regan sort of said it to himself—"old Dan MacCaffery. Who's to tell him?"

Carleton drew a match, with a long crackling noise, under the arm of his chair.

"Me?" said Regan, and his voice broke again. He stopped before the desk, and, leaning, over, stretched out his arm impulsively across it. "I'd rather have that arm cut off than tell him, Carleton," he said huskily. "I don't know what he'll say, I don't know what he'll do, but I know it will break his heart, and break Mrs. MacCaffery's heart—Carleton." He took another turn the length of the room and back again. "But I guess it had better be me," said the little master mechanic, more to himself than to Carleton. "I guess it had—I'd hate to think of his getting it so's it would hurt any more than it had to, h'm?"

And so Tommy Regan told old Dan MacCaffery—that afternoon—the day after pay day.

Regan didn't mean to exactly, not then—he was kind of putting it off, as it were—until next day—and fretting himself sick over it. But that afternoon old Dan, on his way down to the roundhouse—Dan took out the regular passenger local that left Big Cloud at 6.55 every evening, and to spend an hour ahead of running time with the 304 was as much a habit with Dan as breathing was—hunted Regan up in the latter's office just before the six o'clock whistle blew. For an instant Regan thought the engineer had somehow or other already heard the news, but a glance at Dan's face dispelled that idea as quickly as it had come. Dan was always smiling, but there was a smile on the wizened, puckered, honest old face now that seemed to bubble out all over it.

"Regan," said old Dan, bursting with happy excitement, "I just had to drop in and tell you on the way over to the roundhouse, and the missus, she says, 'You tell Mr. Regan, Dan; he'll be rightdown glad.'"

Regan got up out of his chair. There seemed a sense of disaster coming somehow that set him to breathing heavily.

"Sure, Dan—sure," he said weakly. "What is it?"

"Well," said Dan, "you know that—that trouble the boy got into back—back—"

"Yes, I know," said Regan hastily.

"Well," said Dan, "it's taken a long time, a good many years, but yesterday, you know, was pay day; and to-day, Regan, we, the missus and me, Regan, sent the last of that money East, interest and all, the last cent of it, cleaned it all up. Say, Regan, I feel like I was walking on air, and you'd ought to have seen the missus sitting up there in the cottage and smiling through the tears. 'Oh, Dan!' she says, and then she gets up and puts her two hands on my shoulders, and I felt blamed near like crying myself. 'We can start in now, Dan, to save up for old age,' she says, smiling. Say, Regan, ain't it—ain't it fine? We're going to start in now and save up for old age."

Regan didn't say a word. It came with a rush, choking him up in his throat, and something misty in front of his eyes so he couldn't see—and he turned his back, searching for his hat on the peg behind his desk. He jammed his hat on his head, and jerked it low down over his forehead.

"Ain't you—glad?" said old Dan, a sort of puzzled hurt in his eyes.

"I'll walk over a bit of the way to the roundhouse with you, Dan," said Regan gruffly. "Come on."

They stepped out of the shops, and across a spur—old Dan, still puzzled, striding along beside the master mechanic.

"What's the matter, Regan?" he asked reproachfully. "I thought you'd be—"

And then Regan stopped—and his hand fell in a tight grip on the other's shoulder.

"I got to tell you, Dan," he blurted out. "But I don't need to tell you what I think of it. It's a damned shame! The new crowd that's running this road don't want anybody helping 'em to do it after the first of the month that's over sixty years of age. You're—you're out."

Old Dan didn't seem to get it for a minute; then a whiteness kind of crept around his lips, and his eyes, from Regan, seemed to circuit in a queer, wistful way about the yards, and fix finally on the roundhouse in front of him; and then he lifted his peaked cap, in the way he had of doing, and scratched near his ear where the hair was. He hit Regan pretty hard with what he said.

"Regan," he said, "there's two weeks yet to the end of the month. Don't tell her, Regan, and don't you let the boys tell her—there's two weeks she don't need to worry. I'd kind of like to have her have them two weeks."

Regan nodded—there weren't any words that would come, and he couldn't have spoken them if there had.

"Yes," said old Dan, sort of whispering to himself, "I'd kind of like to have her have them two weeks."

Regan cleared his throat, pulled at his mustache, swore under his breath, and cleared his throat again.

"What'll you do, Dan—afterwards?"

Old Dan straightened up, looked at Regan—and smiled.

"I dunno," he said, shaking his head and smiling. "I dunno; but it'll be all right. We'll get along somehow." His eyes shifted to the roundhouse again. "I guess I'd better be getting over to the 304," he said—and turned abruptly away.

Regan watched him go, watched the overalled figure with a slight shoulder stoop cross the turntable, watched until the other disappeared inside the roundhouse doors; and then he turned and walked slowly across the tracks and uptown toward his boarding house. "Don't tell her"—the words kept reiterating themselves insistently—"don't let the boys tell her."

"I guess they won't," said Regan, muttering fiercely to himself. "I guess they won't."

Nor did they. The division and Big Cloud kept the secret for those two weeks—and they kept it for long after that. The little old lady in the lace cap never knew—they ranked her high, those pioneering women kind of hers in that little mountain town, those rough-and-ready toilers who had been her husband's mates—she never knew.

But everybody else knew, and they watched old Dan as the days went by, watched him somehow with a tight feeling in their throats, and kept aloof a little—because they didn't know what to say—kept aloof a little awkwardly, as it were. Not that there seemed much of any difference in the old engineer; it was more a something that they sensed. Old Dan came down to the roundhouse in the late afternoon an hour before train time, just as he always did, puttered and oiled around and coddled the 304 for an hour, just as he always did, just as though he was always going to do it, took his train out, came back on the early morning run, backed the 304 into the roundhouse, and trudged up Main Street to where it began to straggle into the buttes, to where his cottage and the little old lady were—just as he always did. And the little old lady, with the debt paid, went about the town for those two weeks happier-looking, younger-looking than Big Cloud had ever seen her before. That was all.

But Regan, worrying, pulling at his mustache, put it up to little Billy Dawes, old Dan's fireman, one day in the roundhouse near the end of the two weeks.

"How's Dan take it in the cab, Billy?" he asked.

The little fireman rolled the hunk of greasy waste in his hands, and swabbed at his fingers with it for a moment before he answered; then he sent a stream of blackstrap juice viciously into the pit, and with a savage jerk hurled the hunk of waste after it.

"By God!" he said fiercely.

Regan blinked—and waited.

"Just the same as ever he was," said Billy Dawes huskily, after a silence. "Just the same—when he thinks you're not looking. I've seen him sometimes when he didn't know I was looking."

Regan said: "H'm!"—kind of coughed it out, reached for his plug, as was usual with him in times of stress, bit into it deeply, sputtered something hurriedly about new piston rings for the left-hand head, and, muttering to himself, left the roundhouse.

And that night old Dan MacCaffery took out the 304 and the local passenger for the run west and the run back east—just as he always did. And the next night, and for two nights after that he did the same.

Came then the night of the 31st.

It was the fall of the year and the dusk fell early; and by a little after six, with the oil lamps lighted, that at best only filtered spasmodic yellow streaks of gloom about the roundhouse, the engines back on the pits were beginning to loom up through the murk in big, grotesque, shadowy shapes, as Regan, crossing the turntable, paused for a moment hesitantly. Why he was there, he didn't know. He hadn't meant to be there. He was just a little early for his nightly game of pedro with Carleton over in the super's office—it wasn't much more than half past six—so he had had some time to put in—that must be about the size of it. He hadn't meant to come. There wasn't any use in it, none at all, nothing he could do; better, in fact, if he stayed away—only he had left the boarding house early—and he was down there now, standing on the turntable—and it was old Dan's last run.

"I guess," mumbled Regan, "I'll go back over to the station. Carleton 'll be along in a few minutes. I guess I will, h'm?"—only Regan didn't. He started on again slowly over the turntable, and entered the roundhouse.

There wasn't anybody in sight around the pit on which the 304 stood, nobody puttering over the links and motion-gear, poking here and there solicitously with a long-spouted oil can, as he had half, more than half, expected to find old Dan doing; but he heard some one moving about in the cab, and caught the flare of a torch. Regan walked down the length of the engine, and peered into the cab. It was Billy Dawes.

"Where's Dan, Billy? Ain't he about?" inquired Regan.

The fireman came out into the gangway.

"Yes," he answered; "he's down there back of the tender by the fitters' benches. He's looking for some washers he said he wanted for a loose stud nut. I'll get him for you."

"No; never mind," said Regan. "I'll find him."

It was pretty dark at the rear of the roundhouse in the narrow space between the engine tenders on the various pits and the row of workbenches that flanked the wall, and for a moment, as Regan reached the end of the 304's tender, he could not see any one—and then he stopped short, as he made out old Dan's form down on the floor by the end bench as though he were groping for something underneath it.

For a minute, two perhaps, Regan stood there motionless, watching old Dan MacCaffery. Then he drew back, tiptoed softly away, went out through the engine doors, and, as he crossed the tracks to the station platform, brushed his hand hurriedly across his eyes.

Regan didn't play much of a game of pedro that night—his heart wasn't in it. Carleton had barely dealt the first hand when Regan heard the 304 backing down and coupling on the local, and he got up from his chair and walked to the window, and stood there watching until the local pulled out.

Carleton didn't say anything—just dealt the cards over again, and began once more as Regan resumed his seat.

An hour passed. Regan, fidgety and nervous, played in a desultory fashion; Carleton, disturbed, patiently correcting the master mechanic's mistakes. The game was a farce.

"What's the matter, Tommy?" asked Carleton gravely, as Regan made a misdeal twice in succession.

"Nothing," said Regan shortly. "Go on, play; it's your bid."

Carleton shook his head.

"You're taking it too much to heart, Tommy," he said. "It won't do you any good—either of you—you or Dan. He'll pull out of it somehow. You'll see."

There was a queer look on Regan's face as he stared for an instant at Carleton across the table, and he opened his lips as though to say something—and closed them again in a hard line instead.

Carleton bid.

"It's yours," said Regan.

Carleton led—and then Regan, with a sweep of his hand, shot his cards into the center of the table.

"It's no good," he said gruffly, getting up. "I can't play the blamed game to-night, I—" He stopped suddenly and turned his head, as a chair scraped sharply in the despatchers' room next door.

A step sounded in the hall, the super's door was flung open, and Spence put in his head.

One glance at the despatcher, and Carleton was on his feet.

"What's the matter, Spence?" he asked, quick and hard.

Regan hadn't moved—but Regan spoke now, answering the question that was addressed to the despatcher, and answering it in a strangely assertive, absolute, irrefutable way.

"The local," he said. "Number Forty-seven. Dan MacCaffery's dead."

Both men stared at him in amazement—and Spence, sort of unconsciously, nodded his head.

"Yes," said Spence, still staring at Regan. "There was some sort of engine trouble just west of Big Eddy in the Beaver Cañon. I haven't got the rights of it yet, only that somehow MacCaffery got his engine stopped just in time to keep the train from going over the bridge embankment—and went out doing it. There's no one else hurt. Dawes, the fireman, and Conductor Neale walked back to Big Eddy. I've got them on the wire now. Come into the other room."

Regan stepped to the door mechanically, and, with Carleton behind him, followed Spence into the despatches' room. There, Carleton, tight-lipped, leaned against the table; Regan, his face like stone, took his place at Spence's elbow, as the despatcher dropped into his chair.

There wasn't a sound in the room for a moment save the clicking of the sender in a quick tattoo under Spence's fingers. Then Spence picked up a pencil and began scribbling the message on a pad, as the sounder spoke—Billy Dawes was dictating his story to the Big Eddy operator.

"It was just west of Big Eddy, just before you get to the curve at the approach to the Beaver Bridge," came Dawes' story, "and we were hitting up a fast clip, but no more than usual, when we got a jolt in the cab that spilled me into the coal and knocked Dan off his seat. It all came so quick there wasn't time to think, but I knew we'd shed a driver on Dan's side, and the rod was cutting the side of the cab like a knife through cheese. I heard Dan shout something about the train going over the embankment and into the river if we ever hit the Beaver curve, and then he jumped for the throttle and the air. There wasn't a chance in a million for him, but it was the only chance for every last one of the rest of us. He made it somehow, I don't know how; it's all a blur to me. He checked her, and then the rod caught him, and—" The sounder broke, almost with a human sob in it, it seemed, and then went on again: "We stopped just as the 304 turned turtle. None of the coaches left the rails. That's all."

Regan spoke through dry lips.

"Ask him what Dan was like in the cab to-night," he said hoarsely.

Spence looked up and around at the master mechanic, as though he had not heard aright.

"Ask him what I say," repeated Regan shortly. "What was Dan like in the cab to-night?"

Spence bent over his key again. There was a pause before the answer came.

"He says he hadn't seen Dan so cheerful for months," said Spence presently.

Regan nodded, kind of curiously, kind of as though it were the answer he expected—and then he nodded at Carleton, and the two went back to the super's room.

Regan closed the door behind him.

Carleton dropped into his chair, his gray eyes hard and full of pain.

"I don't understand, Tommy," he said heavily. "It's almost as though you knew it was going to happen."

Regan came across the floor and stood in front of the desk.

"I did," he said in a low way. "I think I was almost certain of it."

Carleton pulled himself forward with a jerk in his chair.

"Do you know what you are saying, Tommy?" he asked sharply.

"I'll tell you," Regan said, in the same low way. "I went over to the roundhouse to-night before Dan took the 304 out. I didn't see Dan anywhere about, and I asked Dawes where he was. Dawes said he had gone back to the fitters' benches to look for some washers. I walked on past the tender and I found him there down on the floor on his knees by one of the benches—but he wasn't looking for any washers. He was praying."

With a sharp exclamation, Carleton pushed back his chair, and, standing, leaned over the desk toward Regan.

Regan swallowed a lump in his throat—and shook his head.

"He didn't see me," he said brokenly, "he didn't know I was there. He was praying aloud. I heard what he said. It's been ringing in my head all night, word for word, while I was trying to play with those"—he jerked his hand toward the scattered cards on the desk between them. "I can hear him saying it now. It's the queerest prayer I ever heard; and I guess he prayed the way he lived—as though he was kind of intimate with God."

"Yes?" prompted Carleton softly, as Regan paused.

Regan turned his head away as his eyes filled suddenly—and his voice was choked.

"What he said was this, just as though he was talking to you or me: 'You know how it is, God. I wouldn't take that way myself unless You fixed it up for me, because it wouldn't be right unless You did it. But I hope, God, You'll think that's the best way out of it. You see, there ain't nothing left as it is, but if we fixed it that way there'd be the fraternal insurance to take care of the missus, and she wouldn't never know. And then, You see, God, I guess my work is all done, and—and I'd kind of like to quit while I was still on the pay roll—I'd kind of like to finish that way, and to-night's the last chance. You understand, God, don't You?'"

Regan's lips were quivering as he stopped.

There was silence for a moment, then Carleton looked up from the blotter on his desk.

"Tommy," he said in his big, quiet way, as his hand touched Regan's sleeve, "tell me why you didn't stop him, then, from going out to-night?"

Regan didn't answer at once. He went over to the window and stared out at the twinkling switch lights in the yards below—he was still staring out of the window as he spoke.

"He didn't put it up to me," said Regan. "He put it up to God."

Chapter VII

"THE DEVIL AND ALL HIS WORKS"

Maguire was a little, washed-out, kind of toil-bent hostler in the roundhouse—and he married old. How old? Nobody knew—not even old Bill himself—fifty something. Mrs. Maguire presented him with a son in due course, and the son's name was Patrick Burke Maguire—but the Hill Division, being both terse and graphic by nature and education, called him "Noodles."

Noodles wasn't even a pretty baby. Tommy Regan, who was roped in to line up at the baptismal font and act as godfather because old Bill was a boiler-washer in the roundhouse, which was reason enough for the big-hearted master mechanic, said that Noodles was the ugliest and most forbidding looking specimen of progeny he had ever seen outside a zoological garden. Of course, be it understood, Regan wasn't a family man, and godfathering wasn't a job in Regan's line, so when he got outside the church and the perspiration had stopped trickling nervously down the small of his back and he'd got a piece of blackstrap clamped firmly home between his teeth, he told old Bill, by way of a grim sort of revenge for the unhappy position his good nature had led him into, that the offspring was the dead spit of its father—and he congratulated Noodles.

The irony, of course, was lost. The boiler-washer walked on air for a week. He told the roundhouse what Regan had said—and the roundhouse laughed. Bill thought the roundhouse thought he was lying, but that didn't dampen his spirits any. It wasn't everybody could get the master mechanic of the division to stand up with their kids! Everybody was happy—except Noodles. Noodles, just about then, developed colic.

Noodles got over the colic, got over the measles, the mumps, the whooping cough, and the scarlet fever—that may not have been the order of their coming or their going, but he got over them all. And when he was twelve he got over the smallpox; but he never got over his ugliness—the smallpox kind of put a stop-order on any lurking tendency there might have been in that direction. Also, when he was twelve, he got over all the schooling the boiler-washer's limited means would span, which wasn't a university course; and he started in railroading as a call boy.

There was nothing organically bad about Noodles, except his exterior—which wasn't his fault. One can't be blamed for hair of a motley red, ubiquitous freckles wherever the smallpox had left room for them, no particular colored eyes, a little round knob of uptilted nose, and a mouth that made even the calloused Dutchy at the lunch counter feel a little mean inwardly when he compared it with the mathematically cut slab of contract pie, eight slabs to the pie plate, and so much so that he went to the extent of—no, he never gave Noodles an extra piece—but he went to the extent of

106

surreptitiously pocketing Noodles' nickel as though he were obtaining money under false pretenses—which was a good deal for Dutchy to do—and just shows.

There was nothing organically bad about Noodles—not a thing. Noodles' troubles, and they came thick and fast with the inauguration of his railroad career, lay in quite another direction—his irrepressible tendency to practical jokes, coupled with a lack of the sense of the general fitness of things, consequences and results, and an absence of even a bowing acquaintance with responsibility that was appalling.

The first night Noodles went on duty as call boy, armed with a nickel thriller—that being only half the price of a regular dime novel—and visions of the presidency of the road being offered him before he was much older, Spence was sitting in on the early night trick. There was a lot of stuff moving through the mountains that night, and the train sheet was heavy. And even Spence, counted one of the best despatchers that ever held down a key on the Hill Division, was hard put to it, both to keep his crowding sections from treading on each other's heels, and to jockey the east and westbounds past each other without letting their pilots get tangled up head-on. It was no night or no place for foolishness—a despatcher's office never is, for that matter.

Noodles curled himself up in a chair behind the despatcher—and started in on the thriller. His first call was for the crews of No. 72, the local freight east, at 8.35, and there was nothing to do until then unless Spence should happen to want him for something. The thriller was quite up to the mark, even "thriller" than usual, but Noodles left the hero at the end of the first chapter securely bound to the mill-wheel with the villain rushing to open the gate in the dam—and his eyes strayed around the room.

It wasn't altogether the novelty of his surroundings—no phase of railroading was altogether a novelty to any Big Cloud youngster—there was just a sort of newness in his own position that interfered with any protracted or serious effort along literary lines. From a circuit of the room, his eyes went to the fly-specked, green-shaded lamp on the despatcher's table, then from the lamp to the despatcher's back—and fixed on the despatcher's back.

His eyes held there quite a long time—then his fingers went stealthily to the lapel of his coat. Spence had a habit when hurried or anxious of half rising from his chair, as though to give emphasis to his orders every time he touched the key. Spence was both hurried and anxious that night and the key was busy. In the somewhat dim light, Spence, to Noodles' fancy, assumed the aspect of an animated jumping jack.

Deftly, through long experience, Noodles coiled his pin with a wicked upshoot to the center of attack, cautiously lowered his own chair, which had been tilted back against the wall, to the more stable position of four legs on the floor, leaned forward, and laid the pin at a strategic point on the seat of Spence's chair. Two minutes later, kicked bodily down the stairs, Noodles was surveying the Big Cloud yards by moonlight from the perspective of the station platform.

Noodles' career as a call boy had been brief—and it was ended. Old Bill, the boiler-washer, came to the rescue. He explained to Regan who the

107

godfather of the boy was and what bearing that had on the case, and how he'd larruped the boy for what he'd done, and how the boy hadn't meant anything by it—and could the boy have another chance?

Regan said, "Yes," and said it shortly, more because he was busy at the time and wanted to get rid of Old Bill than from any predisposition toward Noodles. Noodles wasn't predisposing any way you looked at him, and Regan had a good look at his godson now for about the first time since he'd sponsored him, and he didn't like Noodles' looks—particularly. But Regan, not taking too serious a view of the matter, said yes, and put Noodles at work over in the roundhouse under the eye of his father.

Here, for a month, in one way or another, Noodles succeeded in making things lively, and himself cordially disliked by about everybody in the shops, the roundhouse, and the Big Cloud yards generally. And there was a hint or two thrown out, that reached Regan's ears, that old Bill had known what he was doing when he got one of the "big fellows" as godfather for as ugly a blasted little nuisance as the Hill Division had known for many a long day. Regan got to scowling every time he saw Noodles' unhandsome countenance, and he took pains on more than one occasion to give a bit of blunt advice to both Noodles and Noodles' father—which the former received somewhat ungraciously, and the latter with trepidation.

And then one night as it grew dark, just before six o'clock, while Bill and the turner and the wipers were washing up and trying to put in the time before the whistle blew, Noodles dropped into the turntable pit and wedged the turntable bearings with iron wedgings. Half an hour later, when the night crew came to swing it for the 1016, blowing hard from a full head of steam and ready to go out and couple on to No. 1 for the westbound run, they couldn't move it. It took them a few minutes before they could find out what the matter was, and another few to undo the matter when they did find-out—and No. 1 went out five minutes late.

Nobody asked who did it—it wasn't necessary. They just said "Noodles," and waited to see what Noodles' godfather would do about it.

They did not have long to wait. The Limited five minutes late out of division and the delay up to the motive-power department, which was Regan's department, would have been enough to bring the offender, whoever he might be, on the carpet with scant ceremony even if it had been an accident. Regan was boiling mad.

Noodles didn't show up the next day. Deep in Noodles' consciousness was a feeling that his nickel thriller and a certain spot he knew up behind the butte, where many a pleasant afternoon had been passed when he should have been at school, was more conducive to peace and quietness than the center of railroad activities—also Noodles ached bodily from his father's attentions.

Old Bill, too, kept conveniently out of sight down in a pit somewhere every time the master mechanic showed his nose inside the roundhouse during the morning—but by afternoon, counting the edge of Regan's wrath to have worn smooth, he followed Regan out over the turntable after one of the master mechanic's visits.

"Regan," he blurted out anxiously, "about the bhoy, now."

108

"Well?" snapped Regan, whirling about.

The monosyllable was cold enough in its uncompromise to stagger the little hostler, and drive all thoughts of the carefully rehearsed oration he had prepared from his head. He scratched aimlessly at the half circle of gray billygoat beard under his chin, and blinked helplessly at the master mechanic. Noodles lacked much, and in Noodles was much to be desired perhaps—but Noodles, for all that, had his place in the Irish heart that beat under the greasy jumper.

"He's the only wan we've got, Regan," stammered the harassed roundhouse man appealingly.

"It's a wonder, then, you've not holes in the knees of your overalls giving thanks for it," declared Regan grimly. "That's enough, Bill—and we've had enough of Noodles. Keep him away from here."

"Ah, sure now, Regan," begged the little hostler piteously, "yez don't mean ut. The bhoy's all right, Regan—'tis but spirit he has. Regan, listen here now, I've larruped him good for fwhat he's done—an' 'twas no more than a joke."

"A joke!" Regan choked; then brusquely: "That'll do, Bill. I've said my last word, and I'm busy this afternoon. Noodles is out—for keeps."

"Ah, Regan, listen here"—Noodles' father caught the master mechanic's arm, as the latter turned away. "Regan, sure, ut's the bhoy's godfather yez are."

The fat little master mechanic's face went suddenly red—this was the last straw—Noodles' godfather! Regan had been catching more whispers than he had liked lately anent godfathers and godfathering. His eyes puckered up and he wheeled on the boiler-washer—but the hot words on the tip of his tongue died unborn. There was something in the dejected droop of the other's figure, something in the blue eyes growing watery with age that made him change his mind—old Bill wasn't a young man. As far back as the big-hearted, good-natured master mechanic could remember, he remembered old Bill—in the roundhouse. Always the same job, day after day, year after year—boilerwashing, tinkering around at odd jobs—not much good at anything else— church every Sunday in shiny black coat, and peaked-faced Mrs. Maguire in the same threadbare, shiny black dress—not that Regan ever went to church, but he used to see them going there—church every Sunday, Maguire was long on church, and week days just boiler-washing and tinkering around at odd jobs—a dollar-sixty a day. Regan's pucker subsided, and he reached out his hand to the boiler-washer's shoulder—and he grinned to kind of take the sting out of his words.

"Well, Bill," he said, "as far as that goes, I renounce the honor."

"Raynownce ut!" The boiler-washer's eyes opened wide, and his face was strained as though he had not heard aright. "Raynownce ut! Ut's an Irish Protystant yez are, Regan, the same as me an' the missus, an' did yez not say the words in the church!"

"I did," admitted Regan; "though I've forgotten what they were. It was well enough, no doubt, for a kid in swaddling clothes—but it's some time since then." Then, with finality: "Go back to your work, Bill—I can't talk to you any more this afternoon."

"Raynownce ut!" The words reached Regan as he turned away and started across the tracks toward the platform, and in their tones was something akin to stunned awe that caused him to chuckle. "Raynownce ut!—an' yez said the words forninst the priest!"

Regan's chuckle, however, was not of long duration, either literally or metaphorically. During the rest of the afternoon the boiler-washer's words got to swinging through Regan's brain until they became an obsession, and somewhere down inside of him began to grow an uncomfortable foreboding that there might be something more to the godfathering business than he had imagined. He tackled Carleton about it before the whistle blew.

"Carleton," said he, walking into the super's office, and picking up a ruler from the other's desk, "don't laugh, or I'll jam this ruler down your throat. If you can answer a straight question, answer it—otherwise, let it go. What's a godfather, anyhow?"

Carleton grinned.

"You ought to know, Tommy," he said.

"I was running without a permit and off schedule at the time, and I was nervous," said Regan. "What happened, or what the goings-on were, I don't know. What is it?"

Carleton shook his head gravely.

"I'm afraid not, Tommy," he said. "You're in the wrong shop. Information bureau's downstairs to the right of the ticket office."

"Thanks!" said Regan.

And that was all the help he got from Carleton—then. But that night over their usual game of pedro in the super's office, it was a little different. Carleton, as he pulled the cards out of the desk drawer and tossed them on the table, pulled a small book from his pocket and tossed it to Regan.

"What's this?" inquired the master mechanic.

"It's not to your credit to ask—it's a prayer book," Carleton informed him. "Be careful of it—I borrowed it."

"You didn't need to say so," said Regan softly.

"Page two hundred and eight," suggested Carleton. "See if that's what you were looking for, Tommy."

Regan thumbed the leaves, found the place and began to read—and a sickly sort of pallor began to spread over his face.

"'You are his sureties that he will renounce the devil and all his works,'" he mumbled weakly.

"Yes," said Carleton cheerfully. "There's some little responsibility there, you see. But don't skip the parenthesis; get it all, Tommy—'until he come of age to take it upon himself.'"

Regan didn't say a word—nor was the smile he essayed an enthusiastic success. He read the "articles" over again word by word, pointing the lines with his pudgy forefinger.

110

"Well," inquired Carleton, "what do you make of the running orders, Tommy?"

"The devil and all his works!"—it came away from Regan now with a rush from his overburdened soul. "D'ye mean to say that—that"—Regan choked a little—"that I'm responsible for that brick-topped, monkey-faced kid?"

"'Until he come of age,'" Carleton amplified pleasantly.

Regan's Celtic temper rose.

"I'll see him hung first!" he roared suddenly. "'Twas no more than to please Maguire that I stood up with the ugly imp! And mabbe I said what's here and mabbe I didn't, but in any event 'tis no more than a matter of form to be repeated parrot-fashion—and it means nothing."

"Oh, well," said the super slyly, "if you feel that way about it, don't let it bother you."

"It will not bother me!" said Regan defiantly, with a scowl.

But it did.

Regan slept that night with an army corps of red-headed, pocked, and freckled-faced little devils to plague his rest—and their name was Noodles. His thoughts were unpleasantly more on Noodles than his razor when he shaved the next morning, and the result was an unsightly gash across his chin—and when he made his first inspection of the roundhouse an hour later he was in a temper to be envied by no man. His irritability was not soothed by the sight of Maguire, who rose suddenly in front of him from an engine pit as he came in.

"Regan," said the old fellow, "about the bhoy—"

"Maguire," said Regan, in a low, fervent voice, "you bother me about that again and I'll fire you, too!"

"Wait, Regan." There was a quaver in the little hostler's voice, and he appeared to stand his ground only by the aid of some previously arrived at, painful resolution that rose superior to his nervousness. "Wait, Regan—mabbe yez'll not have to. I talked ut over wid the missus last night. I've worked well for yez, Regan, all these years—all these years, Regan, I've worked for yez here in the roun'house—an' I've worked well, though ut's mesilf that ses ut."

"That's nothing to do with it," snapped the master mechanic.

"Mabbe ut has, an' mabbe ut hasn't." The watery-blue eyes sought the toes of their owner's grease-smeared, thickly-patched brogans. "I talked ut over wid the missus. Sure now, Regan, yez weren't thinkin' fwhat yez said, an' yez didn't mean fwhat yez said yisterday about raynowncin' the word ye'd passed. Yez'll take ut back, Regan?"

"Take it back? I'll be damned if I do!" said Regan earnestly.

The little hostler's body stiffened, the watery-blue eyes lifted and held steadily on the master mechanic, and for the first time in his lowly life he raised a hand to his superior—Maguire pointed a forefinger, that shook a little, at Regan.

"'Tis blasphymus yez are, Regan!" he said in a thin voice. "An' 'tis no blasphymay I mean, God forbid, fwhen I say yez'll be damned if yez don't. Before a priest, Regan, an' in the church av God, Regan, yez swore fwhat yez swore—an' 'tis the wrath av God, Regan, yez'll bring down on your head. Mind

111

that, Regan! Fire me, is ut?" The little hostler's voice rose suddenly. "All these years I've worked well for yez, Regan, but I'll work no more for a man as 'ud do a thing loike thot—an' the missus ses the same. Poor we may be, but rayspect for oursilves we have. Yez'll niver fire me, Regan—I fire mesilf. I'm through this minute!"

Regan glared disdainfully.

"Have you been drinking, Maguire?" he inquired caustically.

Noodles' father did not answer. He brushed past the master mechanic, walked through the big engine doors, and halted just outside on the cinders.

"'Tis forsworn yez are, Regan," he said heavily. "Yez may make light av ut now, but the day'll come, Regan, fwhen yez'll find out 'tis no light matter. 'Tis the wrath av God, Regan, 'll pay yez for ut, yez can mark my words."

Regan stared after the old man, his eyes puckered, his face a little red; stared after the bent form in the old worn overalls as it picked its way across the tracks—and gave vent to his feelings by expectorating a goodly stream of blackstrap juice savagely into the engine pit at his side. This did not help very much, and for the rest of the morning, while he inwardly anathematized Noodles, Noodles' father and the whole Noodles family collectively, he made things both uncomfortable and lively for those who were unfortunate enough to be within reach of his displeasure.

"The wrath of God!" communed Regan angrily. "I always said Noodles took after his father, both by disposition and looks! It'll be a long time before the old man gets another job—a long time."

And therein Regan was right. It was a long time—quite a long time— measured by the elasticity of the boiler-washer's purse, which wasn't very elastic on the savings from a dollar-sixty a day.

Old Bill Maguire, perhaps, was the only one who hadn't got quite the proper angle on the "rights" he carried—which were worse than those of a mixed local when the rails were humming under a stress of through traffic and the despatchers were biting their nails to the quick trying to take care of it. Not, possibly, that it would have made any difference to the little worn-out hostler if he had; for, whether from principle, having deep-seated awe for the church and its tenets that forbade even a tacit endorsement of what he considered Regan's sacrilege, or because of the public slight put upon his family—the roundhouse hadn't failed to hear his first conversation with Regan, and hadn't failed to let him know that they had—or maybe from a mixture of the two, Maguire was beyond question in deadly earnest. But if old Bill hadn't got his signals right, and was reading green and white when it should have been red, the rest of the Hill Division wasn't by any means color blind; it was pretty generally understood that for several years back all that stood between Maguire and the scrap heap—was Regan. Not on account of any jolly business about godfather or godfathering, but because that was Regan's way—old Bill puttered around the roundhouse on suffrance, thanks to Regan, and didn't know it, though everybody else did, barring patient little Mrs. Maguire and Noodles, who didn't count anyhow.

Nor did the little hostler even now pass the color test. Short-tongued, a hard, grimy lot, just what their rough and ready life made them, they might have been, those railroaders of the Rockies, but their hearts were always right. In the yards, in the trainmaster's office, in the roadmaster's office they pointed Maguire to the quiet times, to the extra crews laid off, to the spare men back to their old ratings, to the section gangs pared down to a minimum, and advised him to ask Regan for his job back again—they never told him he couldn't do a man's work any more.

"Ask Regan!" stuttered the old boiler-washer, and the gray billy-goat beard under his chin, as he threw his head up, stuck out straight like a belligerent chevaux de frise. "Niver! Mind thot, now! Niver—till he takes back fwhat he said—not av I starrve for ut!"

Regan, during the first few days, the brunt of his temper worn off, experienced a certain relief, that was no little relief—he was rid, and well rid, of the Noodles combination. But at the end of about a week, the bluff, big-hearted master mechanic began to suck in his under lip at moments when he was alone, as the stories of old Bill's futile efforts after a job, and old Bill's rather pitiful defiance began to sift in to him. Regan began to have visions of the little three-room shack way up in the waste fields at the end of Main Street. A dollar-sixty a day wasn't much to come and go on, even when the dollar-sixty was coming regularly every pay day—and when it wasn't, the cost of food and rent didn't go down any.

Regan got to thinking a good deal about the faded little old drudge of a woman that was Mrs. Maguire, and the bare floors as he remembered them even in the palmy days of Noodles' birth when he had attended the celebration, bare, but scrubbed to a spotless white. She hadn't been very young then, and not any too strong, and that was twelve years ago. And he got to thinking a good deal about old Bill himself—not much good any more, but good enough for a dollar-sixty a day from a company he'd served for many a long year—in the roundhouse. There had never been over much of what even an optimistic imagination could call luxury in the Maguire's home, and the realization got kind of deep under the worried master mechanic's skin that things were down now to pretty near a case of bread to fill their mouths.

And Regan was right. Even a week had been long enough for that—a man out of a job can't expect credit on the strength of the pay car coming along next month. Things were in pretty straitened circumstances up at the Maguires.

And the more Regan thought, the hotter he got under the collar—at Noodles. Where he had formerly disliked and submitted to Noodles' existence in a passive sort of way, he now hated Noodles in a most earnest and whole-hearted way—and with an unholy desire in his soul to murder Noodles on sight. For, even if Noodles was directly responsible and at the bottom of the pass things had come to, Regan's uncomfortable feeling grew stronger each day that indirectly he had his share in the distress and want that had moved into headquarters up at the top of Main Street. It wasn't a nice feeling or a nice position to be in, and Regan writhed under it—but primarily he cursed Noodles.

There was nothing small about Regan—there never was. He wasn't small enough not to do something. He couldn't very well ask the yardmaster

113

or the section boss to give Maguire a job when he wouldn't give the old man one himself, so he sent word up to Maguire to come back to work—in the roundhouse.

Maguire's answer differed in no whit from the answer he had made to Gleason, the yardmaster, and every one else to whom he had applied for a job—Maguire was in deadly earnest.

"Niver!" said he, to the messenger who bore the olive branch. "Mind thot, now! Niver—till he takes back fwhat he said—not av I starrve for ut!"

Regan swore—and here Regan stuck. Noodles! His gorge rose until he choked. Kill the brat? Yes—murder was in Regan's soul. But to proclaim Noodles as a godson—Noodles as a godson! He had done it once not knowing what he was doing, and to do it now with the years of enlightenment upon him—Regan choked, that was all, and grew apoplectically red in the face. It wasn't the grins and laughs of the Hill Division that he knew were waiting for him if he did—it was just Noodles.

When Regan had calmed down from this explosion, he inevitably, of course, got back to the old perspective—and for another week the Maguire family up Main Street occupied a reserved seat in his mind.

Carleton only spoke to him once about it, and that was along toward the end of the second week, as they were walking uptown together at the dinner hour.

"By the way, Tommy," said the super, "how's Maguire getting along?"

Regan's thoughts having been on the same subject at that moment, he came back a little crossly.

"Blamed if I know!" he growled.

Carleton smiled. Moved by the same motive perhaps, he had gone into the Cash Grocery Store on the corner the day before and found that Maguire's credit was re-established—thanks to Regan—though Timmons, the proprietor, had been sworn to secrecy.

"One of you two will have to capitulate before very long," he said, with a side glance at Regan. "And I don't think it will be Maguire."

"Don't you!" Regan flung out. "You think it will be me?"

"Yes," laughed Carleton.

"When I'm dead," said Regan shortly. "Had any word from those Westinghouse fittings yet? I'm waiting for them now."

"I'll see about them," said Carleton. "I'm going East this afternoon."

And there wasn't any more said about Maguire.

Meanwhile, if Regan's rancor against Noodles had reached a stage that was acute, Noodles had reached a stage of reciprocative hatred that was positively deadly. So far as elemental passion and savagery had developed in twelve years, and Noodles was not a backward boy, just so far had he developed his malevolence against Regan. Things were in a pretty strained condition in the environment of the Maguire shack; Noodles was unhappy all the time, and hungry most of the time. He heard a good deal about Regan and the depths a man could sink to, and enough about the immutable inviolability of church tenets and ordinances to satisfy the most fanatic disciple of orthodoxy—to say nothing of the deep-seated conviction of the wrath of God that must inevitably fall upon one who had the sacrilegious temerity to profane those tenets.

Mostly, Noodles imbibed this at twilight over the sparsely set table, and when the twilight faded and it grew dark—they weren't using kerosene any more at the Maguires—he could still sense the look on his mother's face that mingled anxiety and gentle reproof; and he edged back his chair out of reach of his father's cuffs, which he could dodge in the daylight and couldn't in the dark—for on one point Regan and the old hostler were in perfect accord.

"An' yez are the cause av ut!" old Bill would shout, swinging the flat of his hand in the direction of Noodles' ear every time his violent oratory reached a climacteric height where a period became a physical necessity.

Take it all round, what with the atmosphere of gloom, dodging his father's attentions, his mother's tears when he had caught her crying once or twice, and an unsatisfied stomach, black vengeance oozed from every pore of Noodles' body. His warty little fists clenched, and his unlovely face contorted into a scowl such as Noodles, and only Noodles, thanks to the background that nature had already furnished him to work upon, could scowl.

Noodles set his brains to work. What he must do to Regan must be something awful and bloodcurdling; and, realizing, perhaps, that, being but twelve, he would be handicapped in coping with the master mechanic single-handed, he sought the means of assistance that most logically presented itself to him. Noodles lay awake nights trying to dovetail himself and Regan into the situations of his nickel thrillers. There wasn't any money with which to buy new nickel thrillers, but by then Noodles had accumulated quite a stock, and he knew them all off pretty well by heart, the essentials of them, anyhow.

Noodles racked his brain for a week of nights—and was in despair. Not that the nickel thrillers did not offer situations harrowing enough to glut even his bloodthirsty little soul—they did—they were peaches—he could see Regan's blood all over the bank vault that the master mechanic had been trying to rob—he could see Regan walking the plank of a pirate ship, while the pirates cheered hoarsely—and he fairly revelled in every one of them—until cold despair would clutch again at his raging heart. They were peaches all right, but somehow they wouldn't fit into Big Cloud—he couldn't figure out how to get Regan to rob a bank vault, and there weren't any pirates in the immediate vicinity that he had ever heard of.

Then inspiration came to Noodles one night—and he sat bolt upright in bed. He would shadow Regan! A fierce, unhallowed joy took hold of Noodles. Noodles had grasped the constructive technique of the thriller! Every hero in every nickel thriller shadowed every villain to his doom. Regan's doom at the end was sure to take care of itself once he had found Regan out—but the shadowing came first.

Noodles slept feverishly for the rest of the night, and the following evening he snooped down Main Street and took up his position in a doorway on the opposite side of the street from Regan's boarding house. In just what dire deed of criminal rascality he expected to trap the master mechanic he did not know, but that Regan was capable of anything, and that he would catch him in something, Noodles now had no doubt—that was what the shadowing was for—he grimly determined that he would be unmoved by appeals for mercy—and his heart beat high with optimistic excitement.

Regan came out of the boarding house; and, barefooted in lieu of gum-shoes, and hugging the shadows a block behind—Noodles had refreshed his memory on the most improved methods—Noodles trailed the master mechanic down the street. Two blocks down, Regan halted on the corner and began to peer around him. Noodles' lips thinned suddenly—it began to look promising already—what was Regan up to? A man came down the cross street, joined Regan, and the two started on again toward the station. A little disappointed, Noodles, still hugging the shadows, resumed the chase—it was only Carleton, the superintendent.

From the platform, Noodles watched the two men disappear through the far door of the station. Free from observation now, he hurried along the platform past the station, and was in time to see a lamp lighted upstairs in the side window of the super's office. Noodles waited a moment, then he tiptoed back along the platform, and cautiously pushed open the door through which the others had disappeared. The door of the super's room on the upper story opened on the head of the stairs and, still on tiptoe, Noodles reached the top. Here, on his knees, his eyes glued to the keyhole, he peered into the room—Regan and the super were engaged in their nightly game of cards. There was nothing to raise Noodles' hopes in that, so he descended the stairs and took up his position behind the rain barrel at the corner of the building, where he could watch both the window and the entrance.

At half past ten the light went out, Regan and Carleton came down the stairs and headed uptown. Noodles, not forgetting the shadows, trailed them. At the corner where Carleton had joined Regan, Carleton left Regan, and Regan went on two blocks further and disappeared inside his boarding house. Noodles, being a philosopher of a sort, told himself that none of the heroes ever succeeded the first night—and went home.

The next night, and the three following nights, Noodles shadowed Regan with the same results. By the fifth night, with no single differing detail to enliven this somewhat monotonous and unproductive programme, it had become dispiriting; and though Noodles' thirst for vengeance had not weakened, his faith in the nickel thrillers had.

But on the sixth night—at the end of the second week since Noodles and Noodles' father had turned their backs upon the roundhouse—things were a little different. Noodles, in common with every one else in Big Cloud, was quite well aware that the super's private car had been coupled on No. 12 that afternoon, and that Carleton had gone East.

Regan came out of his boarding house at the same hour as usual, and Noodles dodged along after him down the street—Noodles by this time, for finesse, could have put a combination of Nick Carter and Old Sleuth on the siding until the grass sprouted between the ties. Noodles dodged along—in the shadows. Regan didn't stop at the corner this time, but he kept right along heading down for the station. Regan passed two or three people going in the opposite direction up the street of the sleepy little mountain town, but this did not confuse Noodles—Noodles kept right along after Regan. There was no

Carleton to-night, and Regan's criminal propensities would have full scope—Noodles' hopes ran high.

Regan reached the station, went down the platform, and disappeared as usual through the same door. A little perplexed, Noodles followed along the platform; but, a moment later, from his coign of vantage behind the rain barrel, he saw the light flash out from the super's window—and his heart almost stood still. What was Regan doing in the super's office—alone! Noodles' face grew very white—Carleton had a safe there—he had got Regan at last! It had taken a lot of time, but none of the heroes ever got the villain until after pages and pages of trying to get him. He had got Regan at last!

Noodles crept from the shelter of the rain barrel stealthily as a cat, and, with far more caution than he had ever exercised before, pushed the outside door open and went up the stairs. There wasn't any hurry; he would give Regan time to drill through the safe, and perhaps even let the master mechanic get the money before giving the alarm—Noodles bitterly bemoaned the fact that he would have to give the alarm at all and let anybody else in on it, but, owing to the fact that he had been unable to finance a revolver with which to hold up the master mechanic red-handed and cover himself with glory at the same time, there appeared to be nothing else to do.

It was just a step from the head of the stairs to the door of the super's room across the hall. Noodles negotiated it with infinite circumspection, and, on his knees as usual, his heart pounding like a trip hammer, got his eye to the keyhole. He held it there a very long time, until he couldn't see any more through hot, scalding, impotent tears; then he edged back across the hall, and sat down on the top step—Regan was playing solitaire.

Hands dug disconsolately in his pockets, playing mechanically with a bit of cord that was about their sole contents, Noodles sat there—and his faith in nickel thrillers was shaken to the core. Noodles' thoughts were too complex for coherency—that is, for coherency in any but one of his thoughts—he hated Regan worse than ever, for he couldn't altogether expurgate the nickel thrillers from his mind on such a short notice, and he could hear Regan gloat and hiss "Foiled!" in his ear.

Noodles' hands came out of his pocket—with the cord. He wound one end around the bannisters, and began to see-saw it back and forth aimlessly in the darkness. There wasn't any good of shadowing Regan any more—but he wasn't through with Regan. Noodles had a soul above discouragement. Only what was he to do? If the nickel thrillers had failed him in his hour of need, he would have to depend on himself—only what was he to do? Noodles stopped see-sawing the cord suddenly—and stared at it through the darkness, though he couldn't see it. Then he edged down another step, turned around on his knees, and knotted one end of the cord—it was a good stout one—to one side of the bannisters, about six inches from the level of the hall floor. There was a bannister railing on each side, and he stretched the cord tightly across to the other bannister, and knotted it there. That would do for a beginning! It didn't promise as gory a dénouement as he thirsted for, and he was a little ashamed of the colorlessness of his expedient compared with those he'd read about, but there wasn't anybody else likely to use those stairs before Regan did, and it

117

would do for a beginning—Regan would get a jolt or two before he reached the bottom!

Noodles retreated down the stairs and retired to the rain barrel. Waits had been long there before, but tonight the time dragged hopelessly—he didn't expect to see very much, but he would be able to hear Regan coming down the stairs, so he waited, curbing his impatience by biting anxiously on the ends of his finger nails.

Suddenly Noodles leaned head and shoulders far out from behind the rain barrel to miss no single detail of this, the initial act of his revenge, that he could drink in, his eyes fastened on the station door—the light in the window above had gone out. Very grim was Noodles' face, and his teeth were hard set together—there was no foolishness about this. The super's door upstairs opened and shut—Noodles leaned a little farther forward out from the rain barrel.

Meanwhile, Regan, upstairs, was not in a good humor. Regan, when alone, played a complicated and somewhat intricate species of solitaire, a matter of some pride to the master mechanic, and that evening he had had no luck—his combinations wouldn't work out. So, after something like fifteen abortive attempts that consumed the better part of an hour and a half, and victory still remaining an elusive thing, Regan chucked the cards back into Carleton's drawer in disgust, knocked the ashes out of his pipe, refilled the pipe for company homeward, and, growling a little to himself, blew out the super's lamp. He walked across to the door, opened and shut it, and stepped out into the hall. Here, he halted and produced a match, both because his pipe was as yet unlighted and because the stairs were dark. He struck the match, applied it to the tamped tobacco, puffed once—and his eyes, from the bowl of his pipe, focused suddenly downward on the head of the stairs. Regan's round, fat little face went a color that put the glowing end of the match, still held mechanically over the pipe bowl, to shame, and the fist that wasn't occupied with the match clenched with the wrath that engulfed him—Noodles!

For a moment, breathing heavily with rage, Regan glared at the cord—then the match, burning his fingers, did not soothe him any, and he dropped it hastily, swearing earnestly to himself. Then he bent down, cut away the cord with his knife, and in grim, laborious silence—Regan was a heavy man, and the stairs had a tendency to creak that was hard to suppress—descended step by step. Regan was consumed with but one desire for the present or the hereafter—to get his hands on Noodles.

Where Noodles had been stealthy, Regan was now positively devilish in his caution and cunning. Step by step he went down, testing each foothold much after the fashion of a cat that stretches out its paw, and, finding something not quite to its liking, draws it back, and, shaking it vigorously, tries again more warily—and the while a fire unchenchable burned within him.

He reached the door at the bottom, found the knob, waited an instant—then suddenly flung the door wide open and sprang out on the platform. Noodles' form, projecting eagerly far out from the rain barrel not five yards away, was the first thing his eyes lighted upon. Regan had no time to waste in

118

words. He made a dash for the rain barrel—and Noodles, with a sort of surprised squeak of terror, turned and ran.

A fat man, ordinarily, cannot run very fast, and neither can a twelve-year-old boy; but, with vengeance supplying wings to the one, and terror imparting haste to the other, the time they made from the rain barrel along the platform past the baggage room and freight shed, off the platform to the ground, and up the track to the construction department's storehouse, a matter of a hundred and fifty yards, stands good to-day as a record in Big Cloud. It was pretty near a dead heat. Noodles had five yards' start when he left the rain barrel; and when he reached the end of the storehouse he had five yards' lead—no more. A premonition of disaster began to twine itself around Noodles' heart in a sickly, dispiriting way. He dashed along beside the wall of the building—and after him lunged Regan, grunting like a grampus, a threat in every grunt.

It was a long, low, windowless building, and halfway up its length was the door—Noodles had known the door to be unlocked at nights for the purpose of loading rush material for the bridge gangs in the mountains to go out by the early morning freight west at 4.10—and his hope lay in the door being open now. The place was full to the ceiling with boxes, bales, casks, barrels and kegs, and amongst them in the darkness, being of small dimensions himself, he could soon lose Regan. He reached the door, snatched at the latch—the door was unlocked—and with an uplift immeasurable upon his young soul, that gave vent to itself in a hoot of derision, Noodles flung himself inside.

Regan, still panting earnestly, the beads on his brow now embryonic fountain-heads that sent trickling streams down his face, lurched, pretty well winded, through the door five yards behind Noodles—and then Regan stopped—and the thought of Noodles was swept from Regan's mind in a flash.

The smell of smoke was in his nostrils, and like a white, misty cloud in the darkness it hung around him—and through it, up toward the far end of the shed, a fire showed yellow and ugly, that with a curious, hissing, sibilant sound flared suddenly bright, then died to yellow ugliness again.

Grim-faced now, his jaws clamped hard, Regan sprang forward toward the upper end of the shed. What was afire, he did not know, nor what had caused it—though the latter, probably, by a match dropped maybe hours ago by a careless Polack, that had caught and set something smoldering, and that was now breaking into flame. All Regan knew, all Regan thought of then, was the—powder. There were fifty kegs of giant blasting powder massed together there somewhere ahead, and just beyond where the fire was flinging out its challenge to him—enough to wreck not only the shed, but half the railroad property in Big Cloud as well.

Up the little handcar tracks between the high-piled stores Regan ran—and halted where a spurt of flame, ending in a vicious puff of smoke, shot out beside him, low down on the ground. It was light enough now, and in a glance the master mechanic caught the black grains of powder strewing the floor where a broken keg had been rolled along. A little alleyway had been left here running to the wall, and the fire itself was bursting from a case in the rear and

119

bottom tier of stores on one side of this; on the other side were piled the powder kegs—and the space between, the width of the alleyway, was no more than a bare five or six feet.

There was no time to wait for help, the powder grains crunched under his feet, and ran little zigzag, fizzy lines of fire like a miniature inferno as the sparks caught them; at any moment it might reach the kegs, and then—Regan flung himself along the alleyway to the rear tier of cases, they were small ones here, though piled twice the height of his head—if he could wrench them away, he could get at the burning case below! Regan bent, strained at the cases—they were light and moved—he heaved again to topple them over—and then, as a rasping, ripping sound reached him from above, he let go his hold to jump back—too late. A heavy casting, that had been placed on top of the cases, evidently for economy of space, came hurtling downward, struck Regan on the head, glanced to his shoulder and arm, slid with a thump to the ground—and Regan dropped like a log.

A minute, perhaps two, it had all taken—no more. Noodles, crouched down against a case just inside the door, had seen the master mechanic rush by him; and Noodles, too, had seen the flame and smelt the smoke. Noodles' first impulse was to make his escape, his next to see if he could not turn this unexpected intervention of fate to his own account anent the master mechanic. Noodles heard Regan moving about, and he stole silently in that direction; then Noodles heard the heavy thump of iron, the softer thud of Regan's fall, and something inside him seemed to stop suddenly, and his face went very white. "Mr. Regan! Mr. Regan!" he stammered out. There was no answer—no sound—save an ominous crackle of burning wood.

Noodles stole further forward—and then, as he reached the spot where Regan lay, he stood stock-still for a second, petrified with fear—but the next instant, screaming at the top of his voice for help, he threw himself upon Regan, pounding frantically with the flat of his hands at the master mechanic's shoulder, where the other's coat was beginning to blaze. Somehow, Noodles got this out, and then, still screaming for help, began to drag Regan away from the side of the blazing case.

But Regan was a heavy man—almost too much for Noodles. Noodles, choking with the smoke, his eyes fascinated with horror as they fixed, now on the powder kegs—whose unloading, in company with a dozen other awe-struck boys, he had watched a few days before—now on the sparkling, fizzing grains of powder upon the floor, tugged, and wriggled, and pulled at the master mechanic.

Inch by inch, Noodles won Regan to safety—and then, on his hands and knees, he went back to sweep the grains away from the edge of the kegs. They burnt his hands as he brushed them along the floor, and he moaned with the pain between his screams for aid. It was hot in the narrow place, so narrow that the breath of flame swept his face from the case—but there was still some powder on the floor to brush back out of the way, little heaps of it. Weak, and swaying on his knees, Noodles brushed at it desperately. It seemed to spurt into his face, and he couldn't breathe any more, and he couldn't see, and his head was swirling around queerly. He staggered to his feet as there came a rush of men, and Clarihue, the turner, with the night crew of the roundhouse came racing up the shed.

"Good God, what's this!" cried Clarihue.

"It's—it's a fire," said Noodles, with a sob—and fell into Clarihue's arms.

They told Regan about it the next day when they had got his head patched up and his arm set. Regan didn't say very much as he lay in his bed, but he asked somebody to go to Maguire's and ask old Bill to come down.

And an hour later Maguire entered the room—but he halted a good yard away from the foot of Regan's bed.

"Yez sint for me, Regan," observed the little hostler, in noncommittal, far-away tones.

"I did, Maguire," said Regan diplomatically. "Things haven't been going as smooth as they might have over in the roundhouse since you left, and I want you to come back. What do you say?"

"'Tis not fwhat I say," said Maguire, and he moved no nearer to the bed. "'Tis whether yez unsay fwhat yez said yersilf. Do yez take ut back, Regan?"

"I do," said Regan in grave tones—but his hand reached up to help the bandages hide his grin. "I take it all back, Maguire—every word of it."

"Thot's all right, thin," said the little hostler, not arrogantly, but as one justified. "I'm sorry to see yez are sick, Regan, an' I'm glad to see yez are better—but did I not warn yez, Regan? 'Twas the wrath av God, Regan, thot's the cause av this."

"Mabbe," said Regan softly. "Mabbe—but to my thinking 'twas the devil and all his works."

"Fwhat's thot?" inquired Maguire, bending forward. "I didn't catch fwhat yez said, Regan."

"I said," said Regan, choking a little, "that Noodles is a godson any godfather would be proud to have."

"Sure he is," said Noodles' father cordially. "He is thot."

Chapter VIII

ON THE NIGHT WIRE

Tommy Regan speaks of it yet; so does Carleton; and so, for the matter of that, does the Hill Division generally—and there's a bit of a smile goes with it, too, but the smile comes through as a sort of feeble thing from the grim set of their lips. They remember it—it is one of the things they have never forgotten—Dan McGrew and the Kid, and the night the Circus Special pulled out of Big Cloud with Bull Coussirat and Fatty Hogan in the cab.

Neither the Kid nor McGrew were what you might call born to the Hill Division; neither of them had been brought up with it, so to speak. The Kid came from an Eastern system—and McGrew came from God-knows-where. To pin McGrew down to anything definite or specific in that regard was something just a little beyond the ability of the Hill Division, but it was fairly evident that where railroads were there McGrew had been—he was old enough, anyway—and he knew his business. When McGrew was sober he was a wizard on the key—but McGrew's shame was drink.

McGrew dropped off at Big Cloud one day, casually, from nowhere, and asked for a job despatching. A man in those days out in the new West wasn't expected to carry around his birth certificate in his vest pocket—he made good or he didn't in the clothes he stood in, that was all there was to it. They gave him a job assisting the latest new man on the early morning trick as a sort of test, found that he was better, a long way better than the latest new man, gave him a regular despatcher's trick of his own—and thought they had a treasure.

For a month they were warranted in their belief, for all that McGrew personally appeared to be a rather rough card—and then McGrew cut loose. He went into the Blazing Star Saloon one afternoon—and he left it only when deposited outside on the sidewalk as it closed up at four o'clock on the following morning. This was the hour McGrew was supposed to sit in for his trick at the key; but McGrew was quite oblivious to all such considerations. A freight crew, just in and coming up from the yards, carried him home to his boarding house. McGrew got his powers of locomotion back far enough by late afternoon to reach the Blazing Star again—and the performance was repeated—McGrew went the limit. He ended up with a week in the hands of little Doctor McTurk.

McTurk was scientific from the soles of his feet up, and earnestly professional all the rest of the way. When McGrew began to get a glimmering of intelligence again, McTurk went at him red-headed.

"You're heart's bad," the little doctor flung at McGrew, and there was no fooling in his voice. "So's your liver—cirrhosis. But mostly your heart. You'll try this just once too often—and you'll go out like a collapsed balloon, out like the snuffing of a candle wick."

McGrew blinked at him.

"I've heard that before," said he indifferently.

"Indeed!" snapped the irascible little doctor.

"Yes," said McGrew, "quite a few times. This ain't my maiden trip. You fellows make me tired! I'm a pretty good man yet, ain't I? And I'm likely to be when you're dead. I've got my job to worry about now, and that's enough to worry about. Got any idea of what Carleton's said about it?"

"You keep this up," said McTurk sharply, refusing to sidestep the point, as, bag in hand, he moved toward the door, "and it won't interest you much what Carleton or anybody else says—mark my words, my man."

It was Tommy Regan, fat-paunched, big-hearted, good-natured, who stepped into the breach. There was only one place on this wide earth in Carleton's eyes for a railroad man who drank when he should have been on duty—and that was a six-foot trench, three feet deep. In Carleton's mind, from the moment he heard of it, McGrew was out. But Regan saved McGrew; and the matter was settled, as many a matter had been settled before, over the nightly game of pedro between the superintendent and the master mechanic, upstairs in the super's office over the station. Incidentally, they played pedro because there wasn't anything else to do nights—Big Cloud in those days wasn't boasting a grand-opera house, and the "movies" were still things of the future.

"He's a pretty rough case, I guess; but give him a chance," said Regan.

"A chance!" exclaimed Carleton, with a hard smile. "Give a despatcher who drinks a chance—to send a train-load or two of souls into eternity, and about a hundred thousand dollars' worth of rolling stock to the junk heap while he's boozing over the key!"

"No," said Regan. "A chance—to make good."

Carleton laid down his hand, and stared across the table at the master mechanic.

"Go on, Tommy," he prompted grimly. "What's the answer?"

"Well," said Regan, "he's a past master on the key, we know that—that counts for something. What's the matter with sending him somewhere up the line where he can't get a drink if he goes to blazes for it? It might make a man of him, and save the company a good operator at the same time—we're not long on operators."

"H'm!" observed Carleton, with a wry grin, picking up his cards again one by one. "I suppose you've some such place as Angel Forks, for instance, in mind, Tommy?"

"Yes," said Regan. "I was thinking of Angel Forks."

"I'd rather be fired," submitted Carleton dryly.

"Well," demanded Regan, "what do you say? Can he have it?"

"Oh, yes," agreed Carleton, smiling. "He can have that—after I've talked to him. We're pretty short of operators, as you say. Perhaps it will work out. It will as long as he sticks, I guess—if he'll take it at all."

"He'll take it," said Regan, "and be glad to get it. What do you bid?"

123

McGrew had been at Angel Forks—night man there—for perhaps the matter of a month, when the Kid came to Big Cloud fresh from a key on the Penn. They called him the Kid because he looked it—he wasn't past the stage of where he had to shave more than once a week. The Kid, they dubbed him on the spot, but his name was Charlie Keene; a thin, wiry little chap, with black hair and a bright, snappy, quick look in his eyes and face. He was pretty good on the key, too; not a master like McGrew, he hadn't had the experience, but pretty good for all that—he could "send" with the best of them, and there wasn't much to complain about in his "taking," either.

The day man at Angel Forks didn't drink—at least his way-bill didn't read that way—and they gave him promotion in the shape of a station farther along the line that sized up a little less tomb-like, a little less like a buried-alive sepulcher than Angel Forks did. And the Kid, naturally, being young and new to the system, had to start at the bottom—they sent him up to Angel Forks on the morning way freight the day after he arrived in Big Cloud.

There was something about the Kid that got the train crew of the way freight right from the start. They liked a man a whole lot and pretty sudden in their rough-and-ready way, those railroaders of the Rockies in those days, or they didn't like him well enough to say a good word for him at his funeral; that's the way it went—and the caboose was swearing by the Kid by the time they were halfway to Angel Forks, where he shifted from the caboose to the cab for the rest of the run.

Against the rules—riding in the cab? Well, perhaps it is—if you're not a railroad man. It depends. Who was going to say anything about it? It was Fatty Hogan himself, poking a long-spouted oil can into the entrails of the 428, while the train crew were throwing out tinned biscuits and canned meats and contract pie for the lunch counter at Elk River, who invited him, anyhow.

That's how the Kid came to get acquainted with Hogan, and Hogan's mate, Bull Coussirat, who was handling the shovel end of it. Coussirat was an artist in his way—apart from the shovel—and he started in to guy the Kid. He drew a shuddering picture of the desolation and the general lack of what made life worth living at Angel Forks, which wasn't exaggerated because you couldn't exaggerate Angel Forks much in that particular respect; and he told the Kid about Dan McGrew and how headquarters—it wasn't any secret—had turned Angel Forks into what he called a booze-fighter's sanatorium. But he didn't break through the Kid's optimism or ambition much of any to speak of.

By the time the way freight whistled for Angel Forks, the Kid had Bull Coussirat's seat, and Coussirat was doing the listening, while Hogan was leaning toward them to catch what he could of what was going on over the roar and pound of the 428. There was better pay, and, what counted most, better chances for a man who was willing to work for them out in the West than there was in the East, the Kid told them with a quiet, modest sincerity— and that was why he had come out there. He was looking for a train despatcher's key some day after he had got through station operating, and after that—well, something better still.

There wasn't any jolly business or blowhard about the Kid. He meant what he said—he was going up. And as far as McGrew was concerned, he'd get along with McGrew. McGrew, or any other man, wouldn't hold him back from the goal he had his eyes set upon and his mind made up to work for. There was perhaps a little more of the youthful enthusiasm in it that looked more buoyantly on the future than hard-headed experience would; but it was sincere, and they liked him for it—who wouldn't? Bull Coussirat and Fatty Hogan in the days to come had reason to remember that talk in the cab.

Desolate, perhaps, isn't the word to describe Angel Forks—for Angel Forks was pretty enough, if rugged grandeur is counted pretty. Across the track and siding, facing the two-story wooden structure that was the station, the bare gray rock of a cut through the mountain base reared upward to meet a pine-covered slope, and then blend with bare, gray rock once until it became a glaciered peak at the sky line; behind the station was a sort of plateau, a little valley, green and velvety, bisected by a tumbling, rushing little stream, with the mountains again closing in around it, towering to majestic heights, the sun playing in relief and shadow on the fantastic, irregular, snow-capped summits. It was pretty enough, no one ever disputed that! The road hung four-by-five-foot photographs of it with eight-inch-wide-trimmed-with gilt frames in the big hotel corridors East, and no one who ever bought a ticket on the strength of the photographer's art ever sent in a kick to the advertising department, or asked for their money back—it looked all right from the car windows.

But sign of habitation there was not, apart from the little station—not even a section man's shanty—just the station. Angel Forks was important to the Transcontinental on one count, and on one count only—its siding. Neither freight nor passenger receipts were swelled, twelve months in or twelve months out, by Angel Forks; but, geographically, the train despatcher's office back in Big Cloud never lost sight of it—in the heart of the mountains, single-tracked, mixed trains, locals, way freights, specials, and the Limiteds that knew no "rights" on earth but a clean-swept track with their crazy fast schedules, met and crossed each other as expediency demanded.

So, in a way, after all, perhaps it was desolate—except from the car windows. Horton, the day man that the Kid was relieving, evidently had found it so. He was waiting on the platform with his trunk when the way freight pulled in, and he turned the station over to the Kid without much formality.

"God be with you till we meet again," was about the gist of what Horton said—and he said it with a mixture of sympathy for another's misfortune and an uplift at his own escape from bondage struggling for the mastery, while he waved his hand from the tail of the caboose as the way freight pulled out.

There was mighty little formality about the transfer, and the Kid found himself in charge with almost breathtaking celerity. Angel Forks, Dan McGrew, way freight No. 47, and the man he had relieved, were sort of hazy, nebulous things for a moment. There wasn't time for them to be anything else; for, about one minute after he had jumped to the platform, he was O.S.-ing "out" the train that had brought him in.

It wasn't quite what he had been used to back in the more sedate East, and he grinned a little to himself as his fingers tapped the key, and by the time he had got back his O. K. the tail of the caboose was swinging a curve and disappearing out of sight. The Kid, then, had a chance to look around him—

125

and look for Dan McGrew, the man who was to be his sole companion for the days to come.

He found McGrew upstairs—after he had explored all there was to explore of the ground floor of the station, which was a sort of combination kitchen, living room and dining room that led off from the office—just the two rooms below, with a ladder-like staircase between them leading up above. And above there was just the one room under the eaves with two bunks in it, one on either side. The night man was asleep in one of these, and the Kid did not disturb him. After a glance around the rather cheerless sleeping quarters, he returned downstairs, and started in to pick up the threads of the office.

Dusk comes early in the fall in the mountains, and at five o'clock the switch and semaphore lamps were already lighted, and in the office under a green-shaded lamp the Kid sat listening to some stray time stuff coming over the wire, when he heard the night man moving overhead and presently start down the stairs. The Kid pushed back his chair, rose to his feet, and turned with outstretched hand to make friends with his new mate—and his outstretched hand drew back and reached uncertainly to the table edge beside him.

For a long minute neither man spoke—staring into each other's eyes. In the opening through the partition at the foot of the stairs, Dan McGrew seemed to sway a little on his feet, and his face, what could be seen of it through the tawny beard that Angel Forks had offered him no incentive to shave, was ashen white.

It was McGrew who broke the silence.

"Hello, Charlie!" he said in a sort of cheerful bravado, that rang far from true.

"So you are Dan McGrew! The last time I heard of you your name was Brodie." The Kid's lips, as he spoke, hardly seemed to move.

"I've had a dozen since then," said McGrew, in a pleading whine, "more'n a dozen. I've been chased from place to place, Charlie. I've lived a dog's life, and—"

The Kid cut him short, in a low, passionate voice:

"And you expect me to keep my mouth shut about you here—is that it?"

McGrew's fingers plucked nervously, hesitantly at his beard; his tongue circled dry lips, and his black eyes fell from the Kid to trace aimlessly, it seemed, the cracks in the floor.

The Kid dropped back into his chair, and, elbows on the table, chin in hands, stared out across the tracks to where the side of the rock cut was now no more than a black shadow.

Again it was McGrew who broke the silence.

"What are you going to do?" he asked miserably.

"What are you going to do? Use the key and put them wise? You wouldn't do that, would you—Charlie? You wouldn't throw me down—would you? I'm—I'm living decent here."

The Kid made no answer—made no movement.

"Charlie!" McGrew's voice rose in a high-pitched, nervous appeal. "Charlie—what are you going to do?"

126

"Nothing!" The Kid's eyes were still on the black, rock shadow through the station window, and the words came monotonously. "Nothing! As far as I am concerned, you are—Dan McGrew."

McGrew lurched heavily forward, relief in his face and voice as he put his hands on the Kid's shoulders.

"You're all right, Charlie, all right; I knew you wouldn't—"

The Kid sprang to his feet, and flung the other's hands roughly from his shoulders.

"Keep your hands off me!" he said tensely. "I don't stand for that! And let's understand each other. You do your work here, and I do mine. I don't want to talk to you. I don't want you to talk to me. I don't want anything to do with you—that's as straight as I know how to put it. The first chance I get I'll move—they'll never move you, for I know why they sent you here. That's all, and that's where we stand—McGrew."

"D'ye mean that?" said McGrew, in a cowed, helpless way.

The Kid's answer was only a harsh, bitter laugh—but it was answer enough. McGrew, after a moment's hesitation, turned and went silently from the room.

A week passed, and another week came and went, and neither man spoke to the other. Each lived his life apart, cooked for himself, and did his work; and it was good for neither one. McGrew grew morose and ugly; and the Kid somehow seemed to droop, and there was a pallor in his cheeks and a listless air about him that was far from the cheery optimism with which he had come to take the key at Angel Forks.

Two weeks passed, and then one night, after the Kid had gone to bed, two men pitched a rough, weather-beaten tent on the plateau below the station. Hard-looking specimens they were; unkempt, unshaven, each with a mount and a pack horse. Harvey and Lansing they told McGrew their names were, when they dropped in for a social call that night, and they said that they were prospectors—but their geological hammers were bottles of raw spirit that the Indians loved, and the veins of ore they tapped were the furs that an Indian will sell for "red-eye" when he will sell for no other thing on earth. It was against the law—enough against the law to keep a man's mouth who was engaged in that business pretty tightly shut—but, perhaps recognizing a kindred spirit in McGrew, and warmed by the bottle they had hospitably brought, before that first night was over no secret of that sort lay between them and McGrew.

And so drink came to Angel Forks; and in a supply that was not stinted. It was Harvey and Lansing's stock in trade—and they were well stocked. McGrew bought it from them with cash and with provisions, and played poker with them with a kitty for the "red-eye."

There was nothing riotous about it at first, not bad enough to incapacitate McGrew; and it was a night or two before the Kid knew what was going on, for McGrew was cautious. Harvey and Lansing were away in the mountains during the daytime, and they came late to fraternize with McGrew, around midnight, long after the Kid was asleep. Then McGrew began to tipple steadily, and signs of drink came patently enough—too patently to be

127

ignored one morning when the Kid relieved McGrew and went on for the day trick.

The Kid said nothing, no word had passed between them for two weeks; but that evening, when McGrew in turn went on for his trick, the Kid went upstairs and found a bottle, nearly full, hidden under McGrew's mattress. He took it, went outside with it, smashed it against a rock—and kept on across the plateau to the prospectors' outfit. Harvey and Lansing, evidently just in from a day's lucrative trading, were unsaddling and busy over their pack animals.

"Hello, Keene!" they greeted in chorus; and Lansing added: "Hang 'round a bit an' join in; we're just goin' to cook grub."

The Kid ignored both the salutation and the proffered hospitality.

"I came down here to tell you two fellows something," he said slowly, and there was a grim, earnest set to his lips that was not to be misunderstood. "It's none of my business that you're camping around here, but up there is railroad property, and that is my business. If you show your faces inside the station again or pass out any more booze to McGrew, I'll wire headquarters and have you run in; and somehow, though I've only met you once or twice, I don't fancy you're anxious to touch head-on with the authorities." He looked at the two steadily for an instant, while they stared back half angrily, half sheepishly. "That's fair warning, isn't it?" he ended, as he turned and began to retrace his steps to the station. "You'd better take it—you won't get a second one."

They cursed him when they found their tongues, and did it heartily, interwoven with threats and savage jeers that followed him halfway to the embankment. But their profanity did not cloak the fact that, to a certain extent, the Kid's words were worthy of consideration.

The extent was two nights—that night, and the next one.

On the third night, or rather, far on in the early morning hours, the Kid, upstairs, awakened from sleep, sat suddenly up in his bunk. A wild outburst of drunken song, accompanied by fists banging time on the table, reached him— then an abashed hush, through which the click of the sounder came to him and he read it mechanically—the despatcher at Big Cloud was making a meeting point for two trains at the Bend, forty miles away, nothing to do with Angel Forks. Came then a rough oath—another—and a loud, brawling altercation.

The Kid's lips thinned. He sprang out of his bunk, pulled on shirt and trousers, and went softly down the stairs. They didn't hear him, they were too drunk for that; and they didn't see him—until he was fairly inside the room; and then for a moment they leered at him, suddenly silent, in a silly, owl-like way.

There was an anger upon the Kid, a seething passion, that showed in his bloodless face and quivering lips. He stood for an instant motionless, glancing around the office; the table from the other room had been dragged in; on either side of it sat Harvey and Lansing; at the end, within reach of the key, sat Dan McGrew, swaying tipsily back and forth, cards in hand; under the table was an empty bottle, another had rolled into a corner against the wall; and on the table itself were two more bottles amongst greasy, scattered cards, one almost full, the other still unopened.

"S'all right, Charlie," hiccoughed McGrew blandly. "S'all right—jus' havin' little game—good boy, Charlie."

McGrew's words seemed to break the spell. With a jump the Kid reached him, flung him roughly from his seat, toppling him to the floor, and stretched out his hand for the key—but he never reached it. Harvey and Lansing, remembering the threat, and having more reason to fear the law than on the simple count of trespassing on railroad property, lunged for him simultaneously. Quick as a cat on his feet, the Kid turned, and his fist shot out, driving full into Lansing's face, sending the man staggering backward—but Harvey closed. Purling oaths, Lansing snatched the full bottle, and, as the Kid, locked in Harvey's arms, swung toward him, he brought the bottle down with a crash on the back of the Kid's head—and the Kid slid limply to the floor.

White-faced, motionless, unconscious, the Kid lay there, the blood beginning to trickle from his head, and in a little way it sobered the two "prospectors"—but not McGrew.

"See whash done," said McGrew with a maudlin sob, picking himself up from where the Kid had thrown him. "See whash done! Killed him—thash whash done."

It frightened them, McGrew's words—Harvey and Lansing. They looked again at the Kid and saw no sign of life—and then they looked at each other. The bottle was still in Lansing's hand, and he set it back now on the table with a little shudder.

"We'd better beat it," he croaked hoarsely. "By daylight we want to be far away from here."

Harvey's answer was a practical one—he made for the door and disappeared, Lansing close on his heels.

McGrew alternately cursed and pleaded with them long after they were out of earshot; and then, moved by drunken inspiration, started to clear up the room. He got as far as reaching for the empty bottles on the floor, and that act seemed to father a second inspiration—there were other bottles. He reeled to the table, picked up the one from which they had been drinking, stared at the Kid upon the floor, brushed the hair out of his eyes, and, throwing back his head, drank deeply.

"Jus'er steady myself—feel shaky," he mumbled.

He stared at the Kid again. The Kid was beginning to show signs of returning consciousness. McGrew, blinking, took another drink.

"Nosh dead, after all," said McGrew thickly. "Thank God, nosh dead, after all!"

Then drunken cunning came into his eyes. He slid the full bottle into his pocket, and, carrying the other in his hand, stumbled upstairs, drank again, and hid them craftily, not beneath the mattress this time, but under the eaves where the flooring met and there was a loose plank.

When he stumbled downstairs again, the Kid was sitting in a chair, holding his swimming head in his hands.

"S'all right, Charlie," said McGrew inanely.

The Kid did not look at him; his eyes were fixed upon the table.

"Where are those bottles?" he demanded suspiciously.

"Gone," said McGrew plaintively. "Gone witsh fellows—fellows took 'em an' ran 'way. Whash goin' to do 'bout it, Charlie?"

"I'll tell you when you're sober," said the Kid curtly. "Get up to your bunk and sleep it off."

"S'my trick," said McGrew heavily, waving his hand toward the key. "Can't let nusher fellow do my work."

"Your trick!" The words came in a withering, bitter rush from the Kid. "Your trick! You're in fine shape to hold down a key, aren't you!"

"Whash reason I ain't? Held it down all right, so far," said McGrew, a world of injury in his voice—and it was true; so far he had held it down all right that night, for the very simple reason that Angel Forks had not been the elected meeting point of trains for a matter of some three hours, not since the time when Harvey and Lansing had dropped in and McGrew had been sober.

"Get up to your bunk!" said the Kid between his teeth—and that was all.

McGrew swayed hesitantly for a moment on uncertain legs, blinked suddenly a sort of helpless protest, and, turning, staggered up the stairs.

For a little while the Kid sat in his chair, trying to conquer his dizzy, swimming head; and then the warm blood trickling down his neck—he had not noticed it before—roused him to action. He took the lamp and went into the other room, bathed his head in the wash-basin, sopping at the back of his neck to stop the flow, and finally bandaged it as best he could with a wet cloth as a compress, and a towel drawn tightly over it, which he knotted on his forehead.

He finished McGrew's abortive attempt at housecleaning after that, and sat in to hold down the rest of the night trick, while McGrew in sleep should recover his senses. But McGrew did not sleep. McGrew was fairly started—and McGrew had two bottles at command.

At five-thirty in the morning, No. 81, the local freight, west, making a meeting point, rattled her long string of flats and boxes on the Angel Forks siding; and the Kid, unknotting his bandage, dropped it into a drawer of his desk. Brannahan, No. 81's conductor, kicked the door open, and came in for his orders.

"Hello, Kid!" exclaimed Brannahan. "What you sitting in for? Where's your mate?"

"Asleep," the Kid laughed at him. "Where do you suppose he is! We're swopping tricks for a while for the sake of variety."

Brannahan stooped and lunged the stub of the cigar in his mouth over the lamp chimney, and with the up-draft nearly extinguished the flame; then he pulled up a chair, tilted back and stuck his feet up on the desk.

"Guess most anything would be variety in this Godforsaken hole," he observed between puffs. "What?"

"Oh, it's not so bad—when you get used to it," said the Kid.

He edged his own chair around to face Brannahan squarely—the wound in the back of his head was bleeding again; perhaps it had never stopped bleeding, he did not know.

130

Brannahan made small talk, waiting for the fast freight, east, to cross; and the Kid smiled, while his fingers clutched desperately now and then at the arms of his chair to keep himself from pitching over, as those sickening, giddy waves, like hot and cold flashes, swept him.

Brannahan went at last, the fast freight roared by, No. 81 pulled out, and the Kid went back to the wash-basin and put his bandage on again.

The morning came and went, the afternoon, and the evening; and by evening the Kid was sick and dropping weak. That smash on his head must have been more serious than he had thought at first; for, again and again, and growing more frequent, had come those giddy flashes, and once, he wasn't sure, but it seemed as though he had fainted for a moment or two.

It was getting on to ten o'clock now, and he sat, or, rather, lay forward with his head in his arms over the desk under the lighted lamp. The sounder was clicking busily; the Kid raised his head a little, and listened. There was a Circus Special, west, that night, and No. 2, the eastbound Limited, was an hour off schedule, and, trying to make it up, was running with clear rights while everything else on the train sheet dodged to the sidings to get out of the way. The sounder stopped for an instant, then came the despatcher's "complete"—the Circus Special was to cross the Limited at L'Aramie, the next station west of Angel Forks. It had nothing to do with the Kid, and it would be another two hours at least before the Circus Special was along.

The Kid's head dropped back on his arms again. What was he to do? He could stick out the night somehow—he must stick it out. If he asked for a relief it was the sack for the man upstairs—it was throwing McGrew cold. It wouldn't take them long to find out what was the matter with McGrew! And surely McGrew would be straight again by morning—he wasn't any better now, worse if anything, but by morning surely the worst of the drink would be out of him. McGrew had been pretty bad all day—as bad as the Kid had ever seen a man. He wondered a little numbly about it. He had thought once that McGrew might have had some more drink hidden, and he had searched for it during the forenoon while McGrew watched him from the bunk; but he had found nothing. It was strange, too, the way McGrew was acting, strange that it took so long for the man to get it out of his system, it seemed to the Kid; but the Kid had not found those last two bottles, neither was the Kid up in therapeutics, nor was he the diagnostician that Doctor McTurk was.

"By morning," said the Kid, with the moan, "if he can't stand a trick I'll have to wire. I'm afraid to-night 'll be my limit."

It was still and quiet—not even a breeze to whisper through the cut, or stir the pine-clad slope into rustling murmurs. Almost heavily the silence lay over the little station buried deep in the heart of the mighty range. Only the sounder spoke and chattered—at intervals—spasmodically.

An hour passed, an hour and a half, and the Kid scarcely moved—then he roused himself. It was pretty near time for the Circus Special to be going through to make its meeting point with the Limited at L'Aramie, and he looked at his lights. He could see them, up and down, switch and semaphore, from the bay window of the station where he sat. It was just a glance to assure himself that all was right. He saw the lights through red and black flashes

131

before his eyes, saw that the main line was open as it should be—and dropped his swooning, throbbing head back on his arms once more.

And then suddenly he sat erect. From overhead came the dull, ominous thud of a heavy fall. He rose from his chair—and caught at the table, as the giddiness surged over him and his head swam around. For an instant he hung there swaying, then made his way weakly for the stairs and started up.

There was a light above—he had kept a lamp burning there—but for a moment after he reached the top nothing but those ghastly red and black flashes met his eyes—and then, with a strange, inarticulate cry, he moved toward the side of the room.

Sprawled in a huddled heap upon the floor beneath the eaves, collapsed, out like the snuffing of a candle wick, as Doctor McTurk had said some day he would go out, dead, lay Dan McGrew—the loose plank up, two empty bottles beside him, as though the man had snatched first one and then the other from their hiding place in the wild hope that there might be something left of the supply drained to the last drop hours before.

The Kid stooped over McGrew, straightened up, stared at the lifeless form before him, and his hands went queerly to his temples and the sides of his head—the room spun dizzily around and around, the lamp, the dead man on the floor, the bunks, a red-and-black flashed whirl—the Kid's hands reached grasping into nothingness for support, and he slipped inertly to the floor.

From below came the sharp tattoo of the sounder making the Angel Forks call, quick, imperative at first—then like a knell of doom, in frantic appeal, the despatchers' life and death, the seventeen—and, "Hold Circus Special." Over and over again the sounder spoke and cried and babbled and sobbed like a human soul in agony; over and over again while the minutes passed, and with heavy, resonant roar the long Circus Special rumbled by— but the man on the night wire at Angel Forks was dead; and the Kid was past the hearing—there were to come weeks, while he raved in the furious delirium and lay in the heavy stupor of brain fever, before a key meant anything to him again.

It's queer the way things happen! Call it luck, if you like—maybe it is— maybe it's something more than luck. It wouldn't be sacrilege, would it, to say that the hand of God had something to do with keeping the Circus Special and the Limited from crashing head-on in the rock-walled, twisting cañon, four miles west of Angel Forks, whatever might be the direct means, ridiculous, before-unheard-of, funny, or absurd, that saved a holocaust that night? That wouldn't be sacrilege, would it? Well, call it luck, if you like—call it anything you like. Queer things happen in railroading—but this stands alone, queerest of all in the annals of fifty roads in a history of fifty years.

The Limited, thanks to a clean-swept track, had been making up time, making up enough of it to throw the meeting point with the Circus Special at L'Aramie out—and the despatcher had tried to hold the Circus Special at Angel Forks and let the Limited pass her there. There was time enough to do it, plenty of it—and under ordinary circumstances it would have been all in the night's work. But there was blame, too, and Saxton, who was on the key at Big

Cloud that night, relieving Donkin, who was sick, went on the carpet for it—he let the Limited tear through L'Aramie before he sent his order to Angel Forks, with the Circus Special in the open cutting along for her meeting point with nothing but Angel Forks between her and L'Aramie.

That was the despatcher's end of it—the other end is a little different. Whether some disgruntled employee, seeking to revenge himself on the circus management, loosened the door of one of the cars while the Special lay on the siding waiting for a crossing at Mitre Peak, her last stop, or whether it was purely an accident, no one ever knew—though the betting was pretty heavy on the disgruntled employee theory—there had been trouble the day before. However, be that as it may, one way or the other, one thing was certain, they found the door open after it was all over, and—but, we're over-running our holding orders—we'll get to that in a minute.

Bull Coussirat and Fatty Hogan, in the 428, were pulling the Special that night, and as they shot by the Angel Forks station the fireman was leaning out of the gangway for a breath of air.

"Wonder how the Kid's making out?" he shouted in Hogan's ear, retreating into the cab as they bumped over the west-end siding switch with a shattering racket. "Good kid, that—ain't seen him since the day he came up with us."

Hogan nodded, checking a bit for the curve ahead, mindful of his high-priced, heavily insured live freight.

"Did ever you hear such a forsaken row!" he ejaculated irrelevantly. "Listen to it, Bull. About three runs a year like this and I'd be clawing at iron bars and trying to mimic a menagerie. Listen to it!"

Coussirat listened. Every conceivable kind of an animal on earth seemed to be lifting its voice to High Heaven in earnest protest for some cause or other—the animals, beyond any peradventure of doubt, were displeased with their accommodations, uncomfortable, and indignantly uneasy. The rattle of the train was a paltry thing—over it hyenas laughed, lions roared, elephants trumpeted, and giraffes emitted whatever noises giraffes emit. It was a medley fit for Bedlam, from shrill, whistling, piercing shrieks that set the ear-drums tingling, to hoarse, cavernous bellows like echoing thunder.

"Must be something wrong with the animals," said Coussirat, with an appreciative grin. "They weren't yowling like that when we started—guess they don't like their Pullmans."

"It's enough to give you the creeps," growled Fatty Hogan.

Coussirat reached for the chain, and with an expert flip flung wide the furnace door—and the bright glow lighted up the heavens and shot the black of the cab into leaping, fiery red. Coussirat swung around, reaching for his shovel—and grabbed Hogan's arm instead, as a chorus of unearthly, chattering shrieks rent the air.

"For the love of Mike, for God's sake, Fatty," he gasped, "look at that!"

Perched on the tender, on the top of the water tank, just beyond the edge of the coal, sat a well-developed and complacent ape—and, as Coussirat looked, from the roof of the property car, behind the tender, another swung to join the first.

"Jiminy Christmas!" yelled Hogan, screwed around in his seat. "The whole blasted tribe of monkeys is loose! That's what's wrong with the rest of the animals—the little devils have probably been teasing them through the barred air-holes at the ends of the cars. Look at 'em! Look at 'em come!"

Coussirat was looking—he hadn't stopped looking. Along the roof of the property car they came, a chattering, jabbering, swaying string of them—and on the brake wheel two sat upright, lurching and clinging for dear life, the short hair blown straight back from their foreheads with the sweep of the wind, while they peered with earnest, strained faces into the cab. And the rest, two dozen strong now, massed on the roof of the property car, perilously near the edges for anything but monkeys, inspected the cab critically, picked at each other's hides, made gestures, some of which were decidedly uncomplimentary, and chattered volubly to their leaders already on the tender. The tender seemed to appeal. Down came another monkey via the brake-rod, and swung by its tail with a sort of flying-trapeze effect to the tender—and what one did another did—the accommodation on the water tank was being crowded—the front rank moved up on the coal.

"Say!" bawled Coussirat to his mate. "Say, Fatty, get up and give 'em your seat—there's ladies present. And say, what are we going to do about it? The little pets ought to be put back to bed."

"Do nothing!" snapped Hogan, one wary eye on the monkeys, and the other on the right of way ahead. "If the circus people don't know enough to shut their damned beasts up properly it's their own lookout—it's not our funeral, whatever happens."

The advance guard of the monkeys had approached too close to the crest of the high-piled coal, and as a result, while they scrambled back for firmer footing, they sent a small avalanche of it rolling into the cab. This was touching Coussirat personally—and Coussirat glared.

Coussirat was no nature faker—he knew nothing about animals, their habits, peculiarities, or characteristics. He snatched up a piece of coal, and heaved it at the nearest monkey.

"Get out, you little devil—scut!" he shouted—and missed—and the effect was disconcerting to Coussirat.

Monkeys are essentially imitative, earnestly so—and not over-timid when in force—they imitated Coussirat. Before he could get his breath, first one and then another began to pick up hunks of coal and heave them back—and into the cab poured a rain of missiles. For an instant, a bare instant, Coussirat stood his ground, then he dove for the shelter of his seat. Soft coal? Yes—but there are some fairish lumps even in soft coal.

Crash went the plate-glass face of the steam gauge! It was a good game, a joyous game—and there was plenty of coal, hunks and hunks of it—and plenty of monkeys, "the largest and most intelligent collection on earth," the billboards said.

Crash went the cab glass behind Fatty Hogan's head—and the monkeys shrieked delight. They hopped and jumped and performed gyrations over each other, those in the rear; while those on the firing line, with stern, screwed up, wizened faces, blinking furiously, swung their hairy arms—and into the cab still poured the hail of coal.

With a yell of rage, clasping at his neck where the glass had cut him, Fatty Hogan bounced forward in his seat.

"You double-blanked, blankety-blanked, triple-plated ass!" he bellowed at Coussirat. "You—you damned fool, you!" he screamed. "Didn't you know any better than that! Drive 'em off with the hose—turn the hose on them!"

"Turn it on yourself," said Coussirat sullenly; he was full length on his seat, and mindful that his own glass might go as Hogan's had. "D'ye think I'm looking for glory and a wreath of immortelles?"

Funny? Well, perhaps. Is this sacrilege—to say it wasn't luck?

Crash! There was a hiss of steam, a scalding stream of water, and in a moment the cab was in a white cloud. Mechanically, Hogan slammed his throttle shut, and snatched at the "air." It was the water glass—and the water glass sometimes is a nasty matter. Coussirat was on his feet now like a flash, and both men, clamped-jawed, groped for the cock; and neither got off scathless before they shut it—and by then the train had stopped, and not a monkey was in sight.

Jimmie Burke, the conductor, came running up from the rear end, as Coussirat and Hogan swung out of the gangway to the ground.

"What's wrong?" demanded Burke—he had his watch in his hand.

"Monkeys," said Hogan, and he clipped the word off without any undue cordiality.

"How?" inquired Burke.

"Monkeys," said Hogan—a little more brittle than before.

"Monkeys?" repeated Burke politely.

"Yes, monkeys!" roared Hogan, dancing up and down with the pain of his scalded hands. "Monkeys—that's plain enough, ain't it? Monkeys, blast you!—MONKEYS!"

To the group came one of the circus men.

"The door of the monkey car is open!" he announced breathlessly. "The monkeys have escaped."

"You don't say!" said Coussirat heavily.

"Yes," said the circus man. "And, look here, we'll have to find them; they couldn't have got away from the train until it stopped just now."

"Are they intelligent," inquired Coussirat in a velvet voice, "same as the billboards say?"

"Of course," said the circus man anxiously.

"Well, then, just write them a letter and let them know when to be on hand for the next performance," said Coussirat grimly. "There's lots of time— we can hang around here and stall the line for another hour or two, anyway!"

Burke and Hogan were in earnest consultation.

"We're close on the Limited's time as it is," said Hogan. "And look at that cab."

"We'd better back up to the Forks, then, and let her cross us there, that's the safest thing to do," said Burke—and swung his lamp.

"Look here," said the circus man, "we've got to find those monkeys."

135

Burke looked at him unhappily—monkeys had thrown their meeting point out—and there was the trainmaster to talk to when they got back to Big Cloud.

"Unless you want to spend the night here you'd better climb aboard," he snapped. "All right, Hogan—back away!" And he swung his lamp again.

Ten minutes later, as the Circus Special took the Angel Forks siding and the front-end brakeman was throwing the switch clear again for the main line, a chime whistle came ringing long, imperiously, from the curve ahead. Fatty Hogan's face went white; he was standing up in the cab and close to Coussirat, and he clasped the fireman's arm. "What's that?" he cried.

The answer came with a rush—a headlight cut streaming through the night, there was a tattoo of beating trucks, an eddying roar of wind, a storm of exhausts, a flash of window lights like scintillating diamonds, and the Limited, pounding the fish-plates at sixty miles an hour, was in and out—and gone.

Hogan sank weakly down on his seat, and a bead of sweat spurted from his forehead.

"My God, Bull," he whispered, "do you know what that means? Something's wrong. She's against our order."

They found the Kid and Dan McGrew, and they got the Kid into little Doctor McTurk's hands at Big Cloud—but it was eight weeks and more, while the boy raved and lay in stupor, before they got the story. Then the Kid told it to Carleton in the super's office late one afternoon when he was convalescent—told him the bald, ugly facts in a sort of hopeless way.

Carleton listened gravely; it had come near to being a case of more lives gone out on the Circus Special and the Limited that night than he cared to think about. He listened gravely, and when the Kid had finished, Carleton, in that quiet way of his, put his finger instantly on the crux of the matter—not sharply, but gently, for the Kid had played a man's part, and "Royal" Carleton loved a man.

"Was it worth it, Keene?" he asked. "Why did you try to shield McGrew?"

The Kid was staring hard at the floor.

"He was my father," he said.

Chapter IX

THE OTHER FELLOW'S JOB

There is a page in Hill Division history that belongs to Jimmy Beezer. This is Beezer's story, and it goes back to the days of the building of the long-talked-of, figure-8-canted-over-sideways tunnel on the Devil's Slide, that worst piece of track on the Hill Division, which is to say, the worst piece of track, bar none, on the American continent.

Beezer, speaking generally, was a fitter in the Big Cloud shops; Beezer, in particular, wore a beard. Not that there is anything remarkable in the fact that one should wear a beard, though there are two classes of men who shouldn't—the man who chews tobacco, and the man who tinkers around a railroad shop and on occasions, when major repairs are the order of the day, is intimate with the "nigger-head" of a locomotive. Beezer combined both classes in his person—but with Beezer there were extenuating circumstances. According to Big Cloud, Beezer wore a beard because Mrs. Beezer said so; Mrs. Beezer, in point of size, made about two of Beezer, and Big Cloud said she figured the beard kind of took the cuss off the discrepancy.

Anyway, whether that is so or not, Beezer wore a beard, and the reason it is emphasized here is because you couldn't possibly know Beezer without it. Its upper extremity was nicotine-dyed, in spots, to a nut brown, and from thence shaded down to an indeterminate rust color at its lower edge—when he hadn't been dusting off and doing parlor-maid work with it in the unspeakable grime of a "front-end." In shape it never followed the prevailing tonsorial fashions—as far as any one knew, no barber was ever the richer for Beezer's beard. Beezer used to trim it himself Sunday mornings—sort of half moon effect he always gave it.

He was a spare, short man, all jump and nerves, and active as a cat. He had shrewd, brown, little eyes, but, owing to the fact that he had a small head and wore a large-size, black, greasy peaked cap jammed down as far over his face as it would go, the color of his eyes could hardly be said to matter much, for when you looked at Beezer, Beezer was mostly just a round knob of up-tilted nose—and beard.

Beezer's claims to immortality and fame, such as they are, were vested in disease. Yes; that's it, you've got it right—disease. Beezer had a disease that is very common to mankind in general. There's a whole lot of men like Beezer. Beezer envied the other fellow's job.

Somebody has said that the scarcest thing on earth is hen's teeth, but the man who hasn't some time or other gone green-eyed over the other chap's trick, and confidentially complained to himself that he could "sit in" and hold it down a hanged sight better himself, has the scarcity-of-hen's-teeth-oracle nailed to the mast from the start. And a curious thing about it is that the less one knows of what the men he envies is up against the more he envies—and the better he thinks he could swing the other's job himself. There's a whole lot like Beezer.

Now Beezer was an almighty good fitter. Tommy Regan said so, and Regan ought to know; that's why he took Beezer out of the shops where the other had grown up, so to speak, and gave Beezer the roundhouse repair work to do. And that's where Beezer caught the disease—in the roundhouse. Beezer contracted a mild attack of it the first day, but it wasn't bad enough to trouble him much, or see a doctor about, so he let it go on—and it got chronic.

Beezer commenced to inhale an entirely different atmosphere, and the more he inhaled it the more discontented he grew. An engine out in the roundhouse, warm and full of life, the steam whispering and purring at her valves, was a very different thing from a cold, rusty, dismantled boiler-shell jacked up on lumbering blocks in the erecting shop; and the road talk of specials, holding orders, tissues, running time and what-not had a much more appealing ring to it than discussing how many inches of muck No. 414 had accumulated on her guard-plates, the incidental damning of the species wiper, and whether her boxes wanted new babbitting or not. Toiling like a slave ten hours a day for six days a week, and maybe overtime on Sundays, so that the other fellow could have the fun, and the glory, and the fatter pay check, and the easy time of it, began to get Beezer's goat. The "other fellow" was the engineer.

Beezer got to contrasting up the two jobs, and the more he contrasted the less he liked the looks of his own, and the more he was satisfied of his superior ability to hold down the other over any one of the crowd that signed on or off in the grease-smeared pages of the turner's book, which recorded the comings and goings of the engine crews. And his ability, according to Beezer's way of looking at it, wasn't all swelled head either; for there wasn't a bolt or a split-pin in any type of engine that had ever nosed its pilot on the Hill Division that he couldn't have put his finger on with his eyes shut. How much, anyhow, did an engineer know about an engine? There wasn't a fitter in the shops that didn't have the best engineer that ever pulled a throttle pinned down with his shoulders flat on the mat on that count—and there wasn't an engineer but what would admit it, either.

But a routine in which one is brought up, gets married in, and comes to look upon as a sort of fixed quantity for life, isn't to be departed from offhand, and at a moment's notice. Beezer grew ardent with envy, it is true; but the idea of actually switching over from the workbench to the cab didn't strike him for some time. When it did—the first time—it took his breath away—literally. He was in the pit, and he stood up suddenly—and the staybolts on the rocker-arm held, and Beezer promptly sat down from a wallop on the head that would have distracted the thoughts of any other man than Beezer.

Engineer Beezer! He had to lift the peak of his cap to dig the tears out of his eyes, but when he put it back again the peak was just a trifle farther up his nose. Engineer Beezer—a limited run—the Imperial Flyer—into division on the dot, hanging like a lord of creation from the cab window—cutting the miles on the grades and levels like a swallow—roaring over trestles—diving through tunnels—there was excitement in that, something that made life worth living, instead of everlastingly messing around with a hammer and a cold chisel, and pulling himself thin at the hips on the end of a long-handled union wrench. Day dreams? Well, everybody day-dreams, don't they? Why not Beezer?

It is not on record that any one ever metamorphosed himself into a drunkard on the spot the first time he ever stepped up to a bar; but as the Irishman said: "Kape yer foot on the rail, an' yez have the makin's av a dombed foine bum in yez!"

Of course, the thing wasn't feasible. It sounded all right, and was mighty alluring, but it was all dream. Beezer put it from him with an unctuous, get-thee-behind-me-Satan air, but he purloined a book of "rules"— road rules—out of Pudgy MacAllister's seat in the cab of the 1016. He read up the rules at odd moments, and moments that weren't odd—and gradually the peak of his cap crept up as far as the bridge of his nose. Beezer was keeping his foot on the rail.

Mrs. Beezer found the book. That's what probably started things along toward a showdown. She was, as has been said, a very large woman; also she was a very capable woman of whom Beezer generally stood in some awe, who washed, and ironed, and cooked for the Beezer brood during the day, and did overtime at nights on socks and multifarious sewing, including patches on Beezer's overalls—and other things, which are unmentionable. The book fell out of the pocket of one of the other things, one evening. Mrs. Beezer examined it, discovered MacAllister's name scrawled on it, and leaned across the table under the paper-shaded lamp in their modest combination sitting and dining room.

"What are you doing with this, Mr. Beezer?" she inquired peremptorily; Mrs. Beezer was always peremptory—with Beezer.

Beezer coughed behind his copy of the Big Cloud Daily Sentinel.

"Well?" prompted Mrs. Beezer.

"I brought it home for the children to read," said Beezer, who, being uncomfortable, sought refuge in the facetious.

"Mr. Beezer," said Mrs. Beezer, with some asperity, "you put down that paper and look at me."

Mr. Beezer obeyed a little doubtfully.

"Now," continued Mrs. Beezer, "what's got into you since you went into the roundhouse, I don't know; but I've sorter had suspicions, and this book looks like 'em. You might just as well make a clean breast of what's on your mind, because I'm going to know."

Beezer looked at his wife and scowled. He felt what might be imagined to be somewhat the feelings of a man who is caught sneaking in by the side entrance after signing the pledge at a Blue Ribbon rally. It was not a situation conducive to good humor.

"There ain't anything got into me," said he truculently. "If you want to know what I'm doing with that book, I'm reading it because I'm interested in it. And I've come to the conclusion that a fitter's job alongside of an engineer's ain't any better than a mud-picking Polack's."

139

"You should have found that out before you went into the shops ten years ago," said Mrs. Beezer, with a sweetness that tasted like vinegar.

"Ten years ago!" Beezer flared. "How's a fellow to know what he's cut out for, and what he can do best, when he starts in? How's he to know, Mrs. Beezer, will you tell me that?"

Mrs. Beezer was not sympathetic.

"I don't know how he's to know," she said, "but I know that the trouble with some men is that they don't know when they're well off, and if you're thinking of—"

"I ain't," said Beezer sharply.

"I said 'if,' Mr. Beezer; and if—"

"There's no 'if' about it," Beezer lied fiercely. "I'm not—"

"You are," declared Mrs. Beezer emphatically, but with some wreckage of English due to exceeding her speed permit—Mrs. Beezer talked fast. "When you act like that I know you are, and I know you better than you do yourself, and I'm not going to let you make a fool of yourself, and come home here dead some night and wake me up same as poor Mrs. Dalheen got her man back week before last on a box car door. Don't you know when you're well off? You an engineer! What kind of an engineer do you think you'd make? Why—"

"Mrs. Beezer," said Beezer hoarsely, "shut up!"

Mrs. Beezer caught her breath.

"What did you say?" she gasped.

"I said," said Beezer sullenly, picking up his paper again, "that I'd never have thought of it, if you hadn't put it into my head; and now the more I think of it, the better it looks."

"I thought so," sniffed Mrs. Beezer profoundly. "And now, Mr. Beezer, let this be the last of it. The idea! I never heard of such a thing!"

Curiously enough, or perhaps naturally enough, Mrs. Beezer's cold-water attitude had precisely the opposite effect on Jimmy Beezer to that which she had intended it should have. It was the side-entrance proposition over again. When you've been caught sneaking in that way, you might just as well use the front door on Main Street next time, and have done with it. Beezer began to do a little talking around the roundhouse. The engine crews, by the time they tumbled to the fact that it wasn't just the ordinary grumble that any man is entitled to in his day's work, stuck their tongues in their cheeks, winked surreptitiously at each other—and encouraged him.

Now it is not to be implied that Jimmy Beezer was anybody's fool—not for a minute—a first-class master fitter with his time served is a long way from being in that class right on the face of it. Beezer might have been a little blinded to the tongues and winks on account of his own earnestness; perhaps he was—for a time. Afterwards—but just a minute, or we'll be running by a meeting point, which is mighty bad railroading.

Beezer's cap, when he took the plunge and tackled Regan, had got tilted pretty far back, so far that the peak stood off his forehead at about the same rakish angle that his upturned little round knob of a nose stuck up out of his beard; which is to say that Beezer had got to the stage where he had decided that the professional swing through the gangway he had been practising every

140

time, and some others, that he had occasion to get into a cab, was going to be of some practical use at an early date.

He put it up to Regan one morning when the master mechanic came into the roundhouse.

Regan leaned his fat little body up against the jamb of one of the big engine doors, pulled at his scraggly brown mustache, and blinked as he listened.

"What's the matter with you, Beezer, h'm?" he inquired perplexedly, when the other was at an end.

"Haven't I just told you?" said Beezer. "I want to quit fitting and get running."

"Talks as though he meant it," commented Regan sotto voce to himself, as he peered earnestly into the fitter's face.

"Of course, I mean it," declared Beezer, a little tartly. "Why wouldn't I?"

"No," said Regan; "that ain't the question. The question is, why would you? H'm?"

"Because," Beezer answered promptly, "I like a snap as well as the next man. It's a better job than the one I've got, better money, better hours, easier all around, and one I can hold down with the best of them."

Regan's eyebrows went up.

"Think so?" he remarked casually.

"I do," declared Beezer.

"Well, then," said Regan, "if you've thought it all out and made up your mind, there's nothing I know of to stop you. Want to begin right away?"

"I do," said Beezer again. It was coming easier than he had expected—there was a jubilant trill in his voice.

"All right," said Regan. "I'll speak to Clarihue about it. You can start in wiping in the morning."

"Wiping?" echoed Beezer faintly.

"Sure," said Regan. "That's what you wanted, wasn't it? Wiping—a dollar-ten a day."

"Look here," said Beezer with a gulp; "I ain't joking about this."

"Well, then, what are you kicking about?" demanded Regan.

"About wiping and a dollar-ten," said Beezer. "What would I do with a dollar-ten, me with a wife and three kids?"

"I don't know what you'd do with it," returned Regan. "What do you expect?"

"I don't expect to start in wiping," said Beezer, beginning to get a little hot.

"You've been here long enough to know the way up," said Regan. "Wiping, firing—you take your turn. And your turn'll come for an engine according to the way things are shaping up now in, say, about fifteen years."

"Fifteen years!"

"Mabbe," grinned Regan. "I can't promise to kill off anybody to accommodate you, can I?"

"And don't the ten years I've put in here count for anything?" queried Beezer aggressively. "Why don't you start me in sweeping up the roundhouse?

Wiping! Wiping, my eye! What for? I know all about the way up. That's all right for a man starting in green; but I ain't green. Why, there ain't a year-old apprentice over in the shops there that don't know more about an engine than any blooming engineer on the division. You know that, Regan—you know it hanged well, don't you?"

"Well," admitted the master mechanic, "you're not far wrong at that, Beezer."

"You bet, I'm not!" Beezer was emphatic. "How about me, then? Do I know an engine, every last nut and bolt in her, or don't I?"

"You do," said Regan. "And if it's any satisfaction to you to know it, I wouldn't ask for a better fitter any time than yourself."

"Then, what's the use of talking about wiping? If I've put in ten years learning the last kink there is in an engine, and have forgotten more than the best man of the engine crews 'll know when he dies, what's the reason I ain't competent to run one?"

Regan reached into his back pocket for his chewing, wriggled his head till his teeth met in the plug, and tucked the tobacco back into his pocket again.

"Beezer," said he slowly, spitting out an undesirable piece of stalk, "did it ever strike you that there's a whole lot of blamed good horse doctors that'd make damn poor jockeys—h'm?"

Beezer scowled deeply, and kicked at a piece of waste with the toe of his boot.

"All I want is a chance," he growled shortly. "Give me a chance, and I'll show you."

"You can have your chance," said Regan. "I've told you that."

"Yes," said Beezer bitterly. "It's a hell of a chance, ain't it? A dollar-ten a day—wiping! I'd be willing to go on firing for a spell."

"Wiping," said Regan with finality, as he turned away and started toward the shops; "but you'd better chew it over again, Beezer, and have a talk with your wife before you make up your mind."

Somebody chuckled behind Beezer—and Beezer whirled like a shot. The only man in sight was Pudgy MacAllister. Pudgy's back was turned, and he was leaning over the main-rod poking assiduously into the internals of the 1016 with a long-spouted oil can; but Beezer caught the suspicious rise and fall of the overall straps over the shoulders of the fat man's jumper.

Beezer was only human. It got Beezer on the raw—which was already pretty sore. The red flared into his face hard enough to make every individual hair in his beard incandescent; he walked over to Pudgy, yanked Pudgy out into the open, and shoved his face into the engineer's.

"What in the double-blanked, blankety-blanked blazes are you grinning at?" he inquired earnestly.

"H'm?" said Pudgy.

"Yes—h'm!" said Beezer eloquently. "That's what I'm asking you."

Whether Pudgy MacAllister was just plain lion-hearted, or a rotten bad judge of human nature isn't down on the minutes—all that shows is that he was one or the other. With some labor and exaggerated patience, he tugged a

142

paper-covered pamphlet out of his pocket from under his jumper. It was the book of rules Beezer had "borrowed" some time before.

"Mrs. Beezer," said Pudgy blandly, "was over visiting the missus this morning, and she brought this back. From what she said I dunno as it would do any good, but I thought, perhaps, if you were going to take Regan's advice about talking to your wife, you and Mrs. Beezer might like to look it over again together before you—"

That was as far as Pudgy MacAllister got. Generally speaking, the more steam there is to the square inch buckled down under the valve, the shriller the whistle is when it breaks loose. Beezer let a noise out of him that sounded like a green parrot complaining of indigestion, and went at MacAllister head-on.

The oil can sailed through the air and crashed into the window glass of Clarihue's cubby-hole in the corner. There was a tangled and revolving chaos of arms and legs, and lean and fat bodies. Then a thud. There wasn't any professional ring work about it. They landed on the floor and began to roll—and a pail of packing and black oil they knocked over greased the way.

There was some racket about it, and Regan heard it; so did Clarihue, and MacAllister's fireman, and another engine crew or two, and a couple of wipers. The rush reached the combatants when there wasn't more than a scant thirty-second of an inch between them and the edge of an empty pit—but a thirty-second is a whole lot sometimes.

When they stood them up and got them uncoupled, MacAllister's black eye was modestly toned down with a generous share of what had been in the packing bucket, but his fist still clutched a handful of hair that he had separated from Beezer's beard—and Beezer's eyes were running like hydrants from the barbering. Take it all around, thanks mostly to the packing bucket, they were a fancy enough looking pair to send a high-class team of professional comedians streaking for the sidings all along the right of way to get out of their road.

It doesn't take very much, after all, to make trouble, not very much; and, once started, it's worse than the measles—the way it spreads.

Mostly, they guyed Pudgy MacAllister at first; they liked his make-up better owing to the black eye. But Pudgy was both generous and modest; what applause there was coming from the audience he wanted Beezer to get—he wasn't playing the "lead."

And Beezer got it. Pudgy opened up a bit, and maybe drew on his imagination a bit about what Mrs. Beezer had said to Mrs. MacAllister about Jimmy Beezer, and what Beezer had said to Regan, and Regan to Beezer, not forgetting Regan's remark about the horse doctor.

Oh, yes, trouble once started makes the measles look as though it were out of training, and couldn't stand the first round. To go into details would take more space than a treatise on the manners and customs of the early Moabites; but, summed up, it was something like this: Mrs. Beezer paid another visit to Mrs. MacAllister, magnanimously ignoring the social obligation Mrs. MacAllister was under to repay the former call. Mrs. MacAllister received Mrs. Beezer in the kitchen over the washtubs, which was

143

just as well for the sake of the rest of the house, for when Mrs. Beezer withdrew, somewhat shattered, but in good order, by a flank movement through the back yard, an impartial observer would have said that the kitchen had been wrecked by a gas explosion. This brought Big Cloud's one lawyer and the Justice of the Peace into it, and cost Beezer everything but the odd change on his month's pay check—when it came.

Meanwhile, what with a disturbed condition of marital bliss at home, Beezer caught it right and left from the train crews, engine crews and shop hands during the daytime. They hadn't anything against Beezer, not for a minute, but give a railroad crowd an opening, and there's no aggregation on earth quicker on the jump to take it. They dubbed him "Engineer" Beezer, and "Doctor" Beezer; but mostly "Doctor" Beezer—out of compliment to Regan. And old Grumpy, the timekeeper in the shop, got so used to hearing it that he absent-mindedly wrote it down "Doctor Beezer" when he came to make up the pay roll. That put it up to Carleton, the super, who got a curt letter from the auditors' office down East, asking for particulars, and calling his attention to the fact that all medical services were performed by contract with the company. Carleton scowled perplexedly at the letter, scrawled Tommy Regan's initials at the bottom of the sheet, plus an interrogation mark, and put it in the master mechanic's basket. Regan grinned, and wrote East, telling them facetiously to scratch out the "Doctor" and squeeze in a "J" in front of the "Beezer" and it would be all right; but it didn't go—you can't get by a high-browed set of red-tape-bound expert accountants of unimpeachable integrity, who are safeguarding the company's funds like that. Hardly! They held out the money, and by the time the matter was straightened out the pay car had come and gone, and Beezer got a chance to find out how good his credit was. Considering everything, Beezer took it pretty well—he went around as though he had boils.

But if Beezer had a grouch, and cause for one, it didn't make the other fellow's job look any the less good to Beezer. Mrs. Beezer's sharp tongue, barbed with contemptuous innuendo that quite often developed into pointed directness as to her opinion of his opinions, and the kind of an engineer he'd make, which he was obliged to listen to at night, and the men—who didn't know what an innuendo was—that he was obliged to listen to by day, didn't alter Beezer's views on that subject any, whatever else it might have done. Beezer had a streak of stubbornness running through the boils.

He never got to blows again. His tormentors took care of that. They had MacAllister as an example that Beezer was not averse to bringing matters to an intimate issue at any time, and what they had to say they said at a safe distance—most of them could run faster than Beezer could, because nature had made Beezer short. Beezer got to be a pretty good shot with a two-inch washer or a one-inch nut, and he got to carrying around a supply of ammunition in the hip pocket of his overalls.

As for MacAllister, when the two ran foul of each other, as the engineer came on for his runs or signed off at the end of one, there wasn't any talking done. Regan had warned them a little too hard to take chances. They just looked at each other sour enough to turn a whole milk dairy. The men told

Beezer that MacAllister had rigged a punching bag up in his back yard, and was taking a correspondence course in pugilism.

Beezer said curried words.

"Driving an engine," said they, "is a dog's life; it's worse than pick-slinging, there's nothing in it. Why don't you cut it out? You've had enough experience to get a job in the shops. Why don't you hit Regan up and change over?"

"By Christmas!" Beezer would roar, while he emptied his pocket and gave vent to mixed metaphor, "I'd show you a change over if I ever got a chance; and I'd show you there was something to running an engine besides bouncing up and down on the seat like balls with nothing but wind in them, and grinning at the scenery!"

A chance—that's all Beezer asked for—a chance. And he kept on asking Regan. That dollar-ten a day looked worse than ever since Mrs. Beezer's invasion of Mrs. MacAllister's kitchen. But Regan was obdurate, and likewise was beginning to get his usually complacent outlook on life—all men with a paunch have a complacent, serene outlook on life as a compensation for the paunch—disturbed a little. Beezer and his demands were becoming ubiquitous. Regan was getting decidedly on edge.

"Firing," said Beezer. "Let me start in firing—there's as much in that as in fitting, and I can get along for the little while it'll be before you'll be down on your knees begging me to take a throttle."

"Firing, eh!" Regan finally exploded one day. "Look here, Beezer; I've heard about enough from you. Firing, eh? There'd have been some firing done before this that would have surprised you if you hadn't been a family man! Get that? The trouble with you is that you don't know what you want or what you're talking about."

"I know what I want, and I know what I'm talking about," Beezer answered doggedly; "and I'm going to keep on putting it up to you till you quit saying 'No.'"

"You'll be doing it a long time, then," said Regan bluntly, laying a few inches of engine dust with blackstrap juice; "a long time, Beezer—till I'm dead."

But it wasn't. Regan was wrong about that, dead wrong. It's unexplainable the way things work out sometimes!

That afternoon, after a visit from Harvey, who had been promoted from division engineer to resident and assistant-chief on the Devil's Slide tunnel, Carleton sent for Regan.

"Tommy," said he, as the master mechanic entered his office, "did you see Harvey?"

"No," said Regan. "I didn't know he was in town."

"He said he didn't think he'd have time to see you," said Carleton; "I guess he's gone back on Number Seven. But I told him I'd put it up to you, anyway. He says he's along now where he is handling about half a dozen dump trains, but that what he has been given to pull them with, as near as he can figure out, is the prehistoric junk of the iron age."

"I saw the engines when they went through," Regan chuckled. "All the master mechanics on the system cleaned up on him. I sent him the old Two-twenty-three myself. Harvey's telling the truth so far. What's next?"

"Well," Carleton smiled, "he says the string and tin rivets they're put together with come off so fast he can't keep more than half of them in commission at once. He wants a good fitter sent up there on a permanent job. What do you say?"

"Say?" Regan fairly shouted. "Why, I say, God bless that man!"

"H'm?" inquired Carleton.

"Beezer," said Regan breathlessly. "Tell him he can have Beezer—wire him I'll send up Beezer. He wants a good fitter, does he? Well, Beezer's the best fitter on the pay roll, and that's straight. I always liked Harvey—glad to do him a good turn—Harvey gets the best."

Carleton crammed the dottle down in the bowl of his pipe with his forefinger, and looked at Regan quizzically.

"I've heard something about it," said he. "What's the matter with Beezer?"

"Packing loose around his dome cover, and the steam spurts out through the cracked joint all over you every time you go near him," said Regan. "He's had me crazy for a month. He's got it into his nut that he could beat any engineer on the division at his own game, thinks the game's a cinch and is sour on his own. That's about all—but it's enough. Say, you wire Harvey that I'll send him Beezer."

Carleton grinned.

"Suppose Beezer doesn't want to go?" he suggested.

"He'll go," said Regan grimly. "According to the neighbors, his home life at present ain't a perennial dream of delight, and he'll beat it as joyful as a live fly yanked off the sheet of fly paper it's been stuck on; besides, he's getting to be a regular spitfire around the yards. You leave it to me—he'll go."

And Beezer went.

You know the Devil's Slide. Everybody knows it; and everybody has seen it scores of times, even if they've never been within a thousand miles of the Rockies—the road carried it for years on the back covers of the magazines printed in colors. The Transcontinental's publicity man was a live one, he played it up hard, and as a bit of scenic effect it was worth all he put into it—there was nothing on the continent to touch it. But what's the use?—you've seen it hundreds of times. Big letters on top:

"INCOMPARABLE GRANDEUR OF THE ROCKIES", and underneath: "A SCENE ON THE LINE OF THE TRANSCONTINENTAL—THE COAST TO COAST ROUTE."

There wasn't anything the matter with the electrotypes, either—nature backed up those "ads" to the last detail, and threw in a whole lot more for good measure—even a pessimist didn't hold a good enough hand to call the raise and had to drop out. Pugsley, the advertising man, was an awful liar, and what he said may not be strictly true, but he claimed the road paid their dividends for one quarter through the sale to a junk and paper-dealer of the

146

letters they got from delighted tourists telling how far short anything he could say came to being up to the reality. Anyway, Pugsley and the passenger-agent's department were the only ones who weren't enthusiastic about the double-loop tunnel—it spoiled the scenic effect.

This is Beezer's story. Beezer has "rights" through to the terminal, and pictures of scenery however interesting, and a description of how Harvey bored his holes into the mountain sides however instructive, should naturally be relegated to the sidings; but there's just a word or two necessary before Beezer pulls out into the clear.

One thing the electrotypes didn't show was the approach to the Devil's Slide. It came along the bottoms fairly straight and level, the track did, for some five miles from the Bend, until about a mile from the summit where it hit a long, stiff, heavy climb, that took the breath out of the best-type engine that Regan, representing the motive-power department, had to offer. And here, the last few hundred yards were taken with long-interval, snorting roars from the exhaust, that echoed up and down the valley, and back and forward from the hills like a thousand thunders, or the play of a park of artillery, and the pace was a crawl—you could get out and walk if you wanted to. That was the approach of the Devil's Slide—on a westbound run, you understand? Then, once over the summit, the Devil's Slide stretched out ahead, and in its two reeling, drunken, zigzag miles dropped from where it made you dizzy to lean out of the cab window and see the Glacier River swirling below, to where the right of way in a friendly, intimate fashion hugged the Glacier again at its own bed level. How much of a drop in that two miles? Grade percentages and dry figures don't mean very much, do they? Take it another way. It dropped so hard and fast that that's what the directors were spending three million dollars for—to divide that drop by two! It just dropped—not an incline, not by any means—just a drop. However—

When it was all over the cause of it figured out something like this— we'll get to the effect and Beezer in a second. Engine 1016 with Number One, the Imperial Limited, westbound, and with MacAllister in the cab, blew out a staybolt one afternoon about two miles west of the Bend. And quicker than you could wink, the cab was all live steam and boiling water. The fireman screamed and jumped. MacAllister, blinded and scalded, his hands literally torn from the throttle and "air" before he could latch in, fell back half unconscious to the floor, wriggled to the gangway and flung himself out. He sobbed like a broken-hearted child afterwards when he told his story.

"I left her," he said. "I couldn't help it. The agony wasn't human—I couldn't stand it. I was already past knowing what I was doing; but the thought went through my mind that the pressure'd be down, and she'd stop herself before she got up the mile climb to the summit. That's the last I remember."

Dave Kinlock, the conductor, testified that he hadn't noticed anything wrong until after they were over the summit—they'd come along the bottoms at a stiff clip, as they always did, to get a start up the long grade. They had slackened up almost to a standstill, as usual, when they topped the summit; then they commenced to go down the Slide, and were speeding up before he realized it. He put on the emergency brakes then, but they wouldn't work. Why? It was never explained. Whether the angle-cock had never been properly thrown into its socket and had worked loose and shut off the "air" from the coaches, or whether—and queerer things than that have happened in railroading—it just plain went wrong, no one ever knew. They found the trouble there, that was all. The emergency wouldn't work; and that was all that Dave Kinlock knew then.

Now, Beezer had been out on the construction work about two weeks when this happened, about two of the busiest weeks Beezer had ever put in in his life. Harvey hadn't drawn the long bow any in describing what the master mechanics had put over on him to haul his dump carts with. They were engines of the vintage of James Watt, and Beezer's task in keeping them within the semblance of even a very low coefficient of efficiency was no sinecure. Harvey had six of these monstrosities, and, as he had started his work at both ends at once, with a cutting at the eastern base of the Devil's Slide and another at the summit, he divided them up three to each camp; and it kept Beezer about as busy as a one-handed paper-hanger with the hives, running up and down answering "first-aid" hurry calls from first one and then the other.

The way Beezer negotiated his mileage was simple. He'd swing the cab or pilot of the first train along in the direction, up or down, that he wanted to go—and that's how he happened to be standing that afternoon on the track opposite the upper construction camp about a hundred yards below the summit, when Number One climbed up the approach, poked her nose over the top of the grade, crawling like a snail that's worn out with exertion, and then began to gather speed a little, toboggan-like, as she started down the Devil's Slide toward him.

Beezer gave a look at her and rubbed his eyes. There wasn't anything to be seen back of the oncoming big mountain racer's cab but a swirling, white, vapory cloud. It was breezing pretty stiff through the hills that day, and his first thought was that she was blowing from a full head, and the wind was playing tricks with the escaping steam. With the next look he gulped hard—the steam was coming from the cab—not the dome. It was the 1016, MacAllister's engine, and when he happened to go up or down on her he always chose the pilot instead of the cab—Beezer never forced his society on any man. But this time he let the pilot go by him—there was something wrong, and badly wrong at that. The cab glass showed all misty white inside, and there was no sign of MacAllister. The drivers were spinning, and the exhaust, indicating a wide-flung throttle, was quickening into a rattle of sharp, resonant barks as the cab came abreast of him.

Beezer jumped for the gangway, caught the rail with one hand, clung there an instant, and then the tools in his other hand dropped to the ground, as, with a choking gasp, he covered his face, and fell back to the ground himself.

By the time he got his wits about him again the tender had gone by. Then Beezer started to run, and his face was as white as the steam he had stuck his head into in the empty cab. He dashed along beside the track, along past the tender, past the gangway, past the thundering drivers, and with every foot the 1016 and the Imperial Limited, Number One, westbound, was hitting up the pace. When he got level with the cylinder, it was as if he had come to a halt, though his lungs were bursting, and he was straining with every pound that was in him. He was barely gaining by the matter of inches, and in about another minute he was due to lose by feet. But he nosed in over the tape in a dead heat, flung himself sideways, and, with his fingers clutching at the drawbar, landed, panting and pretty well all in, on the pilot. A minute it took him to get his breath and balance, then he crawled to the footplate, swung to the steam chest and from there to the running board.

Here, for the first time, Beezer got a view of things and a somewhat more comprehensive realization of what he was up against, and his heart went into his mouth and his mouth went dry. Far down below him in a sheer drop to the base of the cañon wall wound the Glacier like a silver thread; in front, a gray, sullen mass of rock loomed up dead ahead, the right of way swerving sharply to the right as it skirted it in a breath-taking curve; and with every second the 1016 and her trailing string of coaches was plunging faster and faster down the grade. The wind was already singing in his ears. There was a sudden lurch, a shock, as she struck the curve. Beezer flung his arms around the handrail and hung on grimly. She righted, found her wheel base again, and darted like an arrow along the opening tangent.

Beezer's face was whiter now than death itself. There were curves without number ahead, curves to which that first was but child's play, that even at their present speed would hurl them from the track and send them crashing in splinters through the hideous depths into the valley below. It was stop her, or death; death, sure, certain, absolute and quick, for himself and every man, woman and child, from colonist coach to the solid-mahogany, brass-railed Pullmans and observation cars that rocked behind him.

There was no getting into the cab through the gangway; his one glance had told him that. There was only one other way, little better than a chance, and he had taken it. Blue-lipped with fear—that glance into the nothingness almost below his feet had shaken his nerve and turned him sick and dizzy—Beezer, like a man clinging to a crag, edged along the running board, gained the rear end, and, holding on tightly with both hands, lifted his foot, and with a kick shattered the front cab-glass; another kick and the window frame gave way, and, backing in feet first, Beezer began to lower himself into the cab.

Meanwhile, white-faced men stood at Spence's elbow in the despatchers' office at Big Cloud. Some section hands had followed Number One out of the Bend in a handcar, and had found MacAllister and his fireman about two hundred yards apart on opposite sides of the right of way. Both were unconscious. The section hands had picked them up, pumped madly back to the Bend, and made their report.

Carleton, leaning over Spence, never moved, only the muscles of his jaw twitched; Regan, as he always did in times of stress, swore to himself in a grumbling undertone. There was no other sound in the room save the incessant click of the sender, as Spence frantically called the construction camp at the summit of the Slide; there was a chance, one in a thousand, that the section hands had got back to the Bend before Number One had reached the top of the grade.

Then, suddenly, the sounder broke, and Spence began to spell off the words.

"Number One passed here five minutes ago."

Regan went down into a chair, and covered his face with his hands.

"Wild," he whispered, and his whisper was like an awe-stricken sob. "Running wild on the Devil's Slide. No one in the cab. Oh, my God!"

There was a look on Carleton's face no words could describe—it was gray, gray with a sickness that was a sickness of his soul; but his words came crisp and clear, cold as steel, and without a tremor.

"Clear the line, Spence. Get out the wrecking crew, and send the callers for the doctors—that's all that's left for us to do."

But while Big Cloud was making grim preparations for disaster, Beezer in no less grim a way was averting it, and his salvation, together with that of every soul aboard the train, came, in a measure at least, from the very source wherein lay their danger—the speed. That, and the fact that the pressure MacAllister had thought would drop before the summit was reached, was at last exhausting itself. The cab was less dense, and the speed whipping the wind through the now open window helped a whole lot more, but it was still a swirling mass of vapor.

Beezer lowered himself in, his foot touched the segment, and then found the floor. The 1016 was rocking like a storm-tossed liner. Again there came the sickening, deadly slew as she struck a curve, the nauseating pause as she hung in air with whirring drivers. Beezer shut his eyes and waited. There was a lurch, another and another, fast and quick like a dog shaking itself from a cold plunge—she was still on the right of way.

Beezer wriggled over on his back now, and, with head hanging out over the running board, groped with his hands for the levers. Around his legs something warm and tight seemed to clinch and wrap itself. He edged forward a little farther—his hand closed on the throttle and flung it in—a fierce, agonizing pain shot through his arm as something spurted upon it, withering it, blistering it. The fingers of his other hand were clasped on the air latch and he began to check—then, unable to endure it longer, he threw it wide. There was a terrific jolt, a shock that keeled him over on his side as the brake-shoes locked, the angry grind and crunch of the wheel tires, and the screech of skidding drivers.

He dragged himself out and crouched again on the running board. Behind him, like a wriggling snake, the coaches swayed and writhed crazily, swinging from side to side in drunken, reeling arcs. A deafening roar of beating flanges and pounding trucks was in his ears—and shriller, more piercing, the screams of the brake-shoes as they bit and held. He turned his head and looked down the right of way, and his eyes held there, riveted and fascinated. Two hundred yards ahead was the worst twist on the Slide, where the jutting cliff of Old Piebald Mountain stuck out over the precipice, and the track hugged around it in a circle like a fly crawling around a wall.

Beezer groaned and shut his eyes again. They say that in the presence of

150

expected death sometimes one thinks of a whole lot of things. Engineer Beezer, in charge of Number One, the Imperial Limited, did then; but mostly he was contrasting up the relative merits of a workbench and a throttle, and there wasn't any doubt in Beezer's mind about which he'd take if he ever got the chance to take anything again.

When he opened his eyes Old Piebald Mountain was still ahead of him—about ten feet ahead of him—and the pony truck was on the curve. But they had stopped, and Dave Kinlock and a couple of mail clerks were trying to tear his hands away from the death grip he'd got on the handrail. It was a weak and shaken Beezer, a Beezer about as flabby as a sack of flour, that they finally lifted down off the running board.

There was nothing small about Regan—there never was. He came down on the wrecking train, and, when he had had a look at the 1016 and had heard Kinlock's story, he went back up to the construction camp, where Beezer had been outfitted with leg and arm bandages.

"Beezer," said he, "I didn't say all horse doctors wouldn't make jockeys—what? You can have an engine any time you want one."

Beezer shook his head slowly.

"No," said he thoughtfully; "I guess I don't want one."

Regan's jaw dropped, and his fat little face puckered up as he stared at Beezer.

"Don't want one!" he gasped. "Don't want one! After howling for one for three months, now that you can have it, you don't want it! Say, Beezer, what's the matter with you—h'm?"

But there wasn't anything the matter with Beezer. He was just getting convalescent, that's all. There's a whole lot of men like Beezer.

Chapter X

THE RAT RIVER SPECIAL

This is Martin Bradley's story; an excerpt, if you will, from the pages of railroading where strange and grim things are, where death and laughter lock arms in the winking of an eye, and are written down as though akin. There have been better men than Martin Bradley—and worse. Measure him as you will, that is one matter; in the last analysis frailty is a human heritage, and that is another. On the Hill Division they called him a game man.

Bradley was a fireman, a silent, taciturn chap. Not sullen or surly—don't get that idea—more quiet than anything else, never much of anything to say. When a laugh was going around Bradley could appreciate the fun, and did; only his laugh seemed tempered somehow by something behind it all. Not a wet blanket, not by any means—they didn't understand him then, perhaps, didn't pretend to—he never invited a confidence or gave one—but the boys would crowd up and make room for Bradley any time, as they dragged at their pipes and swopped yarns in the murk of the roundhouse at the midnight lunch hour, about the time Bradley used to stroll in, snapping his fingers together softly in that curious, absent-minded way he had of doing—for Bradley was firing for Smithers then on the 582, that took the local freight, west, out of Big Cloud in the small morning hours.

Well set-up, jumper tucked in his overalls, the straps over husky shoulders, thick through the chest, medium height, stocky almost, steady black eyes, a clean-shaven, serious face, the black hair grizzled a little and threading gray—that was Martin Bradley. A bit old to be still firing, perhaps, but he had had to take his turn for promotion with the rest of the men when he came to the Hill Division. He'd have gone up in time, way up, to the best on the division, probably, for Regan had him slated for an engine even then, only— But we'll come to that in a moment; there's just a word or two to "clear" the line before we have "rights" through to the terminal.

Big Cloud in those days, which was shortly after the line was laid through the Rockies, and the East and West were finally linked after the stress of toil and hardship and bitter struggle was over, was a pretty hard burg, pretty hard—a whole lot harder than it is to-day. There was still a big transient population of about every nationality on earth, for the road, just because they could operate it, wasn't finished by a good deal, and construction camps were more numerous than stations. Bridge gangs were still at work; temporary trestles were being replaced with ones more permanent; there were cuts through the gray of the mountain rock to be trimmed and barbered with dynamite; and there were grades and approaches and endless things to struggle over; and—well, Big Cloud was still the Mecca of the gamblers, the dive keepers, and the purveyors of "red-eye," who had flocked there to feed like vultures on the harvest of pay checks that were circling around. It was a pretty hard place, Big Cloud—everything wide open—not much of any law there in the far West in the shadow of the Rockies. It's different to-day, of course; but that's the way it was then, when Martin Bradley was firing on the Transcontinental.

Bradley from the first boarded with the MacQuigans. That's how, probably, he came to think more of young Reddy MacQuigan, who was a wiper in the roundhouse, than he did of any of the rest of the railroad crowd. Perhaps not altogether for young Reddy's sake; perhaps on account of Mrs. MacQuigan, and particularly on account of old John MacQuigan—who wasn't any good on earth—a sodden parasite on the household when he was drunk, and an ugly brute when there wasn't any money forthcoming from the products of Mrs. MacQuigan's ubiquitous washtubs to get drunk with. For old John MacQuigan, between whom and Bradley there existed an armed truce, each regarding the other mutually as a necessary evil, had no job—for two reasons: first, because he didn't want one; and, second, because no one would have given him one if he had. Mrs. MacQuigan, a patient, faded-out little woman, tireless because she had to be tireless, shouldered the burden, and hid her shame as best she could from her neighbors. Reddy? No; he didn't help out much—then. Reddy used to stray a little from the straight and narrow himself—far enough so that it was pretty generally conceded that Reddy held his job in the roundhouse on account of his mother, who did Regan's washing; and, as a matter of cold fact, that was about the truth of it; and, as a matter of cold fact, too, that was why the big-hearted master mechanic liked Martin Bradley.

"I dunno," Regan used to say, twiddling his thumbs over his fat paunch, "I dunno; it's about the last place I'd want to board, with that drunken pickings from the scrap heap around. The only decent thing old John 'll ever do will be to die—h'm? About a week of it would finish me. Bradley? Yes; he's hung on there quite a spell. Pretty good man, Martin. I dunno what Mrs. MacQuigan would do without him. Guess that's why he stays. I'm going to give Martin an engine one of these days. That'll help out some. When? When his turn comes. First chance I get. I can't poison anybody off to make room for him—can I?"

And now just a single word more, while we're getting back the "complete," to say that this had been going on for two or three years; Martin Bradley boarding at the MacQuigans' and firing the 582; young Reddy wiping in the roundhouse, and on the ragged edge of dismissal every time the pay car came along; Mrs. MacQuigan at her washtubs; old John leading his disreputable, gin-soaked life; Tommy Regan between the devil of discipline and the deep blue sea of soft-heartedness anent the MacQuigans' son and heir—and we're off, the tissue buttoned in our reefer—off with a clean-swept track.

It was pay day, an afternoon in the late fall, and, growing dusk, the switch lights in the Big Cloud yards were already beginning to twinkle red and

153

white and green, as Martin Bradley, from the pay car platform, his pay check in his pocket, swung himself to the ground and pushed his way through a group of men clustered beside the car. He had caught sight of Regan across the spur going into the roundhouse a moment before, and he wanted a word with the master mechanic—nothing very important—a requisition for an extra allowance of waste. And then, amongst the crowd, he caught sight of some one else, and smiled a little grimly. Old John MacQuigan, as he always did on pay days, was hovering about first one, and then another, playing good fellow and trying to ring himself in on the invitations that would be going around presently when the whistle blew.

Bradley, his smile thinning a little as old John, catching sight of him in turn, sidled off, passed through the group, crossed the turntable—and halted abruptly, just outside the big engine doors, as Regan's voice came to him in an angry growl.

"Now mind what I say, Reddy! Once more, and you're through—for keeps. And that's my last word. Understand?"

"Well, you needn't jump a fellow before he's done anything!" It was Reddy MacQuigan, answering sullenly.

There was silence for a moment; then Regan's voice again, pretty cold and even now.

"I dunno," he said. "I figure you must have been brought into the world for something, but I dunno what it is. You're not to blame for your father; but if I let a mother of mine, and nearing sixty years, slave out the little time she's got left, I'd want to crawl out somewhere amongst the buttes and make coyote meat of myself. Jump you before you've done anything—eh!" The little master mechanic's voice rose suddenly. "I saw you sneak uptown an hour ago when you left the pay car—one drink for a start—h'm! Well, you put another on top of it, and it'll be for a—finish! I'd do a lot for that fine old lady of a mother of yours, and that's why I've taken the trouble to come over here and warn you what'll happen if you put in the night you're heading for. 'Tisn't because I can't run the roundhouse without you, my bucko—mind that!"

Bradley was snapping his fingers in his queer, nervous way. Reddy MacQuigan made no answer; at least, Bradley did not hear any, but he heard Regan moving toward the door. He had no wish to talk to the master mechanic any more, not just at that moment anyhow, so he crunched through the engine cinders to another door, entering the roundhouse as Regan went out on the turntable and headed across the tracks for the station.

Two pits away, Reddy MacQuigan, with a black scowl on his face, leaned against the steam chest of the 1004. Bradley, pretending not to see him, swung through the gangway and into the cab of the 582. There, for half an hour, he busied himself in an aimless fashion; but with an eye out for the young wiper, as the latter moved about the roundhouse.

The whistle was blowing and Reddy was pulling off his overalls, as Bradley swung out of his cab again; and he was shading a match from the wind over the bowl of his pipe just across the turntable, as Reddy came out. He tossed away the match, puffed, and nodded at MacQuigan.

"Hello, Reddy," he said in his quiet way, and fell into step with the boy.

154

MacQuigan didn't answer. Bradley never spoke much, anyhow. They crossed the tracks and started up Main Street in silence. Here, the railroaders, in groups and twos and threes, filled the street; some hurrying homeward; others dropping in through the swinging doors, not infrequently located along the right of way, where gasoline lamps flared out over the gambling hells, and the crash of tin-pan pianos, mingled with laughter and shouting, came rolling out from the dance-hall entrances.

Bradley, with his eyes in front of him, walked along silently. Upon MacQuigan's young face had settled the black scowl again; and it grew blacker as he glanced, now and then, at the man beside him. Behind them came a knot of his cronies—and some one called his name.

MacQuigan halted suddenly.

"Well, so long, Martin," he said gruffly. "I'll be up a little later."

Bradley's hand went out and linked in the other's arm.

"Better come on home, Reddy," he said, with one of his rare smiles.

"Later," Reddy flung out.

"Better make it now," said Bradley quietly.

The group behind had come up with them now, and, crowding into Faro Dave's place, paused a moment in the entrance to absorb the situation.

"Be a good boy, Reddy, and do as you're told," one of them sang out.

Reddy whirled on Bradley, the hot blood flushing his face.

"I wish you'd mind your own blasted business!" he flared. "I'm blamed good and sick of you tagging me. This isn't the first time. You make me weary! The trouble with you is that you don't know anything but the everlasting grouch you carry around. You're a funeral! You're a tight-wad. Everybody says so. Nobody ever heard of you spending a cent. Go on—beat it—leave me alone!"

Bradley's face whitened a little, but the smile was still on his lips.

"Better draw your fire, Reddy; there's no need of getting hot," he said. "Come on home; you know what'll happen if you don't; and you know what Regan told you back there in the roundhouse."

"So you heard that, eh?" Reddy shot at him. "I thought you did; and you thought you'd fool me by hanging around there, playing innocent, to walk home with me, eh?"

"I wasn't trying to fool you," Bradley answered; and his hand went now to the wiper's shoulder.

"Let go!" snarled Reddy. "I'll go home when I feel like it!"

Bradley's hand closed a little tighter.

"Don't make a fool of yourself, Reddy," he said gravely. "You'll—"

And that was all. MacQuigan wasn't much more than a boy, not much more than that, and hot-headed—and his chums were looking on. He freed himself from Bradley's hold—with a smash of his fist in Bradley's face.

Fight? No; there wasn't any fight. There was a laugh—from old John MacQuigan, who had been trailing the young bloods up the street. And as Bradley, after staggering back from the unexpected blow, recovered himself, Reddy MacQuigan, followed by old John, was disappearing into Faro Dave's "El Dorado" in front of him.

Bradley went home alone.

Supper was ready—it was always ready, as everything else was where little old Mrs. MacQuigan was concerned; and there were four plates on the red-checkered tablecloth—as there always were—even on pay day! Bradley sat down, with Mrs. MacQuigan opposite him.

Not much to look at—Mrs. MacQuigan. A thin, sparse little woman in a home-made black alpaca dress; the gray hair, thinning, brushed smooth across her forehead; wrinkles in the patient face, a good many of them; a hint of wistfulness in the black eyes, that weren't as bright as they used to be; not very pretty hands, they were red and lumpy around the knuckles. Not much to look at—just a little old woman, brave as God Almighty makes them—just Mrs. MacQuigan.

Bradley, uneasy, glancing at her furtively now and again, ate savagely, without relish. There wasn't much said; nothing at all about old John and young Reddy. Mrs. MacQuigan never asked a question—it was pay day.

There wasn't much said until after the meal was over, and Bradley had lighted his pipe and pushed back his chair; with Mrs. MacQuigan lingering at the table, kind of wistfully it seemed, kind of listening, kind of hanging back from putting away the dishes and taking the two empty plates off the table— and then she smiled over at Bradley as though there wasn't anything on her mind at all.

"Faith, Martin," she said, "sure I don't know at all, at all, what I'd be doing not seeing you around the house; but it's wondered I have often enough you've not picked out some nice girl and made a home of your own."

The words in their suddenness came to Bradley with a shock; and, his face strained, he stared queerly at Mrs. MacQuigan.

A little startled, Mrs. MacQuigan half rose from her chair.

"What is it, Martin?" she asked tremulously.

For a moment more, Bradley stared at her. Strange that she should have spoken like that to-night when there seemed more than ever a sort of grim analogy between her life and his, that seemed like a bond to-night drawing them closer—that seemed, somehow, to urge him to pour out his heart to her—there was motherliness in the sweet old face that seemed to draw him out of himself as no one else had for more years than he cared to remember—as even she never had before.

"What is it, Martin?" she asked again.

And then Bradley smiled.

"I've picked her out," he said, in a low voice. "I'm waiting for a little girl that's promised some day to keep house for me."

"Oh, Martin!" cried Mrs. MacQuigan excitedly. "And—and you never said a word!"

Bradley's hand dove into his inside pocket and came out with a photograph—and the smile on his face now was full of pride.

"Here's her picture," he said.

"Wait, Martin—wait till I get my spectacles!" exclaimed Mrs. MacQuigan, all in a flutter; and, rising, she hurried over to the little shelf in the corner. Then, adjusting the steel bows over her ears, with little pats to smooth down her hair, she picked up the photograph and stared at it—at the picture of a little tot of eight or nine, at a merry, happy little face that smiled at her roguishly.

"She's ten now, God bless her!" said Bradley simply. "That was taken two years ago—so I haven't so long to wait, you see."

"Why—why, Martin," stammered Mrs. MacQuigan, "sure you never said you was married. And the wife, Martin, poor boy, she's—she's dead?"

Bradley picked up the photograph and replaced it in his pocket—but the smile now was gone.

"No—I don't know—I never heard," he said. He walked over to the window, pulled the shade and stared out, his back to Mrs. MacQuigan. "She ditched me. I was on the Penn then—doing well. I had my engine at twenty-five. I went bad for a bit. I'd have gone all the way if it hadn't been for the kiddie. I'd have had more to answer for than I'd want to have, blood, perhaps, if I'd stayed, so I pulled up stakes and came out here." He turned again and came back from the window. "I couldn't bring the kiddie, of course; it was no place for her. And I couldn't leave her where she was to grow up with that in her life, for she was too young then, thank God, to understand; so I'm giving her the best my money'll buy in a girl's school back East, and"—his voice broke a little—"and that's the little girl I'm waiting for, to make a home for me— some time."

Mrs. MacQuigan's hands fumbled a little as she took off her spectacles and laid them down—fumbled a little as she laid them on Bradley's sleeve.

"God be good to you, Martin," she whispered, and, picking up some dishes, went hurriedly from the room.

Bradley went back again and stood by the window, looking out, snapping his fingers softly with that trick of his when any emotion was upon him. Strange that he should have told his story to Mrs. MacQuigan tonight! And yet he was glad he had told her; she probably would never refer to it again—just understand. Yes; he was glad he had told her. He hadn't intended to, of course. It had come almost spontaneously, almost as though for some reason it was meant that he should tell her, and—

Bradley's eyes fixed on a small boy's figure that came suddenly streaking across the road and flung itself at the MacQuigans' little front gate; then the gate swung, and the boy came rushing up the yard. Bradley thought he recognized the figure as one of the call boys, and a call boy running like that was always and ever a harbinger of trouble. Instinctively he glanced back into the room. Mrs. MacQuigan was out in the kitchen. Bradley stepped quickly into the hall, and reached the front door as the boy began to pound a tattoo with his fists on the panels.

Bradley jerked the door open.

"What's wrong?" he demanded tersely.

The light from the hall was on the boy now—and his eyes were popping.

"Say," he panted, in a scared way, "say, one of Reddy's friends sent me. There's a wild row on at Faro Dave's. Reddy's raisin' the roof, an'—"

Bradley's hand closed over the youngster's mouth. In answer to the knock, Mrs. MacQuigan was hurrying down the hall.

"What's the matter, Martin?" she questioned nervously, looking from Bradley to the boy and back again to Bradley.

"Nothing," said Bradley reassuringly. "I'm wanted down at the roundhouse to go out with a special." He gave the boy a significant push gatewards. "Go on, bub," he said. "I'll be right along."

Bradley went back into the house, picked up his cap, and, with a cheery good-night to Mrs. MacQuigan, started out again. He walked briskly to the gate and along past the picket fence—Mrs. MacQuigan had the shade drawn back, and was watching him from the window—and then, hidden by the Coussirats' cottage next door, he broke into a run.

It wasn't far—distances weren't great in Big Cloud in those days, aren't now, for that matter—and in less than two minutes Bradley had Faro Dave's "El Dorado" in sight down Main Street—and his face set hard. He wasn't the only one that was running; men were racing from every direction; some coming up the street; others, he passed, who shouted at him, and to whom he paid no attention. In a subconscious way he counted a dozen figures dart in through the swinging doors of the "El Dorado" from the street—news of a row travels fast.

Bradley burst through the doors, still on the run—and brought up at a dead halt against a solidly packed mass of humanity; Polacks and Swedes and Hungarians from the construction gangs; a scattering of railroad men in the rear; and more than a sprinkling of the harder element gathered from all over town, the hangers-on, the sharpers, and the card men, the leeches, the ilk of Faro Dave who ran the place, and who seemed to be intent on maintaining a blockade at the far end of the barroom.

The place was jammed, everybody craning their necks toward the door of the back room, where Faro Dave ran his stud, faro and roulette layouts; and from there, over the shuffling feet of the crowding men in the bar, came a snarl of voices—amongst them, Reddy's, screaming out in drunken fury, incoherently.

Bradley, without ceremony, pushed into the crowd, and the foreigners made way for him the best they could. Then he commenced to shoulder through the sort of self-constituted guard of sympathizers with the house. One of these tried to block his way more effectually.

"You'd better keep your hands off, whoever you are," the man threw at him. "The young fool's been putting the place on the rough ever since he came in here. All Dave wants to do is put him out of the back door, and—"

"Thash the boy, Reddy! Don't lesh him bluff you—saw him change cards m'self. Damn thief—damn cheat—thash the boy, Reddy!" It was old John MacQuigan's voice, from the other room, high-pitched, clutter-tongued, drunken.

Then a voice, cold, with a sneer, and a ring in the sneer that there was no mistaking—Faro Dave's voice:

"You make a move, and I'll drop you quicker'n—"

Bradley's arms swept out with a quick, fierce movement, hurling the man who tried to block him out of the way; and, fighting now, ramming with body and shoulders, throwing those in front of him to right and left, he half

158

fell, half flung himself finally through the doorway into the room beyond—too late.

"Thash the boy, Reddy!"—it was old John's maudlin voice again. "Thash the—"

The picture seared itself into Bradley's brain, lightning-quick, instantaneous, but vivid in every detail, as he ran. The little group of men, three or four, who had been sitting at the game probably, seeking cover in the far corner; Reddy MacQuigan, swaying a little, standing before a somewhat flimsy green-baized card table; old John, too far gone to stand upright alone, leaning against the wall behind Reddy; Faro Dave, an ugly white in his face, an uglier revolver in his hand, standing, facing Reddy across the table; the quick forward lunge from Reddy, the crash of the table as the boy hurled it to the floor and flung himself toward the gambler; the roar of a revolver shot, the flash of the short-tongued flame; a choking scream; another shot, the tinkle of glass as the bullet shattered the ceiling lamp; then blackness—all but a dull glow filtering in through the barroom door, that for the first instant in the sudden contrast gave no light at all.

Bradley, before he could recover himself, pitched over a tangled mass of wrecked tables—over that and a man's body. Somebody ran through the room, and the back door slammed. There were shouts now, and yells—-a chorus of them from the barroom. Some one bawled for a light.

Bradley got to his knees, and, reaching to raise the boy, wounded or killed as he believed, found his throat suddenly caught in a vicious grasp—and Reddy's snarling laugh was in his ears.

"Let go!" Bradley choked. "Let go, Reddy. It's me—Martin."

Reddy's hands fell.

"Martin, eh?" he said thickly. "Thought it was—hic—that—"

Reddy's voice sort of trailed off. They were bringing lamps into the room now, holding them up high to get a comprehensive view of things—and the light fell on the farther wall. Reddy was staring at it, his eyes slowly dilating, his jaw beginning to hang weakly.

Bradley glanced over his shoulder. Old John, as though he had slid down the wall, as though his feet had slipped out from under him, sat on the floor, legs straight out in front of him, shoulders against the wall and sagged a little to one side, a sort of ironic jeer on the blotched features, a little red stream trickling down from his right temple—dead.

Not a pretty sight? No—perhaps not. But old John never was a pretty sight. He'd gone out the way he'd lived—that's all.

It was Martin Bradley who reached him first, and the crowd hung back while he bent over the other, hung back and made way for Reddy, who came unsteadily across the room—not from drink now, the boy's gait—the drink was out of him—he was weak. There was horror in the young wiper's eyes, and a white, awful misery in his face.

A silence fell. Not a man spoke. They looked from father to son. The room was filling up now—but they came on tiptoe. Gamblers, most of them, and pretty rough, pretty hard cases, and life held light—but in that room that

159

night they only looked from father to son, the oaths gone from their lips, sobered, their faces sort of gray and stunned.

Bradley, from bending over the dead man, straightened up.

Reddy MacQuigan, with little jabs of his tongue, wet his lips.

"The old man's gone, ain't he?" he said in a queer, lifeless way.

"Yes," said Bradley simply.

MacQuigan looked around the circle sort of mechanically, sort of unseeingly—then at the form on the floor. Then he spoke again, almost as though he were talking to himself.

"Might just as well have been me that fired the shot," he whispered, nodding his head. "I'm to blame—ain't I? An' I guess—I guess I've finished the old lady, too." He looked around the circle again, then his hands kind of wriggled up to his temples—and before Bradley could spring to catch him, he went down in a heap on the floor.

MacQuigan wasn't much more than a boy, not much more than that— but old enough in another way. What he went through that night and in the days that followed was between MacQuigan and his God. Life makes strange meeting points sometimes, and sometimes the running orders are hard to understand, and sometimes it looks like disaster quick and absolute, with everything in the ditch, and the right of way a tangled ruin—and yet when morning breaks there is no call for the wrecking crew, and it comes to you deep down inside somewhere that it's the Great Despatcher who's been sitting in on the night trick.

Reddy MacQuigan went back to the roundhouse a different MacQuigan than he had left it—sort of older, quieter, more serious—and the days went by, a month or two of them.

Regan, with a sort of inward satisfaction and some complacency, tugged at his scraggly brown mustache, and summed it up pretty well.

"Did I not say," said Regan, "that the only decent thing old John would ever do would be to die? H'm? Well, then, I was right, wasn't I? Look at young Reddy! Straight as a string—and taking care of the old lady now. No; I ain't getting my shirts starched the way Mrs. MacQuigan used to starch them—but no matter. Mrs. MacQuigan isn't taking in washing any more, God bless her! I guess Reddy got it handed to him pretty straight on the carpet that night. I'll have him pulling a throttle one of these days—what?"

Bradley? Yes; this is Martin Bradley's story—not Reddy MacQuigan's. But Reddy had his part in it—had running orders to make one more of those strange meeting points fixed by the Great Despatcher that we were speaking about a minute ago.

It was three months to the day from old John MacQuigan's death that Bradley, in from a run, found a letter waiting for him up at Mrs. MacQuigan's—and went down under it like a felled ox! Not the big thing to do? Well, perhaps not—all that he cared for in life, everything that he lived for, everything that had kept him straight since his trouble years ago, snatched from him without a moment's warning—that was all. Another man might not have lost his grip—or he might. Bradley lost his—for a little while—but they call him to-day a game man on the Hill Division.

White-faced, not quite understanding himself, in a queer sort of groping way, Bradley, in his flood of bitter misery, told Mrs. MacQuigan, who had watched him open the letter—told her that his little housekeeper, as he had come to call the kiddie, was dead. Not even a chance to see her—an accident—the letter from the lawyers who did his business, transmitting the news received from the school authorities who knew only the lawyers as the principals—a letter, trying to break the news in a softer way than a telegram would have done, since Bradley was too far away to get back East in time, anyhow.

And Mrs. MacQuigan put her arms around him, and, understanding as only her mother's heart could understand, tried to comfort him, while the tears rained down the sweet old face. But Bradley's eyes were dry. With his elbows on the table, holding his chin in his hands, his face like stone, he stared at the letter he had spread out on the red checkered cloth—stared for a long time at that, and at the little photograph he had taken from his pocket.

"Martin, boy," pleaded Mrs. MacQuigan, and her hand brushed back the hair from his forehead, "Martin, boy, don't take it like that."

And then Bradley turned and looked at her—not a word—only a bitter laugh—and picked up his letter and the picture and went out.

Bradley went up on the 582 with the local freight, west, that night, and there was a dare-devil laugh in his heart and a mechanical sense of existence in his soul. And in the cab that night, deep in the mountains, Bradley lost his grip. It seemed to sweep him in a sudden, overwhelming surge; and, with the door swung wide, the cab leaping into fiery red, the sweat beads trickling down his face that was white in a curious way where the skin showed through for all the grime and perspiration, he lurched and snatched at his engineer's arm.

"Life's a hell of a thing, ain't it, Smithers?" he bawled over the roar of the train and the swirl of the wind, wagging his head and shaking imperatively at Smithers' arm.

Smithers, a fussy little man, with more nerves than are good for an engineer, turned, stared, caught a something in the fireman's face—and tried to edge a little farther over on his seat. In the red, flickering glare, Bradley's eyes had a look in them that wasn't sane, and his figure, swaying with the heave of the cab, seemed to shoot back and forth uncannily, grotesquely, in and out of the shadows.

"Martin, for God's sake, Martin," gasped the engineer, "what's wrong with you?"

"You heard what I said," shouted Bradley, a sullen note in his voice, gripping the engineer's arm still harder. "That's what it is, ain't it? Why don't you answer?"

Smithers, frightened now, stared mutely. The head-light shot suddenly from the glittering ribbons of steel far out into nothingness, flinging a filmy ray across a cañon's valley, and mechanically Smithers checked a little as they swung the curve. Then, with a deafening roar of thunder racketing through the mountains, they swept into a cut, the rock walls towering high on either side—

161

and over the din Bradley's voice screamed again—and again he shook Smithers' arm.

"Ain't it? D'ye hear—ain't it? Say—ain't it?"

"Y-yes," stammered Smithers weakly, with a gulp.

And then Bradley laughed—queerly.

"You're a damn fool, Smithers!" he flung out, with a savage jeer. "What do you know about it!" And throwing the engineer's arm from him, his shovel clanged and clanged again, as into the red maw before him he shot the coal.

Smithers was scared. Bradley never said another word after that—just kept to his own side of the cab, hugging his seat, staring through the cab glass ahead, chin down on his breast, pulling the door at intervals, firing at intervals like an automaton, then back to his seat agan. Smithers was scared.

At Elk River, the end of the local run, Smithers told the train crew about it, and they laughed at him, and looked around to find out what Martin Bradley had to say about it—but Bradley wasn't in sight.

Not much of a place, Elk River, not big enough for one to go anywhere without the whole population knowing it; and it wasn't long before they knew where Bradley was. The local made a two hours' lay-over there before starting back for Big Cloud; and Martin Bradley spent most of it in Kelly's place, a stone's throw from the station. Not drinking much, a glass or two all told, sitting most of the time staring out of the window—not drinking much—getting the taste of it that he hadn't known for a matter of many years. Two glasses, perhaps three, that was all—but he left Kelly's for the run back with a flask in his pocket.

It was the flask that did it, not Smithers. Smithers was frightened at his silent fireman tippling over his shovel, good and frightened before he got to Big Cloud, and Smithers did not understand; but Smithers, for all that, wasn't the man to throw a mate down cold. Neither was Bradley himself bad enough to have aroused any suspicion. It was the flask that did it.

They made Big Cloud on the dot that morning—11.26. And in the roundhouse, as Bradley stepped out through the gangway, his overalls caught on the hasp of the tool-box on the tender, and the jerk sent the flask flying into splinters on the floor—at Regan's feet.

The fat little master mechanic, on his morning round of inspection, halted, stared in amazement at the broken glass and trickling beverage, got a whiff of the raw spirit, and blinked at Bradley, who, by this time, had reached the ground.

"What's the meaning of this?" demanded Regan, nonplused. "Not you, Bradley—on the run?"

Bradley did not answer. He was regarding the master mechanic with a half smile—not a pleasant one—more a defiant curl of his lips.

Smithers, discreetly attempting to make his escape through the opposite gangway, caught Regan's attention.

"Here, you, Smithers," Regan called peremptorily, "come—"

Then Bradley spoke, cutting in roughly.

"Leave Smithers out of it," he said.

Regan stared for another moment; then took a quick step forward, close up to Bradley—and got the fireman's breath.

Bradley shoved him away insolently.

It was a minute before Regan spoke. He liked Bradley and always had; but from the soles of his feet up to the crown of his head, Regan, first and last, was a railroad man. And Regan knew but one creed. Other men might drink and play the fool and be forgiven and trusted again, a wiper, a shop hand, a brakeman, perhaps, or any one of the train crew, but a man in the cab of an engine—never. Reasons, excuses, contributory causes, counted not at all—they were not asked for—they did not exist. The fact alone stood—as the fact. It was a minute before Regan spoke, and then he didn't say much, just a word or two without raising his voice, before he turned on his heel and walked out of the roundhouse.

"I'm sorry for this, Bradley," he said. "You're the last man I expected it from. You know the rules. You've fired your last run on this road. You're out."

But Regan might have been making some comment on the weather for all the concern it appeared to give Bradley. He stood leaning against the tender, snapping his fingers in his queer way, silent, hard-faced, his eyes far away from his immediate surroundings. Smithers, a wiper or two, Reddy MacQuigan amongst them, clustered around him after Regan had gone; but Bradley paid no attention to them, answered none of their questions or comments; and after a little while pushed himself through them and went out of the roundhouse.

Bradley didn't go home that day; but Reddy MacQuigan did—at the noon hour. That's how Mrs. MacQuigan got it. Mrs. MacQuigan did not wait to wash up the dishes. She put on the little old-fashioned poke bonnet that she had worn for as many seasons as Big Cloud could remember, and started out to find Regan. She ran the master mechanic to earth on the station platform, and opened up on him, fluttering, anxious, and distressed.

"Sure, Regan," she faltered, "you did not mean it when you fired Martin this morning—not for good."

Regan pulled at his mustache and looked at her—and shook his head at her reprovingly.

"I meant it, Mrs. MacQuigan," he said kindly. "You must know that. It will do neither of us any good to talk about it. I wouldn't have let him out if I could have helped it."

"Then listen here, Regan," she pleaded. "Listen to the why of it, that 'tis only me who knows."

And Regan listened—and the story lost nothing in the telling because the faded eyes were wet, and the wrinkled lips quivered sometimes, and would not form the words.

At the end, big-hearted Regan reached into his back pocket for his plug, met his teeth in it, wrenched a piece away without looking at her, and cleared his throat—but he still shook his head.

"It's no use you talking, Mrs. MacQuigan," he said gruffly, to hide his emotion. "I'd fire any man on earth, 'tis no matter the who or why, for drinking in the cab on a run."

163

"But, Regan," she begged, catching at his arm, "he'll be leaving Big Cloud with his job gone."

"And what then?" said Regan. "Mabbe 'twould be the best thing—h'm?"

"Ah, Regan," she said, and her voice caught a little, "sure, 'twould be the end of Martin, don't you see? 'Tis me that knows him, and 'twill not last long, the spell, only till the worst of it is over—Martin is too fine for that, Regan. If I can keep him by me, Regan, d'ye mind? If he goes away where there's nobody to give him a thought he'll—he'll—ah, Regan, faith, Regan, 'tis a lot you've thought of Martin Bradley the same as me."

Regan examined a crack in the planking of the station platform minutely, while Mrs. MacQuigan held tenaciously to his coat sleeve.

"I dunno," said Regan heavily. "I dunno. Mabbe I'll—"

"Ah, Regan!" she cried happily. "I knew 'twas—"

"Not in a cab!" interposed Regan hastily. "Not if he was the president of the road. But I'll see, Mrs. MacQuigan, I'll see."

And Regan saw—Thornley, the trainmaster. And after Thornley, he saw Reddy MacQuigan in the roundhouse.

"Reddy," said he, with a growl that wasn't real, "there's a vacancy in the engine crews—h'm?"

"Martin's?" said Reddy quickly.

"Yes," said Regan. "Do you want it?"

"No," said Reddy MacQuigan shortly.

"Good boy," said the fat little master mechanic. "Then I'll give it to you just the same. Martin's through in here; but he'll get a chance braking for Thornley. You'll run spare to begin with, and"—as Reddy stared a little numbly—"don't break your neck thanking me. Thank yourself for turning into a man. Your mother's a fine woman, Reddy. I guess you're beginning to find that out too—h'm?"

So Reddy MacQuigan went to firing where Martin Bradley had fired before, and his pay went up; and Bradley—no, don't get that idea—whatever else he may have done, Martin Bradley didn't make a beast of himself. Bradley took the job they offered him, neither gratefully nor ungratefully, took it with that spirit of utter indifference for anything and everything that seemed to have laid hold of him and got him in its grip—and off duty he spent most of his time in the emporiums along Main Street. He drank some, but never enough to snow him under; it was excitement that he seemed to crave, forgetfulness in anything that would absorb him for the moment. It was not drink so much; it was the faro tables and the roulette and the stud poker that, crooked from the drop of the hat, claimed him and cleaned him out night after night—all except Mrs. MacQuigan's board money, that they never got away from him. Mrs. MacQuigan got that as regularly now that she didn't need it with Reddy to look after her as she had when she was practically dependent upon Bradley for it all.

Silent, grim, taciturn always, more so now than ever, Bradley went his way; indifferent to Regan when Regan buttonholed him; indifferent to Thornley and his threats of dismissal, meant to jerk Bradley into the straight; indifferent to every mortal thing on earth. And the Hill Division, with Regan leading, shook its head. There wasn't a man but knew the story, and, big under the greasy jumpers and the oil-soaked shirts, they never judged him; but Bradley's eyes held no invitation for companionship, so they left him pretty much alone.

"I dunno," said Regan, tugging at his mustache, twiddling with his thumbs over his paunch, "I dunno—looks like the scrap heap at the end of the run—h'm? I dunno."

But Mrs. MacQuigan said no.

"Wait," said she, with her patient smile. "It's me that knows Martin. It's a sore, hurt heart the boy has now; but you wait and see—I'll win him through. It's proud yet you'll be to take your hats off to Martin Bradley!"

Martin Bradley—a game man—that's what they call him now. Mrs. MacQuigan was right—wasn't she? Not perhaps just in the way she thought she was—but right for all that. Call it luck or chance if you like, something more than that if it strikes you that way—but an accident in the yards one night, a month after Bradley had lost his engine, put one of the train crew of the Rat River Special out of commission with a torn hand, and sent a call boy streaking uptown for a substitute. Call it luck if you like, that the work train with a hybrid gang of a hundred-odd Polacks, Armenians, and Swedes, cooped up in a string of box cars converted into bunk houses, mess houses and commissariat, a window or two in them to take the curse off, and end doors connecting them for the sake of sociability, pulled out for the new Rat River trestle work with Reddy MacQuigan handling the shovel end of it for Bull Coussirat, who had been promoted in the cab—and Bradley as the substitute brakeman on the front end. Well, maybe it was luck—but that's not what they call it on the Hill Division.

Perhaps no one quite understood Bradley, even at the end, except Mrs. MacQuigan; and possibly even she didn't get it all. Inconsistent, to put it mildly, that a man like Bradley would have let go at all? Well, it's an easy matter and a very human one, to judge another from the safe vantage ground of distance—isn't it? Some men take a thing one way, and some another; and in some the feelings take deeper root than in others—and find their expression in a different way. Ditched from the start, Bradley hadn't much to cling to, had he—only the baby girl he had dreamed about on the runs at night; only the little tot he had slaved for, who some day was to make a home for him? But about the Rat River Special—

It was midnight when they pulled out of Big Cloud; and Bradley, in the caboose, glanced at Heney's tissue, which, as a matter of form, the conductor gave him to read. The Special was to run twenty minutes behind No. 17, the westbound mail train, and make a meeting point with the through freight, No. 84, eastbound, at The Forks. The despatchers had seized the propitious moment to send the rolling camp through in the quiet hours of traffic, with an eye out to getting the foreigners promptly on the job in the morning for fear they might draw an extra hour or two of time—without working for it! The Special was due to make Rat River at four o'clock.

Bradley handed back the order without comment, picked up his lantern, and started for the door.

165

"No need of going forward to-night," said Heney, laying his arm on Bradley's arm. "We've only a short train, a dozen cars, and we can watch it well enough from the cupola. It's damn cold out there."

"Oh, I guess it's all right, Heney," Bradley answered—and went out through the door.

There weren't any platforms to the box cars, just small end doors. Once in camp, and stationary on a siding, the cars would be connected up with little wooden gangways, you understand? Bradley, from the platform of the caboose, stepped across the buffer, and made his way through several cars. One was pretty much like another; a stove going, and stuffy hot; the foreigners stretched out in their bunks, some of them; some of them playing cards on the floor; some asleep; some quarrelling, chattering, jabbering; a hard looking lot for the most part, black-visaged, scowling, unshaven, gold circlets dangling in their ears—bar the Swedes.

Bradley worked along with scarcely more than a glance at the occupants, until, in the fourth car, he halted suddenly and shoved his lamp into the face of a giant of a man, who squatted in the corner, sullen and apart, with muttering lips.

"What's wrong with you?" he demanded brusquely.

The man drew back with a growl that was like a beast's, lips curling back over the teeth. Bradley stared at him coolly, then turned inquiringly to the crowd in the car. He was greeted with a burst of unintelligible, polyglot words, and spontaneous, excitable gesticulations. Bradley shrugged his shoulders, and slammed the door behind him.

Outside on the buffer, he reached for the ladder, swung himself up the iron rungs to the top of the car, and, with his lantern hooked in his arm, sat down on the footboard, bracing himself against the brake wheel, and buttoned his reefer—there was another night—to think—ahead of him.

To think—if he could only forget! It was that fearful sense of impotency—impotency—impotency. It seemed to laugh and jeer and mock at him. It seemed to make a plaything of this father love of his. There was nothing—nothing he could do to bring her back—that was it—nothing! Soul, life, mind and body, he would have given them all to have saved her—would give them now to bring her back—and there was only this ghastly impotency. It seemed at times that it would drive him mad—and he could not forget. And then the bitter, crushing grief; the rebellion, fierce, ungovernable, that his all should have been taken from him, that the years he had planned should be turned to nothing but grinning mockery; and then that raging sense of impotency again, that rocked his turbulent soul as in an angry, storm-tossed sea.

Time passed, and he sat there motionless, save for the jolting of the train that bumped him this way and that against the brake wheel. They were into the mountains now; and the snowy summits, moon-touched, reared themselves in white, grotesque, fanciful shapes, and seemed, cold in their beauty, to bring an added chill to the frosty night. Ahead, far ahead, the headlight's ray swept now the track, now the gray rock side, now, softly green, a clump of pines, as the right of way curved and twisted and turned; now,

166

slowing up a grade, the heavy, growling bark of the exhaust came with long intervals between, and now, on the level, it was quick as the tattoo of a snare drum, with the short stack belching a myriad fiery sparks insolently skyward in a steady stream; around him was the sweep of the wind, the roar of the train, the pound of the trucks beating the fish-plates, the sway, the jerk, the recovery of the slewing cars, and, curiously, the deep, brooding silence of the mountains, frowning, it seemed, at this sacrilege of noise; behind, showed the yellow glimmer from the caboose, the dark, indistinct outline of a watching figure in the cupola.

Suddenly, snatching at the brake wheel to help him up, Bradley sprang erect. From directly underneath his feet came a strange, confused, muffled sound, like a rush of men from one end of the car to the other. Then there broke a perfect bedlam of cries, yells, shouts and screams—and then a revolver shot.

In an instant Bradley was scrambling down the ladder to investigate—they could not hear the row, whatever it was, in the caboose—and in another he had kicked the car door open and plunged inside. A faint, bluish haze of smoke undulated in the air, creeping to the roof of the car; and there was the acrid smell of powder—but there was no sign of a fight, no man, killed or wounded, sprawling on the floor. But the twenty men who filled the car were crouched in groups and singly against the car sides; or sat upright in their bunks, their faces white, frightened—only their volubility unchecked, for all screamed and talked and waved their arms at once.

They made a rush for Bradley, explaining in half a dozen languages what had happened. Bradley pushed them roughly away from him.

"Speak English!" he snapped. "What's wrong here? Can't any of you speak English?"

An Italian grabbed his arm and pointed through the door Bradley had left open behind him to the next car forward. "Pietro!" he shouted out wildly. "Gotta da craze—mad—gotta da gun!"

"Well, go on!" prodded Bradley. "He's run into the next car. I understand that—but what happened here? Who's Pietro?"

But the man's knowledge, like his English, was limited. He did not know much—Pietro was not one of them—Pietro had come only that morning to Big Cloud from the East—Pietro had gone suddenly mad—no man had done anything to make Pietro mad.

And then suddenly into Bradley's mind leaped the story that he had read in the papers a few days before of an Italian, a homicidal maniac, who had escaped from an asylum somewhere East, and had disappeared. The description of the man, as he remembered it, particularly the great size of the man, tallied, now that he thought of it, with the fellow who had been in the car when he had first passed through. He glanced quickly around—the man was gone. So that was Pietro!

Bradley started on the run for the next car ahead; and, subconsciously, as he ran, he felt the speed of the train quicken. But that was natural enough—they had been crawling to the summit of Mitre Peak, and, over that now, before them lay a four-percent grade to the level below, one of the nastiest bits of track on the division, curves all the way—only Bull Coussirat was hitting it up pretty hard for a starter.

In the next car the same scene was repeated—the smell of powder smoke, the blue haze hanging listless near the roof out of the air currents; the crouched, terrified foreigners, one with a broken wrist, dangling, where a bullet had shattered it. Pietro, Berserker fashion, was shooting his way through the train.

Bradley went forward more cautiously now, more warily. Strange the way the speed was quickening! The cars were rocking now with short, vicious slews. He thought he heard a shout from the track-side without, but he could not be sure of that.

Through the next car and the next he went, trailing the maniac; and then he started to run again. Stumbling feet, trying to hold their footing, came to him from the top of the car. With every instant now the speed of the train was increasing—past the limit of safety—past the point where he would have hesitated to use the emergency brakes, if there had been any to use—a luxury as yet extended only to the passenger equipment in those days. The Polacks, the Armenians, and the Swedes were beginning to yell with another terror, at the frantic pitching of the cars, making a wild, unearthly chorus that echoed up and down the length of the train.

Bradley's brain was working quickly now. It wasn't only this madman that he was chasing fruitlessly. There must be something wrong, more serious still, in the engine cab—that was Heney, and Carrol, the other brakeman, who had run along the top.

Bradley dashed through the door, and, between the cars, jumped for the ladder and swarmed up—the globe of his lamp in a sudden slew shivered against the car roof, and the flame went out in a puff. He flung the thing from him; and, with arms wide outspread for balance on his reeling foothold, ran, staggered, stumbled, recovered himself, and sped on again, springing from car to car, up the string of them, to where the red flare, leaping from the open fire box in the cab ahead, silhouetted two figures snatching for their hold at the brake-wheel on the front end of the forward car—Heney and Carrol. And as Bradley ran, a thin stream of flame spurted upward from the cab, and there came faintly, almost lost in the thunder of the train, the bark of a revolver shot—and the two figures, ducking instantly, crouched lower.

And then Bradley stood beside the others; and Heney, that no man ever called a coward, clutched at Martin Bradley and shouted in his ear:

"For God's sake, Martin, what'll we do? The throttle was wide at the top of the grade when he threw Bull Coussirat off. We saw it from the cupola. It's certain death to make a move for him!"

But Bradley made no answer. Tight-lipped, he was staring down into the cab; and a livid face stared back at him—the face of the man that he had stopped to look at as they had pulled out of Big Cloud—Pietro—the face, hideously contorted, of a maniac. And on the floor of the cab, stretched out, wriggling spasmodically, Reddy MacQuigan lay upon his back; and Pietro half knelt upon him, clutching with one hand at the boy's throat, pointing a revolver with the other at the roof of the car.

168

Wild, crazy fast now, the speed was; the engine dancing ahead; the cars wriggling behind; the yellow glimmer of the caboose shooting this way and that like a pursuing phantom will-o'-the-wisp; and from beneath the roofs of the cars rose that muffled, never-ending scream of terror from the Polacks, the Armenians and the Swedes—rose, too, from the roofs of the cars themselves, for some were climbing there. It was disaster absolute and certain not a mile ahead where the track in a short, murderous curve hugged Bald Eagle Peak, with the cañon dropping a thousand feet sheer down from the right of way, disaster there—if they ever got that far!

But Bradley, though he knew it well enough from a hundred runs, was not thinking of that. In a calm, strange way there seemed to come one more analogy between Mrs. MacQuigan's life and his—this human thing that looked like a gorilla was choking her son to death, the son that was making a home for her as she had dreamed he would do some day, the son that was all she had to depend upon. Mrs. MacQuigan's son—his little girl. Both out!

There seemed to flash before him the picture of the gray head bowed upon the red-checkered tablecloth in the little dining room, the frail shoulders shaking with the same grief that he was drinking now to the dregs, the same grief that he would have sold his soul to avert—only he had been impotent—impotent. But he was not impotent here—to keep those dregs from Mrs. MacQuigan, the only soul on earth he cared for now. And suddenly Bradley laughed—loud—high above the roar of the train, the shouts and screams of the maddened creatures it was sweeping to eternity, and the human gorilla in the cab shot its head forward and covered Bradley with its revolver, teeth showing in a snarl.

And so Bradley laughed, and with the laugh poised himself—and sprang far out from the car roof in a downward plunge for the tender, reached the coal and rolled, choking with the hot blood in his throat from the shot that had caught him in mid-air, rolled down with an avalanche of coal, grappled with the frothing creature that leaped to meet him, staggered to his feet, struggled for a moment, fast-locked with the madman, until a lurch of the engine hurled them with a crash against the cab frame, and the other, stunned, slid inertly from his grasp. And then for an instant Bradley stood swaying, clutching at his throat—then he took a step forward—both hands went out pawing for the throttle, found it, closed it—and he went down across Bull Coussirat's empty seat—dead.

Only a humble figure, Bradley, just a toiler like millions of others, not of much account, not a great man in the world's eyes—only a humble figure. Measure him as it seems best to you to measure him for his frailty or his strength. They call him a game man on the Hill Division. His story is told.

THE END

Lightning Source UK Ltd.
Milton Keynes UK
UKHW042031080223
416606UK00005B/231/J

9 781647 997953